# AND SHADOWS HAVE THEIR ENDING

ANNOTATED EDITION

PG FORTE

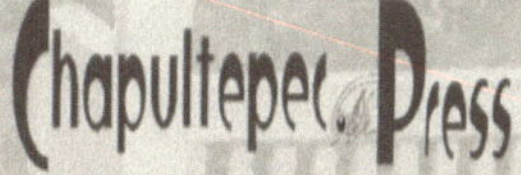

# INTRODUCTION

*Oberon's Midsummer Faire wound slowly down... melting gradually into the warm, mellow gold of a perfect, summer, Sunday afternoon.*

And so we've reached the end of the road. This was always going to be a bittersweet sort of book to write. There are a lot of things I love about this book. I love that the themes/tropes for this book are the same as in the first book in the series; ie, returning to the scene of the crime, getting a second chance at your first love, confronting evils you thought had been defeated, and realizing that your perspective on certain events was completely off-track.

I love how the beginning and end of this book mirror the beginning and end of the first book in the series. I love how I managed to make it reasonable for its main characters (three of whom are teenagers) to try and handle things on their own without asking for help. Hint: I sent most of the responsible adults on vacation.

I'm a little sad that I couldn't fit in one last Crone's Nest scene, but doing so wouldn't have made any sense. But I'm pleased by the multiplicity of happy endings that I managed to squeeze into what is really a very short book...comparatively.

This isn't the definitive end for Oberon. There will be more sequel novellas—my daughter has been waiting for Chenoa's story in particular—and more Christmas stories, as well as additional cross-over books, but this series is absolutely done. And I really don't envision writing a second Oberon series. Although, I suppose I should never say never.

For those of you who have come along with me on this journey, who have fallen in love with Oberon, and who've (metaphorically) taken up residence within its borders, thank you, thank you, thank you.

PG Forte

# LINK TO PLAYLIST

https://tinyurl.com/ShadowsEndingPlaylist

# ACKNOWLEDGMENTS

Oberon is a series that is centered around three women who were friends in high school. So, it would be reasonable to expect me to at least acknowledge my own alma mater in this, the final book in the series.

Unfortunately however, in a recent sickening, saccharine, sycophantic post, my old high school (or whatever nitwit is behind its social media presence) chose to write glowingly about the accomplishments of one of my former classmates—a woman who has recently been appointed to a highly visible position in the incoming administration.

I was appalled by this post. It represents a change in values that I don't condone and refuse to acknowledge.

There are women I went to school with who have lived *truly* commendable lives, who actually *do* embody that "spirit of service" the school claims it "strives to instill" in its students. This ain't it.

*This is the wrong book for this dedication, so instead, I'm going to make it a dedication for the whole series. This series is therefore dedicated to:*

*Jean (Tracey) McBee*
*Kathleen Lucas*
*Nancy (McKeown) Stamberger*
*Roberta Krais*

*Four of my closest friends in high school and the only members of my graduating class with whom I've kept in touch.*
*And, when I say "I've kept in touch," what I really mean is that they've kept in touch with me—because I suck at that sort of stuff.*

*"Types and shadows have their ending*
*for the newer rite is here"*
St. Thomas Aquinas - Pange Lingua Gloriosi

*"For winter's rains and ruins are over,*
*And all the seasons of snows and sins;*
*The days dividing lover and lover,*
*The light that loses, the night that wins."*
Swineburn - Atalanta in Calydon

# CAST OF CHARACTERS

(IN ORDER OF APPEARANCE)

**Seth Cavanaugh:** The last two years have not been kind to Oberon's former golden boy. Tormented by the death of one of his closest friends and still struggling to overcome his accidental addiction, Seth is in no mood to come face to face with the girl who broke his heart.

**Ray Ruiz:** (d) Seth's friend who was murdered the previous April

**Deirdre Delaney Shelton-Cooper:** Deirdre has spent the past two years trying to forget the events that marked her first visit to Oberon, but can you ever really forget the memory of your first love? Deirdre has been looking forward to her reunion with Seth, but his hurtful behavior quickly convinces her that she's been mistaken in her feelings for him.

**Cara Matthews:** Still recovering from the injuries she suffered the previous April, Cara is feeling somewhat lonely of late. Her birthday is coming up soon, but will anyone be there to help her celebrate?

**Rafael (Rafe):** Champion of lovers and travelers, the archangel Rafael (whose name means 'God has healed') is said to rule Sunday, the Second Heaven and the Sun.

**Eric Anderson:** Seth's former friend, Eric is responsible for most of the trouble in Seth's life.

**Jack Connelly:** Lawyer to one of Oberon's nastiest characters, Jack will do whatever he has to do to avoid joining his former friends—either in prison, or the grave.

**Gregg Gilchrist:** Gregg doesn't know for certain if Deirdre is his brother's daughter, but he wants her dead all the same—just in case.

**Dan Cavanaugh:** Seth's father is the first person Deirdre thinks of going to when she needs help. Too bad he's out of town.

**Lucy Greco-Cavanaugh:** Seth's mother. Just because her little boy is all grown up that doesn't mean she's not nervous about leaving him home alone. Who knows how much trouble he might get into on his own?

**Liam McKnight:** Desperately in love, Liam is counting the days until Cara turns eighteen—he won't risk getting involved with her until then. But will he wait too long and miss his chance to win her heart?

**Sinead Quinn:** This former black sheep turned over a new leaf when she became a mother. One of the few people who know about Seth's former addiction, she's determined not to let him back-slide.

**Chayton (Chay) Johnson:** Whose name means Falcon. Chenoa's older brother is still holding a formidable grudge against Liam. A chance encounter with the young cop fuels his decision to keep a close eye on him, just in case.

**Chenoa Johnson:** Whose name means White Dove. Baker, healer, clan matriarch, Chenoa is over her affair with Liam now. Too bad she can't make her brother believe that.

**Maya Hoffman:** One of Chenoa's best friends

**Brent Hoffman, MD:** Maya's father, owner of The Temple Garden

**Ruth Jacobson:** Brent's fiancée

**Jasmine Quinn:** Another of Chenoa's friends. Jasmine and Seth have known each other all their lives

**Brandon Ablemarle:** Jasmine's boyfriend

**Ken Cavanaugh:** Seth's uncle

**Glenn Gilchrist:** (d) Gregg's brother, Jack's friend and co-worker. Glenn was a man with a lot of secrets.

**Camille Johnson:** Chay and Chenoa's aunt

**Erin Davis Allridge:** Chay's girlfriend

**Nick Greco:** It's been a stressful year for Seth's cousin. Make that a stressful couple of years.

**Scout Patterson:** Nick's wife and one of Lucy's best friends.

**Cole Patterson Greco:** Scout and Nick's son..**Amanda (Mandy) Cavanaugh:** Lucy and Dan's daughter.

**Kate Greco:** Nick's daughter. She and Mandy are cousins and best friends.

**Marsha Quinn:** Oberon's leading psychic and one of Lucy and Scout's best friends.

**Sam Sterling:** Marsha's husband. A former stock analyst, Sam is a man who never does anything by halves.

**Frank and Jesse James:** Marsha's twin sons.

**Siobhan Quinn:** Sinead's twin sister, owner of the local Wildlife Rescue Center

**Ryan Henderson:** Siobhan's husband and Nick and Liam's fellow police officer

**Adam Sasso:** Sinead's fiancé and owner of the Lupe e Cervo winery

**Victoria Guinevere Sasso:** Sinead and Adam's new daughter

# 1

## Midsummer

Seth Cavanaugh had been too long at the fair.[1] He'd known it after the first ten minutes, but still he'd stayed for the whole two days of the festival. Even now, as Oberon's Midsummer Faire wound slowly down around him, melting gradually into the warm, mellow gold of a perfect, summer, Sunday afternoon, he made no move toward the exit. Where was the sense in leaving, when he couldn't go home?

He was drunk. But not so drunk that he'd reached the point where he thought he could pass for sober. Or, had he got that backwards? Had he managed to drink himself past the point of delusion? He wasn't sure. And, anyway, what did it matter? Drunk was drunk, after all. And he was drunk enough, and tired enough, to be disoriented by the swirl of noise and color that surrounded him. Even if he *tried* to go home, he probably couldn't find his way.

He cast a jaded eye around at the booths selling food, handcrafts and herbs, and at others that offered a variety of readings—cards, tea leaves, auras, past lives. He had no interest in any of it. It took a moment longer for it to register in his drink-fogged brain that he was alone in the crowd. He'd lost track of his friends. The group he'd been hanging with since yesterday morning had disappeared from sight.

Good. He breathed a sigh of relief. He wasn't in the mood for company, anyhow. He didn't want to party anymore. He didn't want to laugh, or drink, or play around. He was far too disgusted with himself to socialize.

A year and six months. That's how long it had been since he'd had a drink. One year. Six months. And he'd really thought he had it beat. But that was before the night last April when he'd come home to find that one of his best friends had just bled to death on his bedroom floor.

Today would have been Ray's eighteenth birthday. Considering that it was at least partly Seth's fault that his friend was dead, there was no way he could have refused to come here this weekend or to join with the others as they said their last good-byes, as they mourned Ray's passing.

Or, as they toasted his memory again. And again. And again.

They were eighteen years old now (or at least, most of them were) just out of high school and finally able to legally gain entrance to most of the fair's restricted areas, to enjoy most—if not all—that the festival had to offer.

They had stayed awake and partied hard, all day, all night, and on through the next day. All the old crowd. Friends since grade school. Together for what might be the very last time in who knew how long. It was what Ray would have wanted them to do. What he would have been doing *with them*—had he lived.

"Wish you were here, dog," Seth murmured sadly. "Wish it was you above ground now, instead of me."

Why couldn't *he* have been the one to die? How the fuck had things gone so far wrong? He was tired of living. He was sick of the grief and the guilt and the sorrow that marked each moment. Weary from dragging his sorry ass through one day and into the next.

It was one of life's really bad jokes, that Ray should die—that he should be killed in Seth's place—and that Seth should be left behind to deal with the aftermath. It was ugly and wrong and incredibly unfair. But, it was nothing more than what he should have expected from life.

"Seth? Is that you?" A girl's soft voice pierced through the angry haze of his thoughts, startling them into flight. His mind wiped blank, Seth was surprised to notice that his wandering feet had come to a halt. When had he stopped walking? Why had he stopped? And what was causing his heart to pound so fiercely in his chest?

"Seth?" That voice again. Warm. Worried. Familiar. His heart twisted in pain as he recognized the sound.

"Deirdre?" He turned his head to stare in appalled disbelief at the face that had haunted his dreams for two years. At shiny brown hair and bright blue eyes—things he'd told himself he despised. At a smile more hesitant than he'd remembered, but just as sweet. At a bod that he'd claimed in a thousand horny fantasies. "Oh, Jesus." Fuck, this could not be happening. "What are you doing back in Oberon?"[2]

Red flags appeared on Deirdre's cheeks. "I-I live here now," she said, sounding confused as she stumbled into speech. "In Abraxas, actually. I'm going to school there. I don't know why you're so surprised to see me, I mean, you knew I'd be back, right? I-I told you about my plan, didn't I?"

"You told me?" When might that have been?

Deirdre blinked in surprise. "Well, yeah. Didn't I? It's all I've ever wanted to do, ever since I was a little girl. To go to UC Abraxas and become a journalist. Just like my mother did. I'm sure we talked about it. Don't you remember?"

"You think I'm gonna remember some bullshit idea you told me about two fucking years ago?" But, oh, hell, of course he remembered. He remembered everything about her; every moment they'd spent together, every word she'd spoken. Every look. Every kiss. How much easier would his life have been these past two years if he could have only forgotten some of it?

But he hadn't been that lucky. He remembered it all perfectly. The night they'd met, the clothes she'd worn, her laughter, her scent. He'd thought she was the prettiest girl he'd ever seen. But she'd lied right from the start, giving him a fake name and a fake story about why she was in town.

He remembered how he figured out her secret, piecing together clues until he arrived at the truth. She was a runaway. And even though he'd been willing to run away with her; willing to leave his home, his family; willing to turn himself into a liar and a thief and a fugitive—all for her sake—she'd betrayed him. She threw him over the very first chance she got. For a thug. A would-be gangster. A would-be murderer.

Still, he'd been in love, and she'd been in danger. So even though she'd betrayed him, he'd tried to save her from herself. He'd been beaten and drugged and nearly killed for his trouble. He'd lost the respect of his family and his reputation with the whole town. He'd emerged from his ordeal with an addiction he was still struggling to overcome. But that had not been the worst of it.

No, the worst had been the hours he'd spent in the dark; lying on a cold, stone floor; tied up and wracked with pain; forced to listen while, oblivious to his heartache, she made love with his captor in the next room.

Deirdre. Deirdre of the sorrows. In the two years since he'd seen her, he'd done a little reading. She'd been well named. His Deirdre might not be quite as innocent as her namesake, but she was no less skilled at wrecking a guy's life.

"It's been two years," he reminded her again. Two years. And for each time he remembered her and cursed the day they met, there'd been at least that many times he'd prayed that she'd come back to him.

Until the night Ray died, and life became a twisted joke. Now, she was the last thing he needed. The last thing he wanted. The last person he ever wanted to see.

He met her eyes, intending to tell her just that, when his attention was snagged by a shimmer of silver. Two slender teardrop earrings—

earrings he'd bought for her—hung in her ears. He remembered the joy he'd taken in their purchase, his boyish eagerness to see her wear them.

How dare she wear them now. How dare she mock his pain.

"Let's see how much you remember," he said as he reached out and grabbed hold of her arm. He hauled her against him and captured her mouth, moving his other hand to the back of her head and burying his fingers in her hair, determined to hold her where she was until he was done with her.

It didn't take more than a moment to realize that it wouldn't be necessary. She melted against him almost instantly, just like always. Opening her mouth to him. Feeling so right. Tasting exactly as he remembered.

He'd thought he could embarrass her. Or, even better, that he could bring her to her knees, filled with remorse, with sorrow, with regret for what they might have had. Instead, in another instant he'd be the one on his knees, begging her to take him back.

Anger filled him as he realized what was happening. He slid his hand out of her hair and brought it down to palm her breast. She shuddered but made no protest. He squeezed and groped with no finesse and very little tenderness, until at last, he felt her grow restive. Then he pushed her away.

He smirked, pleased with the flush on her cheeks, the confusion in her eyes. "Wow, you're easy. I'd almost forgotten that."

Deirdre gasped. More color flooded her face. The confusion left her eyes, to be replaced by fury. She raised her arm to slap his face, but he caught her wrist before the blow could land.

"Don't even try it," he warned.

Eyes flashing, she pulled her arm from his grasp. He watched in satisfaction as she stormed away. For an instant, the urge to go after her was nearly overwhelming. But what would he do when he caught her? It was not knowing the answer that kept him rooted where he stood.

"Well, you really fucked that up." Once again a girl's soft voice penetrated his thoughts. Not quite so warm. Not even worried. All too familiar. "So, it's not just me you're trying to piss off these days? It's all girls now? That's good to know."

Seth closed his eyes and groaned. "Cara."

Just perfect. Of course he'd have a witness to his behavior. And, of course, it would be her. He opened his eyes and turned to find Cara smiling at him. It was her new lopsided grin, which he had yet to get used to. But, on the other hand, maybe he never would. Maybe the scars that marked her face and neck, her sightless eye, her ruined smile, would seem forever strange. His gaze softened. He smiled ruefully. "How're you doin'?"[3]

Deirdre pushed blindly through the crowd with no clear idea where she was headed, just wanting to put as much distance between Seth and herself as she could. She knew they'd run into each other sometime. With so much unfinished business between them, how could they not? But she hadn't been expecting it today, and she definitely hadn't been expecting something like this.

What had happened to him? The Seth she remembered would never have acted like that. But, they'd known each other for so short a time, maybe she was stupid for having any expectations, for trusting in her memory or her heart. For thinking she knew him.

Her stomach roiled. She felt sick. Hurt. Angry. Confused. Betrayed. And vaguely disgusted by the detached, journalistic part of her mind that continued to observe her reactions, to catalogue her feelings, and which now, apparently, had decided that lonely was a good addition to the list of words by which she might be described.

A sob nearly broke from her throat then, and the tears she would not shed threatened to overwhelm her; tears born of anger and outrage, much more than sadness. So what if she was lonely? She had known when she'd left for Oberon three weeks ago, right after her high school graduation, that she'd be on her own for a while. It had been her choice.

Her friends had declared the gap between high school and college a ten-week-long party, but Deirdre hadn't been interested in partying. Some inner voice had been whispering to her for some time, warning that she was running out of time; that she needed to start living now. Right now. Today.

Her parents may have been dismayed, initially, by her decision, but they'd recovered quick enough. And then, perhaps feeling that someone in the family should be taking the summer after graduation off, perhaps intent on re-living one of the pivotal events of their own youth, they'd gone to Europe in her stead.

In general, Deirdre didn't mind being on her own. A lot of the time she actually preferred it. But there were other times, times like now, when she really wouldn't mind seeing a friendly face.

"Whoops. Careful, now," a voice boomed out, right in front of her, just as she barreled into someone she would have sworn had not been there a moment before. "It doesn't always hurt to look where you're going, you know."

Startled, Deirdre looked up into a familiar face—a familiar, friendly face. "Rafe?"

Two years ago, when she'd run away to Oberon, she'd been befriended by a group of surfers who were camping out near the beach—Rafe among them. They took her in, fed her, gave her a place to stay. She never got the chance to thank them, or even say good-bye. As the memories crowded back, Deirdre surprised herself by throwing her arms around Rafe's neck and hugging him fiercely. The loneliness, the sadness and much of the confusion she'd been feeling receded.

Rafe chuckled softly. "Hey, there, Dee. It's good to see you, too."[4]

She pulled back to look at him. "What are you doing here?" From his sandaled feet to the gold-and-copper curls on his head, he looked just as she remembered. Even his outfit, surfer shorts and a Hawaiian shirt, was reassuringly familiar. "Where are the others?" She glanced around, half-expecting that Ana and Gabby and the rest of the crew would materialize from out of the crowd.

"Oh, they're all busy elsewhere." Rafe lowered his voice conspiratorially. "I'm flying solo this mission."

Mission? Deirdre eyed him curiously. "So, you don't live here now?"

"Heavens, no." He appeared vaguely scandalized by the thought. "No fixed abode for me. I'm just visiting." He cocked his head to the side, eyes twinkling as he added, "Same as you, hmm?"

Deirdre shook her head. "No, actually, I moved down here a couple of weeks ago. I'm over in Abraxas."

Rafe's smile held a hint of challenge. "Yeah? Think that'll last?"

"I hope so." Deirdre stared at him in dismay as doubts assailed her. "I-I think so." All her life had been leading her here. For as far back as she could remember, she'd dreamed of moving to Oberon, of following in her birth mother's footsteps.

But had that been her dream, or Paige's dream for her? She was no longer certain. She'd been learning a lot about her mother lately, and there were a few steps along Paige's path she'd just as soon skip. Giving birth to a child she couldn't raise was one such step. Being murdered was another.

But they weren't the only ones.

She now knew that a big part of the reason Paige had stayed in Oberon was because she was in love with a man who didn't love her back, who'd broken her heart. Seth's father, in fact.

Bile rose in her throat as she remembered Seth's sneer, the coldness in his eyes. Could two years really make that much of a difference? Wasn't it more likely she'd been wrong about him from the start? Just as Paige had been wrong about Dan.

It wasn't too late to learn from her mother's mistakes; to avoid repeating Paige's pattern of wasting her life and her love on some man who couldn't care less. Seth Cavanaugh could go to hell.

"Careful what you wish for," Rafe murmured. He smiled at her sadly. "Don't be so quick to judge, Dee. Remember, things aren't always what they seem at first glance. Most people aren't bad, you know. They're just lost."

Deirdre shrugged. "Maybe." Not that it mattered. If Seth was lost, he could damn well stay that way. And all the dreams she'd had for the two of them, her visions of the future they might someday share, could damn well die.[5]

How many times in the past had she cried over Seth, or wished for the power to magically transport herself back here, just so she could be with him? So many, she'd lost count. Even once was too much.

Rafe sighed. "Don't look so sad. Keep the faith. Eventually, you know, things do work out according to plan."

Not for me they don't. Deirdre shook her head. Never the way I want them to. "I don't have a plan." Not anymore.

Rafe smiled. "Well, that's the beauty of it all, isn't it? You don't need one. The plan has you."

"How am I doing?" Cara's voice held a hint of laughter as she repeated his question and Seth could see amusement gleaming in her one functioning eye. "Better'n you, from the looks of things. So, that's something, I guess."

She was laughing at him? Fucking perfect. "Glad to hear it," he mumbled as he turned and headed away from her.

"Se-*ethh*! Not so fast," Cara whined. "Where you goin'? Wait up."

Wait up? "Nah, I don't think so." He shook his head and kept on going—until the memory of Cara's leg, shattered thigh bone protruding through bloody, torn flesh, rose before his eyes. Oh, crap. It had been a couple of months, but he knew it still gave her trouble. Stop, you jerk. Don't make her chase after you. Guilt and nausea brought him to a dead stop, stomach lurching, festival booths tilting precariously as the whole damn fairground began to spin.

"What d'you want?" he grunted, desperately clenching his jaw in order to keep from spewing.

She limped over to where he'd stopped and peered at him curiously. "Wow. You're really faded, huh? You want a ride home or something? I was gonna hit the cuts soon anyhow. But, listen, no puking in my car, 'kay?"

They were going the same way, but Seth shook his head. "Thanks, but forget it. I'd like to get there in one piece."

"Dude. That's what I'm saying. You're too drunk to drive yourself."

"I know that," he sighed. "But I'm not so drunk I don't remember how badly you drive—even when you're sober."

Cara's smile faded as she pouted at him. "I'm not that bad a driver. Why are you tripping? It's not like I get into tons of accidents, or anything."

"No, but you've got more tickets than...than...than anyone. Isn't your license like...suspended, or something? Why d'you suppose that is?"

"It is not suspended." She crossed her arms and scowled at him. "I told you that. They're letting me do traffic school instead. Remember? I got almost a whole freakin' week of it. Starting tomorrow. Besides, it's the po. They don't like me."

Seth nodded. "I hear that. The cops don't like me much anymore, either." Even despite his cousin being on the force. He frowned. "But, hey, I thought you had a thing going with that guy—what's his name? Can't he do something for you?"

Cara sighed wistfully. "You mean Liam? I haven't seen him since...well, since that one time when you both came to see me in the hospital."

"Really? Well, that's not right." Seth could feel his forehead crinkle up as he tried to think. Liam was a cop—by definition, something of a jerk—but, word was, he'd come close to killing the guy who'd attacked Cara. He'd even shot one of the other cops when they tried to stop him. So, obviously, he had to care about her. "How come you haven't seen him?"

Cara angled her chin and glared at him. "Gee, I dunno. Must be my new look, I guess."

Seth couldn't help wincing. Shit. Her 'new look' included a blind eye and a shitload of scars. He'd be lying if he claimed it didn't take some getting used to, and no doubt she'd call him on it if he tried. But, before he could think of anything to say that might make her feel better, someone passing too close behind her jostled Cara's arm. She gasped and went rigid, all the color draining from her face.

"It's okay. Calm down," Seth murmured, watching helplessly as she trembled uncontrollably. Ever since the night of her attack, Cara had had a problem with being touched, even casually. And there was nothing anyone could do to comfort her, since even hugs were out of the question. But what the fuck was she thinking coming here today? She knew what events like this were like. With tons of people stumbling around half drunk, she was asking for trouble. He shook his head, annoyed, disgusted, too tired to deal with any of it. "Come on, let's get out of here."

Cara looked at him, surprise replacing the pain in her eyes. "Seth, forget it. You're still too drunk to drive."

"I know. You drive."

Her eyes narrowed. "So you're all of a sudden okay with that? How come?"

He smiled at her. "'Cause I just remembered something. I don't want to live that long, anyhow."

# 2

Sunlight glittered on the surface of San Bartolo Bay, dazzling Deirdre's eyes, making them water, forcing her to squint to see the road as she drove back to her apartment in the neighboring town of Abraxas. The confusion brought on by her encounter with Seth had returned full force, along with sorrow, anger, remorse. His coldness left her feeling almost as violated as she'd felt the night, two years earlier, when she'd allowed herself to be all but raped in an effort to save his life.

It was just one of several traumatic events she'd had to deal with during her first trip to Oberon and, if she were honest, not even the worst of them. Still, it had been a sacrifice on her part, one made reluctantly, out of necessity. One she'd often regretted—but never so much as today. One he'd never thanked her for, or even acknowledged.

It's not that she wanted his pity, but a little sympathy wouldn't hurt, a hint of respect, of remorse, of guilt, even–

"Why is that too much to ask?" she demanded angrily of the empty air, wishing Seth was there to answer her question, wishing she'd thought to ask him today when they were finally face to face. She thought about everything she'd suffered, everything she'd given up, so much of it either Seth's fault, or for his sake. "You owe me, you jerk. You'd be dead now, if it weren't for me. How could you treat me this way?"

*Wasn't it really your own fault*? That objective little voice in her head inquired. She had to admit it had a point. Even Paige hadn't been *this* stupid. Dan Cavanaugh might not have loved her mother, but Deirdre knew for a fact he wouldn't ever have behaved like his son. She had only to remember how kind Dan had been to her the last time she was here, to know that...

*"So, it was all a lie?" she'd asked, unable to keep her voice from trembling. She'd been in the hospital, being treated for her wounds after they'd all nearly died—she and Seth and Seth's mom—and she'd just learned that everything she'd grown up believing, everything Paige had told her over the course of her entire lifetime was false.*

*Dan wasn't her father. In fact, up until a few months earlier, he hadn't even known she existed. It was measure of how fucked up, twisted and skewed everything was that she couldn't even tell if that was a good thing. She knew only that the loss of everything she thought she knew about herself, her family, her parents, left her feeling alone and adrift. Rootless. Weightless. Lost.*

*Dan had gazed at her sadly. His wife and son were in the hospital, too, and Deirdre was sure he'd much rather be with them. But they had their friends and family around them and she had no one. So he'd stayed and kept her company instead. He'd held her hand through the tetanus shot, the rabies shot, the anesthetic. He'd distracted her—answering her questions, asking a few of his own—while her mauled arm was cleaned and stitched and bandaged. He'd waited, patiently, while she was bundled into bed and given a compress for the bruise on her face; seeming so solid and supportive, so much like the dad she'd always wanted.*

*Only then, when she was settled and calm, did he tell her the truth. Or, something close to it.*

*"I don't know if it was a lie, exactly," he'd said, letting her down as gently as he could. "Although it sounds like a lot of what you were told may have been exaggerated."*

May have been? *He was being kind, but she wasn't stupid. They'd both known better. A lie was* exactly *what it was. It hadn't taken anything more complicated than a blood test to confirm that. Deirdre felt her face flame with mortification. She'd run away from home. She'd put herself and her parents through hell. She'd come to Oberon in search of the man she'd been told was her father.*

*And somewhere along the way, she'd fallen for his son.*

*How great was that?*

*"I'm sorry for all the trouble I've caused," she'd murmured, blinking back tears, feeling lost and confused. Feeling angry. Feeling cheated. Whichever way she tried to look at it, the answer kept coming out the same: She couldn't have them both. She was either going to lose the father she'd always dreamed of finding, or the boy she'd fallen in love with.*

*And it wasn't even anyone's choice to make. It was a matter of fate, of circumstance, of random cells that may or may not have collided seventeen years earlier. Suddenly the whole Biology is Destiny cliché made sickening sense.*

*"I talked to your friend Rafe about you and Seth," Dan continued, speaking more slowly now, as if he really didn't want to know the answer, but had to ask the question anyway. "You two weren't– I mean that night on the beach, and then at the May Faire you and Seth didn't, uh...?"*

*He was asking whether they'd had sex, and once again she felt her cheeks flame. "Oh! No." She shook her head. "No, we didn't."*

*Dan looked relieved "Oh. Well, good. That's probably just as well. I mean, just in case..."*

*Just in case he was* her *father, too, that's what he'd meant. And even though she was sick at heart, still she had to share in his relief. "Yeah," she said, agreeing quickly. "I know what you mean."* Smiling like she couldn't care less, like none of it mattered, she added, "But you know, if it turns out you're not my father...well, it wouldn't be the worst thing in the world for me."At the time, she really thought she meant that.

She'd just been so horrified in the days before that—when she learned who Seth was, when she thought he was her brother—that she'd gone on to make some of the dumbest mistakes of her life. That day in the hospital, her relief at learning they might not be related after all, had overshadowed everything else.

But right now, things were looking altogether different again. Right now it seemed like that was the day she'd lost everything and gained nothing. Two years of searching had left her no closer to learning who her father might have been. And now Seth–

Damn it, she'd been *in love* with him. She'd cherished the memory of their time together. Did he have to take even that away from her?"

Damn you, Seth," she muttered again as her internal critic jotted down a few more words: guilt, projection, denial. *Who is it you're really angry with? Who's at fault here, anyway*?

Too disgusted to think about it any longer, Deirdre pulled into the alley that ran behind her apartment building and parked her car. She sat for a moment, gazing up at the building through her windshield, waiting for the familiar, happy thrill the sight of it usually brought her. But the joy was gone.

It wasn't that the three story, white stucco building trimmed in mint green and accessorized by brilliant magenta bougainvillea, was all that exceptional to look at, but it was her very first apartment, her own little place and she'd been so excited to have found it. Now, she was wondering if she shouldn't have stayed in Berkeley. She had a bad, bad feeling that, once again, her life was about to change, just when she'd been on the brink of being settled and happy.

And it was all Seth's fault. Again.

Despite what her conscience wanted to believe; Deirdre was sure most people would consider that Seth owed her a big debt from the last time. For two years she'd fantasized that he'd think so, too. That he'd be willing—no, desperate—for the chance to make it up to her, for all she'd lost.

Not anymore. Now, even if he wanted to pay her back, she wouldn't let him. She wouldn't let him touch her, or kiss her or...anything. She was over him. She'd suffered enough. She didn't even care who's fault it was. She was *not* a martyr. She would *not* let him hurt her anymore.As Deirdre exited her car, she was startled to hear a familiar, plaintive meow coming from above her head. She glanced up at her apartment's back window, and froze. Her cat stared down at her from the fire escape.

"Snowball, how'd you get out there?" she asked, still gaping; too surprised, too focused on her pet to even notice the sound of a car starting up. Eyes on her cat, she took one step forward and immediately felt herself lifted and flung backwards. She was slammed against her car, flattened against the side of it as though her clothes were lined with magnets, just as another car flashed past her, missing her with only inches to spare. Darkness rose before her eyes even as the force that had pinned her to her car dissolved. Her knees went weak.

And as she sank toward the ground, she knew a moment of pure disorientation during which she'd swear she could hear Rafe's voice murmur, "That's another thing I came to tell you: Always look both ways."

THE COPPERY TASTE of fear filled Jack Connelly's mouth as he thought about what he had done, what he had *nearly* done, and what he was going to do. It was a feeling and a flavor he hadn't sampled in over twenty years.

As he left the town of Abraxas behind and headed toward home his heart was racing. His glance returned repeatedly to his rear-view mirror as he waited for the wail of sirens behind him, the rotating flash of police lights that would spell disaster.

"I can't fucking believe I'm doing this," he muttered, still appalled at the risk he'd taken, even as, faint but unmistakable, a sensation, half-forgotten, and not entirely unpleasant, began to unfold within him. "Christ, I must be outta my mind."

For most of his adult life Jack had been a model citizen, a pillar of the community. He was a successful businessman, a respected lawyer, a senior partner in the firm his late father had helped found. Every deal he'd made, or touched, or had taken part in had been above board. Or at least that's how he'd made damn sure they appeared. His life and his practice were secure, successful, seemingly above suspicion, beyond scrutiny or reproach. Caesar's wife should look so good, he'd often thought.

Which was not to say he never took risks. Of course he did. One had to, he'd found, if only to keep the juices flowing. Otherwise one got sloppy. And lazy. And careless.

And that was the biggest risk of all.

But, in all those years, the risks he'd taken were small and carefully hedged. The kind that weighed big profits against negligible consequences and always included a scapegoat; someone else to catch the flack if the deal went bad.

There were some lessons you learned fast and never forgot. *Cover Your Ass* was one of those. Whatever else he did, Jack had always, always made sure he had his own back. Or so he believed.

Those twenty years of safety had come to an abrupt halt a little over six months earlier when he'd received a surprising summons from a former friend. Gregg Gilchrist had been the leader of the gang to which Jack had belonged when he was still a wild and impressionable young man.

*With his head shaved, his hands and neck and the back of his skull vividly decorated with grotesque tattoos, the man now known as Rev. Gregg Stevens looked very little like the Gregg that Jack remembered. In fact, if it weren't for those strange, pale eyes, that indefinable* something *in Gregg's manner, and the twisting in Jack's innards when the other man looked at him—a feeling akin to having swallowed a live snake—Jack would never have recognized his old master at all.*

*Were twenty years in prison enough to affect the kinds of changes he was observing now in his former associate's appearance? Jack supposed they might be. But, knowing Gregg as well as he did, he suspected there was more to the story than that. Probably a lot more.*

*Happily ensconced in a blood-colored, leather armchair, his arm wrapped negligently around the barely-clad, barely-legal honey who huddled in his lap, Gregg smiled. "You're looking fit, JJ. Congratulations. You've obviously done well for yourself."*

*JJ. Jack Junior. It was a diminutive Jack despised and had stopped using on the day his father passed. He was pretty sure Gregg's use of it now was, in part, an attempt to remind Jack of their old association; and, in part, a hint that Gregg might want something from him. Jack didn't appreciate the reminder, or the hint, but he held his tongue. The Gregg he used to know hadn't responded well to being crossed, it was a safe bet the new, revised edition wouldn't like it much either.*

*"Thanks, Guts," Jack replied, repaying tit for tat, using Gregg's old nickname, as well. "I uh, I was real sorry about you brother's death. He's missed at the firm. He was an asset to us all." Glenn Gilchrist had been an asset to Jack, for sure. An asset, a sidekick, a potential fall guy, a drinking partner, a scapegoat. In short, a friend.*

*But Gregg waved away the mention of his brother. "Call me Reverend. It's so much more in keeping with my role here at the church, don't you think?"*

*"Oh, of course." Jack nodded, quickly correcting his supposed mistake. "Whatever you say. Reverend it is, then. It's a wonderful thing you're attempting here, by the way. Very spiritual. Uplifting." Wonderful was a relative term, of course, and church an even broader one. What Gregg was running was either a cult or a scam, or a mixture of both. And if Jack were to hazard a guess, he'd imagine that the members of any church presided over by Gregg were likely to drink blood, to invoke demons, to sacrifice virgins at each full moon. Speaking of which–*

*Jack let his gaze linger on the pretty young thing perched on The Reverend's lap. He felt his cock stir and his interest rise as Gregg absently stroked her bare thigh. Was she the flavor of the week? If so, then, alleluia, Jack might just have found religion.*

*Talk about rapture! Assuming Gregg was willing to share, Jack would happily sermonize her sweet, young ass until the last horn sounded. "I'm sure we could all use a little...salvation, now and then," he murmured transferring his gaze to Gregg's face and eyeing him questioningly.*

*Gregg smiled. His arm tightened around the girl's waist and he pulled her closer. "Amen to that." As Gregg's hand slipped between her legs, the girl shuddered, squeezed her eyes shut, said nothing. Jack felt his pulse begin to pound...*

It was pounding now, too, as he recalled that occasion and others just like it. Gregg had teased him with the girl, dangling the idea of her in Jack's mind, letting him think he could have her. It was like a drug, it kept him coming back for more.

Over the next few months, Jack found himself more and more embroiled in Gregg's affairs; setting up trust funds and corporate accounts; protecting Gregg's assets. And compromising his own security in the process. Remembering it now was like remembering a bad dream. One from which he could still not quite awaken.

Jack breathed a sigh of relief as he approached the turn-off to the subdivision where his house was located. He'd made it. For now, he was home free.

His heart was still pounding, and he could still taste the fear. But stronger than either was that other, half remembered sensation: the thrill of exhilaration that could only come from a life lived on the edge.

LUCY WAS FRETTING. She hadn't said anything yet, but Dan Cavanaugh could tell by her vicious treatment of the pillows and towels she was readying for tomorrow's camping trip that his wife wasn't happy.

"What's wrong, babe?" he asked, stepping out onto the porch where she was working. He was pretty sure he already knew the answer, but he'd learned the hard way not to take anything for granted. Especially where Lucy was concerned.

"Nothing," Lucy snapped. Then she unwound a little. "Did Seth get here yet?"

Dan shook his head. "I tried reaching him, but his phone's off. My guess is he's either still out at the festival, or else he forgot."

"Great. Just great," Lucy muttered between clenched teeth. She grabbed a pillowcase from the pile of laundry she was folding and snapped it, startling a hummingbird who'd been feeding among the blossoms of the trumpet vine that grew along the porch. "He promised me he'd drop by this afternoon so I could run through things with him. Now, what's he going to do while we're gone?

Dan sighed. "Well, considering that—other than these last few weeks—he's lived here his whole life, what exactly did you think you were going to tell him that he doesn't already know? I mean, even if he forgets to bring his key when he stops by to check up on things, it won't be a problem. He knows where we keep the spare, doesn't he?"

Lucy glowered at him. "Dan, half the teenagers in Oberon know where we keep the spare key. It's the worst hiding place ever. You might as well tape it to the front door with a note that says, *come on in*. It's a good thing that most people in town are honest."

"True. But since they are, it wouldn't even matter if Seth forgot to come by at all, would it? So, what is it that's really bothering you?"

"Nothing," Lucy repeated. "I just– Well, it's been two weeks since we've seen him, Dan. I thought he'd at least stop by and say goodbye. I thought-"[1]

"You thought he'd change his mind and come with us, didn't you?"

Lucy sighed. "He always used to enjoy it" she answered wistfully.

"It's been a tough couple of months for him, babe. You know that. You can't expect him to get over something like that right away. But it doesn't mean he'll never go camping with us again. It's like your cousin, right? For three years Nick hasn't come with us, and you were so certain he'd never want to come again. Remember? And now you've talked him into it *and* your brother and *my* brother as well. God help us."

"And Marsha and Sam," Lucy reminded him. "Although, I suppose I can't really take too much credit for that."

"Nope," Dan agreed, happy for the change of subject. "Sam's been spoiling for an excuse to use that camper of his ever since he bought it. Not that I'm complaining. You put your cousin and a fully loaded traveling kitchen together and this could be a very memorable trip. Food-wise, anyway."

"Hmph." A small smile made its appearance on Lucy's lips. "*Very* memorable, I'm sure—especially with the ridiculous competition Nick and Scout have going on. Both of them wanting to wear the chef's hat in the family. What is wrong with those two?"

Lucy looked exasperated but Dan was sure his wife was getting a huge kick out of watching as her best friend and her favorite cousin turned their marriage into an Iron Chef Triathlon. How could she not be enjoying it? After all, it was her recipe that had started Scout cooking in the first place.

"They're acting like kids," Lucy said primly, although that rogue smile still flickered at the edges of her mouth.

"Exactly." Dan saw his chance and pounced on it. "So, with all the kids we've got coming on this trip already, we're not likely to miss one more."

"That's different," Lucy snapped, her smile disappearing. "Seth's not just...some random, extra kid we'd have tagging along with us, Dan. He's our own son. Our baby. And he's hurting."

"But, he's *not* a baby, Luce. Not anymore. You can't protect him from the world."

"I can try," Lucy replied stubbornly.

"It's just a week," Dan soothed. "Nothing's going to happen."

"It might." Lucy bit her lip. "And who can he turn to for help if it does? It's next to impossible to reach us by phone with all the interference in the canyon. And there's gonna be no one left in town for him to go to!" She threw the pillowcase into the box she was packing and turned to him, seething. "This is a hell of a time for Siobhan and Ryan to take a second honeymoon. Just 'cause the last one was cut short by a couple of days–"

Dan sighed. "It doesn't matter, does it? You know Seth would sooner die than ask either of them for help." He winced a little, hearing the words that had just left his mouth, but luckily, Lucy had seized on a new idea and didn't seem to notice.

"He'd ask Sinead," she said, face brightening as she thought about it. "Maybe she and Adam haven't left for San Francisco yet. Maybe I can talk her into postponing their trip?"

Dan rolled his eyes. "Lucy, they've had these dates planned for months—since before the baby was born—you know that. They're not going to change them now. Besides, you can't ask for something like that."

Lucy frowned. "I don't know why not. When we agreed to let Seth move out to the winery it was partially because Sinead promised me she'd keep an eye on him. Otherwise, it never would have happened."

"We didn't *agree* to let him move out, Luce. He's eighteen. He made his own decision."

"We could have stopped him, if we wanted," Lucy insisted. "If he had to pay the rent on a place like that, you know he could never afford it. It only works because Sinead has a soft spot for him. Otherwise–"

"Otherwise he'd be living in a hole-in-a-wall somewhere, and you'd be worrying even more," Dan pointed out. "Look, just relax, okay? He'll be fine. It's one week. What could happen in that time?"

"Plenty." Lucy glared at him, scathingly. "A week is long enough for almost anything to happen, Dan. Anything at all."[2]

IT HAD TAKEN Deirdre several minutes, a pretense of patience and a can of tuna fish, to coax her cat back into the apartment. The silver-tipped Persian had lashed his tail and gazed at her warily. He'd looked frightened, furious, frustrated—or maybe Deirdre was simply projecting her own emotions onto her pet. She was still shaken from her near miss in the alley, after all. But, she couldn't deal with that right now, so she put it from her mind and concentrated instead on the question at hand: How had Snowball gotten out?

Had he slipped out the door when Deirdre was leaving to go to the faire? Had he squeezed himself through the window when it had been open earlier in the day? Or was there another, more sinister, explanation? Had someone been in here while Deirdre was gone?

Even living alone, it was hard to tell if everything was just as she had left it. Had she really stacked the mail up so precisely? Or left her hairbrush on the edge of the sink? Had her computer's mouse been moved...or not? The kinds of thing that had bugged her, that caught her eye or appeared out of place, could all be attributed to the cat, or the wind, or simple inattention.

Any other, more sinister explanation made no sense at all.

All the same, as she glanced around, searching for evidence, she was uncomfortably conscious of feeling like she was being watched. It was a sensation she'd had too often in the last few weeks; so strongly, at times, that she'd even begun to wonder if the apartment was haunted. There was nothing conclusive. Nothing she could put her finger on, or point to with surety, but all the same, something felt *off*.

Or was she imagining things? Maybe she just didn't want to admit that she was frightened of being alone?

She made herself a sandwich with the open tuna, hoping to distract herself with dinner. Then she poured herself a glass of iced tea and took that and her plate out on the fire escape.This was where she'd taken to eating most of her meals. The air was sultry and warm and the view—gazing out over the rooftops of downtown Abraxas, facing southeast, toward the foothills and Oberon—was magical.

She had a good view of her car, too, parked right across the alley. She looked down at it, puzzling again over the events of the day. What really happened in the alley tonight? It had all occurred so fast, it was surreal. Like a bad dream. And Rafe—had he followed her here? Had he gotten here ahead of her?

Or had he not been here at all? Had the voice she'd heard been only in her head?

There was no way he could have been waiting in the alley when she got there, not without her noticing him. And there was no way he could have pinned her to her car without her seeing him, either. Except that he had.

Unless it was someone else? Or no one at all?

Bothersome as all those unanswered questions were, even more disturbing was the feeling of déjà vu she'd been experiencing ever since, along with a nagging suspicion of danger.

This was the second time in her life she'd come close to being hit by a car. The first time it was Seth who'd saved her...

*"Hey! Watch out!" Deirdre jumped as she felt a hand close around her arm. She was vaguely aware of a loud, clattering noise as she was jerked back onto the sidewalk. A car squealed by, just inches from where she'd been standing, and disappeared around the corner. She looked up startled, into a pair of furious brown eyes.*

*"Just what the hell did you think you were doing?" Seth demanded; so angry it took her breath away...*

Angry—that's how he'd looked today, too. But why? What the hell was his problem? Maybe bad-tempered was his normal mood these days, but that sure hadn't used to be the case.

There'd been a reason for his anger the day he'd saved her from being run down in the street. He'd been angry because she hadn't called, because he thought she'd forgotten about him. Maybe that was what was bothering him now, too?

Suddenly hopeful, Deirdre considered the idea. After all, they hadn't seen each other in over two years, he could think that, couldn't he? But, no. That was ridiculous. Given the way she'd melted on the spot the moment he touched her, he couldn't possibly believe that was the case.

Thinking about Seth, about that kiss, about the scorn on his face when he pushed her away, put an ache in the pit of her stomach. Her appetite gone, she pushed her sandwich to the side, tucked her knees up to her chest, wrapped her arms around them and stared off into the distance. She was confused by her body's reaction to Seth; annoyed, embarrassed and as much dismayed as she was relieved.

She'd been...aroused, tingling from head to toe, breathless with sensations she hadn't felt in a very long time. So long, in fact, that she'd begun to worry she might never feel that way again. Never again know passion or desire. Never crave to touch or be touched.

Never thrill to a kiss.She'd been startled by her response, by the heat that blasted through her.

She'd been ecstatic, initially, and all too happy to revel in the way she was feeling.It wasn't so much to ask for, was it? To be normal again. To be like anyone else. To have relationships, to fall in love, to someday have a family of her own. And she'd been so afraid that the events in her past had made that impossible, had left her crippled, traumatized for life.

Still, great as it was to realize she'd been mistaken about that, did it really have to be Seth who inspired her recovery? She didn't *want* to want him, damn it. Not now that he'd become such a jerk.

"Easy, am I?" she muttered, and once again felt outraged. "That shows how much you know." It was absurd, ironic, untrue. *Easy* was the last thing she'd been these past two years. If anyone else had told her that, she'd have laughed at their stupidity.

But, coming from Seth, there was nothing funny about it. It was hurtful and cruel. It stung. Much like ripping open old scars and pouring in salt.

Maybe she had been crippled after all, hard-wired to respond only to guys who were cold, unfeeling, hell-bent on causing her pain. Maybe biology *was* destiny, after all, and bad judgement was a trait she'd inherited from her mother.If that was the case...God, she was so screwed.

She didn't want to end up like Paige—alone, unhappy, dead before her time. But how could she hope to escape from her fate while she only had half the picture? She needed to find the missing piece of her puzzle, didn't she? She needed to know who her father had been.

Too bad her search had turned up nothing but roadblocks and dead ends. Neither of the cooperative, nice guys her mother had finally gotten around to listing—in the video Deirdre had received from her upon turning eighteen—had turned out to be her father. The others, long shots and losers, for the most part, were either missing or dead.

After wasting months trying to track them down, writing letters, sending emails, conducting countless computer searches, Deirdre could finally understand why Paige had pinned all her hopes on Dan.

He was stable, locatable, dependable, nice. And a concerned parent, too. Given how unbelievably crappy Seth had acted today, Deirdre was more sorry than ever that Dan was not her Dad.

"Why couldn't he have been?" she asked the evening sky. Why couldn't Paige's plans for them all have worked out? For two years Deirdre had consoled herself with the idea that it was all for the best, that she'd traded Dan for Seth, that it was, in some ways, *better* like this.

But it sure didn't feel better now. So, maybe Paige had been right after all? *That* was the way things should have been. The only way this mess could have turned out right for any of them. Because, the way things were now, just plain sucked.

# 3

Monday afternoon found Officer Liam McKnight fuming. Ever since he'd rejoined the force a couple of months earlier, he'd been pulling the worst assignments imaginable. All part of paying his dues, he figured, for having had the audacity to quit and come back.

Considering that he'd also distinguished himself during his time off by accidentally shooting a fellow officer, he knew there were some who thought he was getting off too easy.

But, Jesus Christ; they wanted him to teach traffic school? Were they fucking kidding? That sucked beyond belief! He wasn't a teacher, damn it. He'd rather be out checking meters—not that Oberon had any. He'd rather be doing just about anything. Manning a speed trap. Writing citations. Even directing traffic. But no such luck. Instead, for the next several days, he was gonna be stuck in a room with a group of disgruntled citizens, trying to pretend that their combined frustration wasn't torquing his nerves into corkscrews.

He stared moodily out the window of the classroom he'd been assigned, ignoring his 'students' for as long as he could, while he waited for the last of the stragglers to arrive. For how much longer would he be drawing the short straw? How many more bullshit assignments could they possibly come up with? If they thought he'd get fed up and quit, they could think again. He hadn't left the force last winter out of choice, it had been a necessity. It was the only thing he could have done, given the circumstances. Now that he was back where he belonged, he was damn sure staying put.

No matter what they threw at him.

Which was not to say that he regretted his actions. However little he liked the outcome, he'd done what he had to do. On the upside, he'd finally laid his ghosts to rest. And if the same situation were to arise again, there were only a few things he'd want to do differently.

He stiffened suddenly, eyes widening, as a familiar looking RX7 sped into the parking lot. Tires squealing, it came to a too hasty stop that left it parked diagonally across two spaces. "What the fuck," he muttered beneath his breath as his heart began to pound and his mouth went dry. *It can't be...can it*? He held his breath and waited while the car's door swung open. Then the driver emerged. He inhaled sharply, exhaled slowly, and smiled. "Cara.

He drank in the sight of her, memories crowding in thick and fast, but his smile faltered as he watched her hurry across the lot toward the building, her gait unsteady, her right leg dragging. "Slow down, damn it," he murmured crossly. "What's the rush? You're gonna hurt yourself."

That was Cara, for you, he supposed. Always in a hurry to get somewhere. But what was she doing here? She couldn't be looking for him. Could she? The thought gladdened his heart, until another, more logical explanation occurred to him. He returned to his desk, picked up the clipboard that held the sign-in sheet and scanned the neatly typed list of names. Sure enough, there it was. Plain as day. Matthews, C. How he'd missed seeing it the first time was a mystery, even given the cursory glance which was all he'd spared the paper until now.

He should have seen it. He should have known. Hell, he should have guessed something like this would happen.

He sank into his seat as he pondered the vagaries of fate. What were the odds of her being assigned to traffic school during the one week he was filling in? Was this some kind of set-up? Was he being fucked with again? Then he considered how badly she drove, and he guessed the odds were actually pretty damn good.

"Can we start now?" a voice inquired from one of the dozen or so desks that filled the room.

Liam frowned at the man—Caucasian, mid-fifties, medium build, moderately expensive suit, clearly annoyed at having to waste his time in this fashion. *Well, join the club.* "Not yet," Liam replied feeling tense, turning his attention to the door just as it was edged open.

And there she was.

Cara hesitated in the doorway, looking as out of place here as she had the first time he'd seen her. A half dozen heads swiveled in her direction. She flinched a little, as though recoiling from their scrutiny. Then a half dozen heads snapped back toward the front of the room as the entire class averted their eyes, shocked and embarrassed by the scars that marked her arms and throat and danced across her face.

Liam felt as though he'd been kicked in the gut. Guilt at having, once again, failed to save her lodged in his chest, making his voice more harsh than he'd intended. "Miss Matthews. It's nice of you to join us."

Cara's gaze flew to his face, her cheeks red, her mouth falling open in surprise. She looked shocked, dismayed and not even a little bit happy to see him.

Steeling himself against his disappointment, Liam forced himself to stay in his seat, while his heart was urging him to cross the room and take her in his arms. He smiled tightly. "Why don't you find yourself a seat?"

He was aware of the curious looks one or two of the others threw his way as Cara scanned the right side of the room, completely ignoring the empty seat on her immediate left. "Something wrong with that one?" he snapped, at last, pointing toward it.

She glanced at him again, blinking fast, her expression startled, angry, hurt. As she turned in the direction he had indicated, practically twisting her whole body around before sighting the chair, it hit him. *Fuck. She can't see?*

Through the roar of blood in Liam's ears, through the shock and the fury and the absolute hatred that blistered his heart, the memories surfaced, taunting, tormenting...

*If it hadn't been for her bare toes peeking out at him from the end of the cast that encased her right leg—toes that still sported the glittery peach polish he remembered so vividly—Liam wouldn't have recognized Cara when he found her. She was almost lost amid the bright, cluttered maze that was the hospital's emergency wing.*

*It wasn't as if the place was chock full of injured teens tonight, either, but her gurney had been pushed into a corner, out of the way of the ordinary ebb and flow, and there was so little of her visible.*

*Just one eye, blackened, swollen. Two lips, also swollen, bruised and split. And those five toes. That was all he had to go on. Everything else was indistinct, either swaddled in blankets or wrapped in bandages...*

Including her left Goddamned eye. Sonofabitch. *No!*

Liam had to close his own eyes as he choked down the bile that rose in his throat. The room grew still. When he'd recovered enough to open his eyes again, Cara had taken her seat. An angry flush still colored her cheeks as she met his gaze with a steady glare, the effect of which was only slightly diminished by the milky cast of her injured eye. How had he not noticed that immediately?

Liam sighed. He wasn't missing it now. In fact, he wasn't missing anything—including her bad mood. She was pissed. He didn't blame her. He dropped his own gaze to his desk. "Okay, then. Since we're all here, let's get started."

Cara felt as though her nerves were about to go to pieces. It was hard enough being out in public these days, all the time feeling like a freak. She didn't need anyone putting her on the spot and drawing even more attention her way.

And Liam, of all people!

She hadn't really meant what she'd said to Seth, yesterday. She didn't know why Liam hadn't come back to see her. They'd been friends, more than friends, and she never thought he'd turn his back on her like that. Certainly not because of her looks. She was sure there was another reason, one he just hadn't gotten around to telling her yet. She'd only said what she did because...well, because if it turned out that really *was* the reason, then she didn't want anyone else saying it first.

She didn't want anyone feeling sorry for her. Why should they?

She was alive, wasn't she? And Gregg was in prison—where he couldn't hurt her anymore. She was free. She was safe. Those were all good things. So what if there'd been a price to pay for that? Wasn't there always?

In time, her scars would fade a little—or so everyone claimed—and her leg would heal. And, maybe, she'd even learn to let people touch her again without freaking out. It was only the loss of her eye that was likely to be permanent. Especially if she let the doctors have their way and take it out altogether.

But that idea seemed so final. She couldn't bear to think about taking that step yet.

She doodled in the margin of her workbook as she listened to Liam talk, not even hearing the words, he probably wasn't saying anything she was interested in, anyway. She just loved the sound of his voice, she always had. She thought back to the few weeks they'd spent together last spring, skipping over all the mistakes his voice had talked her into making. The past wasn't really a better time, but memory had a way of making it seem like it was.

Right now, she was down with that. She wasn't ready to deal with this new version of Liam. Liam the unfriendly. Liam the cop. She didn't need that much reality in her life. She'd much prefer the blue-pill version of the past. At least for this week.

Everyone around her stirred and began to pack up, to get up, to leave. She looked at the clock, startled to realize class was over

"Miss Matthews? If you can stay behind for a couple of minutes," Liam again. "I'd like to speak with you."

Cara gazed at him warily. Why was he acting so weird? He'd called her a lot of things last April, not all of them nice, but none of them *Miss Matthews*. "About what?"

For an instant, Liam looked taken aback. "I, uh, well I had some questions about your license. There are some points against it that, um, I just need to clear some things up. It won't take long.

Her license? Cara shrugged, ducking her head, feigning a disinterest she was far from feeling. "Okay. Sure." Oh, shit, shit, *shit*. He wasn't going to tell her they were going to suspend it after all, was he? They couldn't! She needed her license. She needed it for work, she needed it for school, she needed it to get around. She just plain needed it.

She chewed on her lip, nervously rifling the pages of her book while she waited for the rest of the class to depart. Finally, they were alone.

Liam got up from his seat and went to the door. Cara heard the sound of the lock click. Even without turning, she could feel his eyes on her. She heard him walk toward her and she tensed. His hand reached out. She flinched away. Her heart beat wildly, erratically, like it always did when anyone got too close.

As Liam's hand dropped to his side, Cara felt the blood rush to her cheeks. "Sorry," she mumbled, more embarrassed for him to see her weakness than she was for him to see her scars. It was so stupid of her to act this way, especially with someone she liked, someone whose touch she'd actually longed to feel. Someone like Liam. But her body had a mind of its own these days, and it wasn't taking orders from her heart.

"No, don't be. You're right." Liam's voice was cold, quiet, dull. "This isn't the place for that."

He pulled one of the desks around so he sat facing her. "So. How are you?" he asked.

"Okay." She shrugged. She raised her head and looked at him. It had been so long and she'd missed him so much. His eyes were still as blue as ever and his hair, while shorter than it had been, was still spiky, still looked like it could use a hand to smooth it into place. If she could only focus on his face and ignore the cop outfit he'd look just like the Liam she'd always known. Her Liam. The Liam who teased and tempted, who told her how smart and brave and beautiful she was. The Liam who visited her in the hospital. Who brought her a gift. Who signed his card with love.

*Love, Liam.* That's what he'd written and maybe she'd been childish, believing that he meant it.

*I'll always believe.*

That was something else he'd written, another promise he'd made. And, childish or not, she'd always believe in him, too. And in them. Maybe he didn't love her now, but she was sure he did once. If only a little, little bit.

"You're not gonna take my license away, are you?" she asked, reverting to the topic at hand. Praying that, cop or no cop, he still cared enough to look the other way, to bend the rules for her, the way she'd always done for him.

"YOUR LICENSE?" Liam frowned, surprised by the change in subject. Not that there'd actually been a subject yet. With so much he wanted to say to her, he still didn't know where to start. "What are you talking about? Why would I–"

"Because you said you needed to talk to me about it, that's why."

"Oh. That." He shook his head. "That was just...look, I only said that because I didn't want anyone here to get the idea that we knew each other. That's all."

Cara eyed him suspiciously. "How come?"

The question caught him by surprise. "I don't know. No reason, I guess. Old habit. I mean, you *are* still a minor." Although not for too much longer, thank God. Still, he didn't want anyone to think that he was taking advantage of her.

"Liam!" Cara's brows drew close. "I can't believe you're still hung up on my age."

"I told you last April. Until you're eighteen–"

"And, omigod– You're really a *cop?*" She shook her head. "I mean, I guess I knew that already. But, I just didn't...didn't...wow. That's just...weird."

The disbelief in her tone stung. She'd made her feelings about the police very clear last April, but this was the first time he'd been included in her censure. "Hey, it could be worse," Liam quipped

"Yeah." She nodded in agreement. "I guess. You could be a doctor. Or a paramedic."

Improbably, that hurt even more. He'd heard enough from her friend Seth about how much pain she'd suffered at the hands of the EMTs who'd come to her aid the night she was attacked. But, like he'd told Seth, they were only doing their jobs. Given how badly she'd been beaten, there was probably no way she could have been moved without it hurting her. Still, neither they nor he were ultimately responsible for what had happened to her. He felt a flash of anger. "Really? I was thinking more along the lines of a violent sociopath."

For an instant, Cara's face went blank and Liam was afraid he'd gone too far. But then a trace of her usual smile flashed to the surface. "Well, lucky me. I've had my fill of all three in the last few months."

Liam sighed. "Look, can't we just have a conversation? I want to hear how you're doing, what you've been up to. Stuff like that.

"I'm okay, I guess." Cara shrugged. Then her face brightened. "I graduated High School."

Liam smiled at the hint of pride in her voice. He knew how important that had been to her, mostly because so many people had told her it would never happen. "I know." He'd been there. Lurking in the back of the auditorium. Not wanting her to see him, but yet unable to stay away and miss seeing her moment of triumph.

"Oh, and I'm gonna start taking some classes this Fall, at the Community College," she continued excitedly.

"That's great." She could have no idea how great—not just for her sake, but for his. The news that she was staying in town was exactly what he'd been hoping to hear. "What kind of classes?"

"I dunno. Probably hotel management, or something."

He looked at her, surprised. "Really? That's a new interest, isn't it?"

Cara nodded eagerly. "Well, yeah, because of my job and all. I'm working at the Morning Glory Inn—you know, out at the Lupa e Cervo winery? Seth's friends with the owner. He talked her into letting me stay there after I got out of the hospital. And then, since she needed someone to help her run the place, and I needed a job...it all worked out."

"I see." Liam drummed his fingers absently on the desktop while he tried to tamp down the unreasoning jealousy that seized him at the mention of Seth's name. It was to Seth that Cara had run the night she was attacked. She would have been killed if he hadn't been there to save her. Seth's other friend hadn't been so lucky.

But maybe there'd been more to it than luck. Liam's gaze lingered on Cara's hands and arms, where scars gave testimony to how hard she'd fought for her life. Heart twisting in grief for the pain she'd suffered, Liam reached for her hands, wanting only to hold them. But Cara shrank away from him, crossing her arms over her chest, tucking her hands away where they couldn't be seen.

"So what's Seth up to these days?" Liam asked grudgingly, leaning back in his own chair, forcing himself to keep his distance. "You see him much?" He had no damned business being jealous or resentful of her relationship with Seth. He had no business being anything but grateful. It was Seth who had saved her life. Seth—not him.

Cara blinked in surprise. "Yeah, sure I see him. He's living out there too, you know."

Liam fisted his hand on the desktop as his temper spiked again. "No, how would I know something like that?" He might have no business being jealous, that didn't mean he wasn't. "And how come? Why isn't he still at home?" *Why isn't he miles and miles away from you*? That's what he'd really like to ask. But he couldn't. It wasn't his place to suggest. Besides, he already knew the answer, didn't he? Shit.

Cara's eyes narrowed. "I guess 'cause he likes it better there. Anyway, why not? He's eighteen. Can't he do what he wants?

"Not where you're involved, he can't. You're still underage."

"Only for a few more days."

Liam nodded. Three days, to be exact. "I know." Like he needed reminding of that. Suddenly the very thing he'd been waiting for was the thing he feared the most. "But, until then, you better tell Seth to keep his hands to himself."

CARA STARED AT LIAM, too surprised to speak. She'd almost forgotten how annoying he was about the whole age thing. But, this time, his bitching was completely unwarranted. She wasn't comfortable with people looking at her too hard these days. Letting anyone touch her —even Seth—was totally out of the question.

*Tell him that*, a voice urged softly in her mind. But she couldn't. She was too ashamed. She shouldn't be this weak, this scared, this stupidly sensitive. It was dumb. And childish. And he already thought of her as a child.

"Are we finished?" she asked, feeling like she'd come right out of her skin if she had to sit in this room with him any longer, talking about nothing in particular, not ever coming close to what she wanted to say. "I- I have to go."

"Sure," Liam sighed, his disappointment in her obvious. "I'll see you tomorrow. Try to be on time."

*IT'S NOT FAIR!* Cara thought despairingly as she left the room and headed down the hallway toward the door that led to the parking lot.

*Why now*? She knew the type of women Liam found attractive. Secure, confident, accomplished women. Successful women who ran their own businesses. Someone like her new boss, Sinead Quinn. Which is why Cara could have kissed Seth when he talked Sinead into giving her this job. If she could still have kissed anyone, that is. It gave her just what she needed—room and board, a salary, and a perfect role model. [1]

She was sure that, with just a couple more weeks, or months, of modeling herself after Sinead, she could become exactly the kind of woman that Liam couldn't help but fall in love with, even with the way she looked.

But how could she convince him of that? She hadn't been expecting to see him today. She wasn't ready for him. And, now, she didn't know what to do.

She'd been through a lot in the last couple of months. Not all of the changes were on the surface, not all of them were bad and not all of them were finished. She was no longer the person he used to know, but she wasn't yet the person she hoped to become.

They'd be seeing each other almost every day for a week. Was that a good thing? Or would it ruin her only chance of making him see how different she might someday be?

ALONE IN HIS OFFICE, Jack glanced at his watch and knew a moment of panic. Taking a deep breath, he tried willing himself to let the fear go. What was the point? The situation was out of his hands. Events had been set in motion and he was powerless to stop them, even if he wanted to.

Just a few miles down the road, in the nearby town of Abraxas, there was a young woman, recently returned from her daily workout. For the past two weeks, Jack had been keeping tabs on the girl. He had learned her habits. He knew her routine. On Mondays she worked a split shift in a local coffeehouse. After work she went to the gym. Then she invariably went back to her apartment where she would take a shower prior to getting ready to return to work.

*That's where she is now*, he thought, imagining her in the shower, standing beneath the spray: naked, relaxed, vulnerable. Totally unaware of the incendiary device that was concealed in her bedroom. The one that was set to go off in a few minutes time. The one that would very shortly end her life.

The very same one that could effectively end Jack's life, too, if everything did not go exactly as planned.He ran his hands through his hair and gazed around his office, looking vainly for something with which to distract his thoughts and ease the near-painful racing of his heart.

His office was richly appointed, as befitted his position. It was sumptuous and expensive, if somewhat bland—reflecting the creative vision, or lack thereof, of his ex-wife. A flawless representation of the life he had spent years building, it was also, at the moment, a stark reminder of how terrifyingly fragile that life might turn out to be.

Jack knew that his reunion with Gregg had been a turning point. Prior to that first, fateful meeting his life had been secure, routine, unchanging. As serenely predictable as the earth's orbit around the sun.

Now, it felt more like a meteor, hurtling through space.

In the months following Gregg's surprising return to Oberon, Jack had found himself more and more embroiled in his mentor's affairs. He'd gone to work setting up trust funds and corporate accounts; and protecting Gregg's considerable assets through a variety of other highly creative, quasi-legal venues. Often compromising his own security in the process. Remembering it now was like remembering a bad dream. One from which he could still not quite awaken.

*The old mansion which served as Gregg's headquarters had been abuzz with renovation when Jack arrived there for the very last time. A new security system was being installed and the key code Gregg had given him no longer worked. It was Cara who let him in and escorted him to the large bedroom that housed Gregg's office.*

*As she led the way up the grand staircase, Jack tried, as usual, to engage her in conversation. As usual, the girl's responses were monosyllabic and disinterested, her expression unfriendly. He was not detracted, however. He would bide his time. Though his hands itched to touch her, he wouldn't allow himself that luxury just yet. There was a certain pleasure in self-denial. It was perverse. Painful. Yet, thanks to Gregg's expert tutelage, Jack had come to appreciate the exquisite torture of unsatisfied lust.*

Soon, *he thought to himself, unable to tear his eyes away from her nubile, young form.* Very soon. *His mind was hazy, his body throbbed as he followed her up the last few steps. He was as yet unsure why he'd been summoned. Was today the day Gregg would finally grant him permission to slake his needs?*

*His hopes were quickly dashed.*

*"Good. You're here. It's about time," Gregg said, as he turned off his computer and pushed his chair away from his desk. He dismissed Cara with a curt nod and then turned again to Jack. "Well? What'd you find out? Who is she?"*

*Jack suppressed a disappointed sigh. "I don't think you have anything to worry about," he assured Gregg soothingly. "This girl who's been attempting to contact you is likely a fortune hunter—nothing more. There's no reason to suppose that she's actually Glenn's daughter. If you want my advice, ignore her. There's no need for you to concern yourself with something like this. No need to talk to her or try and reason with her. If she tries to bring suit, the firm will deal with her. Until then, there's really nothing to discuss."*

*"Legal advice?" Gregg frowned. "Is that what I asked for? I'm not interested in what* you *think. What I want is information. Who she is. Where she lives. How I can find her. Have you found any of that out, Jack? Or have you come here to waste my time?"*

*Biting back the protests that rose to his lips, Jack nodded. He'd begun investigating the girl's identity two days earlier, after Gregg called him. She was young. Pretty. In fact, she strongly resembled Jack's own daughter. But if she was hoping to make a career as a grifter she had a lot to learn. She was hopelessly naive, inexperienced, probably doomed to fail. He had no trouble discovering her identify, locating her address or finding out any other basic information about her.*

*Information which, given the predatory look on Gregg's face, Jack would have much preferred not to share.*

*Not that he had a choice.*

*"Her name is Deirdre Shelton-Cooper," he recited dutifully. "She's a kid, Gregg. A high school senior, currently residing in Berkeley, but she's been accepted at UC Abraxas for the Fall semester."*

*"Good." If possible, the gleam in Gregg's eyes grew even colder. "That wasn't so hard, was it? Now, here's what else I want you to do..."*

Jack shuddered as he recalled the rest of Gregg's instructions-- both then and on their subsequent meetings. He glanced again at his watch. It was time. Taking another deep breath, he swallowed down his fear and tried hard not to think about what was happening only a few miles away...

# 4

For practically the whole day, Deirdre had been looking forward to going home; to taking a shower—no, a bath. A long soak in a hot tub filled to the brim with lavender-vanilla bubbles, that's what she wanted; or maybe orange-mint. She'd been having a rotten day. Of course it *was* Monday, and they had a tendency to suck anyway. But, when she really thought about it, things had been going wrong for her ever since the day before. Ever since her encounter with Seth.

There'd been the car that had almost hit her, the cat who had gotten out, the apartment that felt like it had been broken into—and that was only the start.

No matter how hard she'd tried to convince herself that she was safe; that it was unlikely that anyone had been in the apartment, that it was nerves, nothing more, still the uneasy feeling persisted and kept her sleepless for much of the night.

Not surprisingly, she'd woken up late. She wasn't sure how it had happened, but she must have accidentally re-set her alarm so that it didn't go off. As she was rushing around getting ready, the next problem surfaced. Something was wrong with her cat.

Snowball made sure she noticed his distress. When she headed into the kitchen he followed after her, limping and cross. He meowed piteously and licked at his paw—then laid his ears back and hissed when Deirdre tried to take a look at his foot.

Obviously, he'd injured himself during his excursion on the fire escape the day before and, obviously, a trip to the vet was the first order of business. Even though taking the time to drop her pet off at the clinic would surely make Deirdre late for work, what else could she do?

The day's next glitch occurred at the vet's office, when a flea jumped out of the cat carrier and landed on Deirdre's hand while she was rushing to fill out all the required paperwork. It was hard to argue with the receptionist's contention that a flea bath and grooming session were both dire necessities, "since he's already here..."

Since Snowball was usually content to stay in the house, fleas had never been a problem for him before. But Miss Clipboard didn't look like she believed that. "...and we *can't* have him infecting the other pets."

"What choice do I have?" Deirdre muttered, hurriedly signing yet another form when it was handed to her. She could either agree to the grooming, or find another vet.

Some choice.

It meant spending a lot of money that she had budgeted for other expenses, but she took comfort in the thought that if her boss would let her work extra hours for the next couple of weeks, she could almost break even by month's end.

How was she to know that her boss would be in such a bitchy mood that asking him for anything today was a recipe for disaster?

He was bitchy enough to tell her that the idea of giving her extra hours *wasn't gonna work* for him. Bitchy enough to declare that he *didn't give a shit* why she was late. Promptness was an employment requisite. She'd let her personal problems interfere with her ability to do her job—that's all he knew, that's all he needed to know.

Bitchy enough to decide to *fire her ass*, right there on the spot.

Despite the fact that he was leaving himself shorthanded for the day. Despite the fact that she'd been a model employee up until that very morning. Which, she supposed, should make her very grateful for the fact that he was now her ex-boss.

If that was everything that had gone wrong, however, she was sure she could have recovered her mood long before now. She was in Oberon—or close enough to make no difference—where she'd always wanted to be. The weather and the scenery were still as pretty as ever. And she hadn't liked that job much anyway.

But the day was chock full of unpleasant surprises, like the shock she got when she picked Snowball up from the vet.

"Omigod! Are you kidding me? What did you do to him?" she screeched, her voice coming out too sharp, too high, too borderline crazy. If she weren't so upset she would have cringed at the sound. If looks could've killed, she'd have died on the spot. But she was, and they couldn't, so she didn't do either—she just stared in horror at eight pounds of pissed off pet. At what had once been a handsome Persian cat and now more closely resembled a tricked out Chinese Crested.

Except for his head and his paws and the tip of his tail, Snowball had been shaved to the skin. He looked awful. If the icy expression on his face was anything to go by, he thought so too."It's a Lion Cut," the afternoon receptionist explained, sounding surprised and vaguely offended by her reaction. "Isn't that what you asked for?"

"No!" Deirdre wailed. "No, no, no, NO! He was here for a check up. And a flea bath. He'd hurt his foot—did you even find out what's wrong with it?"

"With his foot?" The receptionist pulled the cat's file up on her computer. "Let me see...yes. Apparently he had a partially torn claw. The doctor trimmed it back. And then, to make sure it doesn't happen again, he applied nail caps."

"Nail caps?" Deirdre took a closer look. Sure enough, Snowball's claws looked as though they'd received a thick, shiny coat of polish. Bright blue, to match his eyes. "Omigod. I don't believe this."

The beaming receptionist turned from the screen with a satisfied smile. "So, there you go. He's fine now."

"The hell he is," Deirdre muttered angrily. Tears of rage and self-pity pricked her eyes as she wrote out the check. It would be months before Snowball would be anything resembling fine, and having to pay for his mutilation was the worst part of all. She felt blindsided, broadsided, emotionally battered, humiliated and helpless. As painfully out of control as she had the day before, when Seth had kissed her then shoved her away.

Nothing was going the way it was supposed to—nothing.

It wasn't enough to write everything off as *a bad day*, Deirdre decided as she loaded the cat carrier into the car's front seat and headed for home. She wanted a person to blame. Someone she could yell at, lash out at, *hate*. And, the way she saw it, she had three choices. She could blame herself, her mother or Seth.

She never should have gone to that damn festival. It was there, on those very same fairgrounds, that her life had spun out of control the last time—when Seth promised to meet her and hadn't...

*Where is Seth, Deirdre wondered, chewing on her lip. He'd said he might be late, but had he really meant to come this late?She'd arrived at the fairgrounds just before dark. She'd wandered for a while through the booths where arts and crafts, jewelry, incense, and candles were sold, amazed by everything she saw. By the color and the noise and the crowds of people; many of whom were dressed in strange costumes.*

*Several women, carrying large straw baskets, moved through the crowd handing out condoms. She'd taken one, before she realized what they were. When she did, it was too late to hand it back. So she slid it into her back pocket, wondering if she'd ever get the chance to use it.*

*She took another look at her watch. God, it had been hours. Her feet hurt and she was tired of turning down offers of wine and pot, tired of having her hands grabbed by guys who wanted her to come and dance with them, tired of trying to avoid the drunken revelers who kept stumbling into her.*

*"Hey. Hey, you. I said hey!"*

*She jumped when a hand was waved in her face. She looked up, focused hopefully on the face in front of her, and felt her heart sink as she recognized, not Seth, but the boy from the beach the other night. The one who'd said he was a friend of Seth's. Eric, the toad. Shit.Eric's eyes were bloodshot and bleary. He was wearing a goofy, stoned expression as he shoved the wineskin he was carrying in her face, "Here. Have some mead."*

*"No, thank you," she said, as she pushed it away.*

*"So, what are you doing here? You're not waiting for Seth, are you?" He giggled suddenly and turned to his friends. "This is Cavanaugh's new squeeze."*

*Deirdre started. It was the first time she'd ever heard Seth referred to by his last name, and she couldn't believe her ears. "What did you just say?" she demanded as she grabbed Eric's arm. "That name. Who're you talking about?"*

*"Name?" he repeated blankly. "What name.""You mean Cavanaugh?" one of his friends asked, helpfully.Eric shrugged. "So, what of it? It's just his name."*

*"Whose name? she hissed, swallowing hard."Seth, of course. Why? D'he tell you it was something else?"*

*"No!" she yelled, barely aware that she was still gripping his arm, or that she was shaking it, in her fury. "No, you're lying!"*

*She'd always dreamed of having a brother. Or a sister. Always hoped that, when she found her father, she would find out that she did. But, not like this!*

For just an instant yesterday, when she'd first seen him there, she had the dumb idea she'd been handed a second chance, a do-over. As if all the pain and the crap of the past two years could be wiped out, reversed with one kiss; as if life were a fairy tale. She should have known better.

"Stupid, stupid, stupid," she muttered, berating herself. Snowball whined in misery and, probably, in agreement. "Hey, this is *not* my fault," Deirdre told him. "I didn't tell them to chop all your hair off, you know. I didn't *ask* for this."

She hadn't asked for any of it. All she'd wanted, all she'd come here to find, was the life she'd been promised. The future, the father, the family her mother had sworn would be waiting.

*Get over it*. That's what the last therapist her parents sent her to had said. *The past is past, put it behind you. Move on.*

But it was hard to find peace when your past was a puzzle. Hard to build a future you could believe in or trust, when everything you'd known about yourself kept shifting like sand.

Deirdre was only a few blocks from home when her thoughts were disrupted by the wail of sirens behind her. She pulled to the curb to allow the fire engines to pass, eyes widening as she saw them turn in at her block. Ignoring Snowball's mewl of protest at being left alone, she put the car in park, locked the doors and ran up the street. Fire engines filled the road in front of her. Chattering people crowded the sidewalks to gape at the flames that erupted from one of the buildings. Her building. Shit.

Thick smoke poured from a sooty, cracked window and it was hard, at first, to be sure which one. Or maybe she just didn't want to accept what she already knew. It was her apartment that was engulfed. Her home, her belongings that were being destroyed. She hugged herself tighter as the realization sank in. She was homeless. But worse yet was the realization that, had it not been for the day's unexpected glitches, she'd have been home already. If this had this been another, ordinary day...she'd be dead.

Thinking about that, and about the bath she'd been hurrying home to sink into, had Deirdre sagging against a lamppost, too weak to stand and too stunned to move, until the murmurs of those around her began to register in her mind.

*"I didn't see it happen, but I heard it, all right."*

*"It was like a bomb going off—an explosion. The whole place seemed to ignite at once."*

*"Was anyone inside?"*

*"I don't think they know yet. I certainly hope not."*

*"She must've left the gas on, that's all I can think of. What else would make the place go up like that?"*

*"Could be she was running some type of drug lab. That kind of thing's happened before, you know."*

*"Damn kids. What the hell do they expect's gonna happen when they start fooling around with that sort of stuff?"*

*"Well, I heard it was set."*

*"Arson? Here? How could that be?"*

How indeed? Deirdre slipped away through the crowd before anyone could recognize her. Before they could accuse her of setting the fire or cooking up drugs. Or anything else. How any of this could be happening was beyond believing. How anyone could think she was to blame–

But, why wouldn't they? With her past? With everything that had happened the last time she was here? With the way her luck was running?

Of course they'd think that.

But she wasn't going to stick around and wait to be questioned. Not with her parents in Europe, with no one to turn to, with no one to come to her defense.

No, thank you.

By the time she made it back to her car, she was trembling so hard it took four tries before she got her key in the lock. She turned the car on, doing her best to casual and relaxed, to look innocent. She pulled slowly away from the curb and headed out of town. Leisurely. Unhurried. Like someone with no particular destination in mind. Just out for a drive. Going nowhere.

She had driven several blocks before it hit her. Shit. That wasn't an act, was it? She really did have nowhere to go.

THE LIGHT from the setting sun glinted across the acres of trellised grapevines that surrounded the Morning Glory Inn, gilding the green leaves gold. A faint haze hung in the evening air and the humming of bees and the squeak of the porch swing were the only sounds to be heard.

But the peace and the quiet, the prettiness of the scene, all the things that should be making him feel better, were lost on Seth. Sinead was worried. He could see it in her face as she stared at him, he could read it in her crossed arms and the tense, rhythmic kicks that were keeping the swing in motion.

He leaned against the porch rail, hands jammed in his jeans' pockets and stared back at her, feeling like shit, knowing he was the reason she was worried.

Despite the differences in their ages, Seth had always thought of Sinead as a friend. Someone who'd been there and done that too many times to sit in judgement on anyone else. Someone who might not like everything he did, but who could be counted on to stay cool. To stay quiet.

In the two years they'd known each other he and Sinead had helped each other out of trouble more than once, they'd come to each other's rescue and kept each other's secrets, but that had all ended last April. Ever since her daughter's birth, Sinead's Mothering Instinct had been operating full force.

As demanding as baby Victoria was—even more of a handful than their mutual cousin Cole, from what Seth had seen of both babies—anyone would think she'd be more than enough to occupy her mother's attention. But no such luck. Sinead still had plenty of concern to spare and, these days, it seemed like most of it was focused on him.

It was more bad luck that he'd run into her this morning, while he was still semi-crunked and headed back to bed—where he'd planned to spend the rest of the day with an icepack on his dome and his eyes tight shut against the sunlight. She'd instantly recognized his hangover for what it was, despite his attempt to pass it off as a summer cold.

It was evening now. He was awake and recovered and stone cold sober, yet she was still harping on the same damn subject."Look, it won't happen again," he promised once more. "It was just...it was

Ray's birthday, Sinead, we were toasting his memory. How could I refuse?"

Sinead shook her head. "You have to refuse, Seth. You know that. Because things like that are always going to come up. There will always be an excuse—a reason—to take that first drink, or swallow that pill, or–"

"It wasn't like that," he insisted, angry that she would expect him to shrug Ray's death off like it was no big deal, more angry because...well, maybe she was right, after all. How hard had he tried to say no?

"How would that've looked to everyone?" he demanded. "You know that most of those fuckers already think I had something to do with his death, don't you? You've heard the stories they're telling."

Of course she'd heard them. The whole town had. The stories were ugly and stupid and, worst of all, Seth had no way of proving them wrong. If they even *were* wrong. Shit, even he had questions about some of what had happened that night. Questions that might never be answered...

*It had been an ordinary evening. He and Ray had been hanging out in the apartment Seth had fixed up for himself over his parents' garage. When Seth went out to take his dogs for their walk, he'd left Ray there alone, messing around on the computer like always, like any other night. How could he have known that was the last time he'd see his friend alive? How could either of them have guessed that, in the short time he was gone, Gregg, the psycho, would come hunting for Cara?*

For that matter, why the fuck was Cara there? That was the real mystery, and likely to remain one. Too much of her memory had been destroyed in the attack, she couldn't remember anything of the days leading up to that night.

"There are always going to be people talking about things, Seth," Sinead said sadly. "That's life in a small town. You can't let it get to you."

"I- I don't. Usually." This weekend had been an exception. Why couldn't she see that? Ray had been his friend. His best friend. *Now he's dead!* For two months Seth had held it together. But, Ray's birthday– Shit, he couldn't let that pass unnoticed, could he? He couldn't disrespect his friend like that.

Sinead sighed. "I don't know, Seth. Maybe your mother was right. Maybe it was a mistake letting you move out here. I mean, we're in the middle of a winery. If this is going to be a problem for you–""

No!" The winery wasn't a problem, damn it. The fact that there were bottles of wine, barrels of wine, huge, hulking, stainless steel vats of the stuff just lying around everywhere was *not* gonna make him start drinking again. Living at home, on the other hand, feeling guilty each time that he left the house because he wasn't going out on a gurney, or in a bag; feeling scared each time he came home because of what he might find—that was a nightmare.

"I'll be okay," he promised yet again. "Please, Sinead, don't kick me out yet. I can do this."

"Kick you out? Seth, you know it's not like that! I just– Look, maybe you want to come with us this week? I'm sure Adam wouldn't mind. Maybe a few days out of town would do you some good."

"Go to San Francisco?" Seth stared at her, certain she'd lost her mind. He'd heard her talking to Cara about this trip. She and Adam were planning to visit Adam's mother for a few days before heading out to a Point Reyes retreat for a romantic weekend get-away. Yeah, that sounded like the kind of thing they'd want him tagging along on. Not. "I don't think so."

Sinead frowned. "If this were any other trip, I'd postpone it and stay home. I would. But Adam's mother is counting on us to be there. She hasn't seen her granddaughter yet, you know. But, maybe–"

"I'll be fine," Seth insisted again. "Really." Jeez. She was starting to sound exactly like his mother. And the last thing he needed was– *Oh, fuck. That's it, isn't it?* "My mother called you, didn't she? About the camping trip?"

Sinead's mouth drew tight. "Yes."

"It's this week?" And he'd promised his parents he'd keep an eye on things at home for them, while they were gone.

"Yes."

Seth nodded. Damn it, he was supposed to go over there yesterday, too. He'd forgotten all about that. Probably because it was the last thing in the world that he felt like doing. He sighed. "I'll run by the house in the morning and check up on things."

"I'm sure they'd appreciate that," Sinead said, and Seth had no doubts she would have said more, too, if they hadn't both gotten distracted just then by a sudden blast of noise and dust speeding along the road leading up to the inn.

Seth didn't suppose he'd ever been happier to see Cara in his life. Especially when he felt Sinead's concern-o-meter shift in her direction.

They lost sight of the car as it pulled into the drive, but the slam of the car door closing carried on the still air. From his post on the porch, Seth watched Cara approach. She looked preoccupied, lost in her thoughts. She had one foot on the stairs before she even saw them. Her face quickly assumed the bright, efficient expression he'd come to think of as her *work face,* but her eyes gave her away. Red rimmed, heavy lidded, as though she'd been crying, they also held a wary uncertainty and a spark of alarm.

"Hi." Cara's head swung back and forth as she tried to focus on both of them, before narrowing her gaze on Sinead. "Is everything okay Sinead? I- I thought you'd be gone by now."

Sinead shrugged impatiently. "I know. I did, too. We got delayed. But, it's okay. We'll leave in the morning instead."

Seth felt another twinge of guilt, knowing he was the reason for the delay. "I'm okay now," he said as he pushed away from the rail, putting all the confidence he wasn't feeling into his voice. "Really. I'm over it. It's not gonna happen again."

"I hope not," Sinead replied, sounding doubtful enough for them both."It won't. I promise." He smiled briefly at Cara as he headed down the steps. He'd done her a favor, hooking her up with a place to stay when she needed one. If she could repay him by distracting Sinead long enough for him to make his getaway, they'd be even.

Besides, Cara looked like she could really use a mother right about now, and Sinead was the closest one around. If he stayed, he'd just be in their way. So, he'd go back to the renovated pool house where he was living, get his dogs, and take them all for a nice long walk down by the creek, where they could disappear for a couple of hours. And hope this would all blow over soon.

"Have a great trip," he called over his shoulder to Sinead. "I'll see you when you get back."

If she made any answer, he didn't hear it. Which, he figured, was just as well.

IF THE PAST year had taught Cara anything, it was to always gauge the mood of the people with whom she came in contact, to take note of any changes in the atmosphere around her, and to run at the *first* sign of danger.

The mood on the porch this evening was not bad yet, but it was far from happy. Seth appeared sullen, defensive, a little ticked off, but that was pretty normal for him, especially lately. Sinead, on the other hand, was registering some serious disapproval levels. Not at all like her usual self. And that had Cara more than a little concerned.

In her experience, displeased people had a tendency to strike out at anyone who came within range, and they weren't always picky about who they chose to target. As long as they could reach out and hurt someone, it was all good. It didn't even have to be physical damage they were inflicting, either; it could be mental or emotional.

Cara had been on the receiving end of all three, and if she had to choose, then fuck it, she'd choose to pass. Screw the whole pain thing, let someone else deal with that. She liked her job, she loved where she lived, but at the first hint of trouble, she'd be gone.

"Is everything okay?" she asked again, still hovering on the bottom step—out of reach, out of range, out of danger.

"I don't know," Sinead replied absently. "I hope so." She looked at Cara and a frown creased her brow. "What's wrong? You look upset."

Cara shrugged. "It's nothing. Just traffic school."

"And?" Sinead prompted after a moment.

"Oh, you know," Cara shrugged again. "Turns out I know the guy who's teaching it. It was a surprise."

"Why don't you come up here and tell me about it?" Sinead suggested.Cara climbed the rest of the stairs reluctantly, but that was as close as she felt like getting, even after Sinead moved over to make room for her on the swing.

Sinead's eyes had narrowed. "What do you mean you know him? Know him how?"

*How do I answer that*? Cara had opened her mouth to respond, now she closed it again. *What the hell do I say*?

How would Sinead respond if Cara explained that she'd met Liam early last Spring, when he went undercover in the cult where she lived? Or if she told her about the mistake she'd made of falling in love with him, even though she was living with Gregg at the time and should have known better?

Her. In love with a cop. Could there be anything less likely to work out?

*Did I know he was a cop back then? Had he told me? Had Gregg known, too? Is that why he tried to kill me*?

These were the same questions she'd asked herself a gazillion times already. After the attack, when she saw Liam in the hospital, it seemed like she'd always known what he was. At the time she'd been in too much pain to be concerned about anything like that, but now... She felt her face flush as she thought about Liam. About some of the things she'd said to him. About some of the things she'd done...

*No, I couldn't have known. Why didn't he say something sooner? Why didn't he* do *something? Protect and Serve? Yeah, right. More like harass and betray.*

It made her scars burn just thinking about it. Ghostly reminders of wounds she couldn't remember receiving, but which would mark her forever.

*Why? Oh, Liam, why didn't you stop him before he did this to me?*

"Ohhh. I get it," Sinead murmured.Cara glanced at her questioningly. A smile flickered on the older woman's lips and her voice held understanding and a tinge of humor. But Cara supposed Sinead must have seen something in her face, some trace of guilt or pain, some hint of the embarrassment that always lurked just below the surface of some of those memories, because the humor and the smile both faded.

Sinead frowned. "Is he bothering you? Is that what's wrong? Because, if he is– Look, do you need someone to talk to him for you, to tell him to leave you alone? My brother-in-law's a cop, you know. I'm sure he–"

"No!" Oh, God. Cara's cheeks burned even hotter. She crossed the porch in a hurry and lowered herself onto the porch swing, less concerned with Sinead's temper now than she was by the idea of anyone 'talking to' Liam about her. Especially another cop. "It's okay, Sinead, really. I don't– It's not— That's not how it is!"

Sinead was still frowning. "Cara, honey, are you sure?"

Cara nodded. "He doesn't bother me. Honest."

It wasn't true, of course. Liam bothered her a lot. Just not in the way Sinead meant. What bothered her the most, however, was not knowing how he really felt about her.

"I should cancel this trip," Sinead muttered, biting her lip. "The timing couldn't be any worse. You're upset. And Seth–" She broke off to frown at Cara. "Did you know about his drinking this weekend?"

*Uh-oh.* Cara stiffened. *Is that what this is about*? Of course she knew. There wasn't much that she and Seth didn't know about each other. They were friends, and she liked him more than was smart. She owed him for getting her this job. If everything she'd been told about the night she'd almost died was true, she owed him for a lot more than that. She owed him her life.

But if he thought she was going to take shit for him– Well, he could just think again. He had a home and a family to go back to if things didn't work out for him here. She had nowhere and nothing...and besides, that was something else she'd learned: Never put your ass on the line for someone else unless you're looking to get screwed.

"At the festival?" she asked, doing her best to look innocent.

"Yeah, I...I ran into him there yesterday afternoon. I gave him a ride home."

"Yesterday?" Now it was Sinead's turn to look surprised. "But I saw him come home this morning?"

Cara nodded again. "Well, yeah. 'Cause I drove him back out there earlier today, to pick up his truck." She hesitated a moment. Probably she should stop right there and let Seth dig himself out of his own damn holes, but– "It was kind of a bad weekend for him. What with it being Ray's birthday and all."

Sure enough, Sinead's gaze turned suspicious and Cara found herself wishing she'd had the sense to keep her mouth shut. "And it wasn't a bad weekend for you? Ray was your friend too, wasn't he?"

Cara swallowed hard. "No. Not like that." Had Sinead heard the rumors about her and Ray? Was it possible she believed them?There were some who claimed that she and Ray had hooked up. Or that he'd wanted to, but she'd turned him down. They insisted that it must have been Ray who followed her to Seth's house and attacked her in a jealous rage. And that she'd killed him in self defense. Others maintained that it was she who was jealous. That she'd stabbed Ray out of spite, or in a fit of anger. Or while she was high. That it was Seth who'd beaten her—out of grief—when he saw what she'd done.

There were even those who believed that Seth had killed Ray—and nearly killed her—when he'd come home and found them together.

Even without any clear memory of that night, Cara knew the stories were crap. Nonetheless, a surprising number of people seemed to believe in one or the other version.

"So, were you drinking, too?" Sinead asked.

Cara shook her head. "No." However stupid and lame the rumors were, they did contain one, irrefutable kernel of truth: It was all her fault. If she hadn't been at Seth's house that night, Gregg wouldn't have followed her there. And Ray wouldn't have died.

So, she hadn't expected to be included in Ray's 'party' this weekend. And she hadn't been surprised when she wasn't invited. But this time she was smart enough to keep her mouth shut: Let Sinead think there was a better, more noble reason for why she'd stayed sober.

For several minutes no one spoke. Sinead's gaze was thoughtful, intense. Cara tried not to squirm under her scrutiny.

Finally, "I know you haven't been here that long," Sinead began, sighing just a little as she uncrossed her arms and dropped her gaze to her hands. "So, this is probably not very fair of me to do...

*You're letting me go*? Cara gulped back a protest. *No! You can't!* Her heart began to race as panic set in. Should she argue? Should she beg? Or should she just pack her bags and go?

*Go where*? That was the problem, wasn't it? She had no place to go. No family, no money, no home. That was a big part of the reason she'd stayed with Gregg as long as she had.

"...but I'd really appreciate it if you could keep an eye on things for me while I'm gone."

Cara blinked. "What?"

Sinead shook her head. "I don't just mean with the inn. And, I know we talked already about this being a semi-vacation week for you, too. I purposely didn't book anyone this week, so there's only routine maintenance for you to deal with—that hasn't changed. It's just...look, I know that you and Seth are friends, and I realize this might seem awkward to you. But, the thing is...I'm just so worried about him."

"I know," Cara agreed. "He's a little messed up right now. But it'll pass. He'll be okay."

Sinead sighed. "I hope you're right. But, that's not the point. The bottom line is...I'm afraid I don't feel comfortable leaving him unsupervised. Not the way things are. Do you know what I'm saying?"

"I-I think so."

"I realize I'm putting a lot of responsibility on your shoulders with this. But I don't know what else to do. Besides, you seem like someone who can handle it."

Cara nodded. It was true. When she was with Gregg, she'd run the whole place for him. Those guys at that pathetic *Church* of his couldn't fix a can of soup on their own. She'd had to make their food and shop for supplies and keep everything in order. She'd assigned everyone jobs and rooms, and made sure all the prayer meetings ran smoothly.

She'd been good at it, too. It turned out that there were a lot of things she was good at. But it was still a surprise when anyone noticed.

"So, if you agree to it, and you think you can handle it, I'd like to leave you in charge while I'm gone."

In charge? *Oh, shit. Seth's gonna hate this. I'll have to be real careful how I tell him.*

But whether Seth liked it or not, there was one thing Cara was certain of. This was the chance she'd been waiting for. The chance to prove herself. And she wouldn't let anyone mess that up. She met Sinead's gaze squarely. "I can do it. I'll take care of everything."

Monday night was typically slow at The Temple Garden. On weekends a party atmosphere prevailed as the old Victorian storefront turned Tiki Bar, with live music, a Polynesian buffet, tropical drinks and, not infrequently, plastic leis.

During the week, however, the place morphed back into a rather staid and sleepy Chinese restaurant with a menu that was heavily weighted with dim sum and lo mein. All of which combined to make Monday the perfect night for the owner to rehearse his band in the small, rather airless room behind the kitchen.

Chay Johnson wasn't part of the band, but he sat in with them on a semi-regular basis, so it wasn't unusual for him to be here on a Monday. It was also common to find him afterwards, stopping to wet his throat at the restaurant's bar, before heading home.

But, as Chay was very well aware, the same could not be said about Liam. Spotting the now-and-again cop seated behind a beer at the long, mahogany bar tonight was a surprise, and not a pleasant one. Anything out of the ordinary was usually worth investigating, in Chay's opinion. Especially anything to do with that hothead.

By blood and by training Chay was a warrior. Protector of the land surrounding Oberon, guardian of the creatures who made it their home, and that went double for anyone he considered part of his 'tribe'. Threatening the happiness and wellbeing of any of his charges, was a good way to get on Chay's bad side. And Liam's treatment of Chay's sister, Chenoa, several months earlier, had won him a primo spot on Chay's shit list.

"So, brah, what's happenin'?" Chay inquired genially, as he slid onto the stool next to Liam's, and leaned his back against the bar.

Liam's eyes narrowed. He stared hard at Chay for a moment, and then shrugged. "Not much. How 'bout you?"

"Same ol', same ol'. Don't see you in here that often."

"Nope." Liam picked up his beer and then spun on his seat so that he, too, was now facing the room. "Actually I was hoping I might see your sister. She's not here tonight, is she?"

Chay shook his head with deliberate nonchalance. "No, brah. But, you know, the best place to find her is the bakery. During the day." A nice, safe place, too. Since Chenoa had taken over the bakery their grandfather had founded, business was booming.

Chay was proud of his baby sister's accomplishments, especially if they kept her too busy to fall for Liam a second time.

Liam lifted his beer to his lips. "Yeah, yeah, I hear you."

There was just enough of a defensive edge to Liam's voice to make Chay suspect that he might actually mean it, that he might, in fact, have heard—and understood—both what Chay had said, and also what he'd left unsaid. *Good. You'd better.*

Liam swiveled back to replace his beer on the bar, and then stood. "Well, I guess I'll be going then." He nodded at Chay. "See you around."

"Aho," Chay replied in agreement. His eyes tracked the other man as Liam made his way toward the door. "Count on it," he muttered beneath his breath.

Chenoa had made it clear that she didn't appreciate her big

brother meddling in her affairs, but what she didn't know wouldn't hurt her. Her friendship with Liam might be as innocent and harmless as she insisted it was, or then again, it might not. Only time would tell. In the meantime, the cop warranted a little watching, a little trailing, a little surveillance. And that was something Chay did exceptionally well.He smiled grimly.

"Yah, brah. I will *definitely* see you around."

NIGHT HAD FALLEN before Deirdre found the house she'd been searching for. She'd been hampered by the fact that she'd only been here twice and couldn't recall the address. In the end, she'd had to rely on instinct. But locating the house was only a matter of time. The image of this place, this house, this street, this neighborhood, was imprinted on her brain.

As she pulled into the empty driveway, motion sensitive lights above the garage door and over the back porch flared to life; bathing the surrounding area in a yellow glow. The house itself, however, was dark. Deirdre stared at it uncertainly. *What now*? She hadn't anticipated finding no one home.

The Cavanaughs were the only people she knew in Oberon, or felt like she could trust here. Even if the past two years had turned Seth had into a jerk, still she had to hope that his parents hadn't been similarly affected and that his father, at least, would continue to honor the promise he'd made the day they'd finally come face to face...

*She'd sat huddled on the ground, behind the charred, stone building, fighting back tears. Her arm was throbbing, bleeding, torn where the dogs had mauled it. Beside her, Seth lay unconscious, his head cradled on his mother's lap. Deirdre had never felt so wretched, so alone.*

*And then Dan had arrived, hurrying around the building, looking half-wild with worry. "Lucy? What happened here? Is he okay? Are you?"*

*Deirdre would have known him anywhere, from the pictures her mother had shown her. Despite the concern in his voice and the fact that he had yet to even notice her, she'd felt instantly better, safer.*

*When he looked at her his eyes grew wide, and she'd been so certain that he'd recognized her, too.*

*"Daddy?" Sobbing, she scrambled to her feet and threw herself into his arms, they closed about her protectively. And, for a little while, she felt like everything would be okay.*

*He could have pushed her away. He could have set her straight. He could have told her—right then and there—that he wasn't her father. But he hadn't. He'd waited until things had settled down, until her arm had been stitched up and her parents had been called and were on their way to join her. Then he'd broken it to her as gently as he could—and made the promise she'd never forgotten. The one she'd been hoping to hold him to now:*

*"You'll always have a family here, remember that. Whether we're related or not, if you need us, we're here for you. Always."*

"But you're not here now, are you?" Deirdre murmured, still staring at the empty house and trying not to panic.

Maybe they were out for the day and just hadn't gotten back yet?

*Or maybe they've moved,* an angry little voice in her head suggested. *Maybe this is someone else's house now.*

"I guess I'd better find out," Deirdre sighed, stepping out of her car and heading back down the drive to the mailbox. *Might as well start with the obvious.*Her footsteps sounded loud, accentuating her loneliness. She looked around, shivering slightly. The sky above had deepened to indigo. Pale stars peeked shyly out from behind thin clouds and a soft mist filled the air. Under other circumstances, it would have been a beautiful evening.

The mailbox was full. She pulled out an envelope and held it up to the light. She had time for just one look, before the automatic lights went off again, but it was long enough to read the name. Cavanaugh. Good. That was one less thing to worry about.

But only one, and there were still so many others. Like how long should she wait for them to come home, and where would she sleep, if they didn't?

She'd spent hours driving around aimlessly before she thought to come here. She'd stopped once to buy cat food and a toothbrush, once more to pick up some dinner at a small cafe near the same beach where she'd stayed the first time she was in Oberon. She'd gone there half-hoping to find that Rafe had decided to camp there again, but somehow she'd known all along that she wouldn't find him.

Now, she was here, she was tired, and with no other options available, the idea of letting herself into the house, making herself at home, maybe even pulling a Goldilocks and catching a nap until the bears got back, was starting to look real tempting. After all, wasn't that what families did?

As she walked back to the car, the lights went on again. The lights were new since the last time she'd been here, and damned annoying. They left her feeling like she was in a spotlight. Exposed. Vulnerable. At risk.

What if one of the neighbors happened to look out their window? What if the sight of a strange car in the drive made them suspicious? Or what if the police were looking for her in connection with the fire? What if they drove by, saw her car, recognized the license plate, and decided to check things out?

Did she really want to wake up to the loud pounding of authoritarian fists on the front door? Wouldn't her faux-family prefer it if she didn't make their home a crime scene? And, come to think of it, wouldn't she prefer to skip adding B&E and resisting arrest to the possible drug or arson charge she was already likely to be facing?

She needed to hide her car. Fast. And where better than in a garage? Especially when there was one right here: conveniently located, conveniently empty, conveniently unlocked.

he was feeling a lot better by the time she had her car stowed safely out of sight. But Snowball, still locked in his cage, had stepped up his protests at his continued incarceration. His meows had grown increasingly strident, carrying on the evening air until they were answered with faint but unmistakable annoyance by the area's dogs.

Their barks called up another memory, this one from the first time she'd been here, the night she'd met Seth...

*The fog had been rolling over the road that night, thick and heavy, and she had no idea where they were going, or where the park was where the supposedly wild dogs she kept hearing about were supposed to be. Occasionally, as they walked along the road, a sudden rush of barking would erupt through the fog, barreling closer. The first time it happened she jumped and clutched at Seth's arm.*

*"It's okay," he said. "These yards are all fenced in. He can't get out.""So that's not one of the, you know–"*

*"One of the wild dogs?" Seth grinned suddenly. "Nah. That's just Rusty —the Pearlman's beagle. He's about fifteen years old and almost blind. And, anyway, I thought you weren't worried about them? Weren't you the one who wanted to spend the whole night in the park?"*

*"I didn't say I wasn't afraid of them," she grumbled, dropping his arm again. Yeah, it was real funny all right. Of course she was afraid of the dogs! She'd always been afraid of dogs.*

But nothing like the way she was now, after having been attacked. She shivered again.

"Quiet down, Snowball," she snapped, much harsher than usual. I'll let you out in a minute." She stared at the house, suddenly reluctant to be alone in that big, old house.

*What's wrong with you*, she demanded peevishly of herself. *You think you can stay out here all night? Get in the house. Now! Unless you can think of a better idea.*The lights snapped off again, startling her. She breathed out a shaky breath and breathed in a fresh, spicy-sweet fragrance. Woody. Green. Familiar. It came from the bushes that lined the drive, where she and Seth had once hidden, waiting until the coast was clear...

*Quietly, they'd left the shelter of the hedge and slipped up the flight of stairs at the side of the garage. When Seth stopped to fish a key out of the flowerpot that stood next to the door, Deirdre couldn't help but shake her head in disgust. Good hiding place—not! Jeez, these people would never make it in the city, that was certain.*

*"We can't turn on any lights," he whispered, as she followed him into the dark apartment. "Not if you don't want my parents to know you're here."*

Yes, of course. Perfect. "Now, why didn't I think of that before?" Deirdre asked herself, heart swelling in relief as she glanced up at the window above the garage door. It was the perfect hiding place: safe, secluded, comforting in its familiarity.

It was almost like coming home.

# 5

On Tuesday morning, honoring the promise he'd given Sinead, Seth went home. Not that home was a word he associated any longer with the house where he'd grown up. When he thought of it at all now, which was as little as possible, he thought of it as his parents' house—and even that was a stretch.

*Hell* was a whole lot closer to the way he felt about the place. It was amazing how the memories of one night, two months ago, could overshadow the previous eighteen years. But it had been no ordinary night...

*For a long, horrified moment Seth had stood frozen in his doorway, staring in horror at the scene before him, unable to comprehend what he was seeing. Or maybe just unwilling to believe his eyes.*

This isn't happening. It isn't real. I must be dreaming.

*A bald man dressed in a long, black coat crouched on the floor, partially concealing the motionless, blood-soaked body of the girl who lay pinned beneath him. When the man turned his head, another shock rocked through Seth. Recognition chilled his soul as pale blue eyes in a blood smeared face locked with his. Gregg? Shit.*

I told Cara he was bad news. I warned her. *Over the roaring of blood in his ears, Seth heard himself order his dogs to attack. Snarling, they leaped at Gregg, but before they could reach him, he turned and hurled himself through the second story window. The crash of breaking glass filled the night with its noise.*

*Gulping for breath Seth stared around him, trying to take it all in. The shattered window. The blood spattered wreck of his room. The dogs, still snapping and snarling wheeling in circles, whining in confusion. The gory mess that lay splayed across his carpet.*

Oh, no, please, it can't be–*Cara? Seth took a step forward, stumbled and nearly lost his footing. He looked down and froze. Another body lay crumpled at his feet.* Ray? *Chills of horror dropped him to his knees, begging, murmuring, praying. "Ray? Oh, God. Ray? Ray? Answer me! Please."*

*Seth's fingers were shaking as he touched his friend's neck, his wrists, his chest. Seeking anywhere he might find a pulse. Ray's skin was cool. Too cool. Too pale. Too dead...* [1]

Just thinking about it now made Seth shiver, despite the warm June sunlight streaming in through the truck's windshield, and when the house came into view he felt the familiar twisting in his guts. He pulled into the drive, turned off his engine and took the key from the ignition. Then he froze again. The silence that had settled around him seemed too total. He could feel his heart pounding as adrenaline flooded his system. He could feel sweat beading on his forehead and trickling down his back. He hated the panic, the helplessness, the nausea. Hated most of all that he couldn't make it stop.

After Ray's murder, his parents had begged him to see a therapist, but after having been forced to repeat the story of what had happened endless times—to them, to the police, even to Cara—he was in no mood to talk about it with anyone else. Not last April. Not now. Maybe not ever. He wanted to forget all about the events of that night, and talking only made that harder to do.[2]

He sat in the truck for several minutes longer, trying to will himself out of the vehicle, but his muscles had locked up. He was as good as paralyzed.

"This is so fucked up," he murmured angrily. "What are you scared of, you wuss? There's no one here."

He closed his eyes, took a deep breath and tried to think himself far away; tried to imagine that he was at the beach, or back at the winery, or even out at his family's nursery. Almost anywhere would do, as long as it wasn't here. He reached blindly for the handle and propelled himself out of the truck before he could think too hard about what he was doing. He was so successful in his imagining that when his feet hit the solid pavement of the drive, instead of the dirt and gravel he'd been expecting to find, his eyes shot open and fear seized his insides once again.

He pushed the door closed. Quickly. Before the impulse to jump back into the truck could take hold. He just needed to keep moving forward, that's all. Just take one step at a time.

"It's okay," he muttered, gulping for air. "It's cool. I can do this." His dogs whined impatiently from the bed of the truck. "Stay," he commanded unnecessarily. With their leashes attached to the truck's tie-downs, the dogs weren't going anywhere. He didn't know how long he wanted to stick around, and if he started to freak out again and had to leave in a hurry, he didn't want to have to deal with rounding up four dogs.

He took in another deep breath, filling his lungs with the fresh scent of Arborvitae, from the hedge that grew alongside the drive. His hands were fisted so tight that his keys were digging holes in his palm. "All right," he murmured, "let's do this," and headed for the stairs that led up to his former apartment.

His hands were shaking even harder than before as he unlocked the door at the top of the stairs; tremor after tremor, almost as bad as the knocking of his knees. When he pushed the door open the smell of sawdust, new carpet and fresh paint greeted him, along with fainter fragrances. Cedar. Frankincense. Lavender. Obviously his mother had held some kind of blessing ceremony here—probably hoping to banish any negativity in the atmosphere.

Seth took a step inside, and then another, trying hard to ignore the continued pounding of his heart. The blinds were all shut and it took a minute for his eyes to adjust to the low light. And when they did, he wished to God they hadn't.

*No. It can't be.*

The bed was unmade, rumpled, far too lumpy to be empty. It wasn't. A bare foot, pale and still, and part of a woman's leg protruded out from under the heaped covers.

"Oh, God," Seth mumbled, almost retching as he fell back a step. The blood left his head in such a hurry he had to clutch at the door-frame in order to remain upright. He wanted to run from the room, down the stairs, out to his truck. He wanted to leave and never look back. But his legs refused to carry him, so he stood rooted to the spot. Trembling. Sweating. Praying that this was all an hallucination, that he could blink and make it go away. "No.

He'd stumbled across too many dead bodies during the past two years.

*It can't have happened again. It can't. It just can't...*

Because, if it had, then it was too much. He just couldn't take any more."No. Please, no. Please–"

Suddenly, as if in answer to his prayers, the blankets shuddered to life, the foot was withdrawn, and from beneath the pile of pillows at the opposite end of the bed, a girl's dark head emerged. She turned and sat up and Seth found himself face to face with Deirdre once again. For an instant, shock and relief robbed him of speech.

Then his mind went blank, his temper ignited, he bared his teeth and snarled, "What the fuck are *you* doing here?"

SETH LOOKED at her like a man demented: wide eyes in a chalk white face, one hand fastened, with what looked to be a death-grip, on the molding that framed the doorway, his expression a mixture of horror and fury tinged with disgust.

Still barely awake, Deirdre couldn't help but quail a little in the face of that much rage. "I-I needed somewhere to stay, and this was the only place I could think of." She felt her cheeks grow warm as he continued to glare at her. She angled her chin up proudly. "I got burned out of my apartment yesterday, all right? Is that reason enough for you? It was late. I was tired. And besides, your father said I could come here." That last was a slight exaggeration, but–

"My *father*?" Seth's eyes narrowed. He released his stranglehold on the door frame and propped his shoulder against it. "He told you to stay *here*? When'd you talk to him?"

Deirdre dropped her gaze, unwilling to face the coldness in his eyes any longer. *Couldn't he at least be a little happy to see me? A little concerned?* "Why does it matter when it was? He said he'd be there for me if I needed him. And I do. I-I think someone's trying to kill me."

"*What*?"

"You heard me," Deirdre muttered, crossing her arms. She was uncomfortably aware that the surprise and disbelief in Seth's voice too closely mirrored her own feelings on the subject. The idea that had seemed a lot more believable when she'd first thought of it, late last night.

But, farfetched or not, it still made sense. If she took the fire yesterday, and her close call in the alley the day before that and then added those to the dozen or so other troubling incidents that had all occurred within the last few months, a clear picture emerged.

One of a noose, slowly tightening around her neck.

"You're just out of your fucking mind, aren't you?" Seth sneered. "How many more bullshit excuses d'you think you can come up with?"

"It's not bullshit," she insisted, raising her eyes to his face once more. "I'm serious."

Still lounging in the doorway, Seth shook his head impatiently. "Oh, the hell you are. You did *not* talk to my Dad. You don't even know where he is, do you? And he did *not* tell you to stay here. 'Cause he wouldn't do that! And...*a fire*? Whaddaya think, if you say 'fire' I'm gonna get all sentimental thinking about the fire that nearly killed us both last time you were here? Well, I got news for you, a lot's happened since then. Stuff that makes what happened to you and me seem like nothing. Like kid's stuff. I'm over it. You're just trying to play me. Same as always. You're making shit up just to get to me. But, it's not gonna work!"

Deirdre had to swallow hard to keep from crying. Why didn't he just step on her chest and crush her heart for real? That's how it felt right now, anyhow. *What happened between us meant nothing*? Easy for *him* to say. What had *he* given up, after all?

"I'm not making anything up. Drive over to Abraxas and check it out if you don't believe me. Or look in the papers. [3] They probably all have the story by now. My apartment blew the fuck up. They say it was like a bomb going off. *And* they're saying it's arson.

"Yeah? Who's *they*?"

Deirdre shrugged. "Everyone. The firemen. The cops." She was uneasily aware of the fact that she didn't actually know this to be true.

A short, derisive laugh escaped Seth's lips. "Oh, right. You talked to the cops and they told you...what? 'Sorry, Miss. Your apartment's been toasted and it looks like someone's trying to off you. Why don't you go break into the Cavanaughs' house? 'Cause you're sure to be safe *there*.' As if."

Despite her determination not to let his indifference affect her, Deirdre felt the pricking of tears. Couldn't he be just a little bit nicer? "I just need someplace to stay for a while," she repeated, gazing at him appealingly. "Where is your father anyway? He said–"

"Forget it!" Seth growled, coming away from the doorway. "He's gone. They're all gone. They won't be back 'til next week. You can't stay here."

"Gone where? Can't you call him? And, why *can't* I stay here? I'm not gonna–"

"Because you can't!" Seth's eyes were burning. "I won't let you. I-I don't want you here." The look on his face was gaunt and harsh, totally lacking in sympathy. Deirdre hugged herself tightly. They stared at each other, the silence widening between them, and Deirdre felt all her hopes—for them, for the future—and all the stupid fantasies she'd nurtured for the past two years, stretch right along with it, thinning and fraying until something inside her finally snapped.

"I'm not gonna hurt anything, you know," she murmured at last, dropping her gaze to her lap, giving up, giving in, letting go of her dreams. "I just need help. I need a place to stay."

"That's it," she heard Seth murmur. "I give up. I can't deal with any more of this crap. You know what? You do whatever the fuck you want. If you're still here when my parents get back, make sure you tell them I stopped by."

Stopped by? Startled, she looked up again. "What did you say?"

But he was already gone. She could hear his footsteps clattering down the stairs. An instant later a car door slammed. An engine started. There was a squeal of tires, the engine roared again, grew fainter and fainter. And then silence.Another minute passed, then Snowball clawed his way out from under the bed where he'd been hiding and hopped up beside her. Deirdre stroked his head absently.

"When his parents get back? When do you suppose that's gonna be?"

"That girl is crazy," Seth muttered clutching the steering wheel tightly. "She's fucking nuts." And he had no idea why that should surprise him so much. Didn't he always get stuck with the crazies? But he'd never expected her to pull a stunt like this. To show up at his house? To break in? To tell him some lame ass story about someone wanting to kill her?

She'd better hope that wasn't true. Especially since he hadn't been able to talk her out of staying there—where death had already come knocking. That had to be her dumbest idea yet.

"Fuck it. I'm *not* gonna worry about what happens to her. I'm not."

He took a deep breath and tried to calm down. He had no idea where he was going, but it was definitely taking him too long to get there. If it weren't for the dogs in the back, he'd have floored it by now, just to put as much distance between them as possible, as fast as he could. He wasn't going to worry, and he wasn't gonna go back there again, either. Tough luck on his parents if the lawn died while they were gone. He just hoped to God the grass was the only thing that didn't make it through the week.

And to think that, just last night, he'd been regretting his actions on Sunday. He'd been wishing for a second chance, an opportunity to apologize, to explain, to make things up to her–"I musta been outta my fucking mind."

He'd wanted so much to see her again. To be with her again. But not like this. If only they could both go back in time. Things had been so perfect then. He remembered everything so clearly. Her face had glowed in the light of the campfire. Her eyes had glistened. She smiled at him and his heart stood still. It was magical, as fleeting and fragile as the soap bubbles he used to play with as a kid. And when she kissed him–

"No!" Seth shouted, practically deafening himself in his fury. The past was over. It was done. He'd wasted two years thinking about her, hoping and praying, certain that if he only had another chance, he could make everything turn out right. If she would only come back–

But he'd been wrong. She was back now, and everything was more fucked up than ever.

A stop sign loomed on the road ahead. Seth slowed to a stop and looked around, trying to get his bearings. He was surprised to find himself on the coast road. He hesitated for an instant, and then turned right and headed north, toward Abraxas.

Fine, then. He'd check out this dumb story she'd told him about there being a fire. He'd see for himself whether or not she'd been telling the truth. He'd find out, once and for all, if she was crazy *and* a liar—which is the way he was currently leaning. Or just plain crazy.

*Do whatever the fuck you want.* Well, that wasn't exactly *make yourself at home,* Deirdre reflected, holding Snowball tight against her chest as she explored the empty house she'd just let herself into.

"But, maybe that's how he meant it?" she suggested, lightly scratching beneath the cat's chin. "What do say, Snowy—d'you think that's possible?"

Snowball closed his eyes and purred contentedly, but Deirdre wasn't fooled.

"Yeah," she sighed after a minute. "Me, neither."

She continued her snooping. Peeking first in one room, and then the next, examining the photos on the walls and the books on the shelves. All the little things that revealed so much about a person, or a family.

*Happy families are all alike,* Tolstoy had written. Man, had he ever gotten *that* wrong. She'd always thought her own family was reasonably happy. She was pretty certain Seth's family was, too. But, the two households could hardly be more different.

She paused the longest in the room that had been Seth's. *Tell my parents I stopped by,* he'd said, and that had to mean he no longer lived there, didn't it?

Seth's room looked not so much unlived in, as it did abandoned. Like he'd left without looking back. Like he'd evacuated—fleeing for his life, taking only what he could carry, leaving everything else behind.

Like he never expected to return.

It called to mind her own room in her parents' house—but only because, here again, the two were as different as they could possibly be. The last thing she'd done, before she left for school, was to straighten her room up, knowing she'd be back for the holidays and wanting the place to feel like home when she returned to it.

She'd left everything in its place, except the things she thought she couldn't live without—not even from June to December—those she'd taken with her.

And, wasn't that a joke?

Now, thanks to whomever set the fire in her apartment, those were all the things she no longer had and would never see again. The things she'd likely always miss. The same way she missed her birth mom, and all the stories she used to tell her. About the future they'd never get to share. About the happy family that was supposed to be waiting for her.

This family.

*Tell my parents I stopped by*. It still wasn't *make yourself at home,* but it was feeling a whole lot closer. Combined with what Dan had already told her last time, it added up to an invitation.

If anyone asked, that's just what she'd tell them. That she'd seen Seth and he'd given her his okay. And if that got him in trouble, well too bad. He still owed her for last time. He owed her a lot.

Right now, she needed to collect.

Her tour complete, she retraced her steps to the kitchen, where she put her cat down on the floor beside the bowls of food and water she'd set up for him. She had a plan now—as well as a place to stay. At least for the next four nights. When, according to the calendar on the wall, the family would be returning from their vacation.

Deirdre figured she had until then to figure things out. To find someplace else to stay, or a really good explanation for why she was still here.

In the meantime, she planned on enjoying her fake family's hospitality. Starting with breakfast. And a shower. And after that? Well, then she'd go online and see what she could learn about the fire that had robbed her of even more of her future—as well as a good part of her past.

Tuesday morning found Liam stopping at the Eternal Bliss Bakery for a mid-morning snack—coffee and a cinnamon roll. It was a routine he'd followed nearly every day since he'd rejoined the force.

He'd been hoping to get a few minutes of Chenoa's time, but it was clear she was too busy to chat this morning, so he smiled his thanks, waved good-bye and took his food back out to his car. Which was also pretty much routine.

But today wasn't really like any other day. And, as Liam pulled out his pocket calendar and once again contemplated the date he had circled in red, that fact hit home with enough force to leave him momentarily breathless. The target he'd been working toward for the better part of two months was drawing rapidly near.

Thursday, Cara's eighteenth birthday, was now only two days away.

So close...

Yet, the irony, the cruel reality, was that suddenly, paradoxically, his goal had never seemed so hopelessly out of reach.

It had been a surprise to see her yesterday. A wonderful surprise. But also a shock and a disappointment. He'd been stunned at the extent of her injuries, saddened to the point of tears by the damage that had been inflicted on her. He had no idea she'd been hurt so badly, no idea how spectacular his failure to protect her had really been.

The two times he'd seen her close up since the attack she'd been so heavily bandaged he could only guess at her condition. He'd known about the beating and the knife wounds, about the fractures to her femur and her skull. But, if the scars he'd seen yesterday were anything to go by, Gregg, that sonofabitch, had pretty much sliced and diced her.

"I shoulda killed that motherfucker when I had the chance," Liam muttered, staring blindly through his windshield as he blinked back tears of rage. Not that he hadn't tried to do just that, because he had. Twice he'd tried to put the murderous bastard in his grave. Both times he'd been thwarted.

Once by Gregg himself with the aid of his goons. Once by Chenoa's brother Chay, who'd been on some kind of misguided mission to save Liam from himself.

For two months Liam had assuaged his guilt at having failed Cara with the belief that at least she would recover from her injuries. That, as awful as she'd looked, she hadn't really been that badly hurt.

For two months he'd consoled himself for having failed to kill Gregg, with the hope that now, since he would not be facing a lengthy prison term for ridding the world of a worthless piece of shit, he would at least be free to pursue Cara. That they could be together. Just as soon as she was legal.

Only two days left to go. But had there ever really been any reason to hope that she might care for him in the same way he cared for her? Or had he just been deluding himself?

She'd seemed so cold yesterday, so reserved, so distant. So very different from the Cara he used to know. And her connection with Seth—always something Liam had been a little jealous of, anyway—seemed stronger than ever.He chewed grimly on his pastry, tasting nothing but bitterness. He'd failed to save her. That was the bottom line. And all his feelings for her, all the love he'd tried so hard to deny, what good had that done either of them?

He hadn't been there when she needed him. Just as, years earlier, he hadn't been there to save his sister and brother from another monster.

However much he'd like to believe in the power of redemption, how could he? There was nothing anyone could do to change the past. There was no way to correct his mistakes, to make things right. No reason at all to expect he'd ever be forgiven for his failures.

His appetite gone, Liam shoved his half-eaten pastry back in its bag, crumpled it into a ball and heaved it out the window into a nearby trash can. Half a minute later, he sent his coffee cup flying after it. A minute after that, his calendar joined them both.

Then he turned the car on, backed out of the space, and headed off to work.

He'd give himself the next three days to watch Cara and decide for himself whether there was any reason to hope, any reason to speak his heart, any reason to believe she wouldn't be happier and better off without him.

In the meantime, however, he did not need a calendar to mock him with its naive and foolishly optimistic circle.

And it was a circle, damn it. Even if, as it happened, there was a dip at the top and a point at the bottom, that didn't change anything. It was a circle, nothing more. That was his story, and he was sticking to it.

If Liam had happened to glance in his rearview mirror as he drove away, he might have noticed the car, which had been parked across the street for all this time, as it turned and glided into the parking space he'd just vacated. He might have noticed the driver emerge just long enough to retrieve the calendar that he'd so recently thrown away.

But he didn't look back.

Liam's shadow stood for a moment on the sidewalk, rifling through the pages of the calendar, finding very little of interest until the current month. With one finger the spy traced over the markings Liam had made. A low whistle of surprise escaped from pursed lips, along with a muttered prediction: "Ooh, Gregg's not gonna like this."

Then the driver returned to the car, tossed the calendar onto the passenger seat, and drove away.

Deirdre stood beneath the shower's spray, reveling in the feel of the hot water as it pounded her skin, happily breathing in the steam and the fresh herbal fragrance of the suds with which she was lathering her body. She was thankful to be here, someplace with all the comforts of a real home. It had struck her, while she was getting undressed, that she had only the clothes she'd been wearing and a gym bag in the car that held her workout gear. There was so much she'd have to replace. Clothes. Dishes. Books. Her computer. She didn't even have a toothbrush anymore!

Later, she'd have to think about going into town, getting a few things that she couldn't do without, figuring out how to reach her parents, now that she no longer had her address book or access to the itinerary they'd emailed to her, or...any way to get in touch with them. The thought chilled her a little, even despite the hot water still beating down on her head. So she pushed the thought away. At this moment, she had everything she needed. And that was all she was going to think about right now.

She succeeded for about five minutes, and then went still as it occurred to her that the sudden flurry of noises filtering in from outside—a car door slamming, the barking of several dogs—was a little too close. What was going on? Seth and the calendar both had assured her that the family was not scheduled to return for several days. Had he called them? Had they come back early? Was it to greet her, or to throw her out?

She turned off the water, to better hear what was happening. Sure enough, she could hear her name being repeated, faint and frantic, but coming nearer.

"*Deirdre! Deir-dre! Dee! Where are you?*"

"Seth?" Not certain whether to feel relieved or alarmed by his return, she stumbled out of the shower, grabbed a robe that was hanging on the back of the door and threw it on, quickly knotting the belt around her waist. "Seth? Is that you?" she called as she pulled the bathroom door open. "What's–"

*What's wrong*? That's what she'd planned on saying. But the sight that greeted her on the other side of the door stopped her cold. Words died in her throat. Face to face with her very worst nightmare, she could only scream.

## 6

Seth returned to Oberon in a panic. His trip to Abraxas ad convinced him that Deirdre had been telling something close to the truth, after all. There *had* been a fire, and it *had* been set. But there was one small detail she'd neglected to mention. One that either she hadn't known, or she didn't want *him* to know. That the only person the cops were looking to question was *her*.

So, was she telling the truth about someone wanting to kill her? Had the cops gotten things all wrong, as usual? Or had he just given a wacko arsonist free access to his parents' home?

Given their prior history and his own, bad luck, he'd be damned if he could figure out which of those scenario was more likely to be correct.

He swerved into the drive and braked abruptly, cringing as he heard his poor dogs go sliding, first in one direction, then in another. He leaped from the truck, surprising himself by not freezing, took the stairs two at a time, threw the door open and stopped in dismay. The room was empty.

She was gone?

He glanced around quickly, not even sure what he was looking for. Anything that seemed out of place, he supposed. Would he even know what a fire bomb looked like if he saw one?

It didn't take him very long to determine that everything seemed to be in order. The place wasn't very big—one room, a bath, and a kitchenette. It had been an unofficial clubhouse when he was growing up. For the six months he had lived here, this past winter, it had been his private sanctuary. Remembering how much of that time he'd spent thinking of Deirdre, had him feeling like a chump.

Either he was the world's biggest loser for not being able to shake his obsession with a cold-hearted, lying bitch, or she was everything he wanted her to be and he was an even bigger loser for fucking things up between them. Every. Chance. He got.

*Where has she gone now?* he wondered, his heart heavy as he headed back down the stairs. *How will I find her?* Had she come to him for help, only to have him set her loose with both the po and a killer on her tail? Sick fuck that he was, he knew he'd prefer that to the alternative: That she was a dangerous crazy who wouldn't be happy 'til she got them both killed.

He was still debating what his next step should be when he glanced in the garage window and felt his heart start to race again. Her car was still here. Which meant that maybe she hadn't gone anywhere, after all. Or, if she had, that maybe it hadn't been by choice.

Oh, fuck.

Fear hit him hard and made him dizzy. When he could breathe again, he started calling her name, over and over, with no response. Which meant nothing good.

The dogs were bounding around in the truck, barking and tugging at their leashes. Were they infected by his panic, or did they sense some danger he could not? He didn't know and was too afraid to guess.

When he set them free, hoping they could help him find her, they went straight for the house. He let them inside and then followed, reluctantly. Memories of finding Cara and Ray, of finding altogether *too many* bodies in the last couple of years; of too much blood, too much horror, rose up to haunt him.

He came to a dead stop in the middle of the kitchen, his heart racing, his breathing out of control.He couldn't handle finding another body, especially not hers. *Not her, God, please not her.* Not her, not here, and definitely not while he was alone. *I can't do this any more. I can't! It's too hard.*

Suddenly, a woman's scream tore up the air and ripped the breath from his lungs. Slowing his heart was no problem now, it had damn near frozen in his chest.

*But screaming means life.* Remembering that got him moving again. He rounded the corner at a run and skidded to a stop at the sight before him. The door to the bathroom had been pushed open, three of the dogs filled the doorway, growling menacingly. The fourth, unable to squeeze his way in, paced frantically behind them barking excitedly.

"Outta the way," he ordered, pushing them aside. Deirdre was crouched against the wall sobbing in terror. She had the knuckles of both hands jammed against her mouth and her eyes looked huge and unfocused. "What happened?" he asked as he fell to his knees beside her. "Why are you crying?" He peered at her anxiously, she appeared unharmed, but she didn't even acknowledge his presence. Her eyes remained fixed on the doorway. He reached out a tentative hand and stroked her arm, alarmed by her lack of response. "Deirdre? Can you hear me?" Gently, he pried her hands away from her face and held them. "What's wrong? Talk to me."

For a moment, lips trembling, she continued to stare blindly at nothing at all, then she transferred her gaze to his face. "Th-th-the d-dogs." She choked out the words, gulping back a sob. "M-make th-them go. Make them go!"

"What?" Seth blinked in surprise. He felt his heart sink. *You, too*? Why did everything have to be about his dogs? They were good dogs, damn it, despite their reputation. He'd raised them himself, from cute little pups—all except for the few months when his disgust with Eric's side business had kept him away from the abandoned cottage where the dogs were hidden. That had been a near-fatal lapse in judgement, one for which he'd probably never stop paying.

Everything bad that had happened to him since then had sprung from that one decision. In his absence, Eric had taught the dogs to hunt and track prey, to kill on command. It wasn't their fault that they did as they were told. It was Eric's fault, for issuing the orders. And it was his own fault, a little, for having trained them so well. But the dogs themselves were blameless.

"Stop crying. They're not gonna hurt you."

"Yes, they will," Deirdre sobbed, her voice rising with each repetition. "They will. They *will.*"

"Stop saying that!" he snapped, dropping her hands and glaring. He was so disappointed he could barely speak. He turned to the dogs and ordered them out of the room, then turned back around to face her. "See? They're good dogs. They just do what they're told. And I don't care what you've heard. They've never hurt anyone."

Abruptly, Deirdre left off crying. Her last sob ended in a strangled gasp as her face went from ashen to brick. "Wh-what did you say?"

Seth frowned. "They got a bad rap, that's all. So, c'mon, cut the drama."

"*Drama*?" Deirdre shoved him away, straight arming him in the chest, hard enough to knock him off balance so that he landed on his ass. "I'll show you drama, you son of a bitch."

Startled, he watched as she pulled her right arm free of the robe and thrust it in his face. "They never *hurt* anyone? Then what's this, asshole? Or don't I count?"

DEIRDRE WATCHED as Seth's eyes grew wide. "Are, are you saying *m-my dogs* did that to you? B-but when? H-how?"

The tenderness in his voice made her nuts. If that soft little quaver had been for her, if his concern had been on her behalf, she'd have forgiven him anything. But it was only those monsters he cared anything about.

"Yes, *they* did this," she snarled, shivering as his fingers traced over the gashes on her arm. He had some nerve accusing her of being dramatic. And...*his* dogs? She should have guessed. If they were *his* dogs, that meant this was *his* fault. One more thing he owed her for. Still, it was hard to stay angry when he touched her that way.

"Ask your mother, if you don't believe me. I brought her there to save your ungrateful ass. But Eric came back before we could leave and, and–"

She broke off, gulping for breath, furious with herself as she felt her lip begin to tremble again. "And then they, they...he...he told them to, to–"

Seth's face had gone white with shock, his eyes looked stricken. Deirdre felt her gaze falter along with her voice. She didn't want to cry, but as her memories flooded back, she couldn't help it...

*She'd paced anxiously around the cottage's back room as Seth's mother worked to cut the ropes that bound her son's wrists. Seth looked even worse today than he had the night before. He'd been repeatedly beaten, drugged, and the few times he'd regained consciousness, he'd been almost incoherent. Not a good sign. They had to get him out of here before he died. But she didn't know how they were going to do that.*

*He couldn't walk, they couldn't carry him, and if they didn't go soon–*

*Shit. She broke off pacing as the door in the cottage's front room squeaked open. Her heart jumped up and clogged her throat as she heard Eric's voice calling her name.She moved swiftly toward the door hoping to deflect him, to buy them some more time. "Hey, good, you're back," she said, brightly, holding onto the door in a vain attempt to block his view. "C'mon, let's go in the other room and I'll tell you what happened."*

*But the dogs came lunging past Eric to barrel into the room, wrenching the door out of her hand, almost knocking her over.*

*She never even saw the blow. But his slap sent her flying. She smashed against the wall and fell to the ground, hard enough to knock the wind from her lungs."Stupid bitch," Eric snarled, his face distorted. "I'll teach you to mess with me." And then he called to the dogs.*

*It was a short command, she never could remember what he'd actually said, but the dogs responded instantly, leaping on top of her, teeth bared. Growling, biting, tearing, chewing...*

"Oh, God." She covered her face with her hands, trembling uncontrollably, as a sob broke from her throat.

Seth scrambled forward and wrapped his arms around her. "I'm sorry," he groaned as he held her tight. "I'm so sorry. Please don't cry. Please..."

Deirdre nodded, as she hiccuped softly. Not crying sounded like a great idea to her, too. And not that hard, really. She'd gotten good at putting those memories behind her. It had taken therapy and determination and a whole lot of sessions with the bio-feedback machine her parents had bought for her. But she'd done it. It was just the shock of seeing the dogs again that had got her unwound.

But now, as he held her close, she couldn't help but calm down again. She was almost shocked by how good it felt, how soothing. The beat of his heart. The rise and fall of his chest. The warmth of his skin on her bare arm and back. It was better than Valium.

This time, when she shuddered and lost her breath it wasn't from tears. It was from the intoxication of being locked in his arms. She closed her eyes and smiled. "Seth," she whispered his name, hardly daring to believe that he was real. Not a memory. Not a dream. It felt like a dream, though—better than she'd imagined or remembered. Not to mention that, finally, he wasn't being cruel, or rude, or mean.

"I didn't know," he murmured sadly. "I swear I didn't. No one ever told me. I never would have let them hurt you, if I knew. I would've done anything to stop them. I–"

"But, you did," she said, pushing away enough to look at him. "You woke up and...you made them stop. You saved me."

He'd come to suddenly, just long enough to order the dogs away from her. Then he'd passed out again.

Seth shook his head. "Not soon enough." His gaze dropped to her arm. He stiffened suddenly. Color flared in his cheeks. His eyes went dark. "Uh, Deirdre..?"

She followed his gaze. Shit. It wasn't just her arm she'd bared, was it? She was showing a lot more skin than she'd realized. As her nipple hardened under their combined scrutiny, she knew she was blushing.

"Excuse me," she muttered through gritted teeth as she shoved him away again and wrapped the robe around herself once more.

"Any time." Seth's voice held a hint of humor and even before she looked, she knew he was grinning.

The comfort she'd been feeling a moment earlier had all but evaporated now. She felt embarrassed, vulnerable. She wanted to smack that smile right off his face.

"What are you doing here, anyway?" she demanded angrily.

His eyebrows rose. "What?"

"I thought you left. What are you doing back?"

"*Me*?" His mouth dropped open. He was staring at her now like she was crazy. Or like she'd just said something incredibly stupid. "What am *I* doing here?"

"Yes, you. And don't look at me like that. I'm not the one disturbing people's showers, rolling deep with vicious dogs, coming and going with no explanation."

"They're not vicious," he insisted, "I just, just–" And then he stopped, his face changing back to angry as he scrambled to his feet. "I was worried."

"About me?" she asked, feeling somewhat mollified. Well, that was better. And, about time, too.

He started to pace. "You were right. That fire– That fire was set. On purpose."

"I told you it was."

"Yeah, well, that's not all." He stopped in his tracks and looked at her hard for a minute. "Did you know the police are looking for you?"

Uh-oh. Her stomach tightened. The accusation in his tone made her feel almost...guilty. She opened her eyes wide, trying hard to look as innocent as she was. "They are? What for?"

"The fire. They think you set it."

"Really?" She got to her feet, deliberately avoiding his gaze, shoving her hands deep into the robe's pockets so he wouldn't see how hard badly they were shaking. "And what do you think?"

"I don't know."

*He didn't know*. "Well, that's just great." *Just shoot me now, and get it over with*. Because, shit, if even Seth suspected her, what were the odds she'd be able to convince anyone else? She sighed and shook her head. "So, then why don't you just go away again and leave me alone?"

"I can't," he snapped as he started to pace again.

She stared at him moodily. "Oh? Why not? You left fast enough before."

"Because! If you didn't set the fire...well, then who did, huh?"

And wasn't that the question? "I dunno. Someone who wants me dead?"

"Exactly. But who?"

"I don't know."

Deirdre." He frowned at her impatiently. "You *have* to know. Something like that...how could you *not* know?"

"I don't," she insisted, glaring right back at him. "Why would anyone want to kill me?"

It was the stupidest idea she'd ever heard of. Well, the second stupidest, anyway. Right after the really dumb idea that she'd actually go and set her own stuff on fire. And even though it had been her idea in the first place, she still couldn't believe it was true. Not really.

He frowned harder. "Why're you asking me for? How would I know?"

Right. Stupid question. She shrugged, embarrassed by her outburst. "It was rhetorical."

"Oh." He stared at her for a moment longer, looking confused. And then reverted right back to this morning's pet topic.

"Well, either way, you can't stay here."

*Great. Back to that, are we*? She stomped her foot in frustration. "Seth! Why not?"

"Because I can't– It's not– Fuck! Will you just take my word for it? Please?"

"But I have nowhere else to go. All my stuff is gone. No one believes I didn't blow up my own apartment. *You* won't help me. Your folks aren't here. And I can't go back to Berkeley, because there's no one home there right now, either."

Seth nodded. "I know. I got all that. And, I've been thinking. Maybe you can come out to the winery with me. It's a big place, lots of room. It's miles away from here. There's not a lot of people around. You can stay there until we figure out what's going on."

"A winery?"

"Yeah, why not? That's where I'm staying. And, besides, I figure no one will think to look for you there, right?"

"You're saying you live in a winery?"

He sighed again. "It's a long story, but yeah, pretty much."

Deirdre glanced around wistfully. Well, it had been nice being here. A winery didn't sound nearly as homey. Or as comfortable. Or as safe. But, if she had no choice–

Suddenly, the quiet was shattered. A loud wailing filled the air and set the dogs barking. Seth's face turned white. "What was that?"

But Deirdre didn't need to ask. With her heart lodged in her throat once again, she pushed him out of her way and ran.

SETH FROZE. The scream, the barking, the fear on Deirdre's face had brought it back again; all the blood and horror of that night. Ray's eyes, open and sightless, staring at the carpet, at the dark pool in which he lay. Cara's gurgled moans of distress as she struggled to breathe without choking to death. His heart pounded. Sweat trickled down his face, his back.

*No*, he yelled, as Deirdre moved suddenly, shoving past him. *Wait. Come back! Don't go out there. It's not safe!* But the words never made it past his lips. He shot out a hand to stop her, but nothing happened. His body refused to respond to his mind's command. His arms remained motionless at his sides.

*Go*, he ordered himself, *Go after her! Run!* But his feet were rooted in place.

It was only after another scream split the air, accompanied by the sound of glass breaking and Deirdre's voice yelling his name, "Seth! Come help me," that he managed to force himself into motion.

"Hurry!" she urged, frowning at him as he caught up with her in the living room. "Make them stop. They're gonna kill him!"

Him? Seth looked around. Except for the two of them and the dogs, the room seemed empty. Then a flash of motion near the top of the drapes caught his eye.

Before he could focus on it, the small gray something that had been hanging there, launched itself from the curtain rod to land on the mantle, dislodging several framed pictures and one of his mother's brass candlesticks. The dogs vaulted over the sofa in pursuit. The falling candle glanced off Vulcan's head. Mars slammed into Zeus and both dogs connected with the coffee table, sending books and a basket of dried flowers flying.[1]

Deirdre turned on him. "Why are you just standing there? Get them out of here—now!"

Seth put two fingers in his mouth and whistled to get the dogs' attention. He had to repeat the order twice, before three of them gave up and retreated from the room. Mouth, never as well trained as the others, turned and bounded back toward him, as if hoping for a reprieve. Deirdre shrieked and fell back a step as the dog approached.

Seth spoke sharply, ordering Mouth away again, and then turned to glare at her. Guilt made him angry. It wasn't Mouth who'd attacked her two years ago, that much he knew for a fact. If she'd had a problem with some of the dogs, well, he supposed could understand her being upset. But did she really have to take it out on all of them? "Relax. I told you. I won't let any of them hurt you. They were just chasing after that...that thing up there.

Deirdre's eyes flashed fire. "That *thing* happens to be my cat!"

"That's a cat?" Seth took a second look. "Christ, are you sure? I thought it was a mutant squirrel." Too big to be a rat, too long-legged for a possum, it looked like a cross between a chinchilla and a poodle.

"Yes, I'm sure," Deirdre snapped as she picked her way through the scattered books and blossoms. "For your information he's a silver-tipped Persian."

"A Persian? You're kidding, right?" Frowning, Seth shook his head at the mess. His mother was gonna kill him unless he cleaned this stuff up before she got home. Oh, crap. Just what he needed. "Aren't Persians supposed to have long hair? What happened to him?"

Deirdre sighed. "I took him to the groomer yesterday. They gave him a lion cut."

*What*? The mess and his mother forgotten, Seth stared at her, appalled. *She'd made it look like that on purpose*? Great. Just when he thought things were gonna start making sense. "Watch out," he warned as Deirdre reached for the cat. Seth was sure he saw a flash of blue as the cat swiped at Deirdre with one paw, and then quickly backed up, sending the other candlestick, and another of the small framed pictures that were lined up on the mantle, crashing to the floor. Seth winced as more glass broke. His mother would more than kill him. He'd never, *ever* hear the end of this. "Would you hurry up and get him before he wrecks the whole house? I want to get out of here."

"I can't get him," Deirdre complained anxiously. "He won't let me near him."

*Well, not if you're going to approach him that way*. Sighing, Seth strode across the room. If there was one thing he'd learned from all his hours of community service work at the local wildlife rescue center, it was how to handle injured and potentially hostile wildlife. He plucked the cat from the mantle by the scruff of the neck, getting scratched only once in the process, before he captured the creature's hind legs in his other fist, and held him immobile. "You got something I can put him in?"

Deirdre nodded. "Just don't hurt him," she cautioned as she hurried back toward the doorway.

"I won't," Seth promised, staring in horrified fascination at the cat's front claws, which really *were* blue. Bright, sparkly, neon blue. Goddamn! This thing between them—it was never gonna work, was it? How could he have fallen for someone who would paint their pet's nails? And blue, no less! Unless maybe she'd been drunk when she did it. Or if she did it as a joke.

"So, like, are his nails supposed to match his eyes, or something?" he asked when Deirdre returned with the cat's carrier.

"Yes. Apparently," she replied, frowning at him as if he was stupid for having to ask.

"Nice," he muttered, quickly shoving the fashion failure into its box, and slamming the door shut.

He swept the room with another glance. He'd have to come back another time and straighten things up. Or maybe, if he was lucky, he could find someone else to do it for him. But, either way, he couldn't stay here any longer. The guilt was becoming overwhelming.

"Come on," he sighed. "Let's get going."Deirdre nodded. "Okay. But, I need to stop in town first."

He frowned at her impatiently. "What are you talking about? What for?"

"I dunno...food? A toothbrush? Clothes, maybe? Lots of stuff. There was a fire, remember? I lost *everything*."

Jeez. She really was crazy, wasn't she? "I know there was a fire," Seth snapped. "That's why you can't hang out in town. What if someone sees you?"

Deirdre's shoulders sagged. She looked so sad, so demoralized, so defeated. "I know," she murmured. "You're right. It's just–"

"It won't be forever, you know. Just until we figure out what to do."

She nodded again and tried to smile. She didn't quite make it.

Seth sighed, relenting as much as he dared. "Okay, look, we can probably stop and get you something to eat. All right? And maybe a toothbrush, too. But, that's it. And *I'll* do the shopping, okay? You're gonna stay in the truck—out of sight."

Out of sight? Deirdre shook her head in disgust. What the fuck had Seth been thinking? Following his orders, she was scrunched down in her seat, trying to look invisible. *Right. Like that's gonna work.* She couldn't be more conspicuous if she tried. He'd parked his glowing white truck right smack in the middle of Main Street. And left her with one very angry, very vocal cat on the seat beside her, and four, slobbering dogs chewing and pawing at the window, acting like they were getting ready to eat the truck for breakfast and then munch on both her *and* her cat for lunch. *Out of sight, my ass.*

Her arm throbbed with remembered pain. Her head ached with tension. And every noise, every voice, every car that passed on the street behind her caused her gut to tighten in fear. Until all her nerves were screaming at her to run, to hide, to get undercover. *Get out of here—now!*

She was stupid to have asked him to stop in town. And he was even stupider, for having gone along with the idea.

And where was Mr. Out-of-Sight now, while all her nerves were going to pieces? Standing in the middle of the freakin' sidewalk, that's where; arguing with some skinny-ass redhead.

Yeah, like that's not gonna draw attention.

*Nervousness*, her imaginary inner observer noted in clinical tones as she jotted the emotion down in an official looking ledger.

"Goddamn right I'm nervous," Deirdre muttered, drumming her fingers on top of Snowball's carrier as she stared out the window and chewed on her lip. She glared at the arguing couple. If only there was a way she could get their attention without drawing any more attention to herself. "C'mon, c'mon," she growled anxiously, as the pain in the pit of her stomach grew worse. "Get over yourselves. Kiss and make up. Let's go."

*Anger*, the list continued. *Hypocrisy. Nausea. Impatience. Jealousy. Fear.*

Jealousy? Oh, hell, no. Deirdre blew out an angry breath, crossed her arms and slumped lower in her seat. She was *not* jealous, damn it. Why should she be?

Just because Seth had, apparently, forgotten all about her existence, along with his mission to get her into hiding, the minute Red had appeared. Just because their body language screamed 'we've had sex' even despite the fact that the two of them hadn't touched each other once. Was that any reason for her to feel jealous?

No. Not at all. She couldn't care less about either one of them.

*Denial.* Her inner recorder continued unabated. *Frustration. Loneliness. Pain.*

Oh, bullshit, Deirdre thought, breathing a sigh of relief as Seth—finally—turned toward the truck. *Well, it's about time. And, oh, look: He's frowning again. Now there's a surprise. Not.*

"Something wrong?" She inquired as he climbed into the truck. He tossed her a paper bag filled with doughnuts that she'd never be able to swallow now, and then slammed the door shut.

"No," he replied shortly, turning the key in the ignition and shoving the gears into reverse. The tires screeched as he peeled out of the parking space.

She probably shouldn't ask, but she just couldn't help herself. "So who was that you were talking to?"

"No one," he snapped, and then shrugged. "A friend."

A friend huh? "She didn't look all that friendly just now."

"She's not," Seth replied. He glowered silently for the space of several blocks and then, "She's being a bitch. She won't let you stay at the inn."

Inn? "What inn? I thought–"

"The inn at the winery."

"Oh." There was an inn at this winery where he supposedly lived? Now, why hadn't he said that in the first place? That sounded a lot more comfortable. Not that it mattered, she supposed, since she couldn't stay there, anyway.

"C-can she do that?"

He sighed. "I guess so. I guess I've gone and pissed everyone off this week."

Everyone? Silence fell between them again, broken only by Snowball, whose complaints grew louder with every mile.

"Hey, cat!" Seth pounded his fist on the top of the carrier. "Shut up in there!"

"Stop that," Deirdre ordered, shoving his hand away. "Can't you see he's already upset?"

Seth snorted. "Yeah, I'd be upset too, if I looked like that. What d'you call him anyway?"

Deirdre sighed. "There's nothing wrong with the way he looks—normally. It's just...we both had really bad days, yesterday. And his name is Snowball."

"Snowball?" Seth took his eyes off the road for much too long as he stared at her. "Where'd that come from? He's *gray*. What kinda snow have *you* been looking at?"

"He's silver," she snapped. "And it's not about what color he is. He's actually Snowball III."

"Ohhh. I get it." Understanding dawned in Seth's brown eyes and when his mouth turned up in a big smile that lit up his whole face, Deirdre swore she felt her heart stop beating. "Like the cat from The Simpsons. Right?" [2]

Deirdre could only nod.

"Now that's pretty funny." Still smiling, Seth turned back to watch the road, but Deirdre was having a difficult time taking her eyes off him.

This was the Seth she remembered, the one she'd fallen in love with. *Where's he been hiding*? Several minutes passed before she could tear her eyes away. When she did, she glanced out the window and frowned. Fields full of trellised plants stretched along both sides of the road, for as far as she could see. "Seth...where are we going?"

"To the winery, remember? How many times I gotta say it?"

"But I thought you said–"

"I *said* you couldn't stay at the inn," he corrected, his jaw clenching as his expression darkened once again.

"I don't care who Cara thinks she is, she's *not* gonna start making decisions for me. What is she, my mother? If she wants the inn to stay empty all week, that's her call. But, she can't tell me what I can and can't do anywhere else. You can stay in the pool house. With me."

"Oh." Deirdre turned away so he wouldn't see her smile. "Okay," she said, meekly. Cara. The name sounded vaguely familiar, but Deirdre couldn't recall if she'd met her here last time, or not. Were Cara and Seth a couple? Did they have a fight? *Was it over me*?

She knew it was wrong to feel good about causing trouble between them, maybe even breaking them up, especially if they'd been living together, which is kind of how it sounded. But, on the other hand, it was hard to feel too bad about it, either. Something warm and happy had blossomed to life within her. He must care for her, after all, to go to this much trouble.

Seth sighed again, sounding anything but happy. "Look, don't worry, okay? It's like I told you before. I'm not going to let them hurt you."

Them? Deirdre turned a puzzled face his way. What did he know that he wasn't telling her? "Them, who?"

Seth nodded toward the back of the truck. "My dogs."

"Oh." A little of the happiness she'd been feeling drained away. Was that the only reason he was doing this? He felt guilty?

She bit her lip and gazed out the window. The dogs. Shit. She could still remember the hot smell of their breath on her face as they clambered on top of her. She remembered their weight on her chest as they pinned her to the ground, the pain as their teeth sank into her arm...

Afterwards, she'd been promised that they would never hurt anyone again. That they'd be rounded up and put to sleep. Clearly, that hadn't happened. She'd been lied to. Why?

"Wh-where do they stay?" she asked, although she could already guess what his answer would be.

"With me," he replied firmly, just as she figured he would, in a voice that did not invite further discussion. "They stay with me."

# 7

For the first several minutes after Seth left, Cara was too upset to even move from where she stood on the sidewalk. The argument they'd just had replayed itself, over and over again, in her mind...

*Seth had emerged from The Eternal Bliss Bakery, bag in hand, just as she was about to go in.*

*"Oh, Cara, hey, I'm glad I ran into you," he'd said, the pensive frown on his face smoothing out into a somewhat guarded smile.*

*"What's goin' on?" she'd asked, getting her stupid hopes up again, even though she should have known better by now. It was two days before her birthday, and here he was coming out of a bakery. Was it too much to hope that he'd been thinking of her, that he'd been ordering something special... like a cake, perhaps? Apparently so.*

*"I got a friend who's gonna be staying at the inn for a few days. Which room d'ya want me to give her?"*

*What? Cara blinked. Her? Who, her? "What are you talking about? I can't– I mean, I'm pretty sure Sinead doesn't want me taking in any guests while she's gone. She said last night that she hadn't taken any reservations on purpose."*

*Seth frowned. "Well, she wouldn't be a guest, exactly. I don't even know if she has any money, come to think of it. But she, uh, well, she sorta had a problem with her apartment, see? And now she needs a place to stay. Just until we can sort things out."*

*"No money? Seth, I can't make that kind of decision! I don't own the place, you know. I just work there. And I don't think Sinead would appreciate it, either, if I just started giving rooms away for free."*

*"Ah, that's crap. This is an emergency. Sinead wouldn't care."*

*"Bullshit." Of course Sinead would care. No doubt this was exactly the kind of thing Sinead had been worried about last night, and with good reason, too. She hadn't been gone more for than a few hours and already Seth was acting like The Morning Glory was his personal crib.*

*"Look, I'm not asking you to do anything for her. It's not like she's expecting something fancy, just a place to sleep and, you know, hang out. It's only until the end of the week. I'll square it with Sinead when she gets back, if that's what you're worried about. But, I'm tellin' you, it'll be fine. Chances are she won't even know about it, anyway."*

*"She'll know," Cara ground the words out through clenched teeth. She crossed her arms tight and hoped like hell Seth would let the subject drop. Sinead would definitely know about it because Cara would definitely tell her. Coming clean about something like that was part of being left in charge, wasn't it? And Cara was not gonna fuck that up.*

*But, still, she'd rather not have to tell Seth that, right now, and watch him explode.*

*"How is she gonna know?" Seth asked, a little absently, glancing up and down the street. "Unless we tell her."*

*But he really didn't look like he expected her to answer that. So she didn't.*

*"Look," he said at last, lowering his voice and leaning in closer—a little too close for Cara's comfort. Her heart started to pound, making his words hard to hear. "I gotta do this, Cara. It's important. Yesterday, someone burned down the apartment building where she lived. The po think it was her, but I think maybe someone's trying to kill her."*

*"Seth!" Cara took a step back and stared at him, openmouthed. Was this some kind of test? Or a really bad joke? Or maybe a trick? Or was he actually serious? "What if the cops come to the inn looking for this chick,*

*huh? Have you thought about that? What if they decide to arrest us, too?"*

*Seth shook his head. "For what? Running an inn? Is that a crime now?"*

*"No, not for– Stop being stupid! For hiding a fugitive, or aiding a criminal, or whatever the fuck they call it." Cara felt her stomach turn over at the thought of handcuffs clamped around her wrists. Of rough hands and rude stares and–* Oh, God, no! No, I can't! I can't! *"What are we supposed to do then?" Seth had his parents to bail him out. Who did she have?*

You could call Liam, *a little voice in her head suggested, but oh, yeah, that'd work real well too, wouldn't it? She could* not *call Liam. Liam was trying to pretend he didn't know her. "Look, could just stop stressing? Nothing's gonna happen, okay?"*

*"Sure, that's easy for you to say. And, hold on a minute– Wh-what do you mean, 'you don't think she did it'? What if she did? Who is this chick? Do you even know her?"*

*"Yeah, I know her." Seth glanced quickly at his truck and then away again. "I'm just not sure how much I trust her. But, either way, I need her someplace close, you know? To keep an eye on her."*

*An eye? Right. More likely a hand or two. Cara shook her head. "No. I don't know what you're thinking but, no. Forget it, Seth. You can't do this. It-it's too risky."*

*A potential fire bug in an old, wooden house, crammed full of brittle, dry antiques, why was it not clear to Seth how really bad an idea that was?*

*"Besides, what if you're right and someone really is trying to kill her? Have you thought about that? What if he follows her out there? He could do that, you know. Then what? What if he, if he..." her voice trailed off, as she caught sight of Seth's expression. His eyes burned with some emotion she could not identify. His lips were curled in a bitter sneer. Suddenly, Cara found it hard to breathe.*

*"What if he...*what?*" Seth asked, his voice soft, angry, mocking. "What if he follows her out there and hurts someone? Kills someone? Yeah, I guess that could maybe happen, huh? Imagine that."*

*Cara sighed. Okay, so he'd thought of that. They'd both thought of that. In fact, she supposed they'd both thought of very little else in the past two months except how Gregg had followed her to Seth's. How he'd killed Ray there. How he'd nearly killed her.*

*Cara was pretty sure that most of the people they both knew wished it had been the other way around, but that's not how it had worked out. She'd been given a second chance that night, and she was damn sure not going to throw it away.*

*"Look, Seth, I'd like to help you—I would, really. But Sinead left me in charge of things and...and I just don't think you should be moving people onto her property without asking her. There must be some place else this chick could go."*

*He shook his head. "Nope. There is no place else. If there was, I'd have thought of it by now.* [1] *I can put her in the pool house with me, I guess. If I have to. It's gonna suck, though 'cause she's afraid of the dogs. But if this is how you're gonna be about it, I guess I have no choice, do I?"*

*He looked like he was getting ready to blow a rod or two and Cara knew she should just shut the fuck up now, before he lost it completely and started shouting at her. She really couldn't stop him, could she? But she couldn't back down, either. "What about Sinead? Don't you care at all about her feelings? What's she gonna think when she–"*

*"No!" Seth yelled, exploding right on schedule, just like she figured he would. "God damn it, I don't care—all right? At this point...I really don't give a fuck what Sinead thinks about this. Or you either. And it don't matter if you're in charge of the inn, or the whole friggin' planet, Cara, because you're not in charge of me. So get that straight. I lost enough friends this year and I've seen enough blood to last me a lifetime. Ten lifetimes. So, no more. I'm done. I'm not losing anyone else!"*

*Cara opened her mouth to speak, but, really what answer could she make to that? Did Seth really think she needed any more reminders that it was her fault Ray was dead? It hadn't been her intention. She hadn't wanted it to happen. But, even if there was something she could do to change things now, to go back in time and do things over, do things differently...well, she wouldn't, either. She'd been hurt real bad and she had to live with that every day. But she did not want to be dead. She did not want to take Ray's place. Maybe nobody in Oberon wanted to hear that, but it was the truth.*

*They stared at each other for a moment longer, while Seth continued to seethe. Finally, he shook his head in disgust. "Screw this. I gotta go," he muttered as he turned to walk away from her.*

*Cara's heart twisted in pain.* Here we go again. *She always hated that moment when they turned away like that, when they walked away, when they left her without a backward glance—any of them, all of them—as if she meant nothing.*

*She nearly called him back then, just to make herself feel better. But she swallowed the impulse down. How long would that last? She wasn't going to change her mind and give in. She wasn't going to let his friend stay at the inn just because he'd made her feel guilty about Ray. And he probably wasn't gonna change his mind, either. So that was that. Dead end. So much for their friendship—they'd really flushed that guppy.*

*She was just glad that she'd finally gotten over him, because otherwise this would've hurt a whole lot more...*

The bell over the bakery door jingled suddenly, as the door was pushed open from inside.

"Hi there."

The sound of a woman's soft voice shook Cara from her reverie. Feeling suddenly self-conscious, she turned her head. Warm, brown eyes in a sympathetic face met her gaze.

"Were you coming in here?" the woman asked. "You look like you could maybe use a snack, or a cup of tea or...someone to talk to perhaps?"

Cara knew who she was immediately. Chenoa Johnson. Healer, medicine woman, successful business owner, and Liam's friend. The woman he'd talked about in glowing terms last April.

Cara shook her head. "No. I uh, I just wanted to order a cake."

Chenoa nodded. "I see. Well, you're in the right place for that, aren't you? Come on, in."

Cara studied Chenoa surreptitiously as she followed her into the bakery. *So, this is what I need to become*. Chenoa was everything Liam admired and Cara aspired to: mature, talented, successful. She was also pretty, petite and possessed of a graceful, full figure that left Cara feeling awkward, unattractive, gangly and damaged.

Because all the aspiration in the world couldn't fix those flaws.

"So? What kind of cake are you interested in?" Chenoa asked cheerfully as she slipped behind the counter and turned to face Cara once more. "Is it for a special occasion?"

Cara nodded. "Yes. It is. I don't know what kind of cake I want yet, exactly. But it's for my birthday. On Thursday.

"Chenoa's eyes brightened. "Well, happy birthday. How old will you be?"

Cara sighed. "Eighteen." She didn't want to like Chenoa. She didn't want her to be nice—as well as friendly and pretty and all those other traits that Liam found so fascinating.

*Can't I ever catch a break? Isn't there ever going to be* something *that makes me special or different or...just plain better than someone else? Than anyone else?*

"Wow. Eighteen. That's a big one, isn't it?" Chenoa looked thoughtful for a moment, then she smiled.

"Okay, chica. I guess what I want to do is set up a little taste test. That way, we can figure out exactly what kind of cake you want for your big day."

She opened one of the refrigerated cases behind the glass cabinet and pulled out a tray of mini-cupcakes. "That sound good to you?"

Cara was almost too surprised to answer. "Sure."

"Great." Chenoa gestured toward the corner counter. "Why don't you pour yourself a cup of coffee and then us grab a table, 'kay? I'll be with you in a minute."

"Okay," Cara answered, touched in spite of herself. It *wasn't* every year that she turned eighteen. And, considering the fact that she'd spent most of seventeen expecting to die, she was really in the mood to celebrate this birthday.

Of course, it would've been even nicer if she had someone to celebrate with her. *But, I guess you can't have everything, can you?*

"Hey, girlfriend," Chenoa called to her. "How many people are you looking to feed with this cake, anyway?"

Cara shrugged and busied herself with the coffee urn. "Oh, I don't know. A couple? Not too many. Just...a few, maybe."

Just herself and whoever happened to turn up. Just herself and...well, probably just herself. Though she was not about to admit it, especially not to Chenoa, this cake was her Field of Dreams.

She was buying it in the hope that, if she had one on hand, all ready to eat, maybe someone would show up to share it with her.

"Well, I think that's a great idea," Chenoa said as she joined her at a small table in front of the window. Cara wasn't sure which was more surprising—Chenoa's words, or the large assortment of cupcakes she'd provided for Cara to sample.

"You do?"

"Sure. It's *your* birthday, isn't it? With a small group, you can think about yourself. You can indulge your own tastes, rather than worrying about what a lot of other people are going to like. An occasion like this—that's how it should be. Don't you think?"

"I guess," Cara sighed. "Maybe."

Funny, that was exactly what she always seemed to get grief about —considering her own needs first. But, why not? There was no one else looking out for her. Or, at least, not too often.

It would have been real nice if this could have been one of those times. She'd been secretly hoping Sinead would do something to mark the occasion. She seemed like the kind of boss who could be expected to make a big deal over an employee's birthday. And maybe she would have, too, if she'd been in town. But Sinead and Adam had scheduled this trip months earlier, before they even knew who Cara was.

She'd been hoping Seth might remember as well, but now that she'd gone and pissed him off? Ha! Fat chance of that happening.

And then there was Liam—but, no, she wouldn't even go there.

Now that she'd actually met Chenoa, face to face, well, what was the point? If this was the kind of woman Liam was used to hanging out with, how could Cara even hope to compete?

Chenoa didn't look that old, maybe three or four years older than Cara. But, in terms of accomplishments, she seemed light years ahead. She could cook, too. Cara ate her way through several different bite-sized cakes, each more delicious than the last, before making her decision. "That one."

Chenoa nodded. "Good choice. The spice cake is my favorite, too. How does a double layer of it, filled with caramel creme and frosted with a brown sugar buttercream sound to you?"

"It sounds good," Cara answered, her voice tight. Her spirits had been feeling inexplicably brighter until that one word. *Caramel.* It sent a tiny pang, like a razor tipped arrow, zinging straight to her heart. And it sent her memories spiraling back three months in time...

*It was late at night. The old mansion that housed Gregg's church was dark, cold and quiet. Everyone was asleep, except for Cara, and she was alone in the kitchen, hunched over the table, trying to study. She was so tired, so blurry eyed, that the numbers on the page kept running together, until nothing made any sense.*

*For the past few months, Seth had been helping her, tutoring her on Saturday afternoons and a couple of days a week after school. But now, he was all of a sudden too busy to help. And, without help, she was just lost.*

*Suddenly, a sound from the doorway made her look up. And there he was.*

*"Liam? What are you doing down here?" she asked, startled by the odd look on his face—angry, sad, lonely—she didn't know what the look signified. Their eyes met for only a moment, before he looked away.*

*Well, hey, looky here," he drawled as he crossed the room and headed toward the refrigerator. "If it's not Suzy Sunshine. What's up, Caramel, can't you sleep, either?"*

*Had there really been a tender warmth to his tone, a gentleness that belied the coolness of his words? Or did she only hear what she wanted to hear? Either way, his voice found its way deep inside, into the loneliest, coldest corner of her heart, and soothed her pain.*

*Tears filled her eyes. Feeling foolish, she tried to use her sleeve to wipe them away but he turned just then, and he saw them, anyway.*

*"Hey, what's wrong?" he asked, crossing the room to crouch beside her. "C'mon, I was just joking around. You know that, right? I didn't mean to hurt your feelings, or anything."*

*"Huh?" She gazed at him, mystified. Hurt her feelings? What was he talking about?*

*He used his thumb to wipe away her tears. "I'm sorry I called you names."*

*She shook her head. "Don't be stupid. It's not that."*

*Still sniffling, she gestured at the books in front of her. "It's all this...stuff. I suck at school work. I always have. And now, my tutor's too busy to help me and...and..."*

*She broke off, overwhelmed by the look of concern on his face. Her lip trembled and she swallowed hard to keep from bursting into tears.*

*He grabbed a chair and planted himself next to her. "Okay, well, why don't you tell me what you're having trouble with, and maybe I can help?"*

*"You?" She gazed at him doubtfully.Liam frowned.*

*"Well, yeah, me. Why not? I'm pretty good with this stuff, you know." He shook his head. "That is, if I can still remember any of it. It has been a while."*

*Cara laughed at that—he was maybe half a dozen years older than her. "Yeah, a real long while, huh?"*

*"Well, it was," he protested, looking so adorably solemn that she had to smile. "It was another lifetime."*

*And then, for a long moment, he said nothing at all, as though he was lost in thought.*

*"Well?" Cara asked at last, nudging his arm to get his attention. "Are you gonna just sit there?"*

*He shook his head, and tried to smile. "Sorry, Caramel, I guess my mind musta wandered."*

*Then as now, the word caught her ear. She blinked in surprise. "Wh-what did you just call me?"*

*Liam's eyes widened in a show of innocence. "What? I said Caramel. Isn't that what you said they all call you around here?" She tried hard to look stern as she corrected him. "It's Cara-ma."*

*Liam smiled. "That's what I said. Caramel."*

*She set her teeth and frowned harder. "That's not–""Cause you're so sweet, right? Just like candy?"*

*Her breathing stalled. Her face flamed red. She crossed her arms and looked away, not knowing whether to laugh or cry. "Now, you're making fun of me," she muttered, hoping it wasn't the case*

*"No, I'm just trying to make you laugh." Liam bumped her shoulder with his own. "C'mon, you're too young to be so serious all the time."*

*"I'm not too young." She looked at him for a moment, still uncertain, but she could see no malice in his eyes. "You're just not that funny, that's all."*

*"Sure I am." His eyes were twinkling as he added, "Caramel."*

*"Stop it," she growled, lips quirking. She picked up her highlighter and nodded toward the book. "Now, help me."*

*He didn't move.She looked at him. She could tell he was waiting for her to cave. That was so not gonna happen.*

*She shook her head. "I told you. I'm not gonna laugh. You're not funny."*

*He grinned. "Oh, yeah? So, why are you smiling, then?"*

*"I'm not," she tried to insist, but, oh, hell. Yes she was. And he knew it, too. She clamped her mouth shut and forced her face back into a scowl.*

*But Liam only grinned wider. "Yeah, you are. I can see it in your eyes." He leaned in close and whispered mockingly, "Help us, Caramel, you're our only hope. We're out of coff-ee. We need the keys to the ga-ate. Pleeeaase, Caramel. Please think for us; we're too stoopid to think for ourselves."*

*His act was dead-on perfect. He'd caught the words, the tone, the whiney, sleep-deprived stupidity of the other cult members with crystal accuracy.*

*"Stop!" she squawked, as she tried to cover her ears, but it was too late. One single snort of laughter escaped her, and it was all over. She dissolved into helpless giggles, while Liam sat back, smiling even wider now, apparently satisfied with his results...*

"Hey, are you okay?" Chenoa asked softly, reaching a hand out toward her arm. "What's wrong?"

Cara pulled back quickly. Oh, God. She'd been so lost in her memories, she'd forgotten where she was. "Nothing. I'm fine." She reached behind her for her purse and pushed away from the table, anxious to put as much space as she could between herself and the other woman. She did not want to be touched. And she definitely did not want to start crying. Not now, not here. She couldn't bear it."So how much do I owe you for the cake?" she mumbled, digging in her purse for her wallet.

"Why don't you worry about that when you pick it up?" Chenoa suggested, leaning back in her seat, her expression surprised, dissatisfied, curious.

"Okay." Cara nodded, heading for the door as swiftly as her gimpy leg would allow. "Great. See you Thursday."

CHENOA GAZED SPECULATIVELY at the fleeing teen. *What just happened here*? She was usually pretty good at reading people, their energy levels, their auras, their hidden pain. And, when it came to healing heart wounds, she was better than good.But this girl was a puzzle. There'd been a closed, pinched look to both her aura and her face when she'd first come in. But then she'd gradually opened up, like a flower unfurling its petals in the sunlight.

For several minutes, while the girl sampled cupcakes, Chenoa had stayed focused, channeling her energy into the girl's aura, smiling at the transformation. She'd been pleased when her work was rewarded with a slight flush on the girl's cheeks, with a fresh sparkle in her eyes. And then, suddenly...*poof!* All her efforts were undone in an instant.

*Ah, well.* Sighing, Chenoa stood and began to clear the table. So much of the work she did here was a mystery. As was life itself, come to think of it. Which was why it was important not to become too attached to the outcome. "I did the best I could for her, Grandfather. But she's in Your hands, and what will be, will be."

Cara drove through town a little slower than usual. Partly because she was in no hurry to get to the police station, partly because her meeting with Chenoa had left her unsettled. She needed time before she saw Liam again. She needed to think. To grieve. To put her pain behind her.It had been nice, for a few minutes, to remember a time when she could smile and laugh like anyone else.

A time when loneliness was a fleeting, transitory thing; a chill that could be warmed away with nothing more than a smile, a word, a touch; not a glass-walled maze she couldn't fight her way out of, no matter how hard she tried.

She'd been fooling herself thinking Liam cared for her. Sure, he'd been kind—so had Chenoa. That's just the way they were. But he saw her as a kid back then, someone to be babied and teased. Why should that have changed?

Her feelings for Liam hadn't changed much, either. They were as strong as ever. But her fear of being touched, of being hurt again, was stronger still. Too strong to be overcome. Even by him. That had been obvious last night.

She arrived at the station with time to spare. Heat dazzled her as she stepped out of her car and all she could focus on, or think about, was getting to the shaded walkway that ran alongside the building. She was almost at the door when the sound of footsteps reached her ears and, suddenly, a hand appeared from out of the void on her left hand side and touched her arm.She swallowed a scream as her body jerked instinctively away from the threat.

Stumbling over the bent stump of a rosemary bush, she felt her leg twist. Pain sheared through her and she came down hard on the edge of the concrete bench. Her nose was filled with a pungent smell of rosemary, damp earth and fear. Terror distorted her sight and, for a moment, Gregg's face swam above her. If she hadn't lost her breath in the fall, she would have screamed.

Thankfully, her vision cleared before her lungs had a chance to re-fill. "Liam?" Relief sluiced through her, followed by embarrassment and then by rage. Her hands tightened into fists. "What the fuck are you doing sneaking up on me like that?"

"What?" He looked down at her startled and confused. "I didn't–"

"You did. You were in my blind spot. You know I–" She broke off as his face went dark and a look, almost of hatred, blazed in his eyes. Shit. He didn't know. And, she hadn't wanted to tell him about that, either. She didn't want to admit to her weaknesses, to her childishness, to her defects. "I-I didn't see you. It-it-it surprised me."

He looked away, his jaw clenching. "Sorry," he muttered. After a minute, he turned back again, frowning now. "You know, if you...if you...if it's this much of a problem for you to see, maybe you shouldn't be driving?"

"What?" Oh, no. Not that again? "Why can't any of you ever give me a break?" she snapped, slamming her hands down on the concrete for emphasis. "I'm learning, aren't I? I'm getting better every day. It's just–" Slam. "Why can't you give me some time, huh?" Slam. "Why does everything have to be right now?" Slam, slam, slam–

"Stop that!" He shook his head. "Look, I just meant–"

"It's not fair!" Her palms stinging, she folded her arms across her middle and hugged herself tight. "I just can't fix everything, do everything, be everything you want me to be—I can't, all right? I just...can't. Not yet."

"I know that." His voice was quiet, his expression unhappy. "All I meant is that, maybe someone else should drive you places– just for a while. That's all. Just until you're comfortable with...with the way things are."

"Drive me places?" Cara snorted at the idea. "Oh, yeah. Good idea. Like who's gonna do that?"

Liam's jaw clenched again. "What's wrong with Seth? Is he too busy to drop you off? I could always drive you back out to the inn afterwards, you know, if he can't stick around and wait for you. Or if he doesn't want to make two trips."

Cara's breath caught. For a moment, her hopes became reality. If he drove her home on Thursday she'd have an excuse to ask him in for cake, wouldn't she? But then reality turned predictably dull. Right. Like *that* was ever gonna happen.

What was she thinking? He'd told them that yesterday, hadn't he?

Thursday and Friday were his days off. That's why the last class of the week was going to be on Saturday. She wouldn't be seeing him at all on Thursday, or Friday either.

She shook her head sadly. It didn't matter. By now Seth was no doubt back at the winery, getting it on with Miss Fugitive-from-Justice Girl. A fact that was sure to land Cara in a shitload of trouble if Liam ever found out. And if he remembered that he was a cop.

And if Liam didn't remember, or if he chose to look the other way? Well, that could land *him* in trouble, couldn't it? Cara didn't want that on her conscience, either.

*Or, maybe neither of us will get in trouble. Maybe Liam will just lay all the blame on Seth, and leave me out of it?*

Cara pushed that mutinous thought aside as well. It *was* possible. Liam might feel he owed her that much loyalty. But it wouldn't really help either, would it? Because she owed Seth, too. Besides, Sinead might be annoyed with Seth for the moment, but that didn't mean she'd be happy to see him get arrested. Especially not on Cara's watch. No, the best thing she could do, the only thing, really, was to keep Liam as far away from the inn as possible. Sometimes responsibility just plain sucked.

"No. Thanks, anyway. I can drive myself."

Her voice was so soft, so sad, but its impact on Liam was anything but gentle. It tore at his heart. He took a step forward, reaching for her without a single thought for where they were, or who might be watching. But, as usual, she was way ahead of him. "Don't touch me."

He felt his eyes widen as she flinched away from him. "No, I– I'm not. I just...I just wanted to help you up," he lied.

She shook her head. "I don't want any help. I'm fine here."

"Okay." His chest tight, he fought for breath, as he backed up a pace. "It's almost time for class to start. Why don't we go inside?"

Cara bit her lip and looked away. "You go ahead." She gestured toward the metal ashcan. I uh, I just want to have a smoke before I go inside. You know how that is, right? Us nicotine addicts, we, uh...we need our fix, you know?"

Liam felt himself frown. She was a smoker now? Since when? Was that Seth's influence?

"You'd better not. You're still seventeen, you know. Technically, you're not supposed to smoke."

"Two days, Liam," Cara snapped as she turned to scowl at him, slapping her hands against the bench again, so hard he winced at the sound. "So would you please just...just shut the fuck up about that. For once? Please? I'm not a child! I– Oh, just go away. Leave me alone."

Once, he would have argued. Once, he would have stayed and teased her into a better mood. But this was neither the time nor the place. Maybe there would never be a right time or place for that again? "All right. I'll see you inside. Don't be late."

*Don't touch me? Leave me alone*? These weren't things he ever thought he'd hear her say. Not to him. Not after everything they'd been through together, after everything they'd said and done.

And...a child? No, God help him, she wasn't. She definitely wasn't. Except that, legally, she was. And there were some laws he was bound to honor.

For the last three months, even longer, if he were honest, all he'd wanted to do was to go to her, to be with her, to wrap his arms around her. To hold her close and never let her go. He'd wanted to love her. To comfort her. To care for her.

Instead, he'd kept his distance, because, more important than what he wanted was what she needed. Time to heal.

A child? No. Not for much longer, anyway. She was young woman, and there were decisions she needed to make so that she could get on with her life. He'd wanted to be fair. He didn't want his feelings to take precedence over what was right for her. He didn't want to influence her choices or limit her options...

So he'd given her space. He'd given her time. Maybe too much of both. And, now?

"What'd you expect?" he asked himself angrily, as he unlocked the door to the classroom and switched on the lights. Fluorescent tubes flickered slowly to life. The cool air smelled faintly of ammonia and acetone. "What'd you think was gonna happen, asshole?" Did he think she'd just forget that he'd failed her? That she'd forgive him, when he could not forgive himself? "What's done is done."

He'd made mistakes, that was for sure. Now, he'd have to play the cards that fate had dealt him. But he wasn't giving up. Not yet. He hadn't expected it to be easy. It wasn't like he thought he could just show up at her door on the morning of her eighteenth birthday and jump her bones. It was just...harder than he'd thought it would be. Much harder than he'd imagined. He hadn't expected her to be so cold to him. And he'd never, ever realized it would be quite so painful letting go.

"WELL? WHADDAYA THINK?" The young punk who'd invaded Jack's office asked him. "Are those shots gonna bake Gregg's beanie, or what?"

Jack took his time studying the photos he'd just uploaded to his computer, trying hard to disguise the slithering disgust that made him want to twitch. Of all the things Gregg had talked him into, dealing with this piece of slime was probably the worst. Not that he'd actually been given a choice."I don't think he'll be too disturbed," he replied in an even tone. "They don't look that cozy, do they?"

There was a gap of several feet between Cara and the cop. And the anger on both their faces was hot enough to ignite the screen. But why was he thinking that? Fire was the last thing he wanted on his mind today.

"Cozy?" His informant chuckled. "What kind of candy-ass word is that? Anyway, it's not your call to make, is it? Besides, the pansy drew a heart around her name in his calendar—what does that tell you?"

*It tells me he's not half the pansy you are*, Jack thought, bitterly. He glanced at the book on his desk once again and shrugged.

"I don't see a heart. I see a circle. It's a little lopsided, but still–"

"Ah, bullshit," his visitor scoffed as he got to his feet. "Look at it! It's red. It's a heart and you know it. Anyway, I've done my job, so pay up."

*Gladly*, Jack thought, taking his key from his pocket and unlocking the side drawer of his desk. *Anything to get you the fuck out of my office*. He shot a quick, suspicious look at the punk who appeared to be studying his nails, and then removed the sealed envelope of cash.

"Here," he said as he tossed it onto the desk. "It's all there. You can count it, if you like."

The young man grinned. "Nah, s'okay. If Gregg trusts you, that's good enough for me."

Jack nodded. There might not be much honor between thieves, but there was fear aplenty. Messing with one of Gregg's people was just the same as messing with Gregg—at least from Gregg's perspective. Jack knew that, and so did the shithead who was finally leaving.

As the door swung shut, Jack turned back to the pictures once again. He traced his fingers over the figure on the bench and waited for the familiar hardening of his cock. Cara. He barely recognized her now. She'd been so pretty once, and he'd been so hot to have her, he'd have done almost anything Gregg asked. Now, he couldn't even get a rise from the thought of her.

Still, it was a relief knowing that all Gregg wanted was to have her watched. Not touched. Not hurt. Not threatened. Not yet. And not killed, either. Not like the other one.

Jack jumped and bit his tongue as the door to his office burst open once again.His visitor reappeared. "Oh, yeah. Almost forgot. There's one more thing you should know."

"What now?" Jack demanded, scowling at the pain. His tongue

throbbed and if the shit-eating grin of amusement on the punk's face was any indication, the bastard knew it, too.

"Didn't know if you'd heard yet, but your shot went wide."

Jack's gaze flickered toward the open door. "What are you talking about?"

The slimeball's eyebrows rose in mock surprise. "You missed, man. You fucked up. You know that fire? Over in Abraxas?" He shook his head. "No good, Jack. No body. Tough luck, huh?"

Jack could feel the blood as it drained from his face. "I don't know what you're talking about."

The punk shrugged. "'Course you don't. A nice, respectable lawyer like yourself, what would you know about arson or attempted murder, right?" He stopped and smiled. "This is what you get when you hire amateurs. I warned Gregg something like this could happen. I told him to let me deal with it. See, I'd have done her at night, when she was all tucked up in her bed." His eyes glinted as he added, "That way you know you got her. I'd have gone in ahead of time, too. Made sure that's where she was. Made damn sure she wasn't in any condition to run, either."

Jack's fingers twitched as he considered the gun in his center drawer. Could he get away with claiming the man was a stranger who'd broken in and tried to rob him? The day was close to being over, not too many people around...still, it was probably better not to chance it. Not this time. He took a deep breath and forced himself to stay calm. "Get out of here."

The punk nodded. "I hear you," he said as he turned once more to go. "I'll be in touch." And Jack had no doubt that he meant what he said.

Jack waited until the door was closed for the second time and then he leaned back in his chair and scrubbed his hands over his face. This couldn't be happening. His nice, tidy life was starting to come apart. He didn't want that.

He thought again about the hairs he'd removed from the girl's brush on Sunday. Some of them he'd already sent to a lab for a DNA test, to determine if she really was Glenn's daughter. But the others...those he'd held onto. Somehow, some day, he *would* find a way to bring Gregg down. He had to. Only then would he finally be safe.

In the meantime, much as he hated Gregg, much as he hated what he'd been forced to do, he had to keep his cool and play along. It had been fun, he'd admit that much. He hadn't felt this alive in a long, long time. He'd been surprised by how much he'd missed it.

But enough was enough. Once, when he was still just a kid, he'd broken into a friend's house on a dare and stole the grocery money from his mom's purse. He'd been young enough that the only thing he could think to buy with the money was a shitload of candy.

He'd always had an insatiable sweet tooth. Always. But, as he'd learned that day, as he was learning now, too much of a good thing could make you sick. He had to stay cool. He had to cover his butt. He had to end this. Soon.

# 8

Seth had little to say on the way to the winery. He didn't appear to be brooding, Deirdre decided, after slanting several curious looks in his direction, but he did seem distracted.

*What's he thinking about*? Was it still the dogs? Was he replaying the conversation he'd had with the girl he'd run into downtown? Or was there something else on his mind?

Her own mind seemed to have gotten stuck on two little words: *With me*. That's where he said she'd be staying. And where the dogs would be staying. All of them together, apparently, like one big, furry family. *Won't that be fun*?

She cast a quick glance out the back window at the truck bed where the monsters had hunkered down for the ride. They looked calm enough, at the moment. And she felt a whole lot safer with Seth here to control them, but if these really were the same dogs who'd attacked her—and she had no reason to think otherwise—then why weren't they dust by now? She'd been told that they'd be put down. Both she and her parents had been assured that would be the case.

She felt confused and betrayed, but she couldn't think about that now. If she thought too much about that subject, she knew she'd only end up losing her temper. So she put it from her mind.

She would have loved to question Seth about it though—and about what kind of sleeping arrangements he envisioned for the two of them—but his expression, while not exactly grim, didn't welcome conversation. Besides, bed was another topic she wasn't sure she wanted to get into right now. She didn't know what she wanted to do about that yet, either.

For two years she'd fantasized about what sex with Seth would be like, about how different he'd be from Eric, or any of the guys she'd gone out with since then. How he'd awaken everything that had been dead inside her, and give her back everything that had been taken away.

Her therapist had told her she was only fooling herself. But that couldn't be true! The way she'd felt this morning, when Seth held her, had her convinced she was at least partially right.

That still didn't mean she was ready to jump into bed with him though. If he pushed too hard for that, he'd ruin everything. And if he didn't push at all, if he wasn't even interested? Well, that would be even worse, wouldn't it?

She might never know what love was like then. She might spend her whole life alone. Sighing in frustration, she settled back in her seat and tried to distract herself by gazing at the scenery.

They were traveling between two seemingly endless rows of Eucalyptus trees. Their papery trunks and blue-green leaves only partially obscured the surrounding fields. Miles and miles of sun-drenched orchards and staked grapevines, extended across the valley floor, all the way to the green and gold foothills.

Beyond the hills she could see mountains: slate blue, verging on purple, only slightly darker than the clouds that lowered above them.Finally, there was a break in the trees, and a large sign welcomed them to Lupa e Cervo.

As they passed through the winery's wrought iron gate, she saw another, smaller sign directing them left, toward what appeared to be a castle. But rather than turn there, as indicated, Seth veered to the right, following a narrow, two lane road that meandered northeast through the vineyard.

There were no trees to shelter them here from sun or rain or wind, and the air blowing in through the open windows was so hot and dry that it seared Deirdre's eyeballs.

After several minutes, a classic, two-story, Victorian farmhouse shimmered into view. From its gingerbread trimmed eaves to its white picket fence, it was picture perfect.

Deirdre smiled eagerly when yet another sign identified it as The Morning Glory Inn. The tree shaded front porch and the cool green of the lawn promised relief from sun, from heat, from just about anything unpleasant.

She was dismayed when Seth failed to pull into the drive. "Wait. Where are you going?" she blurted in surprise.

He shot her a swift, questioning glance. "Around back, why? I told you. I live in the pool house."

"Oh." Deirdre gazed out the window, hoping her voice did not betray her disappointment. "Right."

Pool house. The name conjured thoughts of wet tile and damp terrycloth, of mildew and chlorine and locker rooms. What kind of place was that to be living? She felt a serious grudge starting to form against the redhead. What the hell was that girl's problem? The inn seemed close to heaven. The pool house, not so much.

As the truck bounced down a rutted dirt track, Deirdre clutched at the armrest and tried not to frown. *At least it's shady here*, she thought, glancing up at the ancient, moss and lichen encrusted Live Oaks that loomed overhead. But, on the other hand, shady was also the *most* she could say for the place.

The ground beneath the trees was dry and rocky, littered with dead leaves. She knew just what that meant. Snake country. The yard behind the inn was enclosed by a ramshackle fence that looked likely to collapse at any second. Paint, the color of butter, peeled from the weathered boards. [1]

As they rounded the corner of the property, Deirdre could see where the fence had been extended recently. The new section was more sturdily built, but equally utilitarian. What appeared to be a barn, or a shed of some sort, seemed to occupy most of the added area. It stretched across the back of the yard, its corrugated tin roof, painted brick red, jutted above the fence-line. From where she sat, it looked about as habitable as a chicken coop.

Seth pulled his truck alongside the other vehicles parked against the fence. Deirdre noted a couple of jeeps, an old truck, a small trailer.

*What kind of place is this*, she wondered. *It looks so ghetto.*

She could imagine chickens on the other side of the fence, scratching for bugs in the dust. Maybe a cactus or two. But very little else.

Seth turned the car off, then looked at her. “Wait here a minute. I’ll be right back.”

Deirdre turned to watch him as he got out and went to the back of the truck. He unhooked the dogs from their leashes and then gestured toward a path that seemed to run downhill toward some kind of ravine.

Deirdre heaved a deep sigh of relief as the dogs leaped from the truck and took off down the path. She hadn’t realized it until that moment, but she’d been holding her breath.

“Come on,” Seth said, returning to the truck’s cab. “It’s hot out here. Let’s get inside.”

He reached for the handle of Snowball’s carrier, but Deirdre forestalled him. “Thanks. I’ll take that.”

Seth nodded. “Okay.” He grabbed the duffel bag with her exercise clothes, instead, along with the grocery bag that held Snowball’s food and bowls, as well as Deirdre’s new toothbrush.

“So, where’d your dogs go?” Deirdre asked glancing nervously at the path they’d taken as she followed him to the gate. He was right about the temperature. Even in the shade the air felt almost too hot to breathe. Snowball was already panting.

“I sent them to play in the creek,” Seth replied. “I figured they could use a cooldown, and I wanted to get them out of the way until we got you settled in.”

“Oh. Good idea.” Deirdre nodded, watching as Seth inserted a key into the gate’s surprisingly substantial looking lock. Given how rundown the place appeared, that much security seemed a little excessive.

*Don't be so quick to judge, Dee. Remember, things aren't always what they seem at first glance.* Rafe had said that, just the other day. It was a good point, Deirdre thought ruefully, as Seth pushed the gate open and she got her first glimpse of what awaited her.

On the other side of the fence, the ghetto view faded. There were no chickens, no cactus, just a lush, tropical garden, almost a jungle. A hedge of bright, red and yellow hibiscus covered one wall, a thick growth of honeysuckle, and several potted fruit trees, trailed along another, the heady scent of blossoms perfumed the air. [2]

"Wow," Deirdre murmured, looking around in a daze. A vine covered pergola extended from the back of the farmhouse. Three or four small tables, shaded by yellow umbrellas, shared the brick terrace with a burbling hot tub.

Closer at hand was the pool house. A one-story structure, painted a deep, olive-sage, trimmed with mustard and blue, it blended seamlessly into the garden. Despite the tin roof, this was definitely no shed. In fact, Deirdre could only conclude that its name referred merely to its proximity to the pool.

With no less than three sets of French doors leading out to the terrace the house was light-filled and airy, definitely no place for chickens. It looked more like something a tornado, perhaps the same one that had transported Dorothy to Oz, might have picked up in Mazatlan or Port au Prince and deposited here.

The pool itself, half-hidden behind giant banana trees, resembled an enormous, liquid emerald. Deirdre got only a peek at it as she followed Seth into the house. It looked so refreshingly cool, she wanted to drop everything and dive right in.

She sighed wistfully. If only she'd had time to pick up a bathing suit while they were in town. If only she didn't need to buy yet another new suit. Not that she had anything against shopping, of course, but it was still a little overwhelming to remember that everything she once owned was gone.

She sighed again, thought of all the stuff she'd lost in the fire, and felt her chest tighten. *They're just things*, she reminded herself, refusing to give in to despondency. *They can be replaced. They're not like people. Their loss shouldn't matter so much.* But, all the same, it did. It did.

"What's wrong?" Seth turned his head to glance over his shoulder at her.

"Nothing," she said, shaking the thoughts away. It was nothing she could bear to talk about, or even think about, right now. She looked around, hoping to distract herself. "Don't worry about it."

They were in a small sitting room, made to appear larger by the sparse furnishings. Built-in shelves, packed with books and a flat screen TV, took up most of one wall. A narrow writing desk, a CD rack and stereo occupied the wall opposite it. In the space between them, an upholstered wicker couch and two comfortable looking armchairs beckoned invitingly.

Deirdre balanced Snowball's carrier on the back of the couch as she continued to look around. Toward the rear of the building, and separated from the main area by a glass and wrought iron breakfast bar flanked with stools, was a modern and efficient looking kitchen. Above her head, the blades of a ceiling fan turned slow, lazy circles, barely stirring the warm air. Beneath her feet, polished terracotta tiles, and a few scattered rugs, tied the room together.

The whole place had been thoughtfully, tastefully, expensively arranged. But it was not what she'd expected of him. How could they be so different?

She forced a polite smile. "Nice place."

"I guess," Seth replied without much interest.

Still curious, Deirdre nodded at the crowded bookcase. "Did you read all those books?"

Seth frowned. "Did I what? No, of course not. Listen, I figured you could take my room for now." He pointed toward one of two doors that led from this center room into the other portions of the building. "That way, if we keep the door closed, you won't have to worry about your cat getting out."

Touched by his thoughtfulness, Deirdre smiled again, more genuinely this time. "Thank you."

Seth looked surprised. "Sure," he said, shrugging a little. He shot her a puzzled glance, then turned and led the way into the other room.

*Now, this is more like it,* Deirdre thought, eyes widening in surprise, as she caught sight of the bedroom. She put Snowball's carrier on the floor and looked around happily. The room was dark and slightly messy, but at least it looked lived in.

A hamper stuffed with clothes stood beside the dresser. Magazines lay piled on the floor beside the unmade bed. And on the cluttered desk, amid a welter of books and notebooks, cables and Sharpies, and other things she couldn't even start to recognize, was something she absolutely did.

"Hey, can I use your computer to go online?" she asked eagerly. Why hadn't she thought of this before? What better way to contact her parents? They'd taken a laptop to Europe with them, and she knew how obsessive they both were about checking their email.

"I–I guess so," Seth replied, uncertainly. "D'you mean now?"

"No." Deirdre shook her head and tried to calculate the time difference. Was Europe ahead or behind, and why couldn't she ever remember? "Just...at some point." It wouldn't do any good to try and contact them in the middle of their night.

"All right."

There was a hint of wariness in Seth's voice, but Deirdre couldn't be bothered wondering what that was all about. She had other things to think about. Like how much she should tell her parents, when she finally reached them. And how much to keep hidden.

"Look, I'm sorry the bed's such a mess," Seth blurted suddenly. "I'll get some clean sheets for it when Cara gets back. And some towels, I guess."

Deirdre nodded. "That would be good." But she wasn't really listening. She'd tell them about the fire, of course, and let them know she was okay. But she wouldn't tell them that someone was trying to kill her.

What was the point? They wouldn't believe her anyway.

"*That's Paige's story,*" they'd tell her, "*not yours. You're not your mother. You've got your own life to live, Deirdre, your own decisions to make. You can't base everything on what Paige did.*"

They'd said that about her decision to move here, to go to school at Abraxas, to become a journalist. They'd said it about a lot of things.

"And I can get you a box with some sand in it, for your cat," Seth said. He gestured to the door next to the closet. "Maybe you could put it in the bathroom, or something?"

Again Deirdre nodded. "Okay, sure." She couldn't tell them that the police were looking for her, either.

"*Well, if that's the case, then you should go down to the station and clear things up. Do it now. Before things get more complicated. You don't want this turning into another Runaway Bride, do you?*" That's what they'd say about that.

They'd tell her to stand up for herself. To demand her rights. To demand an investigation. And, if she really thought she was in danger, not just imagining things because Paige had been killed, to demand protection for herself.

"*Hiding does not make you look innocent,*" she could hear her father saying that now. "*It makes you look complicit—which you don't want. No one can help you if you don't let them. Besides, they're not going to be looking for the real culprits, if they're busy looking for you.*"

But going to the police was the last thing Deirdre wanted to do. Especially on her own. She remembered the cops here from last time. They hadn't all been that nice to her, which she could kind of understand, given some of the trouble she'd caused. This time she hadn't done anything wrong, but were they likely to believe that?

"So, what else do you need?" Seth was starting to sound impatient, Deirdre thought, as she shook her head once again.

"Nothing. Except...when are your parents getting back?"

Seth's family knew the cops. And as for his father, well, if Dan was even half as understanding, or half as supportive, as he'd been two years ago, Deirdre knew she'd have nothing to worry about, would she? Dan would take care of everything, just like a real father.

Unlike his son, who huffed out an angry breath and scowled. "End of the week. Why?"

She looked at him, surprised by his sudden show of temper. "I just wanted to know, that's all. I just thought– Oh, forget it."

He probably didn't like being reminded that his father and her mother had once been lovers. She didn't blame him for that. She didn't want to think too much about it either, come to think of it.

They gazed at each other unhappily. Before Deirdre could think of anything to say, a clattering on the living room's tile floor alerted her that the dogs were back. She gasped as they appeared in the doorway.

Seth turned and spoke sharply. The dogs stopped in their tracks, looking so crestfallen Deirdre almost felt sorry for them.

"Look, I gotta go hose them down," Seth said, turning to face her again. "Before they track mud all over the place. After that, I thought I'd make us something to eat. Are you hungry?"

Deirdre nodded. She'd been too upset to eat the doughnuts Seth had bought, which meant she hadn't eaten anything since yesterday. "Starving."

"Okay, well, I'll see what I've got." He looked at her fiercely for a moment and then added, "They're not gonna hurt you."

Of course he'd say that. He probably even believed it, too. She, on the other hand, was far from convinced.

But she didn't want to argue, so she nodded again. "Okay."

"Okay, good." Seth expelled another deep breath, this one sounded relieved, and headed toward the door. "I'll let you know when the food's ready."

SETH HAD REMOVED his shirt and his shoes before going back outside, to keep them dry. Now, the afternoon sun beat down on his back and shoulders and the hot bricks of the patio stung his feet as he ran water from the hose over the last of his dogs. But he barely noticed. He was used to the heat. After all, he'd spent most of his summers out at his family's nursery, in one of the canyons outside of town.

Besides, he had other things to think about. Like the gigantic lump that had just risen in his throat. Mist sparkled in the atmosphere, adding to the tropical enchantment of the garden. He'd inhaled a lungful and the green and earthy scent had rendered him instantly homesick.

He liked his job at the winery well enough, and he loved the success he was making of his own dog-walking and training business, but there were times when the fields and greenhouses of his family's nursery seemed like the best part of his childhood. Like a favorite toy, or a sweater he'd outgrown. Something he'd broken. Something he'd lost. Something he wished he could somehow fix or retrieve or still fit into.

Not that his father wouldn't welcome him with open arms if Seth decided to return, but it wouldn't be the same and he just couldn't do it.

He knew his parents were disappointed by a lot of the choices he'd made lately—to move out of the family home, to discontinue his education, to work here. That was hard enough to deal with from a distance. Working alongside them both, day in and day out, witnessing their disappointment up close and in his face, was more than he could handle.

"Stay still," he murmured as Zeus wriggled impatiently beneath the spray. The big dog wanted to be set loose to play with his brothers, but Seth knew better than to let himself be rushed. The soft silt from the creek bed had a nasty tendency to collect between the dogs' toes and along the creases where their legs joined their torsos. Fine as powder, the sand didn't wash off easily. But if it stayed there it would either rub the surrounding skin raw; or mix with oil from the dogs' skin to become a paste that, once ground into the inn's rugs and carpets, was all but impossible to remove.

The other dogs, all newly washed, scampered around the terrace snapping and snarling. Jaws gaping, they sparred with each other, until Seth's nerves were frayed.

"Down," he ordered when he couldn't take any more. The sight of their teeth bared in play had never disturbed him before, but now, with Deirdre's voice fresh in his head, describing her attack, that was all he could think about.

Which of them had done it? Fists clenching, he gazed at the four dogs arrayed before him. Ears pricked forward, they waited expectantly for his next command. He'd never wanted to hurt an animal in his life. Until now.

There had been eight dogs in all, originally. And Seth could rule out only two: Mouth, who'd been elsewhere when Deirdre was attacked, and Athena who was already dead. It could have been any of the others—or all of them. And he might never know for certain.

But, at least now he could understand why his cousin Nick always acted like keeping the dogs from being killed had been such a big deal.

At the time, Seth had thought that Nick, and everyone else in town, was simply out to bust his balls; threatening to destroy his dogs for no other reason than to punish him for being such a jerk. It would have done that, all right. They might as well have gone ahead and killed him too, while they were at it. It would have saved him the trouble of doing it himself. Which was exactly what he'd told them—Nick, his parents, anyone who'd listen, anyone he thought might care.

And, if they'd carried through with their threats, he'd have damn sure made good on his own. What other choice were they leaving him? They had to know he could never have lived with the guilt.

But if he'd known what had happened to Deirdre, would that have made a difference? Would that have made him care less about the dogs, or worry less about their fate? Would it have made it any easier to let them go to their deaths?

Maybe. But not without a case or two of tequila to help numb the pain. "Shit." Disgusted with himself, he tossed down the towel and the hose and went to turn off the water.

Just remembering that portion of his life had him craving a drink, and probably it always would. The truth was, he didn't know what kind of difference it would have made if he'd known. Maybe it would have made things worse. It would have been like...trying to choose between two things that he loved. How could anyone make a choice like that? Which was maybe why no one had told him.

*Deirdre*. He glanced toward the house, not sure whether there'd been a flash of motion behind the shutters, or if that was just what he wanted to think, that she was in there watching him. That, beneath all the craziness, the wild stories, the betrayal, her feelings for him were the same as his feelings for her.

Or maybe not quite the same. Less confused would be good—it would be nice if at least one of them could still think straight. He still couldn't get used to the idea that she was really here. He'd dreamed about her coming back for so long, and now that she had, he wasn't sure how he felt.

He wished he knew what it was about the girl that made him want her like he did, or why he couldn't get the thought of her out of his head. His life had been pretty much perfect, up until the night she first came to town. And if they'd never met? Then maybe the other stuff would never have happened either. Maybe his life would still be perfect.

That wasn't the only reason he shouldn't want anything to do with her, but it was a good one. Besides, it wasn't like she'd ever tried to make him like her. Her behavior toward him had always run hot and cold, and he saw no signs of that ever changing.

She'd barely said two words the whole ride out here today. She'd mostly stared out the window looking glum. When she wasn't stealing worried looks at his dogs, that is. Or at him. The look on her face brought to mind the first night they'd met...

*The fog was not too thick yet, but it was setting in fast and Seth was about to call it a night when one of the kids he was skating with nodded toward a slowly approaching vehicle, its headlights just visible through the mist.*

*"Check it. Here come the po."Seth turned around just as the unmarked car slid to a stop alongside them.*

*"Hey there, Seth. How's it going?" Ryan Henderson called from behind the wheel.*

*Okay," Seth replied, rolling closer, playing it cool. He knew the other kids would be watching, eyes riveted on him. And on the cop.*

*"Lots of kids out tonight," Ryan observed needlessly. "Everybody behaving themselves?"*

*Seth shrugged. "I guess."*

*"You know, we' had some problems down here a couple of weeks ago, some kids from out of town looking to cause trouble. Nothing like that tonight, is there?"*

*Seth pretended to look around. "Nope. Just locals here tonight, as near as I can tell." Just the locals and one, as of yet, unidentified girl. Deirdre. Although, at the time, he knew her only as Monica.*

*"Can't you and your friends find anything better to do than play in traffic?" Ryan asked, and Seth had to work hard to keep from rolling his eyes.*

*Playing?* What was this, pre-school? *"Not that much traffic this time of night."*

*"Still. Why don't you guys just stay in the park?"*

*Seth shook his head.* Well, that's obvious, isn't it? *"Not enough concrete. And anyway...we probably won't be here too much longer. We'll probably be heading home soon."*

*The car started to roll forward as Ryan eased up on the brake. "Sounds like a good plan. You do know to stay out of The Greenbelt, though, right?"*

*Despite his best intentions, Seth couldn't help but grin at that. "'Cause of the wild dog thing? Yep. Know all about 'em."*

*He was still grinning as he watched Ryan drive away.* Old people. Sheesh. *Imagine getting that worked up about a few harmless little pups.*

*He turned and skated back to the ledge where his friends had retreated, along with Deirdre, who was huddled on a nearby bench, watching him with a hard, suspicious look in her eyes. Maybe she didn't think he noticed, but he did. Just like he'd noticed all the other oddities in her manner.*

Something's definitely wrong there. *He felt a trace of annoyance. She'd glommed onto him right quick tonight, and while he wanted to believe it was his charm that had attracted her, he knew better. There were discrepancies in her story. Things that just didn't add up the way they should.*

She wants something. But what? *Although she claimed she was supposed to be meeting a friend here tonight, Seth was almost certain that was a lie. Unless he was mistaken, she was a runaway, and a pretty damn helpless one, at that. Not like it was his job to try and save her, but all the same–*

*"What'd the cop want?" Ray had asked when Seth skated back to join them. Seth shrugged. "Not much. Just saying hello. He's friends with my cousin."*

*"So you want to skate some more?" David, another friend, had asked.*

*Seth shook his head. "Nah. I've got work tomorrow. I'm gonna head home."*

*He waited until his friends had skated away before he turned to the girl. "So, listen...I've been thinking. Why don't you come home with me? I mean, you gotta go somewhere and it's obvious you're not gonna connect with your friend tonight, so...how 'bout it?"*

*"What about your parents?" she asked, cautiously. "Are they away or something?"*

*He shook his head. "No, but they'll be okay with it. They're usually pretty cool about me doing stuff like that."*

*His parents were used to kids spending the night. Not that he'd ever brought home a girl before, but there was an extra bed in his sister's room, so that was okay. The only problem was, they weren't that dumb, either. He'd have to do some pretty fast talking if he was going to spin a story they'd be likely to believe about Monica and her missing friend.*

*The girl's eyes widened. "I dunno, Seth...me and parents? We don't usually hit it off too well."*

*That got him pissed. Didn't she realize he'd seen through her act? That he was offering her a way out of the mess she was in? Did he really have to spell it out for her?*

*"Well you can't stay here all night, can you?"*

*She shrugged. "Why? It's not so bad. If it gets too cold I'll just go hang in the bus station."*

*Now, there was some great logic. That was a sure way to stay unno-*

*ticed—not. "You just try hanging around the bus station all night. Someone's sure to call the cops if you do that."*

*"Maybe I can find some money for a motel room."*

*"What do you mean 'find' money? How d'you think you're gonna do that?"*

*Her gaze dropped from his face. "Well, you know, someone could maybe give me some."*

*He stared at her in surprise. "Like who? I thought you didn't know anyone here?"*

*"I know you."*

*That stopped him. She thought he had money? Was that the only reason she'd been hanging around him all night?Hurt and angry—with himself as much as with her—he scowled. "Hey, don't look at me. I don't have that kind of bank."*

*"Fine." Frowning, she tossed her head. "So, I can always stay in the...what do ya call it? The Greenbelt."*

*"Right. The Greenbelt." Seth shook his head. Why'd he always have to get stuck with the crazy ones? Maybe this was one time when the dogs' bad rep might work to his advantage? "I don't know if you've heard, but there's supposed to be packs of wild dogs hiding in The Greenbelt. Big, ugly dogs. With fangs. Maybe even rabies. I think you'd probably stand a better chance with my parents, but, if you don't want to..." He shrugged and let his voice trail off. Surely, now, she'd get the picture?*

*But she merely crossed her arms, looking nervous, but unconvinced.*

*Seth sighed. "Okay, listen, how's this? We've got an apartment over our garage. I could sneak you up there, and then no one would have to know. You wouldn't have to deal with anyone, all right? No parents. No wild dogs. No cops."*

*"No, just you. Right?"*

*The sudden note of venom in her tone took him by surprise.* Oh, hell, no. *If she was going to be that difficult, then shit—*she can stay here. *"Yeah, well, what can I tell you?" he said, giving it up as a hopeless cause. "That's the best I got. It's your call. Take it or leave it."*

*She looked at him then. A long, cold, angry look that—at the time—he hadn't at all understood. They stared at each other for a moment, then, at last, she'd looked away.*

*"Okay. Sure. Why not?" She got up from the bench and tossed her backpack at him. "Let's go," she snarled impatiently.*

*Her tone had taken Seth by surprise. All of a sudden, she was acting as if she were the one doing him a favor! What the hell's up with that?*

What was up was typical for them. It was a classic case of miscommunication—the first of many. It was also a warning, one he'd often wished he'd heeded.

When he offered to let her spend the night at his house it never occurred to him that she might think he wanted something in return. But she had. She'd somehow gotten it in her head that he expected her to sleep with him in exchange for the favor. She'd been desperate enough to agree to it, especially after he'd scared her, but she hadn't been happy about it.

She couldn't be worried about the same thing now, could she? He considered the idea for several minutes as he rolled the hose back on its hook. The way she was acting, and her questions about his parents' return, sure made it seem so.

And, this time around, if sex was an option, he'd damn sure take it. Except...fuck. Maybe he wouldn't, either. Getting sex in trade for something else might be loads of fun if you were on the receiving end, but he was in no hurry to find out. He'd tried it the other way and it was no good at all.

Besides, if that's what she thought of him...it was his own fault, wasn't it? That would be just what he deserved, for acting like such an asshole at the Faire.

*Yeah, ese. So what d'you think she's gonna do when she turns on your computer and her face pops up on the desktop, eh? Or if she learns that you have her blog bookmarked, or finds the folder with all the pics of her that you had me download for you? She's gonna be righteously pissed, bro.*

Yeah, she would. "Shit." Seth's stomach clenched. Not because he was hearing Ray's voice in his head—that was nothing new. But, because, as usual, his friend was correct. And, even more so, because downloading those pictures was the last thing he and Ray ever did together.

Deirdre's photo was on his computer screen when Ray was killed. Her face, her smile, that's what Seth had clung to when the horror around him was too much to bear. As he sat on the floor beside Cara, begging her to stay alive, when the paramedics arrived and he was shunted aside, but not allowed to leave, not allowed to escape hearing Cara's screams, it was Deirdre's face he'd concentrated on. In hopes of keeping his sanity. And, for a while, it actually worked. But nothing could drown out the memory of Cara's anguish entirely. Even now, just thinking about it made him want to puke.

*If Cara had been just a few months older, the EMT's wouldn't have used that collar to stabilize her neck. Those fucking assholes. There was nothing wrong with her neck—they'd even admitted it! And anyone could tell from listening to her, how much it hurt. He'd begged them to stop. He'd pleaded with them not to use it. But they did it anyway.*

No wonder she'd chosen to forget what happened that night. If he could have erased his memories, he would have forgotten about it, too. In a heart beat. No matter what else he had to lose—days, weeks, months—he'd give them up gladly. But, he didn't have that option. Not only did it all remain crystal clear in his mind, but, hell, he couldn't even bring himself to delete that picture from his computer, even though it seemed forever linked with that night. With the sights and the sound and the sorrows...

*Deirdre of the sorrows.* Whoever had named her that was either really smart, or had a sick sense of humor. He supposed it wasn't her fault that every time he got around her he lost another piece of his heart—or his mind, or his fucking appetite—but it sure felt like it was, and he'd had enough of it.

So, from here on in, maybe he'd just try and keep his distance, keep his cool. Just stay the fuck away from her. Maybe then he could find a way to survive.

"Seth?" Deirdre called hesitantly from the doorway. "Are you almost done out here?"

At the sound of her voice the dogs' heads pivoted in her direction.

"What's the matter?" Seth asked as he, too, turned to look at her. He felt his chest tighten. She'd changed her clothes and was now wearing a vaguely familiar yellow T over black track shorts and it was all he could do to tear his gaze away from her long, bare legs. So much for keeping his cool.

"N-n-nothing's wrong," she stammered. "Why'd you think that?"

Why? Seth's eyes narrowed suspiciously as his gaze fixed on her face. There was the stammer, the hitch in her voice, the slight flush on her cheeks. What else should he think? There was something wrong, all right. But what?

They stared at each other and, for a moment, neither of them said a word. Finally, "Are you hungry?" she asked. "I made sandwiches."

He nodded. "Sure. I'll be right in."

Hopefully, whatever was wrong could wait until after they'd eaten. He'd probably think better on a full stomach, anyway. Truth was, about the only times he wasn't hungry was if he'd just finished eating, if he was about to puke or, like just happened a few minutes ago, unpleasant memories were curdling his insides.

He felt fine now, he realized, with a pleasant shock of surprise. Somehow, just the sight of her had sent the memories of that night back into hiding.Thinking about that made him feel like smiling for the first time in several hours. Things were definitely looking up. Maybe he'd been on the wrong track before. Maybe keeping his distance from Deirdre was not what he needed after all.

# 9

Deirdre slanted a curious sideways glance at Seth as he sat beside her a short while later, eating one of the sandwiches she'd made. He'd put his shirt back on, which was something of a disappointment, but probably for the best.

The sight of his naked, wet torso, bronzed, glistening, completely unexpected, had already turned her into a bug-eyed, stuttering idiot at a distance of ten feet. Faced with all those muscles at this close range, she'd likely be too distracted to eat. She'd be so busy staring she'd probably miss her mouth and wind up spilling food all over herself. Not the kind of move that was likely to impress a guy. Even if it was his fault.

She thought he was hot when she'd met him two years ago, but it had been more than his looks alone that had captivated her. It had been his smile, his laugh, his manner, the gentleness in his eyes. On the other hand, she hadn't seen him without his shirt on then, either.

Had he always looked like this? Or had he morphed into a god over time? She was pretty sure he'd gained an inch or two in the intervening years, and certain he'd put on a few pounds. Now, she cast her thoughts back in time, trying to recall what else she might have been missing. Instead, the image that sprang to mind was an all too familiar one...

*Trapped in the corner of the room, with two, snarling dogs standing guard, Deirdre watched helplessly as Eric aimed another kick at Seth's midsection. Already unconscious, thanks to a lucky blow to the head from Eric's baseball bat, Seth didn't move.*

*"Stop it!" she begged, sobbing in frustration and fear. "You're killing him!"*

*A cruel smile curved Eric's lips. "Nah, he's not dead." He kicked him again. Seth's body jerked, a soft groan escaped his lips. "See? What'd I tell you? Besides, I thought you didn't care about him. Isn't that what you said last night?"*

*Deirdre tore her gaze away from Seth's recumbent form. She'd been lying last night, but, since that still seemed to be the only way to save them both from further injury, she met Eric's eyes and nodded. "Well, yeah, but that doesn't mean I want to watch while you beat him to death. Th-th-that's disgusting."*

*"Okay." Eric shrugged. "Have it your way." Grabbing some rope from a crate by the door he began to bind Seth's arms and legs. "If you're gonna be squeamish about it, I'll just drag him into the back room. That way you won't have to watch."*

*Deirdre's stomach roiled. "That's not the only reason," she said, thinking quickly. "He's no use to either of us dead. His parents have money, don't they? I bet they'd pay to get him back. Why don't you hold him for ransom?"*

*Eric paused and looked at her thoughtfully. "You know, that's not such a bad idea. You're pretty smart, aren't you? I like the way you think."*

*Smart? Deirdre dropped her gaze to the floor before Eric could read the truth in her eyes. She wasn't smart. In fact, at the moment, she was feeling like a total loser in the brains department. Anyone with even half a brain would have known better than to go anywhere with Eric.*

*If she'd been thinking at all last night, she'd have stayed right where she was. She would have waited at the fairgrounds until dawn, if she had to. Until Seth arrived. Until she had confronted him with her suspicions, and heard the truth from his own lips. But, she'd been too cowardly for that.*

*She'd been reeling from a sense of betrayal and loss, desperate to leave, unwilling to face him. Now, she had only herself to blame for the mess she'd gotten them both into...*

Her appetite gone, she pushed her plate away. That memory of Seth, bloody, beaten, unconscious, still haunted her nightmares, even two years later. She guessed no one looked too much like a god when he'd just gotten the crap kicked out of him.

Seth stopped chewing. "Aren't you gonna eat that?"

Deirdre shook her head. "No."

"Why not? It's really good."

"Thanks." She nodded at the untouched half of her sandwich. "D'you want it?"

He frowned. "How come? I thought you were starving?"

"I got over it." She didn't want to talk about her sudden lack of appetite, or its cause, she just wished she could get back to the mood she'd been in just a few minutes earlier.

Glancing over her shoulder, she cast a wistful look at the door leading out to the terrace. If she could only think of a way to lure Seth back outside again. And into taking his shirt off again, as well. Maybe that would dispel the other, sickening image.

There had to be some way she could clear away the memory of how scared she'd been, how certain that, unless she did something drastic to save him, Seth would surely die. She needed to put an end to the shadows that clouded her past, and move forward, into the sparkling sunshine of a bright new day. But, how?If she had a bathing suit, she could maybe have talked him into going for a swim with her. But she didn't and, barring that, no bright ideas were springing to mind.

"Stop worrying about the dogs," Seth blurted suddenly.

She glanced at him in surprise. "I wasn't."

"Yeah, right." He shook his head, then popped the last bite of his sandwich into his mouth and chewed savagely.

"Can we talk about something else?"

He looked at her for a moment, as though considering her request. "Sure. Where'd you get that shirt you're wearing?"

Deirdre blinked. Whatever she'd been expecting, that wasn't it. "I, uh, it was in your closet."

Seth nodded. "I thought it looked familiar. It must be Cara's."

"Oh." Deirdre felt a stab of jealousy. Was Cara in the habit of leaving her clothes at his place, or was there another explanation for its being here?

Once again, Deirdre found herself wondering about Seth and the redhead. Exactly what kind of relationship did they have? "I hope she won't mind that I borrowed it?"

Seth shrugged. "I guess it's her tough luck if she does, if she'd wanted it that bad, she should have taken it with her when she moved out."

"Moved out?" They'd been living together? "When'd she do that?"

"I dunno. A few weeks ago, I guess."

Seth reached for the plate that held her sandwich. "Are you sure you're not gonna eat this?"

Deirdre nodded. She couldn't care less about food at the moment, she had far too much else on her mind. Besides, it was a little hard to eat with bitterness clogging your throat. What had she expected, anyway? It had been two years since she'd seen him. Had it really never occurred to her until now that he'd maybe gone on with his life? Did she think he'd stop living, and do nothing but wait for her to return? She sighed as the memories rose up again. Would she never be free of the past?

Seth stopped eating and looked at her. "What's the matter now?"

Deirdre shook her head. Even if she wanted to tell him, what could she say? That she was sick with loss? That she'd only just realized they could never go back to the way things were, could never pick up where they'd left off? Time had changed them. They'd never again be the people they'd been before. Right now, she wasn't sure who either of them was.

She sighed again. "Nothing. I don't suppose Cara happened to leave a bathing suit behind when she left?"

It was family night at Genovese's Pizza and Pub and the whole place was abuzz with noise. Children ran about between the tables while pizza, the animated film that played on both TVs, and the menagerie of balloon animals being produced by a rainbow-costumed clown who'd set up shop in the rear of the restaurant vied for their attention.

Jack observed the scene with distaste. Genovese's was not his usual hangout—for precisely this reason. But, tonight, nothing was as usual. The punk had been right. It hadn't taken more than a couple of phone calls to confirm that the girl wasn't dead. Even worse, she appeared to have gone missing. Now, in order to escape Gregg's wrath, Jack would have to find her before the cops did and silence her in a way that wouldn't look suspicious.

"And just how, in God's name, am I supposed to do that?" he wondered angrily.

He wasn't even aware he'd spoken aloud, until the stranger seated beside him replied, "You know, I would not have said there was anything that could not be done in His name. I see now that I was mistaken. I thank you, friend. I am indebted to you for showing me the error of my thinking."

The noise around him seemed to recede as Jack favored the wise guy with a quelling scowl. "Do you mind?"

The stranger smiled genially. "No. Not at all. I'm just doing my job."

"Your job?" Jack's gaze swept over the man; taking in his long hair and the clothes he was wearing, shorts, sandals, Hawaiian shirt, with a single glance. "Why? Is the circus in town?"

An eager expression brightened the stranger's eyes. "Is it? I haven't heard. I hope so. I always liked the lions."

"Whatever." Not wishing to be suckered into any more of this absurd conversation, Jack turned back to his Merlot. The wine was just barely passable and he doubted that even consuming an entire bottle of it would produce the desired, anesthetizing effect. He'd have much preferred a good scotch, or a vodka martini. But he'd eschewed his usual choice of drink for the same reason he'd steered clear of his usual bar. He did not want to be seen drinking heavily tonight. He did not want to appear distressed or concerned. Apparently, however, that plan was not working out quite as well as he'd hoped.

"Perhaps there's a reason you do not see your way clear in this endeavor, Jack. Perhaps your heart is urging you to turn away, to choose another path?"

Annoyed, Jack turned and glared at the man. "I'm sorry, have we met before?"

The stranger's smile turned wistful. "Once. But, it was long ago. I do not wonder at your not remembering."

Jack shook his head. No, he didn't remember but, given the other man's apparent lack of years, it couldn't have been *that* long ago, either.

"*Consider this*," the young man recited softly, "*that in the course of justice, none of us should see salvation. We do pray for mercy, and that same prayer doth teach us all to render the deeds of mercy*."

"The Merchant of Venice." Jack stared, as much surprised that he could recall the passage's provenance as he was by the memory of the first time he'd heard it read aloud, back when he was still in junior high.

His teacher's voice, laden with emotion, had stirred Jack's young soul. '*It is an attribute to God, himself; and earthly power doth then show likest God's when mercy seasons justice*.' It had made his father's profession seem suddenly so noble.

The stranger smiled. "I thought, being a lawyer, you'd appreciate the wisdom of Portia's offer. '*Be merciful, take thrice thy money, bid me tear the bond*'."

Startled, Jack stared more closely at his companion. Despite the firm, and definitely masculine, angle of his jaw, there was something incongruously gentle, almost feminine, about his expression. Perhaps, it was just his youth. Though he'd appeared, at first glance, to be in his mid-twenties at most, but there was something in his eyes, an odd awareness that made Jack reconsider his initial assessment. The man beside him seemed somehow...ageless.

"I don't know what you're talking about," Jack said, as he rose from his seat. Hands shaking, he pulled his wallet from his pocket, counted out some bills and tossed them on the bar. "I have to go."

"Wait." Jack froze. He eyed the other man warily. *What now*?

Deliberately, the stranger extended his empty hand, closed it into a fist and then slowly re-opened it. A small box of matches lay nestled in his palm. The glossy yellow paper and green type of its label caught Jack's eye and kept his gaze riveted as, one-handed, with motions that were suddenly too swift and dexterous for Jack to follow, the stranger rotated the box, extracted a match and struck it. Fire flared.

Jack felt his eyes widen in fright, as he continued to stare, not at the match, but at the box itself, which bore the logo of the coffee shop where the girl, Deirdre, had worked.

*No*. Jack's throat spasmed, he worked to clear it. "You know, given your obvious sleight of hand skills, and your choice of clothing, I'm surprised you're not plying your trade at The Temple Garden. I think the atmosphere there would be more to your liking."

"Perhaps you're right." The flame's reflection danced in the stranger's eyes as he smiled. "Thank you. I shall take your advice. Might I hope that you'll take mine, as well?"

"What advice is that?" Jack asked. Despite the quailing of his heart, his voice sounded surprisingly calm.

"Choose again," the young man urged quietly. "Turn away from this path. There is still time."

Chills raced across Jack's skin as, his head spinning, he turned and stumbled away from the bar and out into the street.

"HEY! PUT THAT OUT," the bartender called to the man with the match. "There's no smoking in here."

Smiling, the magician in the Tiki shirt closed both hands into fists, clapped once, and then re-opened them to reveal...nothing.The bartender shook his head and returned to his work.

Impressed, Liam watched as the other man picked up the pint glass in front of him. He regarded it thoughtfully for a moment before taking a sip. Then, as though aware that he was being scrutinized, he turned his head and met Liam's gaze.

"Nice trick," Liam said. Despite the bad mood that had dogged him ever since his encounter with Cara, he found himself intrigued.

The other man shrugged modestly. "A small matter. Not at all in the same category as, say...extricating yourself from bondage."

Liam felt himself grow momentarily lightheaded as a memory surfaced. Freeing himself from ropes was something he knew a little about...

*It was a technique he'd taught himself when he was still a boy, and as useful as the skill had proven to be, he'd never before felt an urge to give thanks for the events that had forced him to master it. But, right now, all the tortures he'd endured as a kid seemed worth it and he was more than thankful, he was glad for those years he'd spent trapped in his stepfather's private hell. The lessons he'd learned back then just might spell the difference between life and death. Not just his, but Cara's, as well.*

*It had been years since he'd tried anything like this, and for a moment he was afraid he might have forgotten too much. It was more difficult than he recalled and it took longer than he could afford, possibly because he was larger and less limber than he had been. Or perhaps because Gregg and his goons had just gotten through using him as a punching bag.*

*His head felt woozy and it was enough of a struggle staying conscious, but he had no choice. He had to stay awake long enough to free himself. He had to find a way out of the compound. He had to get to Cara. The thought of that mad man on her trail scared him like nothing he'd ever known. He only hoped that he could find her before Gregg did. And the likelihood of that happening was so slim, he couldn't bear thinking of it. He had to get to her first. He had to...*

For an instant, Liam felt blinded by his rage. Because he hadn't found Cara in time, had he? Despite his best efforts, Gregg had gotten to her first.

"Fret not," the man at the bar murmured quietly. "Just because things do not turn out the way you hope or expect them to, that doesn't mean they don't turn out as they should. Sometimes you just need the right perspective."

"No," Liam muttered savagely. "You're wrong." There was no perspective that could make sense of this, or make Cara's being hurt any less tragic.

"There are many kinds of lessons, you know; including some that are only reached through hardship. There are gifts that must be won at great price. Places you'd never willingly go. Understandings you'd never arrive at, if you weren't brought to them by force."

Too heart-sick to respond this time, Liam merely shook his head. Theoretically? Sure, that made sense. But in practice? No. It was a nice thought, nothing more. If things had turned out the way they 'should' have done, if the universe was really just, then Gregg would be dead by now, Liam would be in prison for his murder.

And Cara would be alone.

Could it be the stranger was right? Maybe there was a reason Liam had been prevented from killing Gregg. *Maybe Cara's supposed to be with me, after all? Bullshit*, the jealous little voice he'd never been able to completely silence whispered; *that's just what you want to believe. She wouldn't be alone, she'd be with Seth.*But, bullshit or not, Liam decided to take it as a sign. The world was full of young women, let Seth find someone else.

His companion smiled gently. "Be of good cheer. Seize the day. Embrace uncertainty. It's part of what makes life so interesting."

"Interesting?" Liam repeated, finding his voice again, with difficulty. "Like the Chinese curse, you mean? *May you live in interesting times.* [1]Well, they certainly were that.

"Even so." Still smiling, the other man leaned closer. "Can I let you in on a secret?" he asked, lowering his voice conspiratorially.

Liam nodded. "They're all interesting. To the people living through them, each age is the most interesting time of all."

CARA STOOD at the inn's back door, shortly after dusk, breathing in the warm, sultry air, gazing out across the terrace. Tiny, white lights twinkled in the pergola above her head, and in the surrounding trees. The lights were on in the pool house, as well. The French doors stood open and she could hear music and the soft murmur of voices coming from within.

Loneliness clawed at her heart.

All she'd ever wanted in life was to fit in, to belong—to somebody, to some place. Sure, she'd come close, but never for long. Time and again, her goal had seemed within reach, only to elude her. She felt betrayed tonight. Left out. Abandoned. Homesick. Which was a stupid way to feel about a place that she'd lived in for a little less than two months.

She'd moved into the pool house the day she was discharged from the hospital. It was Seth who'd set things up—saving her, once again, when life had turned against her. In view of her age, and in order to save the State the trouble of arranging for foster care, she'd been made an emancipated minor when it was discovered that her father, never the most reliable of people in the first place, had left town and disappeared.

She was sure he'd fled to avoid being stuck with her hospital bills, even though, according to the neighbors, he'd moved out of the house they'd shared long before that, while she was still with Gregg.

Her aunt, who'd been named legal guardian following the death of Cara's mother a few years earlier, had been all too happy to relinquish her responsibility. She certainly didn't want Cara moving in with her.

Faced with no money, no resources and no clue where to turn,

Cara had begun to panic. And then Seth had come through for her, talking Sinead into letting her stay in the spare bedroom in the pool house—just until she got on her feet.

Up until then, the building, which also housed Sinead's office, was used as a lounge and overflow accommodations for guests. Cara still hadn't been ready to return to school, however, and she still couldn't drive, but Seth came by every evening with groceries, and to help tutor her, so that she could graduate with her class.

They'd never talked about why, but, somewhere along the line, Cara had tumbled to the fact that Seth was looking for reasons not to go home. A fact that became real obvious when he began spending the night there, making excuses to delay leaving until it was too late, until he was too tired to drive, and then falling asleep on the couch.

Whatever it was that was motivating him, Cara knew it had very little to do with his feelings for her—although Sinead had been a little harder to convince.

"I'm beginning to think that you're a lot more like your cousin than I ever realized," Sinead had told him; managing to appear both frustrated and amused.

Cara didn't know what *that* was all about, and she didn't much care. Apparently, however, Seth did. He'd flushed and turned sullen and Cara hadn't had the nerve to press him for information. But, since her tenure there was based on her friendship with Seth, and on Seth's friendship with Sinead, she read the writing on the wall and figured her days there were numbered.

Which was why it had been such a surprise when, not long afterwards, Sinead offered to hire her as her assistant, to give her a salary and pay her to stay at the inn. Though they never discussed that subject, either, Cara knew she owed Seth for that decision, too. At least, this time, his motivation seemed clear: sure, he'd done it in part for her, but he had to be looking to free up some space for himself, as well.

He'd helped Cara move into the inn on a Saturday and, then, by Sunday evening, he'd moved his own stuff into her old room in the pool house.

Despite the fact that they were now neighbors, Cara had seen very little of Seth in the weeks that followed. Graduation was looming ahead and her new responsibilities kept her too busy to be lonely. But, now, with her schooling behind her, Sinead out of town, and the inn standing empty, she suddenly found herself at loose ends, missing the time she and Seth had shared.

Which was why her heart sank when she arrived home tonight, following her therapy session, to find the brief, impersonal note he'd left taped to the inn's front door, asking her for a clean set of sheets and some extra towels.

*So*, she thought, as she read and re-read the words he'd written; *he's done it. He's brought that girl home with him, just like he said he'd do.*

For the life of her, Cara couldn't understand why that surprised her. If there was one thing she knew she could pretty much always count on Seth for, it was to follow through—on his threats as well as his promises.

She wasn't jealous. Really she wasn't. Even though once, long ago, and for a really long time, she'd thought herself in love with him. That was over now. It had been hard, at first, but she'd finally accepted the fact that she'd never convince him to love her back.

Oddly enough, she felt a weird kind of freedom about that now. No matter what she did, it wouldn't change how he felt about her. In a way, it was almost a relief, of sorts.

But, if she lost even that? If they stopped being friends? That would be unbearable. So, even though she still thought his moving the girl in here while Sinead was away was a bad idea, and a really shitty thing to do, she'd been on her way to bring him his sheets just the same.

Maybe they could be a peace offering. Maybe he'd invite her to stay and hang out with him and his friend. But something about the cozy domesticity of the scene in front of her was making her hesitate.

Maybe she wasn't quite ready to put their friendship to the test. Maybe she should give him a little more time to cool down? And, speaking of which, she wouldn't mind cooling down a little, herself.

Even though it was past eight p.m., the temperature still hovered above ninety degrees. The air was warm, a gentle, soft caress against her skin, not so different from the feel of cotton candy. Dry. Soothing. And thick, somehow, like a gigantic terrycloth towel. She felt almost as if she could lean on it, as if the air that surrounded her could also hold her erect.

In the absence of human touch, she'd begun to crave whatever sensations her body would allow: wind, water, sunshine, mud between her toes...

Her mind made up, Cara grabbed a set of keys from behind the door and set off across the terrace. She'd leave the sheets and towels outside the door, where Seth could find them—all except the topmost towel, she'd need that for herself. Then she'd let herself out of the gate, and take the trail that led down to the pond.

It was a spot she'd discovered shortly after she'd moved here; it was now her most special place in the world. There, she could dream. She could ponder her life and plan for the future. Or, she could swim. Naked. Unafraid. Unashamed. With no one to see her but the stars.

"Hottie alert," Maya leaned toward Chenoa to whisper.

Chenoa glanced up from her plate of Peking Duck to meet her best friend's gaze. "What'd you say?"

Maya nodded toward the bar. "Serious eye candy at seven o'clock."

Doing her best to be discreet, Chenoa turned her head as far to the left as she could manage. "Hmph. Not bad."

The dude seated at The Temple Garden's mahogany bar was undeniably handsome, but, for some reason, Chenoa wasn't getting any vibes—good, bad, or otherwise—from him. She stared at him curiously.

"Why don't you send him a drink?" Maya urged. "Or, maybe I could invite him to join us?"

"No. That's all right," Chenoa replied hurriedly, turning back to her meal. "I'll pass. We're here to celebrate your birthday, remember? Let's keep it at that, okay?"

"Good plan," Chay murmured. "It's about time you learned to curb your impulses."

Chenoa bristled. She felt a perverse urge to reverse her decision, just to piss her brother off. "Shut up, Chay. My impulses are my own, damn business."

Maya pouted. "Don't be such a spoil-sport, Chay. Why shouldn't she have some fun?"

"Because the last time she had fun, she nearly lost her head," Chay replied. Eyes narrowed, he turned back to Chenoa. "And, speaking of Mr. Spring-fling, what's his deal? You talk to him lately?"

Chenoa eyed her brother sourly. She'd grown tired of fielding questions about Liam—and Chay knew it. They'd talked the subject to death. "Not that it's any of your business, but, I don't know what he's up to. He stops by the bakery fairly regularly, but we've been swamped. I haven't really spoken to him in weeks."

Truth was, she'd been avoiding it. Though she'd never admit it to Chay, she'd harbored a little resentment toward Liam, herself. It wasn't fair, and she knew it, but it had taken her a while to forgive him for his part in the mistake they'd both made last April. But, she was over it now. It was her pride that had been injured, after all, not her heart. Such wounds didn't take that long to heal.

"Omigod," Maya moaned, still scowling. "We're not gonna talk about that again, are we? Change the channel, Chay. Don't make me sorry that I invited you to my party."

Chay smiled fondly at her. "You didn't invite me. Your father did. He didn't want to be the only guy stuck at a table full of women all night."

"Not at all," Brent Hoffman said quickly. He glanced at the women around him, Maya, Chenoa, his girlfriend, Ruth, and smiled. "I can't think of any better company to be in."

"Too bad Erin couldn't be here," Ruth observed, fixing Chay with a quiet smile.

"Hey, that's right." Brent glanced at Chay inquiringly. "I knew someone was missing. Where is the lovely Erin tonight?"

Chenoa felt Chay stiffen. "Guatemala. Remember? She got that research grant she'd applied for. She'll be back in a couple of weeks."

"Ah, right, right." Brent resumed his meal. "Good. I was forgetting about that."

"Well, I'm relieved," Ruth murmured, eyes twinkling. "I was beginning to be afraid you'd misplaced her somewhere."

Chay's eyes flashed and Chenoa grabbed for her cup and gulped tea to keep from laughing. Poor Chay, she thought, as her brother, looking anything but amused, pushed back his chair and got to his feet.

"I'll go see about getting us a refill," he said, picking up the teapot and heading toward the bar.

Brent glanced up in surprise. "We do have a wait staff," he remarked, sounding vaguely affronted.

"He knows that, Daddy," Maya chided. "You embarrassed him."

"What?" Brent shook his head. "No way." He turned to Ruth for confirmation. "I didn't. Did I?"

"Yes." Ruth nodded. "We both did. But, don't worry, dear. He'll get over it."

"Family troubles?" the man at the bar inquired as Chay waited, impatiently, for his tea pot to be refilled.

Chay nodded, thinking of all the other things he could be doing tonight. He loved his friends and family and enjoyed their company. But, more often than not, he found that a small dose went a long way. The only exception to that rule was Erin.

"You know, if you can't laugh at yourself, maybe you're taking life too seriously," the stranger observed.

Chay glanced at him, surprised. "Aho," he muttered in agreement.

It was his own personal motto, after all, the very thing he'd always said. But, for some reason, tonight, he wasn't in a laughing mood. It wasn't hard to find the reason for that. Erin. His world had gone off-kilter the night they met. It was an imbalance. One he couldn't correct. One that got worse—not better—the more they were apart.

"Here, have a fortune cookie," the stranger said, tossing a cellophane wrapped package his way.

Chay caught it and nodded his thanks, then picked up the tea pot and went back to the table.

In his absence, the conversation had moved on to less controversial subjects. Relieved, Chay settled back in his seat and opened his cookie.His eyes widened as he read his fortune. It was surprisingly brief; just a single word. *Ask.*

Puzzled, he glanced back toward the bar, but the stranger had disappeared. Chay slipped the paper into his pocket, and poured himself a fresh cup of tea. He still didn't feel like laughing. He could think of only one question he might have for Erin, upon her return. A very serious question. One he'd have to think long and hard about before he asked it.

Suddenly, two weeks seemed like no time, at all.

# 10

It was too hot to sleep. Less than two hours after Deirdre had succumbed to exhaustion, she found herself awake again, pulled from a dream of being smothered to find it wasn't a dream, at all. Her twisting and turning had left her snared in a tangle of sheets and Snowball had taken advantage of her immobility to curl himself upon her chest with his head lodged hard beneath her chin.

Even after removing the cat, unwrapping the sheets, reversing her pillow, she could find no peace. The air was stifling, stale, unmoving. The fan hung motionless above her head and she had no idea where the switch to turn it on was located. Fear of the future weighed on her mind. Concerns for the present nipped at her nerves.

She sat up and swung her feet to the floor, unable to lie still any longer, as all the events of the past few days crashed in on her again. The fire. The dogs. Seth.

He was here. Only steps away. On the other side of the door. *So close!* She grabbed up the robe she'd borrowed from his parents' house and crossed the room, shoving her arms in its sleeves. She tightened the belt around her waist and then paused, with her hand on the door.

She wanted to see him, to touch him, to prove to herself that this, too, wasn't a dream. But, did she dare? What if he was sleeping? She imagined tip-toeing over to the couch, gazing at his face in the moonlight, maybe waking him with a kiss...and getting mauled by the dogs in the process.

And, even if he was awake...what excuse could she make for invading his privacy? Could she confess to all the longings that even two years apart hadn't cured? Or all her dreams? Her hopes? Her memories of him?

Not with the way he'd been acting. When he already looked at her like she was crazy whenever she tried to talk to him about *anything*...no, she couldn't tell him about any of that.

She turned away from the door and glanced around the darkened room. *His* room. It was so tempting to explore; to start opening drawers, peeking in his closet...but, with her luck, the noise would wake him and then she'd have to explain the reason for her snooping.

And, in the meantime, she still couldn't breathe. She glanced around once more but the switch for the fan remained hidden. She crossed to the glass door that led out to the terrace and pushed it open. The air outside was warm, as well, but fresh and sweetly scented.

At the sound of Snowball dropping off the bed, Deirdre stepped outside and closed the door behind her. She couldn't risk his getting outside, getting lost.

The night was soundless. Not a cricket chirped. Not a leaf stirred. The sky above her head looked vast, immense, spangled with more stars than she had ever seen. The same stars glistened in the water of the pool, luring her closer.She dipped her toes into the starry depths and sighed with pleasure. The water was warm, but not too warm. She took another step. Little waves lapped around her ankles, caressing, tempting. She paused. Listened. Glanced around. The darkness seemed to hold its breath along with her.

She undid her belt and tossed the robe aside, moved deeper. With the water at mid-thigh, she paused again; sifting the sparkling droplets through her fingers, her heart pounding out a steady beat: just do it, just do it, just do it.

*Why not?* She reached for the hem of her T-shirt, pulled it off, balled it between her hands and lofted it. It sailed through the air and landed atop the robe. Perfect. She slipped deeper in the water. Waist deep. Chest deep. Higher. She held her breath and let it close over her head. Then she pushed off from the bottom, moving with swift, sure, silent strokes towards the far side of the pool. It was paradise. Silver heaven. Liquid bliss.

When her outstretched fingers brushed the concrete wall, she surfaced. She filled her lungs with a deep breath of the floral-chlorinated air, opened her eyes...and found herself nose to nose with a big, black dog.

Shrieking, she back-peddled frantically, stopping when she was in the center of the pool, when the realization that she was all but surrounded by dogs hit her hard in the chest and stole her breath away. Four sets of eyes glowed weirdly, reflecting the shimmering water, and then abruptly turned to an iridescent, greenish-black as lamps, set along the porch, and within the pool as well, snapped on, flooding the terrace with light.

Deirdre gulped back another shriek when the door flew open and Seth appeared, wearing nothing but a pair of khaki shorts.Gasping in embarrassment, Deirdre crossed her arms over her bare chest and immediately sank. She had to kick hard to re-surface; had to keep kicking, just to stay afloat. She blinked the water from her eyes and met Seth's gaze.

Color stained his cheeks. His expression was unreadable."What's going on?" he asked. "Are you all right? Wh-what are you doing out here?"

"It was too hot inside. I-I couldn't sleep. I thought a swim would help." She swallowed hard as her eyes cut to the dogs who continued to watch her, panting slightly, as though waiting for her to venture within range of their jaws. *Not likely*. "I just, I just...I didn't think that..."

Frowning, Seth turned his head, issued a sharp command and the four dogs melted into the shadows. He turned back to face her. "So, uh...how's the water, anyway?"

“It-it’s fine,” she stammered, as her face grew even warmer. “It’s nice. Warm.” Was he thinking about joining her? Heat shafted through her. Her legs shook. She imagined him diving in, surfacing in front of her. The water beading on his lashes. The heat blazing in his eyes. His lips would be firm, wet...

Her heart pounded harder. More than anything, she wanted him to join her; more than breathing, more than life. More than she could stand.

“G-go away,” she murmured helplessly; too frightened by her feelings, by the unaccustomed need that pooled like liquid fire between her legs. If he didn’t leave soon, she was going to pass out—just from wanting him so much. Or her legs would seize up and she’d sink. Either way, she’d drown; a victim of her own desire. “Go back inside.”

“I could turn the lights off,” he suggested. “And you could put your shirt back on. We could take a little swim together. It would be fun.”

She shook her head. “No.”

He had crouched by the edge of the pool, and now, as he trailed his fingers in the water, Deirdre jolted. Blood pounded in her veins.

He gazed at her wistfully. “C’mon, let me join you. Why not, huh? I’m hot, too, you know.”

Oh, God, did she know! “Please, Seth,” she gulped, shaking her head and staring helplessly. “I-I’m done here. I’m tired. I don’t want to swim anymore tonight.”

His expression darkened. He held her gaze for another instant, then stood and turned and strode away. Deirdre flinched as the door slammed shut behind him. Echoes ricocheted around the terrace.

Before they ceased, she’d reached the stairs, grabbed up her clothes and fled back to her room. She dressed with shaky hands while Snowball sniffed suspiciously at her ankles.

She scoured the room until she finally found the switch for the fan—hidden behind the drapes. The fan swirled slowly to life, but it would take awhile for the room to cool. And, in the meantime, she figured she had a fence or two to mend.

THE TV WAS on when Deirdre emerged from the bedroom. Seth was lying on the couch flipping through the channels.

He turned his head and gazed at her in surprise. "What's wrong now?" he asked, sounding angry.

Deirdre shook her head. "Can't you sleep either?"

For the space of several heartbeats, he said nothing. Finally, "No. I can't." He gestured at the pitcher on the coffee table. "I made iced tea. You want some?"

She nodded gratefully, and went to the kitchen for a glass. He sat up and made room for her as she came to join him, but otherwise he ignored her. She poured herself a glass of tea and then curled up in the space he'd vacated. The pillow at her elbow was still warm from his head. Deirdre snuggled against it as she sipped her tea. She studied his profile in the flickering light of the TV. He looked glum. Unhappy.

"What are you watching?" she asked after a moment.

Seth shrugged, still surfing. "Nothing." Click. Pause. Click. Pause. Click. Pause. Several minutes passed in silence as he scrolled through the channels. Movies, commercials, familiar re-runs of shows she'd watched her whole life, passed in an endless stream. Star Trek. The Simpsons. The Real World. Friends. Seth's thumb hovered. His expression softened.

Deirdre found herself giggling as Joey's grin lit up the screen. *How you doin*?

"He sounds like you," she told him.

Click. Law and Order. Click, click. CSI.

Deirdre bit her lip. Okay, so maybe he didn't want to be reminded of the night they met; of his impersonation of Joey; of her own retaliation—telling him her name was Monica.

Click. The cooking channel. Some chef she didn't recognize was grilling fish.

She couldn't stand the silence."Seth? Do you remember that night on the beach?"

It was the next night, the night *after* the night they'd met. Rafe and the others had caught fish that day, she and Seth had joined them for a barbecue...

Seth turned his head to look at her, his expression hard, suspicious. Their eyes met, locked, held. Something shifted in his gaze. He nodded. "I remember this," he said, leaning close enough to touch his lips to hers in a kiss that was tender and sweet. Just like the first time.

"Me, too," she murmured, swallowing hard, heart thumping as he twisted toward her.

Still searching her eyes, he reached a hand up to her face. He touched her hair, her cheek. Then he kissed her again, still with that same exquisite gentleness. As he pulled away, she shuddered softly and gulped for breath. Her eyelashes fanned her cheeks.

She felt a tug as he took hold of the glass in her hand. She relinquished her grip, felt it slip from her grasp as he took it from her. He put it down on the table and twisted back toward her, framing her face with his hands as his lips covered hers once again; firmer this time, warm, demanding. So right. *Yes!*

Deirdre's hands fluttered aimlessly before coming to rest; first on his chest, and then, when he released her face to gather her into his arms; on either side of his neck."I want you," he murmured as he pulled her down to lie beneath him.

She licked her lips. Nodded. "I know." She loved the sturdy, warm weight of him as it surrounded her. She felt secure in his arms, protected. Safe. Not trapped there. Not terrified. Not like last time.

He brushed the collar of her robe aside. As his fingers grazed her bare flesh she shivered. But she didn't feel vulnerable. She didn't feel exposed. Clothes were a restriction, a distraction. They were only getting in the way. She didn't need them. It was all so right, so perfect. She was glad, now, that she'd waited. For him. For this.

His lips trailed kisses across her shoulder. His fingers traced the swell of her breast. He didn't squeeze or grope her, as he'd done on Sunday; or as Eric had done two years ago. He wasn't rough with her, or careless. She knew she'd be cherished by him tonight, not abused. Cared for, not taken.

Still, as his thumb teased her nipple's tight point and hot waves of desire began lapping at her core, she felt a small qualm. Despite his gentleness, there was a certainty to his actions that hadn't been there two years ago. He knew just how to touch her now. And where. And when. He knew how to put her at ease, how to please her. This wasn't the first time for either of them, but for him, it might not be the second. Or the third. Or, even, the fourth.

Deirdre felt a pang of loss. She missed the fumbling hesitancy that had marked their earliest explorations with each other, back when sex was a mystery and love was still brand new. She knew she could never get back what Eric had taken from her; what he had cheated them both out of sharing.

But, though it couldn't be *the* first time, it would still be *their* first time—and she was determined that they not lose the magic of that, as well."Seth, wait." Breathless, she pushed at his arms. "We can't do this." Not now. Not like this. She wanted it to be pure. Romantic. Perfect. Everything she'd always dreamed it could be.

"What's that?" he murmured, moving up to nip gently at her ear lobe.

"It's too soon." This wasn't something to be rushed into or hurried through. It was something to be planned and savored. Something to be cherished forever. Something they needed to talk about first.

Seth nodded. "Okay. Sorry. I'll slow down."

"No." She pushed him away again. "That's not– Stop. This isn't right."

He raised his head and looked at her; his expression doubtful, confused. "What are you saying?"

"I'm saying stop. I'm saying it's too soon."

"Deirdre–" He shook his head. "No." It was a whisper, a groan. Not a refusal, exactly; more like a plea. "No, no, no. Don't tell me this now."

"I want it to be special." In a bed. With candles, maybe, and flowers. And with a clear understanding of all it might mean—to both of them.

"Special?" For a moment more, he stared at her in disbelief. Then, he pushed himself away from her. He sat up again, fisted his hands in his hair and closed his eyes. "Shit. I don't believe this."

Deirdre sat up, too; curling back up in her corner, pulling the robe closed. Tentatively, she reached a hand out and touched his shoulder.

"Don't," he growled. He picked up the TV remote and turned his back on her. Click. Click. Click.

"Seth–"

"It's late. I'm tired. Why don't you go back inside so I can get some sleep?"

"We need to talk."

Seth shook his head. "I don't wanna talk right now. Go back to bed, Dee."

"No," she insisted."Listen–"

He turned his head. "I think you'd better go. I have to let the dogs in now, anyway."

Deirdre gasped. He did *not* need to let the dogs in. He was just saying that. To threaten her. To punish her. She hated that he'd stoop so low; that he'd lie, that he'd use her own fears against her. "Forget it. I'm not leaving."

"Oh, no?" His jaw clenched. "Well, then, fine. I will."

He surged off the couch. She jerked backwards in surprise, and then watched as he stormed across the room. *Boom!* The French door slammed open. He disappeared into the night. Half a minute later, she heard a huge splash as he hit the water, then a seemingly endless series of smaller splashes as he began to swim, and swim, and swim...

From the private sundeck off her second floor suite, Cara watched Seth as he swam. His body knifed through the water, arms and legs pumping furiously, churning up waves all around him.

He couldn't have caused more commotion if he had a school of piranha on his heels. Even the dogs had come out to watch. They appeared puzzled by his behavior.

Cara wasn't puzzled, however. She'd been out here for a while. She'd seen the first act in this drama: *Go away, Seth. Go back inside. I don't wanna swim anymore tonight*. The little bitch.

Given the amount of frustration Seth appeared to be feeling, it wasn't hard to fill in the blanks. It was an old story. As old as boy meets girl. Whoever the chick was, he wanted her, she didn't want him.

Cara sighed and shook her head. Once, she would have taken satisfaction in Seth's unhappiness. It was only fair, wasn't it? She always knew that, someday, someone would come along and break his heart like he'd broken hers. There was even a song like that, wasn't there? She tried to recall it, but her mind remained blank. In any case, it didn't matter. She wasn't in a singing mood tonight, anyhow.

Maybe she'd grown up some, after all. Because she felt nothing right now but sympathy. She remembered how bad it had hurt. She wouldn't wish it on her enemy. And she really couldn't wish it on Seth.

"Stupid bitch. Why don't you give him a break, huh? He'll make it worth your while. He'll treat you right." And, even more importantly, "He's a good guy. Whatever he did to you, he doesn't deserve this. So, quit playing games."

Cara had recognized the girl. She was the same one who'd gotten pissed at him last Sunday. At the Faire. When the hell had they hooked up again? And, given how unhappy they seemed to make each other, why?

Seth continued to swim, back and forth across the pool. Cara stared, mesmerized by the sight; by the purity and grace. Damn, he was something to look at, too. That girl didn't know what she was missing.

But, Cara did. She knew just what she was missing. What they were both missing. Hell, what they were all missing tonight, come to think of it. She missed sex.

Where was the bad, after all? It was mostly good, occasionally great. And, even when it wasn't quite so good, it was rarely so awful that she couldn't just chalk it up to experience and try again.

Right now, more than anything, she wished she could go down there and offer herself to Seth. Even knowing it wasn't exactly what either of them wanted, it would still feel better than what they had now—which was nothing.

It would help Seth out. It would teach that silly bitch of his a thing or two. But, even for that, even to make a point, she couldn't do it. 'Cause what would happen was this: She'd be fine until he touched her, then she'd freak. She'd go rigid and she'd start to shake. Start to panic. Start to cry. And, wouldn't that be fun for them both?

A sudden noise made her jump. Seth had howled—whether in anguish or in rage, she couldn't tell—and was now attacking the water even more ferociously than before.

Cara took a deep breath, tried to still the racing of her heart. She knew Seth wasn't about to go postal. He wouldn't hurt her. He wouldn't hurt anyone. Not really. But, still, even at this distance, that much anger was frightening.

Maybe Gregg had been that mad the night he beat her? Maybe that's what she was remembering now? She didn't know. She couldn't recall anything about that night. But, remembered or not, something was starting to nibble at her mind, was starting to worry her, was starting to creep her out real bad. Fear, like tiny spiders, crawled across her skin, making her itch. She cast one, final look at Seth, and hurried back inside.

Seth continued swimming, hopping the exertion would clear his mind. So far, it wasn't working. He felt confused, betrayed and angry. So angry. *Special. Too soon*. What the hell was Deirdre talking about? *No*, she'd told him. *Stop*, she'd told him. *This isn't right*.

She hadn't said any of that to Eric though, had she? She hadn't said anything to him but *yes*. Then they'd done it on a smelly, old mattress, in a derelict cottage—how special was that?

He howled again and swam faster; pouring everything he had into each stroke. *How could she do it? How?*

How could she care so little? How could she treat him like this—again and again? And what the fuck was wrong with him that he kept falling for it, that he kept coming back for more?

Schmuck. Asshole. Loser. Jerk. That was him, all right.

He was stupid. That had to be the answer, didn't it? He was too stupid to know any better, too stupid to learn. Anyone that dumb, deserved whatever he got.

He kept swimming. Back and forth, back and forth. Until he was tired and spent, and cold. Until the stars had begun to fade and it was all he could do to drag himself out of the water and into the house.

He stripped out of his shorts and collapsed on the couch, pulling the sheets around him, falling asleep even as his head hit the pillow.

# 11

"Seth, wake up." As the sound of his name, whispered over and over again, filtered into his consciousness, Seth groaned.

What now? He was pretty sure he'd only just fallen asleep a short while ago. So, he ignored the voice. And, when something nudged at his shoulder, he ignored that, too. He kept his eyes tight shut. Whoever this was, she was gonna have to go away, 'cause there was no way he was waking up already.

"Se-*eth,*" the girl's voice came again. This time he recognized it. Cara. That whine—Jesus.

She wasn't gonna start with that again, was she? But, she was, and he knew it. Reluctantly, he opened his eyes. "What's wrong?"

"We need to talk."

Oh, fuck. He closed his eyes again. "No way." What was it with these girls and talking? Couldn't they think of anything else?

"Come on, Seth. It's important."

"No."

Something poked him in the ribs. He swatted at it, felt his hand connect with hers, and opened his eyes again, frowning. "Damn it,

Cara." Given how she couldn't stand being touched, it must be *real* important. "What?"

"Shh!" she cautioned. Her gaze cut to the bedroom door. She shook her head. "Not here. Get dressed and meet me at the inn. In the kitchen. Hurry." And then she left.

Seth sat up slowly. His shorts were still a soggy pile on the floor at his feet. The rest of his clothes were conveniently locked in the bedroom with Deirdre. Just great. Giving up, he wrapped the sheet around him and followed Cara back to the inn.

It was even earlier than he'd realized, the sun was just now coming into view. The morning was gloomy and gray, with the kind of dank, clammy fog that would probably burn off by lunchtime, but which could also turn into one of the rare, summer lightning storms; the kind that, all too often, started fires in the surrounding hills.

Cara was standing at the kitchen counter, staring at the coffee maker and shifting restlessly from foot to foot. As though the news bubbling up inside her wouldn't let her keep still.

"All right, I'm here" he told her. "Now, what's up?"

"Well, finally!" She turned to look at him. Her eyebrows rose. "Nice look. What's that you're wearing—a toga?"

"Don't start," Seth sighed, sinking wearily into a chair. "Can I at least get some coffee?"

Cara nodded. "Yup. Almost done."

A minute later she'd deposited two of the inn's signature cups—shaped and painted to resemble morning glories—on the table in front of him. Seth grabbed for the nearest cup and gratefully gulped down half its contents.

Then he looked at her. "So, tell me already. What's so important that you had to come get me this early?"

She'd seated herself across from him. Now, she gazed at him earnestly. "This girl you brought home with you. Seth...she really can't stay here. You gotta get rid of her. Now."

Seth groaned in disbelief. "Cara, what is this shit? Give me a break, huh?"

"I mean it, Seth. I recognize her. I remember where I've seen her before. She's trouble."

"God damn it." For one, brief moment, Seth considered leaving. If he could just go back to bed, maybe he could pretend the whole thing had been nothing but a bad dream. There was only one flaw in that plan, "I *know* you didn't drag me over here just so we could replay yesterday's conversation. What's happened?"

"She knows Gregg."

Seth's mouth dropped open. "What? Impossible." It was a measure of Cara's sincerity, however, that she'd mentioned the bastard by name. Like Sauron, or Voldemort, it was something they both avoided doing, whenever they could. "No, she doesn't. What are you talking about?"

Cara nodded. "She does. He had her picture on his computer. I saw it. She emailed him last spring."

"No. Cara, that's not– That was *my* computer. That's where you saw it, that, that night. That's what you're remembering."

"Se-*eth*!" Cara whined again, sending his nerves into hyper-shock. "Would you fucking listen to me? I know what I'm talking about. She's his daughter! 'Least, she thought maybe she was."

"No, no, no!" Seth slammed his fist against the table, making the cups jump. *She couldn't be. She just couldn't. But...shit, it would sure explain a lot, if she was. Wouldn't it?* "Not possible. She doesn't know who her father is." At least...she hadn't known two years ago. Maybe more had changed since then than he wanted to admit?

Cara shrugged. "Yeah, well, for what it's worth, Gregg said she wasn't, either. But, you can't take his word for something like that, can you?"

"I don't care," Seth sighed, wearily. "I don't care if she is, or not. I don't care about any of it. It doesn't change anything."

"Are you crazy?" Cara stared at him. "It changes *everything!* You said someone's maybe trying to kill her, right? Well, what if it's him? What if *he's* the one who's after her?"

"No." Seth shook his head once more. "That makes no sense. His daughter–? And, how's he gonna do that, Cara, huh? Gregg's in prison. He's locked up. He's not still running around loose somewhere, setting fire to places."

"Well, sure, I know that. I didn't mean he's doing it himself. But he still could be behind it, couldn't he? What if he's got someone working for him?"

"Like who?" Seth asked, nearly tripping over his sheet as he got up to pour himself another cup of coffee. "Everyone connected to him died last April, remember? I told you about that while you were in the hospital. That house where you all were living got blown to shit. You and Liam were just about the only ones who made it out in time." Other than Gregg, himself.

Cara brushed his argument aside. "That doesn't mean anything. Not everyone who knew him lived there. There were others, too, you know. I'll have to think about who it could be."

Chewing on her lip, Cara lapsed into a thoughtful silence. Seth sipped his coffee and considered this new twist. He could find only one bright spot: his morning probably couldn't get much worse.Or, so he thought, until he saw the way Cara was looking at him. "What now?"

"Why'd *you* have her picture on your computer for?" she asked, eyes narrowed suspiciously. "How do you know this chick, anyway?"

Oh, like that wasn't the last subject Seth felt like discussing this morning. "Never mind. I just do, that's all. I know her from a while ago."

Cara frowned at him for a moment longer, then her eyes widened. "Omigod. This is her, isn't it? That girl you told me about? The one you thought you'd never see again?" *The one you said you were in love with.*

She didn't say that last part, but they both knew it's what she was thinking. And Seth was pretty sure he saw a trace of pity in her gaze. Which was just what he wanted—not.

"Yeah," he muttered, turning away, swallowing the last of his coffee, putting the cup in the sink. "That's her, all right. But she's got no connection to Gregg." *At least I hope she's not.* "And this has nothing to do with him, you got that? It's got nothing to do with him, it's got nothing to do with you, so just drop it. Let it go.""Se-*eth*!" Cara glared at him, exasperated. But, this time, Seth wasn't gonna bite. He'd heard enough.

"No. Forget it," he muttered as he gathered up his sheet and headed for the back door. "I'm outta here. We're done. Conversation over."

CARA SAT AT THE TABLE, after Seth left, gnawing on her thumbnail. "Over? It's not over, you jackass."

She should have figured he'd be stubborn about this. Seth might be smart, but he was still a guy; which meant that, when it came to some girl he was hot for, he had a blind spot the size of a small planet. Especially *this* girl. Shit.

Well, Cara had a blind spot, too. A *real* blind spot, and a pretty damn big one. In the process of getting it, she'd learned a real important lesson. It didn't matter what you wanted to believe about a person. Wishes didn't stand a chance against cold, hard facts.

And, the fact of the matter was, she had a bad, bad feeling about this.The anxiety that had started nagging at her mind last night had led to dreams. Horrible, fitful dreams that wouldn't come clear. Then, shortly before dawn, it all fell together and she awoke with a start, with a razor-sharp memory replaying in her head...

*Gregg hadn't so much as glanced in her direction when she entered the bedroom they shared. He was seated at his desk, staring at the paper in his hand. His expression was one Cara didn't recognize, but which made her uneasy, all the same. So, she tip-toed up behind him, curious to see what he was finding so fascinating.*

*It was a picture of a girl. A teenager, no older than Cara, herself; holding a big, gray cat. "Hey, what ya got there" she asked, reaching over his shoulder to take the photo away from him. But, then the subject line on the email message open on his computer desktop caught her eye. She stared in surprise.* Are you my father?

*"Omigod. Gregg? Is this for real? You're a daddy?"*

*"No." He plucked the photo from her hand, and put it down on his desk. "It's a mistake. She's looking for someone else."*

*"Oh." Cara wasn't sure whether to believe him or not. Isn't that what guys always said about things like this? Why would the girl think he was, if he wasn't? Her eyes flickered back and forth, from his face to the picture, to the monitor screen, and then back again, searching for clues. For a resemblance. For something. It wasn't jealousy she was feeling, it was fear—the fear that she'd be replaced, abandoned. She smiled tentatively. "Well, don't look so sad. You can pretend you're my daddy, if you want"*

*She swiveled his chair until he was facing away from the desk and then perched herself on his lap. Smiling, Gregg wrapped his arms around her waist. "Why would I want a slut like you for a daughter?"*

*"It was just a game," she murmured, feeling more hurt by his words than she had any right to be. In spite of the way he treated her, she'd convinced herself that he loved her—in his own way. "I thought we decided you were going to try and say nice things to me, for a change?"*

*"That was your idea," Gregg reminded her. "I say what I feel like saying. If you don't like it, you can always leave."*

*"Would you really let me go?"*

*He shook his head. "You know better than that, don't you?"*

*But she didn't. That was something she'd recognized early. Gregg liked to keep her guessing. So there were a lot of times when she felt like she didn't know the first thing about him.*

*A fact that was driven home only a moment later when he looked deep into her eyes and said, "I want you to do something for me."*

*"Great," she replied, wondering what was coming next. "What do I have to do now?"*

*His answer was nothing she'd been expecting: "I want you to fuck Liam for me."*

At the time, Cara had been terrified that Gregg had discovered her secret. She hadn't meant to fall in love with Liam, she hadn't tried to...but she had, all the same. Unfortunately, she wasn't at all certain how Liam felt about her...

*"What if he doesn't want me?"*

*Gregg looked at her curiously. "You think he might not? Why?"*

*She shrugged. "I don't know. He's not like most other guys. He doesn't just sleep with anyone."*

*"And how would you know that? Have you talked about it with him?"*

*"Not exactly," she answered cautiously, remembering the conversation they'd had, just yesterday, how Liam had told her about his attraction to women who weren't shallow; his need to connect with a woman on a lot of levels, before he'd have sex with her. "Just sort of in general."*

*Gregg's gaze turned thoughtful. "I guess, you'll just have to do the best you can then, huh? Maybe take one of those nightgowns you're so fond of buying with you. Pick out one you think he'd like."*

But, just as Cara suspected would be the case, her best was not good enough...

*She'd gone to wait for Liam in his room She'd been lying on his bed, trying to read, trying to keep her mind off the reason why she was there, feeling anxious, apprehensive, excited, when she heard the door behind her swing open.*

*"Cara? What are you doing here?"*

*Smiling nervously, she turned to face him. "Hi."*

*"Do you need help with your schoolwork, or something?" he asked, glancing at the backpack she'd dropped on the floor.*

*"Not really. Maybe later." She studied him for a moment longer. "I guess we should talk, or something."*

*His eyebrows rose. "About what?"*

*"Well, you don't seem real happy here," she said, repeating the words Gregg had used earlier. "And...I guess...I was thinking...that maybe I should do something. Or give you something. Or, you know, try to change that?"*

*"Give me something." Liam looked confused. "Like what?"*

*"Like...something that would keep you busy. Or happy. Or, you know, make you hang around more."*

*"You mean, some kind of chores?"*

His cluelessness had her rocking with laugher. "No, Liam. No. Nothing like that."

He sighed. "Okay, look, I'm a little tired for games right now. So, why don't you just tell me what you want, okay?"

Smiling, she crooked a finger at him. "Why don't you come over here, and I'll show you what I want?"

Liam shook his head. He looked neither amused, nor interested. "I don't think so."

Frowning self-consciously, Cara sat up. "Wh- why not?"

"Because it's not a very good idea, that's why." He looked at her curiously. "What's this all about, anyway?"

"I told you. I want you to be happy here. And, and you're not. Are you? Gregg thinks you're not."

His eyes narrowed. "So you're here to make me happy. Is that it? Kinda like the way you make Gregg happy, d'you mean?"_The anger in his tone was not a good sign.

She looked at the floor and shrugged. "Yeah. Sort of."

Liam shook his head. "Just what do you suppose Gregg'll have to say about something like that? I know you like to bend the rules, Caramel, but I don't think either of us is up for that much trouble right now."

"Is that all you're worried about?" Relieved, she got up from the bed and sauntered toward him.

"Stop it, Cara," he warned. "Don't be stupid."

"Shhh. I'm not." She silenced him with a finger against his lips. "Really, no one's going to get in trouble this time, okay? Gregg's not gonna be upset. I promise."

"Oh? Why not?"

She smiled. "Because it was his idea."

"His idea?" Liam's face congested. "You're telling me Gregg sent you here to sleep with me?" He shoved her away and paced angrily to the center of the room. "How many others?" he demanded as he whirled around to face her.

She stared at him in surprise. "How many other what?"

"Men, Cara." He scowled at her. "Who else have you been 'making happy' around here?"

*"Don't be disgusting, Liam. This isn't like that!"*

*"The hell it's not."*

*"It's not," she insisted. And then, seeing that he was still waiting for an answer, "None. Okay?"*

*He shook his head. "Wrong answer. Don't lie to me, Cara. I want names."*

*"Why should I lie? I do what I want to do. And if I wanted to hook up with every guy here, what's it to you?"*

*He sighed. "You're a kid. You shouldn't be doing things like that."*

*"I am* not *a kid!"*

*"Well, you're not eighteen, yet, are you? That makes you a kid in my book. And you shouldn't be 'hooking up' with anyone."*

*"Get real, Liam." She frowned at him for a moment and then, "I don't know what this age thing is all about with you. Gregg's like twice as old as you are. He doesn't have a problem with it."*

*"Gregg's old enough to be your father."*

*She nodded. "I know. That's my point. In fact, there's some chick who's like my age who just emailed him, 'cause she can't find her father and she thinks maybe he's it. So, if that's okay, then–"*

*"It's* not *okay. That's what I–" And then he stopped. His face changed. He crossed back to where Cara was standing and took hold of her shoulders. "What girl? Who is she? Do you know her name? Did she leave an address, some way to contact her?"*

*Cara couldn't believe her ears. "What do you want to know about* her *for?"*

*He shrugged. "I just do, okay? Now, could you please just–"*

*"No." She glared at him moodily. "I won't. I'm tired of all the time having to listen to guys talk up other girls when they're with me. First Seth, then Gregg and now you, too? And you don't even know this chick. So just forget it."*

*"Cara–"*

*"It's not fair, Liam. What's so wrong with me that everyone always wants someone else, instead?"*

*"Nothing's wrong with you," he murmured as he pressed a kiss to her forehead. "And I don't want someone else."*

*"Right. You just don't want me."*

*He shook his head. "I don't want anyone tonight, okay? I just want information."*

*"Well, too bad. Because I don't have any. It was just one email and a picture of some chick holding a cat. For all I know he could have deleted both of them by now."*

*"A picture? Is there any way you can get me a copy? And the email, too?"*

*Cara's mouth dropped open. "Oh, sure. And then I can get my butt tossed out of here for messing with Gregg's stuff. Are you nuts? Why the fuck would I do something like that?"*

*"Because. It's important. You have to trust me."*

*"Trust you?" She shook her head. "Why should I trust you, Liam, when I know you don't give two shits about me?"*

*Liam frowned. "What are you talking about? Of course I do. I care about you a lot."*

*"Yeah, sure you do. That's why you're kicking me out of bed, right?"*

*"It's not because I don't want to," he said. "It's because you're under age."*

*"If you really cared about me, that wouldn't matter."*

*But, he shook his head. "You're wrong. It will* always *matter."*

*"I don't believe you." She wanted to, though. She wanted to so much.*

*"C'mere," he sighed as he pulled her to him, sliding his hand around to cup the back of her neck and lowering his mouth to hers.*

*As the taste and feel of him flooded her senses, she caught her breath. For one, blissful moment, she really thought she'd won him over. It was like a little slice of heaven, being kissed like that—being kissed by him. It was like a dream come true. He made it all seem so real. Like he really did want her. Like he really did care. "Now do you believe me?" he rasped as he pushed her away.*

*Dazed and heated, she stared at him, wanting him like she'd never wanted anyone. "Yes."*

*"And will you get me the email? Please?"*

*Reluctantly, knowing how much trouble she could get into; hating that he didn't seem to consider that a problem, she whispered, "I'll try."*

*"Good." He snagged her backpack from the floor and thrust it toward her. "Now, go on. Take your stuff and get out of here."*

*Cara's heart sank as her happy little dream came to an end. He didn't care, did he? He was just using her. She looked at him sadly. "But, why?"*

*"Because I can't," he said as he nudged her toward the door. "And, I won't. Not until you're older. And not until you're here for the right reasons."*

But, what were the right reasons, Cara wondered now; how much older did she have to get? And, "Omigod, what is it about that girl?" She must be something special, all right, to make all the men in Cara's life go insane.

For that reason alone, Cara wanted to kick her to the curb.

Deirdre looked up from the orange she'd been juicing when Seth came in from the terrace. At the sight of him, her stomach started turning cartwheels. She'd been wondering where he'd gone, now that she saw what he was wearing, she wondered even more. "Hi. Where were you?"

He looked at her, a faint flush on his cheeks, a stymied, confused expression in his eyes. For several minutes, it looked as though he could find no answer to her question. Finally, "I just...I...nowhere. Never mind. I just had to see Cara about something."

"Oh?" Deirdre's eyebrows rose. Cara again? Dressed like that? Deirdre supposed it wasn't any of *her* business, of course, but, "What about?"

He shook his head. "Nothing. I don't wanna talk about it."

Right. "Of course not." Suddenly furious—at him for being such a jerk, at herself for caring—she picked up the knife she'd been using and started cutting oranges. One orange. Two. Three. Slice, slice, slice.

He was never gonna want to talk about anything, was he? She

could guess what they'd been doing, though, he and Cara. It made Deirdre's heart ache, just thinking about it. And, he had a lot of nerve, too! After the way he'd been acting, after the way he'd kissed her last night and...and all that time he'd been keeping Cara on a string? Damn him. She didn't know which of them she felt sorrier for, herself or Cara.

"Look" she told him, "you can't just ignore something, because it's unpleasant. You won't make things better by not facing them. I should know. Keeping your mouth shut, keeping your eyes closed, telling yourself pretty stories about what's really going on—that's never solved anything."

"Yes, it does. Sometimes." He scowled at her. "And quit that! Stop waving that knife around."

"Why?" she challenged, pointing it in his direction. "Are you worried? Think I might hurt someone?"

Seth gaped. He glared. His face went white, then red, then settled on a ghastly shade of purple. "Unnhh!" he growled, fisting his hands in his hair, almost losing his sheet in the process. He snagged it as it started to slip, held it at his waist, stormed into the bedroom and slammed the door shut, grumbling, "I don't fucking believe this shit."

Deirdre stared after him, wishing he'd been just a little slower on the grab. But, Jesus, what was it with him and doors, anyway? He was gonna break something if he didn't stop soon. He might even shake the whole house to the ground. Then neither of them would have to worry about anything, ever again. It sounded peaceful. "Jerk," she muttered, as she poured herself a glass of juice.

She leaned her hip against the counter while she drank it down, feeling gloomy and hopeless and...frustrated. He couldn't avoid the subject forever. They needed to talk about things. About the two of them. About Cara. About where they all stood, where they were going...

"And, that's another thing," he shouted, reappearing suddenly from the bedroom, dressed in jeans and a faded red T, breathing so hard his chest heaved. He pointed at the door which he'd once again slammed behind him. "What kind of crazy person'd do something like that to a cat? That's just, just– Do you have any idea how stupid he looks?"

Deirdre's eyebrows rose. "Well, yeah! Hello? I told you Monday was a really bad day for us. What did you think I was talking about?"

He frowned suspiciously. "But...wasn't it your idea?"

"What?" Now it was her turn to feel outraged. "*My* idea? You think I–? Seth! My own cat? I'd have to be a, a psychotic freak to do something like that! Are you insane?"

Seth's eyes went wide. His lips twitched. The next thing Deirdre knew, he was hooting with laughter.

"It's not funny," she grumped, feeling sour. "And you're such a jerk. I can't believe you thought something like that." Nothing was going right for her lately. Nothing. And, now, on top of everything else, he was laughing at her.

"Yes it is." Still laughing, Seth collapsed onto one the breakfast stools. "You don't know how funny."

He wiped his eyes, feeling lightheaded with relief. Of course she wasn't crazy enough to do something like that. How could he have been so stupid? She probably wasn't violent or dangerous, or a pyromaniac, either. And, no matter how many knives she felt like waving in his face, he'd still bet anything she wasn't the daughter of a crazy, violent, dangerous, murdering psychopath. He'd really have to thank Cara for putting *that* idea in his head!

But, while Deirdre might not be crazy, she sure did look angry. For once, he didn't have to wonder why. "I'm sorry. I wasn't laughing at you. It was just something Cara said earlier."

"Oh, well, that's so much better," Deirdre muttered, in a voice that dripped sarcasm and scorn.

"So, I gotta ask you something," he said, hoping to change the subject.

Still pouting, she leveled a suspicious gaze his way. "Like what?"

"How long would it take you to get ready to leave? I have to go to work, and I think you should come with me."

Deirdre looked startled for a moment, then she shrugged. "I could be ready now, I guess. It's not like I have any other clothes to change into."

He nodded. "Yeah, I know. That's what I was thinking. And, I think maybe I've figured out a way we can get you some. It won't cost anything and I don't think we'll run into anyone while we're doing it. 'Least, no one who'll tell the cops that they saw you."

Her eyes widened. "How're we gonna do that? Is there a used-clothing-store-for-the-blind you plan on breaking into, or something?"

Seth grinned. "Not exactly." He didn't want to get into any long discussions this morning, he had too much on his mind. "You'll see," he promised as he got to his feet. "C'mon, let's go."He had several reasons for wanting to take Deirdre with him this morning—beyond the fact that he just liked her company, when she wasn't making him crazy. But, it still wasn't anything he wanted to talk about.

Despite the fact that he was feeling a lot better about things, for the moment, he didn't really want to leave her here alone. And he wanted to leave her here with Cara even less. But, there was also the small matter of the dogs. He understood now why she was so afraid of them, but it wasn't healthy. She needed to get over it. And, since it was his fault she'd gotten frightened in the first place, the way Seth saw it, that made it his responsibility to put things right.

And, that was just exactly what he intended to do.

# 12

Deirdre couldn't believe how much cooler it was here at the beach. Ten, maybe fifteen degrees. Everything seemed fresher, brighter. More green. The sand beneath her bare feet was soft and damp. The air was brisk. The sky a cloudless, brilliant shade of blue. Her heart was so weightless she felt like flying or dancing, or...something.

She couldn't help but remember another beautiful morning, two years ago, on this same beach. She remembered sitting on a log; watching her friends surf; thinking about Seth, whom she'd only just met. She'd been happy then, too.

"Don't you love it here?" she asked now, throwing her arms out and pirouetting in place. "It's just...so...pretty."

"So are you," Seth said. She stopped spinning and turned to look at him. The smile in his eyes made her knees go weak. She'd have kissed him, if it weren't for the dogs that surrounded him; not his dogs, which he'd left back at the winery, but six smaller dogs, all wagging their tails at once and looking at her with bright, black eyes.

Deirdre stared back at them for a moment, then raised her gaze to Seth's face. "So, this is what you do for work, huh? You walk dogs? Every day?"

Seth nodded, watching her carefully. "Yep. Just about."

"And, you've been doing it how long?"

"Couple of months."

"You like it, huh?"

He shrugged. "Sure. What's not to like? It's fun. I get to be my own boss, set my own hours. I get to be outside every day."

"It's not boring?"

"Uh-uh. Every day is different. Walking multiple dogs is more of a skill than you'd think. You gotta know what you're doing. You need to make sure the dogs you take out together are a good fit. Some dogs make a great walking team, they walk at the same speed, stop for the same smells; they either all go at the same time, or they wait patiently for each other. Some dogs can never successfully be walked together. Maybe they're just not compatible, or maybe they want to fight with everyone else."

Deirdre nodded. "I guess that's like people, too. Some can get along with each other, some can't." *I wonder which kind we are?*

"You wanna try?" Seth asked, as they turned and started back. She looked at the hand he'd extended, then at the two dogs whose leashes he was offering her. They were small and calm looking; not at all threatening. But, just the same, "Mm-mm. Maybe some other time, 'kay?"

He nodded, accepting that. "Will you come out with me again later? I have another walk scheduled for this afternoon."

"Maybe." She glanced around, took another deep breath of sea-scented air. "Are you coming back here?"

"No. Somewhere else."At the note of something wistful in his voice, she turned to look at him again. He was still smiling, but his expression seemed a little strained, somehow; a little regretful.

"Where?"

"Someplace special," he said quietly. "I haven't been there in a while but..."

Well, that piqued her curiosity. "Special, huh?"

He nodded. "Real special. Just about my most favorite place to be."

And, how could she pass up a chance to see something like that? "Okay, sure. But, what about my clothes?"

"We'll get those first," he promised. "In fact, that's where we're going right now."

"I DON'T GET IT," Deirdre murmured, staring in surprise at the cedar-shake cottage. "The sign says Wildlife Rescue. What made you think they have clothes here?"[1]

Seth smiled. "I don't think it. I know." He finished tying the dogs up to the cottage's porch railing, pulled his keys from his pocket and headed for the door. "Trust me, okay? I worked here. Besides, the owner's out of town, so it's even more perfect. We don't even have to worry about who we might run into."

Or, then again...maybe not.

He felt his eyes widen as the door swung open, even before he touched the handle. Crap. Maybe he'd spoken too soon?

"Hi, Seth. What are you doing here?" Jasmine Quinn, the daughter of his mother's best friend, Marsha, inquired.

Holy shit. For an instant, Seth was too surprised to answer. *Me? What the hell is* she *doing here?*

"I uh, Jasmine, hi. This is my friend Monica," he said at last, nodding at Deirdre and hoping she was smart enough to play along. "She needs to use the bathroom."

"Oh. Okay," Jasmine waved them inside. "Sure. C'mon in."

Seth pushed Deirdre ahead of him. "Here," he said as he handed her the backpack he'd brought with him. "Bathroom's that way. You'll find everything you need there." What she'd find—he hoped—was the cabinet full of spare clothes which Siobhan, Jasmine's aunt, kept on hand for the benefit of anyone—volunteers, field trip attendees, stray visitors—who found themselves in need of dry clothes.

Deirdre nodded, frowning slightly, as she took the bag.

"Seth! It's a bathroom. What could she *need*?" Jasmine asked, laughing at him. "I mean...other than the toilet."

Seth shrugged. "I dunno. Water? Paper towels? Whatever. I'm sure she'll find it in there, right?"

"Soap." Deirdre held up her hands. "See, we were on the beach with the dogs and they um, they got into some...some stuff. Some dead stuff. You know? And then I had to– to–"

"Oh!" Jasmine's eyes widened. She looked surprised and vaguely ill. "Oh, ewww. Gross. Sure, we got soap and, and towels and uh...yeah, go ahead." She waved Deirdre toward the bathroom.

Seth watched her go. That was a pretty good story. A little too good, maybe. She'd almost had him believing it. Which made him wonder how many other made up stories she might have told him? But, this was no time to start thinking about that.

He just hoped she didn't take too long in there, or start trying stuff on. She needed to just pick out a few things, enough so she'd have a couple of outfits to change into, not so many that it would be obvious that she'd raided the place.

He turned to find Jasmine eyeing him curiously, a puzzled smile glimmering on her lips. "Okay, dish. What's really going on? Who is that girl? She looks familiar."

"I just told you her name," he said, trying to bluff it out. "And, anyway, what are you doing here? I thought you went camping with your mom and my folks?"

Jasmine shrugged. "I was supposed to. Except, Siobhan needed someone to keep an eye on things while she and Ryan were in Hawaii. But, never mind that. C'mon, tell me. You guys didn't come here to, you know, use my aunt's place, or anything, while she's away, did you?"

Seth looked at her in surprise. She thought they'd come here to screw? That thought had never entered his head. But, now that it had...oh, fuck. Is that what everyone'd think? If word of this got around, he'd never hear the end of it.

Before he could answer, Jasmine shook her head. "No, wait, of course you're not. What am I saying? You've got your own place now, don't you? Out at the inn?"

Seth nodded. Right. The inn. Which just happened to be run by another of Jasmine's aunts: Sinead. He'd heard Jasmine's boyfriend complain that she had too many relatives, Seth was beginning to see Brandon's point.

Jeez, the Quinns weren't even really part of his family, and he still couldn't get away from them. Once the sisters got back in town and started talking to each other, comparing notes– Holy shit.

"Jasmine– You gotta keep quiet about this. Just...don't tell anyone you saw us here, okay? It's important."

The curious gleam in Jasmine's almond shaped eyes shimmered brighter. "I know. Why don't you tell me what this is all about, hmm? And then I'll decide if I should keep my mouth shut about it or not."

"I can't." He gazed at her pleadingly. "Not yet. And you *have* to keep quiet."

Jasmine pursed her lips, looking doubtful. "Gee, Seth, I don't know. Without knowing the details? I'm not sure if I can do that."

"I'll tell you later, okay?" Seth promised. "As much as I can. But right now–"

"As much as you can? Naw, that doesn't sound very fair."

Seth squeezed his eyes shut. "Jasmine...come on. I–I can't."

Laughter bubbled out of Jasmine's throat. She punched him lightly on the arm. "Seth! Don't you know when I'm kidding around? Stop stressing. I'll keep your secret. Same as always, right?"

Relieved, he opened his eyes. "Thanks."

A mischievous smile had curved Jasmine's lips. "For now, anyway. But, I do expect to get the 411 on it all someday."

Seth nodded. "Okay, you got it."

Jasmine's gaze strayed toward the bathroom, then back to his face. "So, this girl. Did I meet her somewhere before? Where do I know her from?"

"You don't." He looked at her, surprised. She couldn't, right?

Jasmine shook her head thoughtfully. "Are you sure? It seems to me...well, maybe you showed me a picture?"

A picture? Sure, he had one of those. In his room at home. But, he didn't known when Jasmine could have seen that. Unless...oh, right. Fuck. Two Christmases ago...

*"So, what do you do for fun these days?" Jasmine asked him. "Fun?" Seth looked at her in surprise. She'd been prowling restlessly around his room for several minutes now, looking at everything, touching everything. He kinda wished she'd stop.*

*"What do you mean, fun? This is Oberon. There's never been anything to do here, remember? That's why you wanted to leave."*

*"Oh. Right." She continued to snoop. Picking things up. Opening boxes and drawers—*

Including his night table drawer, where he'd kept his picture of Deirdre. That had to be it—didn't it? "Maybe." He shrugged, his mind still stuck in the past... "

*Where do you keep your booze, anyway?" Jasmine had asked, as she peered into his closet. "Maybe we could have a drink to celebrate the holiday."*

*"Can't," he muttered shortly. "I'm out."*

*"Since when? I thought you were party guy; the booze king of Oberon? Isn't that what you said the other night"*

*The question stung—even if it was no more than what he, himself, had told her. "I'm trying to quit," he mumbled, feeling like crap.*

*"Oh. Well, whatever." Jasmine shrugged, without much interest. As she lifted a book from his shelf, a handful of condoms that had been stuck between the pages fell out and tumbled to the floor. She smiled. "Oops. Sorry."*

*"Oh, Christ. What the hell are you doing?" he groaned, wishing she'd just sit the fuck back down and stop touching things.*

*Normally, he liked Jasmine. But she was sure in a weird ass mood today, and she was turning the afternoon into the longest Christmas of his life. Or, at least, the most depressing.*

*"So, you got a girlfriend, Seth?" Jasmine asked, as she gathered the condoms back up.*

*And wasn't that another fantastic topic? He sighed unhappily, his thoughts having turned to Deirdre. "No. Not in forever."*

*Jasmine looked surprised. "So, I guess you don't really need these, then, do you? I mean...if you don't have a girlfriend or anything–"*

*He felt himself frown "What's that got to do with anything?"*

*"Oh." She sat back down on his bed and stared at him thoughtfully. "Do all guys think like you? Do they all want to have sex with girls they don't really care about?"*

*Seth shrugged. Had he* said *he thought something like that? Although, he supposed– "I guess? Maybe? I haven't really thought about it."*

*"Why is that? I mean, it's called making love. Shouldn't it have something to do with being in love?"*

*"Love's bullshit," he growled, as anger ignited inside him. "Fucking is...I don't know...easier. And, what are you talking about guys for? Most of the times I've had sex, it was the girl's idea to do it."*

*Jasmine flashed him her most ironic smile. "Oh, and you couldn't say no, right?"*

But no was not something guys said, was it? It was what girls like Deirdre said to guys like him. *Not to Eric, she didn't*, a demon voice in his head just had to whisper. No, with guys like Eric, things were a whole lot different...

*"What is it about guys like that?" Seth remembered having asked Jasmine on another occasion. "Why is it girls like them so much?"*

*Jasmine stared at him. "What makes you think they do?"*

*"Well, they sure seem to." Certainly Deirdre had. And, Cara, too, for that matter, although she'd claimed later that it wasn't Eric she'd been interested in, it was all the shit he'd gotten her hooked on.*

*Seth had never been sure how much he believed that. Eric had gotten him hooked, too, for that matter. And, while it had led to his making some really bad choices, it hadn't ever left him wanting to fuck Eric, that was for sure.*

*Jasmine shook her head and gazed at him pityingly. "I don't know who these girls are that you're hanging with, Seth. But, I think maybe you ought to broaden your horizons a little."*

"Seth? Are you okay?" Jasmine peered at him curiously. "What's wrong?"

Before he could think of an answer, however, the sound of footsteps crossing the floor made them turn their heads.

Deirdre looked at them both questioningly. "Did I miss something?"

"No." Seth grabbed her hand. "C'mon, let's get going. I gotta get the dogs back."

"Thanks for letting me wash up," Deirdre told Jasmine as Seth hauled her out the door.

"Uh-huh." Grinning, Jasmine waggled her fingers at them. "Bye-bye you ghosts. Have fun."

"Ghosts?" Deirdre looked at Seth questioningly, after he'd gotten the dogs and they were heading back to his truck. "What'd she mean by that?"

But Seth was in no mood, now, to discuss Jasmine. Or anything else, for that matter. "Never mind. Did you get some clothes?"

Deirdre was silent for a moment. "Yeah. I did. That was a good idea you had. But, won't someone notice there's stuff missing?" "Nope." Seth shook his head. "Not for a while anyway. It's Summer, so no fieldtrips. Not that many people around."

They'd reached the truck by then. Seth started lifting the dogs into the bed and securing their leashes to the tie-downs. Deirdre went and sat in the truck. Was it his imagination, or was she a little too quiet?

"So, what were you and Jasmine talking about?" Deirdre asked, once they'd pulled out of the parking lot and were back on the road.

Seth glanced out the window before answering. It was a pretty day, sunny and warm. Still, a few small clouds hung over the landscape, casting shadows on the surrounding hillsides. Just like all the stray wisps of doubt and depression that cast shadows on his soul.

*We talked about you,* he thought of saying. *About love. About how fucked up my life is.*

Instead, he shrugged. "Oh, you know, just stuff."

"Oh." Deirdre turned to gaze out the window and said nothing more. And there was nothing else Seth could think of saying either. He pushed down a little harder on the gas, then remembered the dogs in the back, and forced himself to slow down. The warm, spicy smell of chaparral floated in through the open windows. Usually, it made him feel better. Today it didn't.

"So, I guess you two used to work together, huh?" she asked, her voice low.

Seth frowned. "Who?"

"You and Jasmine? Isn't that where you know her from?"

"From work?" Seth shot her a surprised look. "Oh. No. We're just...I dunno...friends, I guess." More like family, really. Except that they weren't actually related. "We kinda grew up together."

"Oh. I guess you must have a lot of friends, don't you?"

Seth sighed. "Not really." Once he had. Once, it seemed like everyone he knew wanted to be his friend. But, lately? Not so much. Thanks to Eric. And Cara. And, Deirdre, herself, come to think of it. "What about you? How many friends do you have in Oberon?"

Her eyebrows rose. "Here? I- I don't, really."

"What about family, then?"

"What?" She was frowning now. "Seth, what are you talking about? You know I don't..."

"I'm just trying to get things straight, that's all. Didn't you tell me last time that you had family here?"

A flush of red stained her cheeks. "Yeah, I– I– Probably, but..."

"Oh." She'd been lying. Right. "Didn't you ever find out who your father was?"

He held his breath, wondering what she'd say, and which would be worse: yes, or a lie.

Deirdre's eyes flashed. "No. Why are you asking all these questions?"

"I told you. I'm trying to figure out what's going on. I mean, if someone's really after you–" Crap. He sounded just like Cara, now. "It's gotta be someone you know, right? Who else do you know in town? Who else knows you're here?"

"No one!" She scowled at him for a moment, and then her expression turned uncertain. "I mean, other than the obvious: school, my landlord, my former boss, the people I worked with... Oh, and Rafe, I guess. Do you remember him? I ran into him on Sunday."

"Rafe? How? You're saying he lives in Oberon now, too?" Seth felt as though a shard of glass had just lodged in his heart.

Jealousy, he supposed. Last time she was here, she'd stayed at the beach with Rafe and a bunch of others: male and female. Fool that he was, Seth had actually believed her when she'd said they were all just friends. Now, he wasn't so sure.

Deirdre shrugged. "No, I don't think so. I just...like I said, I ran into him. Literally, in fact. At the fair and then...well, that was it, really."

But, something about her expression said that wasn't it, not even close. "So, you're saying he *doesn't* live here then?" But, Seth already knew the answer to that. Of course he didn't. Small as Oberon was, if Rafe were living here, Seth would have had to run across him, at least once or twice, in all that time. "He just happened to turn up two years ago, and then again on Sunday? How come?"

"I told you: I don't know. I asked but, I don't really remember what he said. I don't know anything about him, really. I haven't seen him or talked to him in two years. Why are you acting like this? And why does it have to be someone I know? Why can't it just be some random crazy person?"

They'd left the coast road behind them now. Seth slowed the truck even more. He sighed. "And, that doesn't seem at all strange to you, does it? You don't find it the slightest bit...suspicious?"

"Find *what* suspicious? What are you talking about?"

"Rafe. The way he keeps turning up—it's like he's following you around."

Her eyes narrowed. "You don't trust anyone, do you?"

Seth shrugged, doing his best to keep his face from changing, to keep the pain that weighed on his heart from showing. "I trust some people. It's just...a lot of people, lately, haven't given me much reason to trust them."

Once, he'd trusted everyone. Once, when he was young and idealistic...and an idiot. He'd trusted the wrong people and ended up here.

In a world where he didn't know who to trust, or what to believe in. In a world where not a lot of people trusted or believed in him.

He wanted his old world back, his old life back. Because this one sucked.

"YES, Miss Matthews? Can I help you with something?"

Despite the worried look on Cara's face, Liam couldn't help smiling when she approached him after class. He'd been in a surprisingly good mood all day, ever since his conversation last night, in the bar.

*Be of good cheer,* The stranger had counseled. *Seize the day. Embrace uncertainty.* And, somewhere in the course of an otherwise sleepless night, Liam had fallen asleep with those words whispering in his head. He'd awoken this morning feeling lighthearted, carefree, and more determined than ever to take that advice to heart.

"You- you're really gonna make us take a test on Saturday?" Cara asked.

He nodded. "Yes. I have to. It's part of what you agreed to when they let you into this program, you know."

"I know," she sighed. "It's just– What if I don't pass? Liam, I'm not good at tests."

He smiled at her encouragingly. "Don't worry. You'll do fine. Just like always, right?"

Cara shook her head. "No, not always. Almost never without help."

Liam tried to hide his smile. Tomorrow, when he showed up at her door, maybe he'd tease her about this. Maybe he'd tell her the only reason he was there was to help her study. That the flowers and balloons were study aids. Or for someone else. Or that he'd just found them somewhere, by the side of the road, and hadn't even realized it was her birthday.

It didn't matter what he told her as long as, eventually, he got to see her face go from sullen or annoyed to pink and pleased when she realized that he hadn't forgotten, that he'd been planning this all along. "Well, you still have two days to study for it. Maybe you can find someone to help you."

"I guess. Maybe."

For almost a minute, neither one spoke. Liam watched as Cara scratched with her thumbnail at a spot of dried paint on his desktop. What was making her frown like that? "Is there something else you wanted to talk to me about?" he asked gently.

Cara shrugged. "Yeah, sorta. Do you remember that girl you were so curious about last April? The one who'd emailed Gregg? Remember, you wanted me to steal her picture for you?"

He nodded, trying hard to ignore the dull ache that had started in his chest. "I remember." Vividly. "Why?"

"Well...yeah. That's what I'm asking. Why were you so interested? What was she to you?"

"No one. That's...really not important anymore."

"Well...but, what if it was?" she asked quietly. "What if she, or maybe some other girl, was here in Oberon and what if Gregg was trying to have her...you know, killed, or something."

"Cara–" He stared at her, hating the nervous way her teeth worried her lip. Feeling helpless to make things right for her.

"And what if...what if this chick had a problem with the cops. Or, you know, what if she just didn't like 'em much–

"Some chick, huh? "You mean like you?"

She nodded. "Yeah, you know. It's not like she did anything wrong, or anything. It's just–"

"Cara, are you worried about Gregg getting out of prison and coming after you?"

She blinked down at him; one eye widening in surprise, one eye staring over his shoulder, as though disinterested. "Well, yeah, sure. A little. I mean, who wouldn't be?"

He shook his head. "Well, don't. I mean it. He's not getting out. Not ever."

She nodded, still looking worried. "Still, he could maybe send someone else to do it, don't you think?"

"No. That'll never happen. And you can't go through your whole life looking over your shoulder, you know. You're safe now. It's over."

He stretched out his hand, intending to cover hers, to offer some comfort, but she snatched her hand back quickly and jammed it in her jeans' back pocket.

"Okay, look," he told her. "How about this. I promise you, it's never gonna happen. But, if it did, if Gregg were to get out somehow, I swear I will be the first person to hear about it. And I will *personally* track him down and kill him before he ever gets anywhere near you. D'you believe me?"

A small smile flickered on Cara's lips as she nodded. "I guess, sometimes, being a cop has advantages, huh?"

"Yeah. Sometimes." Liam studied her face for a moment, wondering if he shouldn't just invite her out to dinner now, tonight. What difference did a few hours really make, after all? And, who was ever gonna know? But, before he got the chance–

"But why was it so important?" Cara pressed, reminding him just how persistent she could be. Like a terrier, once she got hold of an idea, she just couldn't let it rest. "You seemed really curious about this girl. You *said* it was important."

Sighing, Liam nodded. However painful it was to speak about, he owed her an explanation. An explanation and just about anything else she might care to ask him for. "Okay, it's like this. I had a sister once. She'd have been the same age as you. I lost touch with her years ago but, the last anyone heard of her, she was in a cult that was...well, a lot like Gregg's."

"Your sister?" Cara's eyes widened. She looked at him searchingly. "You mean..."

"Yeah. That's why I was there. I was hoping I could find her. Or find some information about her."

"Are you...well, are you still looking for her?"

"No." Feeling overwhelmed, he closed his eyes, giving himself a moment to pull himself together. "No, she's dead. She died a long time ago, actually. Which I knew all along. I mean, some part of me knew it. I just...I just wanted to keep believing there was a chance, I guess."

TEARS PRICKED at Cara's eyes. She bit her lip. "I'm sorry," she whispered, wanting to say more but not knowing how. She struggled to find the right words and, finally, "B-but, in a way, I'm– I'm glad you believed."

He looked at her questioningly.

She nodded. "Yeah, 'cause...you know, if you hadn't, you wouldn't have had any reason to be there, right? I mean, you wouldn't have been at Gregg's 'Cause, you wouldn't have been looking for anyone."

Liam frowned a little, looking puzzled. "True."

She shrugged. "Yeah, and then...then you and I might never have met."

A sad smile curved his lips. His gaze traveled over her face. "Yeah. A fat lot of good that did you, huh?"

"Well, it did," Cara insisted, a little surprised that she had to say it. Did he really not know how she felt? She thought he was smarter than that. "You helped me study. And that was great. 'Cause, you know, otherwise..."

"Helped you study?" Liam's eyes filled with pain. "God, Cara, I nearly got you killed! Don't you realize that?"

"What do you mean?" She frowned uncertainly. He'd gotten her into a shit load of trouble, that was for certain. But, killed? "How'd you do that?"

The look in his eyes intensified, more pain, more guilt. Which could only mean one thing. Oh.

"You know, Liam, if you're talking about that...that night...I uh, I can't really remember much about it, you know. I don't...I still don't even know what happened?"

"I wish I had that problem," he muttered as he lowered his gaze to the top of his desk. He folded his hands on the blotter and studied his thumbs. "Well, I don't know what to tell you. Other than I– I messed up. I came back to the compound that evening and...and I found you there, with your face all bruised, spouting some nonsense about having tripped down the stairs. That's when I knew it was over. I'd been fooling myself for weeks, thinking I could keep you safe, without blowing my cover and making you leave. But, after that–" He shook his head.

"I finally got you to admit what really happened," he continued sadly. "Big surprise: Gregg had hit you. And then...then I tried to get you to leave. I tried to bully you into it. I just wanted to get you somewhere safe, I swear, that's all I wanted. But I went about it all wrong and...you got scared. You made up some excuse about needing to get the remote for the gate, and took off without me. Then, when Gregg found out you were gone, he uh, he locked me in the basement and went after you."

"Oh." Startled, Cara tried to pull her thoughts together. Some of what he said made sense. An image of her face, bruised, swollen, staring wide-eyed back at her from a mirror, flashed through her mind.

But...the idea that she'd have been afraid of him? That didn't sound right at all. She'd spent two solid months listening to stories about that night that made no sense at all, she knew when she was hearing another one.

But, that wasn't important right now. She took a deep breath and asked, "So, I uh, I guess you must've felt kind of bad about that, huh?"

Then she waited for the answer, which could never be right, no matter what he said. Because, if Liam blamed himself for what happened, if that was the only reason he'd come to see her in the hospital, the only thing between them–

Her thoughts stalled as he raised his head. And when those blue, blue eyes of his met hers, she felt like everything inside her had just caught fire. Breathing was almost impossible. Thinking, even more so. "Yeah," he said harshly. "You could say that."

Cara nodded, dropped her gaze, slid her purse strap over her shoulder, cleared her throat. So, she was right. That was why he'd come to see her in the hospital—only once, and never again. Guilt.

Pity. Her two least favorite emotions. Just exactly what she'd been hoping for, what she'd always wanted him to feel for her—not.

"Yeah, well...don't." She tossed her head to show it didn't mean anything to her, that she was over it. She even managed a small, brittle smile. Then she turned and headed quickly toward the door, only knocking into two chairs on her way.

"Cara." Liam said her name softly, so softly it was like a touch. It stopped her in her tracks.

She turned and glanced at him over her shoulder. "I mean it, Liam. Stop stressing, we're chill." She shrugged, and smiled once again. "Forget all about it, dude. I have."

## 13

After the morning at the beach, the afternoon—in yet another canyon—seemed twice as hot as yesterday. Not that Seth seemed to mind the heat, Deirdre thought, sneaking a sideways glance at him as they stood, hand in hand, in a lush, green field. The grim, unhappy expression he'd worn all the way back from the beach had begun to smooth out shortly after they arrived here at his *special place*: the nursery his family had owned and operated for generations.

Despite the bright sun beating down on her face, the incessant shrill of insects, the heady, warm scent of growing things that thickened the air, Deirdre couldn't help but smile.

Seth turned and caught her looking at him. "What?"

She shook her head. "Nothing. It's just...you look happy."

"Happy." He repeated the word after her, as if he were uncertain of its meaning. As his gaze flickered over her lips, the question in his eyes grew more pronounced. "I could be happy," he murmured as he tugged on her hand.

Deirdre let herself drift closer, smiling encouragement. When his lips met hers in one of those gentle, sweet kisses he did so well, she sighed in contentment.

He pulled back and nodded at their surroundings. "So? What do you think?"

"Its beautiful here," she said, glancing around once again, trying to take it all in. "And this whole place is yours, huh?"

"Well, it's my family's, but yeah, pretty much."

"Wow." She couldn't help but think about how close she'd come to being a part of his family, a part of this place. Not close at all, really. "Must've been nice, growing up here."

"Some of the time it was," he answered wistfully. Then his gaze shifted and he frowned. "Hey! That's far enough." He put two fingers in his mouth and whistled loudly. "Zeus. Vulcan. Bring 'em back now."

A snarling commotion erupted at the edge of the field. As it moved toward them, Deirdre pressed herself against Seth's side. He squeezed her hand reassuringly. He dug in his pocket with his other hand, for a moment, and then extended it toward her. "Here. You want to feed 'em?"

Chopped up pieces of what appeared to be jerky filled his open palm. She shook her head. "No. That's okay."A minute later, they were surrounded by dogs; only two of Seth's this time, along with five other, mid-sized dogs that they'd picked up on their way out here.

Deirdre watched as Seth doled out the treats. The dogs' eyes were riveted on him, totally focused on the food in his hand. One or two of them eyed her speculatively at first, but once they figured out she didn't have anything to give them, they totally ignored her.

Still, as they continued to jump and bark and mill about impatiently, she found herself having to take slow, deep breaths in order to stay calm.

Seth shot a swift, somewhat worried glance in her direction. "You okay?"

She nodded. Even if it wasn't completely truthful, it was what she wanted him to think. "So, do you bring the little dogs out here, too?"

Seth shook his head. "Nah, the ground's too uneven. Their leashes get all tangled up in the vegetation and stuff. It's a mess trying to walk them through here."

“Can’t you walk them off leash? You know, just let them run around like these guys are doing?”

Seth smiled. “Yeah, that’d be fun, until I tried to round them all up. Or until a hawk decided one of them looked like he’d make a good snack.” He shook his head again. “They’re too small. It’d be too hard to keep track of them out here. It’s tricky enough with this size.”

“I thought that’s why you brought your two along.” She pointed at the black dog who had startled her in the pool the other night, and the big brown one he called Zeus. “To keep the others together?”

The smile disappeared from Seth’s face. “I did. It doesn’t work the same with little dogs.”

“Why not?”

“Because it doesn’t, that’s all.” He took more jerky from his pocket and began to throw it; hurling pieces of it over the dogs’ heads, making them work for their treats.

Deirdre said nothing, knowing there was more, hoping if she just waited long enough...

Finally, he shrugged. “Look, dogs are predators, all right? They’re descended from wolves. And, sometimes, when they get out here and start running around, they forget what they’re doing. They forget they’ve been domesticated. It’s called Predatory Drift.[1] The little dogs...they don’t always realize what’s happening. They’re looking at the big dogs and thinking, *let’s be friends*.”

“And the bigger dogs?” she prompted when his voice trailed off. “What are they thinking?”

Seth sighed. His eyes met hers reluctantly. “I dunno Probably...*time for lunch*.”

Lunch? “Oh.” For a moment, Deirdre feared she might lose hers.

“And I’m not just talking about mine, either, you know,” Seth insisted, gesturing at the pack of dogs, who’d gone back to playing. “Any of these can turn savage. Even the little ones can. It’s not that they’re mean, or anything. They’re not trying to hurt anybody. They’re just being...dogs.”

He shot a rueful glance in her direction, and then shook his head. “Fuck. It was a mistake bringing you out here, today, wasn’t it?”

"No!" She clutched at his arm. "It wasn't. Really. It's just...well, let me ask you something. About your dogs."

He met her gaze and nodded. "All right. What do you want to know?"

"I know you say they're not dangerous. But, that's not what they told me when I was in the hospital. They asked all kinds of questions about them, Seth. They said they'd been looking for them for a while. And, that's why– Well...how come they're not dead? I mean, I know how much they mean to you but...they told me they'd be, you know, p-put down. They promised me they'd be rounded up and...and I– I mean–"

"What?" Seth's eyes had widened in alarm.

Deirdre shrugged. "I don't know...maybe they were lying. Maybe they just said it 'cause they thought my parents' insurance company was going to sue them, or something. But–"

"Who said it?" he demanded. "Who told you they were going to do that? Was it my father?"

"No, not him. But...well everyone else, really. The police. The people in the hospital—the doctors, nurses, social workers, psychiatrists... I don't know who they were, but they all told me the same thing. That's why I was so surprised when I–"

"Crap." Pulling his arm from her grasp, Seth turned away. He aimed one vicious kick after another at the ground at his feet, disintegrating big clods of dried dirt, filling the air with dust. "I don't fucking believe this."

Watching him, Deirdre couldn't help but feel wretched and worried...even a little bit scared. "Seth?"

"I didn't know. I mean, Nick—my cousin—he kept saying what a big deal it was, but I just– Fuck. I didn't believe it. He acted like it was such a huge favor he was doing for me. And I didn't know why he made it out to be so freakin' hard! He gave me so much grief for it, and I mean, shit! Yeah, I knew people had flipped out a little when they thought the dogs were just running around loose in the parks, killing everything they ran across. But, Nick knew that's not how it was—I *told* him that! They were always under control, it's just that, for part of the time, they were under Eric's control. And he was being a total dick."

Eric. At the mention of his name, Deirdre felt her stomach turn over.

Seth appeared not to notice."I thought they were just out to bust my balls and...I couldn't let that happen, you know? I couldn't let the dogs take the blame for my mistake."

He looked at her, eyes wide and full of pleading. Deirdre could think of nothing to say. "You want to know why they didn't kill them? How I finally got them to back the fuck off?" he asked, his voice raspy and hoarse.

She nodded. "Yes."

He shook his head. "God, I'm such an asshole. But, I didn't know anything back then. I- I told my parents I was gonna kill myself if they didn't do something, if they didn't find some way to save my dogs. And I would've too. They knew I wasn't playing."

He turned away again, speaking more softly now, so that she had to strain to catch his words. "I didn't know that the dogs had hurt you, but...even if I did, it wouldn't have mattered." He broke off again, breathing hard.

"Seth, it's okay," she said, putting her hand on his shoulder, forcing him to turn around, to face her again.

But, his eyes were so troubled, she couldn't bear looking at them. "I can't believe I did that," he whispered. "I was just so stupid. Maybe it was the drugs. I musta scared the shit out of my parents, and it wasn't even their fault!"

Deirdre slid her arms around his waist and laid her head on his chest. "I'm sorry. I shouldn't have said anything. I didn't mean to upset you, Seth. It's just...I didn't understand either, you know? I thought everyone was lying to *me*. And, I thought you–" *I thought you cared more about the dogs than you did about me.* She still wasn't sure about that, was she?

"It's not your fault," he murmured. "I should've known better. But, they're my dogs, Deirdre. I found them when they were just puppies;

just a little of puppies someone had abandoned in the woods. I raised them. And, if it wasn't for fucking Eric and his stupid drugs–"

Eric again. Deirdre gagged and clutched Seth tighter, willing him to put his arms around her, to hold her and comfort her. To make the memories of that awful night go away. "How'd you get mixed up with him, anyway? W-were you really friends?" she asked, not knowing how it was possible, but almost not caring when Seth slid one arm around her waist, absently tangling the fingers of his other hand in her hair.

"Well, yeah. Sort of, I guess. Off and on. He could be fun, you know, to do stuff with? He wasn't boring, that's for sure. But something always went wrong. He just couldn't help messing with my stuff. And, after a while...well, it just seemed like, if anything was mine, he wanted it."

Deirdre squeezed her eyes shut, still fighting the churning sickness in her gut. *If anything was mine, he wanted it.* She hadn't thought anything could make her feel worse about that particular event. Apparently, she'd been wrong. She'd thought that at least Eric had wanted her for her own sake. But, no. She'd just been one more thing he could take from Seth.

"I guess I should've been used to it by then," Seth sighed, still stroking her hair, oblivious to the flood of fresh pain his words had started. "I should've known better than to let it get to me, but when he started messing around with Cara– Ah, it just pissed me off."

"With Cara?" Deirdre frowned. "Mm. We were sorta dating, you know? But he got her hooked on that shit he was cooking up in his lab, got her to dump me for him. 'Least that's what she says now. I'm still not sure I believe her. I sure didn't back then. I was so freakin' angry with the both of them–"

He shook his head. "So, I took one dog, because that was our deal. We'd each keep one, and we'd sell the rest and divide whatever money we made between us. I chose Mouth, 'cause he was the smallest and Eric was already picking on him, trying to make the other dogs fight with him and stuff. And I split. I walked away, left

Eric with the rest of the dogs...it was months before I went back, even to check on how they were doing. Worst fucking mistake of my life."

"I'm sorry," she whispered, wishing there was some way she could make either of them feel better.

"Me, too," he sighed. "Too bad that doesn't help anything, huh?" He pulled away, smiling faintly. "C'mon, let's get out of here. It's time I got these guys back home."

BY THE END of the day Deirdre felt wilted. The pool beckoned; sun-dazzled, glimmering, more irresistible than ever. She still didn't have a bathing suit, but she was tired and cross and she just didn't care. As soon as they got back to the inn, she changed into one of the T-shirts she'd picked up earlier today, and dove in.

The water was warmer than it had been last night. She slipped seamlessly between the elements, feeling both refreshed and caressed as she swam briskly for several minutes, and then turned on her back and just floated. Water rising and falling beneath her. Sun beating against her closed eyelids. Heat reflecting from the surrounding brick drying her face. Finally, she felt herself begin to relax.

The sound of running footsteps slapping against the brick got her eyes open. She stood up quickly and spun around, just in time to see Seth arc through the air and plunge into the pool.

Water surged, pushing her back a step. Her heart hammered in her chest as he swam straight toward her, surfacing when he was only inches away. His hands felt warm on her hips as he pulled her toward him. She had time for just one look into his eyes, but it was enough to make her lose her breath.

His lips were wet against hers. His body felt solid and strong, slippery in her arms. She was acutely aware that there was nothing at all between them but one, thin layer of nearly transparent, wet cotton.

He deepened the kiss, pressing her close, molding their bodies together; and, wonderful as it was, she couldn't help but remember Sunday. His cruelty. Her anger.

She pushed him away, ducking her head, refusing to meet his eyes as she murmured, "And, just for the record, I am *not* easy."

He was still for an instant. Silent. And then, "Is that what all this is about? Is that why you said no to me last night?"

It wasn't really, but, all the same, she shrugged. "Partly."

With a finger beneath her chin, he urged her to look at him. "Dee? You know I didn't really mean that, right?"

"Then why'd you say it?" she asked. "I don't understand. Why would you treat me like that?"

Seth shrugged. He looked embarrassed. "I dunno. I guess...I was drunk. I was tired. I was upset. I was having a really bad day."

*That's it*? Deirdre felt her gaze darken. "*That's* your excuse?"

He shrugged again. "Well, yeah, it seemed like one, at the time."

A bad day. *Was he really*? Furious, Deirdre crossed her arms over her chest. "I see."

Seth sighed. "C'mon," he murmured as he pulled her back into his arms. "I'm sorry, all right? Besides, that was days ago. Let's not talk about it now, okay?"

"That's the problem with you," she complained. "You never want to talk about anything!"

He nuzzled her neck. "Sure, I do. There's lots of things we could talk about. Try me."

But, just then, his mouth found the sensitive spot where her neck met her shoulder. He bit softly and she just gave up. She couldn't really think of anything she wanted to talk about just now anyway. "Forget it."

Closing her eyes, Deirdre reveled in the feel of Seth's hot mouth on her neck; of his soft, wet hair, cool against her cheek and between her fingers as she slid her hand up his neck to tangle in the slippery locks.

As his hands roved over her back she canted her hips into his, hoping to ease the throbbing tension in her lower body. It didn't really help, however, because, as soon as she did, he moved his hands lower, cupped her ass, ground against her. And made everything throb and ache—even worse than before.

Deirdre gulped for breath. "I really like you Seth," she whispered, trying to pull away yet going nowhere, trying not to dig her fingernails into his arms, digging anyway. "You know that, right?"

He bit her neck again and murmured, "Mm-hm."

She waited, sure he'd say more, but he didn't. Finally she did pull away. She backed up half a step. Uncertainty shimmered along her nerves, igniting her temper. If she wasn't standing almost chest deep in water, she'd have stamped her foot—much as he had done out at the nursery. "Seth!"

He looked down at her, the glint in his eye belying his innocence. "What?"

"This might be a good time for you to say something back, you know."

A dimple appeared on his cheek as he smiled. "Umm...you mean something like...*I really like you, too*?"

"Yes," she said, trying hard not to fall for the dimple or the smile or the hope that he might actually mean it. "Something like that."

He took a step towards her. "Well, you know I do. Why do I need to say it?"

She backed up again, pushing at his chest to keep him away. "Because. It's nice to hear. That's why."

"Okay then." Eyes gleaming, he slid closer. "I like you." She backed away some more. "I like you a lot." She grunted in surprise as her back hit the edge of the pool. Shit. She was out of room. "I like you a whole lot." Seth's hands clutched the tile on either side of her, caging her where she stood.

She looked up at him, breathless again.

He smiled. "Now, c'mere, and let me show you how much."

As he pressed himself against her, she melted. But then his hands found the hem of her T-shirt and started to tug it upwards. She balked. "Stop! W-we can't– Not here!"

Seth paused and glanced around. "Why? What's wrong with here? Haven't you ever done it in the water before? It's nice."

"We're outside—in broad daylight. Someone might see."

"We're in the country," he corrected, "miles from anywhere." His eyes locked with hers again, intensely dark, hypnotic. "The only one who's gonna see anything is me. And I want to see everything. Now. Please?"

"No." She shook her head, tightening her grasp on his wrists, embarrassed by the trembling that had seized her, by the thunder beating in her heart, by the urge to let go and– "No. You're rushing me. Stop it."

Seth stilled. "How'm I rushing you? It's been *two years*. Longer, even!"

Annoyed, she did let go of his wrists then, and shoved at his chest. "So? What's that supposed to mean? It's not like we've been together all that time, is it? We haven't seen each other or...or...or even thought about each other all that much."

It wasn't true, of course. Not for her. The sun was in her eyes as she squinted up at him, hoping to see something in his expression; anything that would let her know that it wasn't true for him, either. But his face was shadowed, it told her nothing.

"Well?" she pressed, growing impatient with his silence. "We haven't have we?"

"I guess not," he muttered at last, falling backwards into the water, staring up at the sky. "Fine. Have it your way." Then he pushed off from the bottom, spun around, and swam for the far end of the pool.

"Where are you going?" she called as he heaved himself out of the water. He turned again, and looked at her. "I'm hungry. I'm gonna go make some dinner. You want a burger or something?"Deirdre nodded yes, then watched as he walked away. She leaned her crossed arms on the edge of the pool, idly scratching at the grout between the tiles with the edge of her thumbnail. Her mind and body were in total turmoil.

Two years. And, despite what she'd just got finished saying, in all that time not a week had gone by when she hadn't thought about

Seth at least once. His name had wormed its way into nearly every therapy session she'd attended. His face appeared in far too many of her dreams. Every time she saw the scars on her arm, she remembered him, even every time she saw a dog.

Whenever a friend gushed about a new boyfriend, or groused about an old one; and, even more so, on those rare occasions when she, herself, went on a date...it was like he was right there, somewhere in the back of her mind, watching her. "Like a friggin' ghost," she muttered, wondering why she'd never had the sense to try and exorcise him.

Maybe that's what she should do now. If the therapists were right, if the reality would never live up to the fantasy she'd created, why shouldn't she just give it up, walk away, find someone new. Just like they'd been telling her to do for years.

But, what if they were wrong? If she gave up now, how would she ever know? How would she ever know, in any case? Unless she gave in. Unless she gave him what he wanted—what they both wanted, if she were going to be honest. Maybe she should just sleep with him now, and get it over with.

Was that the answer? "What's the worst that could happen?" she asked, speaking to the Lady Bug that had just landed on her arm. The worst thing she could imagine happening was that she'd find out that she'd been wrong to blame her sexual problems over the last two years on Eric.

That she'd learn for sure that she was the one responsible for her own unhappiness. The only one. And she'd have to accept that there was no cure, no end in sight, that the loneliness that had haunted her for two years was something that would last her whole life.

The Lady Bug fanned her wings, but said nothing. Not that Deirdre had expected anything more. Despite Oberon's reputation for being magical, she was pretty sure that, even here, some things were just plain impossible. Maybe too many things.

SETH CHOPPED savagely at the ground beef browning in the pan, using the spatula like a cleaver as he took out his frustrations on the dinner he was making; reducing the meat to hash. So, he'd said he was making burgers—so what? *Change of plans. Deal with it.* And if she was disappointed? If she didn't like it, or if she didn't want to deal? Well, then she could damn well feed herself.

He wasn't in the mood to shape the meat into nice, round patties, or to even think about anything that might require that much patience or restraint, two things he was pretty much out of, at the moment. So, all the little details, things like slicing onions, hunting up pickles, toasting rolls or waiting for the friggin' ketchup to drip out of the bottle, were flat out not gonna happen. They were all completely beyond his abilities to deal with. Not to mention inquiring as to how Deirdre might want her meat cooked.

He didn't want to inquire about that. He didn't want to inquire about anything. So, with his plans to make hamburgers gone to hell, like everything else in his life it seemed, he did what he always did when things got tough. He wussed out. He turned to his family for assistance.

A batch of his mother's tomato sauce, one of several with which she'd stocked his freezer, simmered in the smaller of his two saucepans, while the water for pasta bubbled away in the other. He paused in his massacre of the meat to add some salt and a pound of rotelli to the water, then went back on the attack. Not that the beef needed to be further subdued, but he was just so...fucking...pissed...*off!*

He was furious—with the world in general, and with women in particular.

He was angry with Cara for waking him up too early this morning, for filling his mind with all her stupid, lame-brained, half-baked theories, for confusing the hell out of him.

He was angry with Jasmine for being at the center today—when it should have been empty. For being helpful. And cheerful. And too damn smart.

But, first, last and always, he was angry with Deirdre. For being too good of a liar. For dropping that bombshell on him about the dogs. For acting so concerned when he'd gotten upset, for sounding so sincere, looking so sweet. And for the way she thought he could just turn his feelings for her on and off at will, *like I'm some kind of fucking light switch*—that most of all.

Time and again he'd gotten his foolish hopes up, only to have them shot down. Something—the words she'd say, the way she'd act —would make him think the two of them were going somewhere; but the minute he responded– *Wham!* Like a knee to his balls she'd smash his hopes flat. *Take that, sucker! Blam!*

As he mashed at the meat, grease splattered the stove. God, he was pissed! He was angry, horny, miserable and...confused.

What the hell was he doing wrong, all of a sudden? How come nothing he tried seemed to work with her? He never had *that* problem before. [2]All the other girls he'd hooked up with had melted for him, with almost no effort at all; even the ones who'd had a reputation for being cold. Not that there'd been many of those. And they'd all seemed to like sex at least as much as he did, too.

But, shit, what did he know? He'd never even left Oberon for more than a few weeks at a time. Maybe Jasmine was right. Maybe there was just something wrong with the girls he'd been hanging with. Or maybe it was Deirdre who was screwed up.

"Want some help?" she asked, coming up behind him.

He was so angry, he hadn't even heard her come in. As she laid a hand on his back, he flinched away.

"Seth? What's wrong?" She looked surprised by his reaction, maybe even a little hurt.

*She has to be kidding, right*? If anyone should be feeling hurt right now, it was him. "Nothing. Just...don't do that anymore."

Under normal circumstances, or even half an hour ago, he'd have been perfectly happy to let her touch him—as much as she wanted.

For two whole years it he'd daydreamed endlessly about it: in bed, in the shower, when he was with other girls. In vivid detail he'd imagine how it would to feel if he were with Deirdre instead, if it were her hands touching, stroking, squeezing him...

But, now, when she was here and making him crazy? When she'd just gotten through admitting that she hadn't thought of him at all while she was gone? When she'd, only a few minutes earlier, been complaining that he was rushing her? And when she wouldn't let him touch her back? Now, having her touch him was hell.

"Sorry," she mumbled biting her lip, looking like, any minute, she might start bawling. And, oh, fuck, no. He couldn't deal with that tonight, either.

He grabbed a large bowl from one of the cabinets and shoved it into her hands. "Here. Why don't you make us a salad, okay?"

"Okay." She took the bowl and headed for the refrigerator. "I thought you said you were making hamburgers?"

"Yeah. I changed my mind." He turned off the heat under the pan and added the mostly-pureed meat to the sauce. "I didn't feel like it. We're having spaghetti."

"Oh. Well, whatever it is, it sure smells good. Did you just make that sauce?"

"What?" He turned to stare at her in disbelief. "In ten minutes? Of course not. Don't you know it takes *hours* for sauce to cook?"

Deirdre shrugged. "No, not really. I just always used the stuff that comes out of jars."

Of course she did. Shaking his head in disgust, Seth turned back to the stove. He thought briefly about offering to teach her to cook, but then changed his mind. He didn't want to teach her anything. He didn't even want to talk to her at this point. The pool house had never seemed as small or as crowded as it did this minute. He had no idea how he was going to get through the night. Especially if it was anything like last night.

"This is delicious," Deirdre murmured several minutes later in an attempt to break through the silence that had gripped them. But, despite the quiet, her voice sounded low and uncertain, even to her own ears.

Seth shrugged and kept on shoveling pasta into his mouth. He'd been glum and uncommunicative ever since she'd come in from the pool. His attitude was doing nothing to help settle Deirdre's nerves. Here she was, attempting to gear herself up to take the plunge; preparing to put her hopes and fears on the line, to put her heart, her future, her *self*, in Seth's hands, the least he could do was say thank you when she paid him a compliment.

If he kept this up, she was going to change her mind again. The thought was surprisingly depressing. She picked moodily at her food.

Finally, his plate empty, Seth leaned back in his seat and glared at her. "You know, if you don't like it, you can just say so. You don't have to lie about it."

Lie? Deirdre's mouth dropped open. "I'm not lying. I said it was good and I meant it."

Seth stared meaningfully at her plate. "Yeah, it looks like it."

Deirdre pushed it away. "I guess I'm just not hungry."

Seth's gaze softened. "There's still some meat left. Do you want me to make you a burger?"

She shook her head. "No, thank you." Her parents had been on-and-off vegans for years, so red meat had never been high on her list of favorites. That wasn't the issue at the moment, however. The fluttering in her stomach had gotten so bad she doubted she could eat anything at all.

"Well, what *do* you want?" Seth asked sounding plaintive.Sensing an opportunity, Deirdre took a deep breath, opened her mouth...and promptly chickened out again. "Something to drink, maybe?"

Alcohol was rumored to make people's clothes fall off, wasn't it? If she could just relax a little bit–

Seth glanced at her untouched glass of water. "That's not from the tap, you know."

"I know. Don't you have anything else?"

"Well, sure. Same as before. Soda. Tea. You don't want milk, do you?"

Deirdre shook her head.

Seth sighed. "I think there's some juice in the freezer. You want me to make that?"

"Anything else?""Like what?"

"I dunno. Wine, beer...tequila, maybe?" She smiled a little as she said the last word. If she was remembering correctly, tequila was what he'd been drinking that night on the beach, the first time he'd kissed her. He'd been drunk and sweetly goofy and he couldn't take his eyes off her.

Come to think of it, maybe they *both* should have a drink... Or not.

"Are you kidding me?" Seth scowled. "No. I've got nothing like that here."

Deirdre felt herself starting to blush. "H-how come?" she asked, trying to make a joke of it. "This is a winery, isn't it?"

"Because I don't drink, that's why."

Now who was lying? "Oh, yeah? What about Sunday?"

Seth scowled harder. "That was a mistake."

Deirdre nodded. It was hard to argue with that. They stared at each other unhappily for a moment, then a frown creased Seth's brow. "Is that why–" he began, then he stopped again.

"What?" she prompted.He shook his head. "Nothing. Never mind."

He glanced at her plate, and then at her face. "You know," he said gently, leaning towards her, "if you have some kind of problem, with drinking, or, or anything..."

A problem? Deirdre's face flamed. This conversation was going nowhere that she'd imagined. "I don't."

"Well, if, if you did...I know some people who could maybe help you."

"You're not my brother, Seth," she snapped, too annoyed to think about what she was saying. "So, quit acting like it."

The softness disappeared from his face, he sat back in his seat like he'd been shot. "I can't believe you went there."

To be honest, she couldn't either. Embarrassed, Deirdre dropped her gaze. Shit. She hadn't even meant it that way. She was just angry at him for acting so superior.

"And for the record? Just so you know, my father would *never* cheat on my mother."

Deirdre shrugged. "Yeah, well, that's not what my mother told me."

"Your mother was a troublemaking bitch," Seth growled. "I remember her. She was a kook."

Deirdre clenched her fists and blinked back tears. Paige might have been a kook, but she was *her* kook. As a child, Deirdre had idolized her. And even though there were times when she hated Paige—for being unreliable and a liar, for the stories she'd told her, the plans she'd made—still her death was a blow from which she'd yet to recover. Stung, she snapped at him. "You just don't like *anyone*, do you?"

Seth's eyes widened. "What are you talking about? Of course, I do. I like...I like lots of people."

"Oh, really?" Deirdre replied. "Who? You told me Jasmine was a friend and then you lied to her about my name, and what we were doing there. You said you and Eric were friends—and just look how well that worked out! And then there's poor Rafe–"

"Hey! Rafe's *your* friend, not mine. I just think it's weird the way he only shows up when you're in town."

"So, it's a coincidence. What's so weird about that? It's like I said this morning. You don't trust him."

"Why should I?" Seth challenged. "In fact, why should *you*? You keep telling me someone's trying to kill you and you don't know who it is, well, why shouldn't it be him?"

"Because." She stared at him, stymied, unable to account for the certainty she felt. She couldn't explain why it was, but she knew, instinctively, that she could trust Rafe. "I just trust him, that's all. He's my friend."

"That's it." Seth pushed away from the table and got up. "I can't listen to any more of this."

"Where are you going?" Deirdre asked as he headed for the door.

"Over to the inn."

Deirdre ran to the door. "Going to see Cara?" she called after him.

"Might as well."

"So, do you trust *her*?"

For an instant, Seth's steps slowed. "Yeah," he replied, sounding vaguely surprised. "Yeah, actually, I do."

Something cold and wet brushed Deirdre's ankle. She looked down and saw one of the dogs sniffing at her leg. A shudder ran through her. Shit. She'd forgotten all about them. She backed away slowly, relieved when the dog didn't seem interested in following.

Just the same, she didn't feel like taking chances. She'd lock herself in the bedroom and wait until Seth got back. However long that might take.

# 14

*Did he trust Cara*? Deirdre's question, and his own response, had caught Seth completely by surprise. So much, in fact, that it continued to occupy his mind as he knocked at the inn's back door and waited for a reply.

It seemed seriously wacky that he should count Cara as someone he trusted when, for most of the time he'd known her, he'd have ranked her as one of the most *un*trustworthy people he'd ever met.

If he'd been asked to give a rating, he'd have given her low scores in every category but one: Looking out for her own self interests. That was one subject where she was totally trustworthy. In fact, she excelled at it.

But things had changed in the course of the last year. Maybe he'd just gotten to know her better, or maybe it was something else entirely. Because now, as he'd only just discovered, she was one of the few people he *did* trust.

She still hadn't answered the door though, so he tried the handle. And, finding it unlocked, he let himself in.

Another of the things he liked about Cara was the way she always laid things on the line. Yeah, it was true the trait had annoyed him plenty in the past, but the nice part of it was that he knew just where he stood with her. How many others could he say that about? Other than his parents? No one.

He finally found her in the inn's sitting room, face down on the red leather sofa, crying her eyes out."Hey. What's wrong?" he asked, noting the open wine bottle on the coffee table. *Great, Sinead'll love this. Maybe I should call Deirdre over and set her up with a glass as well.*

"I-I'm lonely," Cara sobbed.

"Yeah, I know what you mean." Seth seated himself in a chair on her right, where she'd be able to see him. "Join the club."

It had occurred to him at dinner that if he took Deirdre's erratic mood swings into account, factored in her perpetual lack of appetite and added them both to her request for alcohol, then shit. Was she addicted too? And was it Eric who'd gotten her started, just like he'd done with Cara?

"What?" Cara had lifted her head and was staring at him, open-mouthed. "Se-*eth*! No. What the hell? You mean you and that crazy chick aren't doing it *yet*?"

From anyone else the question would probably have sounded rude. He shook his head. "Nope."

Improbably, Cara began to cry again, even louder than before.

"Now what's wrong?" Seth was startled into asking.

"I wish I could fuck you. We could do it in the pool, right under her nose. That would show her, wouldn't it?"

"Uh, yeah." It would show her something, all right. What, he had no idea. "But, that's okay—really. I appreciate the thought, but—"

Cara shook her head. "No, it's *not* okay. 'Cause I-I c-can't. You know I can't."

"I know," Seth answered quietly.

"And, I want to, you know? I miss it. I really *miss* sex."

"Yeah." Seth sighed. And wasn't this what he'd just been thinking about earlier? This was exactly the attitude he'd come to expect from girls. How come Deirdre couldn't feel this way?

"But, come on," he told her. "It's only been a few months. Give yourself a little more time. I'm sure you'll get over this touching thing soon, and then you'll have lots of guys, right?"

Cara continued sobbing. "I don't want lots of guys. Just L-L-Liam."

"Yeah, so? What's the problem? He likes you, doesn't he?"

Cara shook her head. "Not like that. We're j-just f-friends."

"Oh." Well, that sucked. Seth tried to imagine how he'd feel if Deirdre told him she just wanted to be friends. It wouldn't ever stop him from trying to change her mind, that was for sure.

"But, you know, I'm not so sure you're right about that," he said. "I saw him at the hospital the night you were attacked. He was super upset. I think he likes you more than you think he does."

She shook her head. "No. That was just guilt. He thinks it was his fault Gregg went after me the way he did."

Seth sat up straighter. This was something he hadn't heard before. "Well, was it?"

"Se-*eth!*" Cara's whine had a tone that made rusted hinges sound soothing. "I don't *know*!"

"Right. You're right. I know that." Seth settled back in his seat, wondering how long this crying jag would last. With Cara, you just couldn't tell. Especially since his gaze had just discovered a second wine bottle that had rolled beneath the coffee table. "And, what are you doing taking Sinead's wine for? Do you know how pissed she's gonna be about this? Besides, when's drinking ever helped anyone feel less lonely?"

She swung her feet to the floor and sat up. "That's not why I'm drinking," she said, pouting just a little.

"Oh, it's not?"

"Mm-mm. I'm celebrating."

"You're what?"

"It's my birthday. You weren't going to remember were you?"

"No, I– uh..." He shook his head sadly. With so much going on, how could he remember everything? Still, he felt bad. He'd meant to remember. He'd thought about it only this past weekend. But then... "Hey, wait a minute. Your birthday's *today*?"

"Okay, tomorrow, actually."

Seth frowned. "You're starting the party a little early, don'cha think?"

Cara shrugged. "Not really. Day starts at midnight, right?"

"Yeah. It's not midnight, though. So what's your point?"

She giggled suddenly. "Well, it has to be midnight *somewhere*." As she started to reach for her glass he leaned in quick and slid it out of reach.

"Cara, stop it. Don't screw things up. And don't screw Sinead, either. She gave you a chance. She trusted you."

Slowly, Cara sat back. She folded her arms across her chest. Tears tracked slowly down her cheeks. "I know. But...what does it matter if, if..." After a moment a worried frown appeared on her face. "Do you really think she'll fire me?" she asked in a very tiny voice.

"Fire *you*?" Seth propped his feet up on the table and snorted. "Nah. But she's for sure gonna kick *my* butt out of here this time."

She looked startled. "You? Why?"

"Well, sure. Think about it," he said, thinking about it himself and getting even more depressed. "She doesn't know about your history with drugs and stuff, but she knows all about mine. Who d'you think she's gonna think took 'em? Me. That's who." And coming right on the heels of Monday's promise that he'd stay sober? Of course she'd kick him out. And he'd be back in hell. Just fucking perfect.

A faintly cautious look had crept into Cara's expression. "You didn't tell her about that when you talked her into giving me this job?"

Seth shrugged. "I don't know what I would have said if she'd asked, because you're both my friends, but, luckily, the subject never came up. Besides, *I* didn't talk her into hiring you. The first I heard about it was when you asked me to help you move in here."

Cara's look changed to startled. "But, wasn't it your idea?"

He shook his head. "Nope. 'Fraid not."

"But, but...then why–?"

He smiled at her surprise. "I guess, when she got to know you, she figured you'd be good at it. Looks like she was right, huh?"

Seth's grin dissolved as Cara's face turned stricken. "Hey, that wasn't sarcasm, all right? I wasn't talking about tonight; I meant in general."

She nodded absently, and continued to stare at the wine bottle as if it were a live snake.

"Look, I knew you were feeling stuck in the hospital. Everyone was acting like a dick and no one seemed to care if you found a place to stay, or not. I asked my parents if you could move into our house, but that would have meant you'd be sharing a room with my sister and my mom wasn't too chill with that."

Cara shrugged. "She doesn't trust me after what I did last year. I can't really blame her for that."[1]

His mother didn't like Cara for a whole lot of reasons, none of which Seth felt like discussing. "Well, I could probably have talked her into it, but I knew Sinead had just renovated the pool house, so I told her if she'd let you stay there 'til you got back on your feet that I'd landscape the terrace for her.

"I told her I could talk my father into giving her the plants and supplies at cost and that I'd do all the labor myself and wouldn't charge her for any of it. She went for it, and that was that. But, I didn't do anything about a job. I didn't even think of it."

"You did all that for *me*?" Cara asked, and the quaver in her voice made him want to squirm. He wasn't trying to be a hero, or anything. It had just seemed like the right thing to do.

"S'okay, I like landscaping, you know? Besides it kept me away from my parents' house, too. So it was all good."

"I could kiss you," she told him, and then, because he knew she couldn't, he grinned and said, "Careful. I might take you up on that someday."

To his surprise she shook her head. "Nope." She folded her legs under her and gazed at him primly. "If I ever get better, I'm changing my game. I'm gonna be one hundred per cent faithful."

Now, that was something he never thought he'd hear. He studied her with interest. "You mean to Liam?"

Her gaze faltered. "Mm. Or, you know, whoever," she mumbled unconvincingly.Seth took his feet off the coffee table and sat up.

"Look, have you told him how you feel?"

She shook her head.

"No?" So much for lay-it-on-the-line Cara. "Well, how come? You never had any trouble telling *me* how you felt, did you?"

An unexpected blush climbed Cara's cheeks. "That was different."

"Different how?"

"Just different, okay?" she said, getting excited.

"Okay. Chill." He gazed at her curiously. Obviously a change of subject was in order. "So tell me what you have planned for your big day?"

She shrugged. "Nothing really."

"What? You give me crap for not remembering and now you're saying this," he gestured at the wine bottles, "is all you're doing to celebrate?"

Cara sighed. "Well, I did order a cake. One of those really fancy ones from the bakery downtown? But that's about it."

"Oh." Seth studied her thoughtfully. Considering how disappointed she'd been acting all night, especially when the subject of a certain, dickhead cop came up, he'd bet anything she'd planned to invite Liam over to eat it with her. Either he'd turned her down, or she'd chickened out and hadn't asked him. Either way it had to suck, buying a cake like that and then having no one to help you eat it.

"Well, good. That's one of the reasons I came over here tonight. I wanted to ask you what you wanted for dinner. I figured I'd cook you something special after work tomorrow, and we could maybe eat it out on the terrace, or something. But I don't really bake."

Cara's eyes narrowed suspiciously. "You said you forgot it was my birthday."

"Well, yeah, that's 'cause you got me so confused I thought you meant *today* was your birthday and I'd missed it."

She continued to stare at him. "You really didn't forget?"

"Uh-uh," he lied, smiling innocently.

Finally, she shrugged. "Wow. Thanks. Th-that'd be nice."

"So? What d'you want?"

She shrugged again. "I don't know. You know I don't know much about food. Why don't you just pick something, okay?"

Seth nodded. "Sure, I can do that."

"And...instead of the terrace...can we eat in here?"

"Here?" Perplexed, he glanced around the sitting room.

"No, I mean in the dining room. With the good dishes and all?"

"Well, yeah, if you want. I guess that'd be okay."

"You can invite that girl—what's her name?""Who—you mean, Deirdre? Okay, sure. I could do that."

Cara's eyelids were starting to droop. "You look tired," Seth observed. "D'you want me to leave now?"

"Not yet," she murmured snuggling into the corner of the couch.

Seth felt a stab of pity. "Want me to stay 'til you fall asleep?"

Eyes closed, she nodded. "Yes, please."

It didn't take very long. While he waited, Seth occupied the time by reaching his hand slowly, slowly, slowly toward Cara's head. By the time his finger tips grazed the surface of one bright red curl, Cara was asleep.

He hated the idea of leaving her here, however. He'd slept on this couch once himself. It hadn't been comfortable. Besides, he had a suspicion that her phobia was more about consciousness than about contact. So, he opened the door to the inn's closest bedroom, turned down the covers on the bed closest to the door, then went back and got Cara.

As he'd hoped, she didn't wake and she didn't freak out, she didn't do anything but snuggle slightly into his arms.

He put her down on the bed and covered her up. The second bed beckoned invitingly. It had to be more comfortable than the couch in the pool house, and his odds of sleeping through the night would be greatly improved if he could put even a little distance between himself and Deirdre.

It took less than a minute to decide. He turned off the light, shucked out of his clothes and was asleep within seconds.

From across the terrace, Deirdre watched as the lights in the inn went out. She blew out the candles she'd lit at either side of the bed, then she scooped Snowball up and cuddled her close. She tried not to think about what might be happening over at the inn, tried not to feel hurt or abandoned. Or betrayed. She curled up on her side and closed her eyes and just tried really hard not to feel anything at all.

# 15

The pounding of someone's fist on the inn's front door, early the next morning, roused Seth from a pleasant sleep. He was halfway across the foyer before it occurred to him that answering the door in his underwear might not be the best idea in the world, and certainly *not* what Sinead would have wanted.

By then, however, it was too late to go back and dress. Whoever was on the other side of the frosted glass panel would have already seen him coming.

He pulled open the door and immediately had to shield his eyes against the glint of sunlight on Mylar balloons.

"Seth..." Liam stared at him, his expression one of blank surprise.

"Hey. Whazzup?" Seth inquired, still squinting. Besides the balloons, the cop was also carrying a big bouquet of flowers. *Nice.*

"Is Cara here?"

Seth nodded back toward the bedroom from which he'd just come. "Yeah, sure. She's still asleep. You want me to wake her?"

Liam glanced toward the bedroom. "N-no, that's okay. I..."

"Well, you wanna come in and wait then?"

"No, I– Here." Liam thrust the balloons at Seth. "Just give her these." He pulled something from the bouquet and then shoved the flowers at him, too. "And...tell her happy birthday."

Then he turned and hurried across the porch and down the path.Seth felt a rush of anger. *What's this bullshit all about? He brings her all this stuff and then just...leaves?*

He took a couple of quick steps out onto the porch. "Hey! Wait a minute."

Liam stopped and pivoted to face him. "Yes? What is it?"

Seth indicated the balloons and flowers. "So, what's the deal with you two, anyway? I mean, do you like her, or what?"

Liam's gaze traveled to the inn and back to Seth's face. "Of course I like her."

"Like, how much? A lot?"

Liam's mouth tightened. He nodded. "Yes. A lot. Okay?"

Seth smiled in satisfaction. "Thought so."

Liam nodded again, turned and left. Seth went back inside. He still thought it was bogus that the cop couldn't be bothered waiting until Cara woke up, but maybe he was on his way to work and didn't have time to stay. At least he'd remembered her birthday. And at least he'd admitted that he liked her more than Cara thought he did. That had to count for something.

Seth found a vase for the flowers, and then he took some time arranging them and the balloons on the dining room table. When he was done, he wrote a note:

*Happy Birthday from your 'friend'. See? What did I tell you? Seth*

Finally, he went back to the bedroom. Cara was still asleep. As he pulled his clothes on, he took a wistful look at the bed where he'd been sleeping. He'd been having such a good dream, all about kissing Deirdre. It would be nice to go back and get a little more of that. But, the reality would be even nicer.

LIAM'S HEART was filled with disappointment as he drove back to town. This was *not* how he'd envisioned the day turning out. He'd thought that, by now, he'd have Cara in his arms. That he'd be kissing her again—finally—for the first time in months. *Really* kissing her, with no reservations, nothing held back. Not like before when the timing had always been wrong.

*So, do you like her*, Seth had asked. Even though the question burned it had felt good to admit the truth. He'd been hiding his feelings for too long. Liam supposed he should have assured Seth that he understood how things were; that he'd respect their relationship, keep his distance, stay out of their way.

But the truth was, that wouldn't have been the truth. The truth was...he didn't know what he was going to do now. Other than to go see Chenoa and get a little energy work done, get his chakras balanced and his equilibrium restored. After that, he'd think about what to do next. Just as soon as the pain in his chest receded.

DEIRDRE WAS in the kitchen when Seth returned to the pool house. She leveled a frosty glare in his direction. "Next time you take off like that, take your dogs with you. I felt like a prisoner in here last night. I was afraid to move."

"Sorry." Seth glanced curiously around the room. All four dogs were sprawled, dozing on the floor. "You look like you're doing all right now."

Deirdre indicated four bowls lined up along the wall. "I fed them the leftover spaghetti. I figured if they had real food maybe they wouldn't be looking quite so much like they wanted to eat me instead."

Seth stifled the annoyance that always came with learning that someone had messed with his dogs' diets. What was more important, right now, was that Deirdre was obviously growing more comfortable with them.

Grinning, he crossed to where she was viciously beating eggs. "I guess you might want to give me some real food too, then," he suggested, bending to kiss her neck.

"Stop that." Eyes blazing, she wrenched herself away from him. "What do you think you're doing? You come here—right out of some other girl's bed—and think you can just start kissing me?"

She glared at him angrily, but Seth was too surprised to answer. After a minute, Deirdre added, "Well, you can't. Maybe these other girls don't mind how you treat them, but I won't be played like that. You're going to have to choose between us."

Seth felt his eyes widen. "No, I won't." He grinned at the shocked expression on her face. "I didn't sleep with Cara last night. I didn't even kiss her. And I don't have any plans to. We're just friends. I told you that."

"Friends with benefits, you mean?" Deirdre asked, chin angled up at him. "I know you've slept with her. I could tell just by looking at you two."

Seth considered the idea. It wasn't how he'd ever thought of the sex he'd had with Cara. He'd pretty much figured they were both just using each other. Friends with benefits sounded...friendlier, somehow. Nicer.

"Yeah, maybe," he said, feeling instantly better about a situation he'd never felt particularly good about. "Once. But that's over now."

Deirdre gazed at him doubtfully as he backed her into the corner between the kitchen sink and the stove. "You were there all night."

Seth nodded. "The inn's full of beds, all of them empty, and I didn't feel like sleeping on that couch again."

"I thought she wouldn't let anyone stay there? How'd you get her to change her mind?"

"I didn't. I just waited until she fell asleep." Seth smiled as he crowded closer. "Besides, I think you're the one who has to choose."

"Choose what?" she asked, sounding breathless.

He tired to kiss her but she squirmed away."What you want. What we're doing here. Whether or not you're gonna let me have you."

"That's a good question." Deirdre straight armed him in the chest. "What *are* we doing here, Seth? I can't just hide out here forever, you know."

"It's not forever," Seth answered, giving up. He pulled a bowl from the cabinet and started to fix himself some cereal. "Just a few more days."

"And what's that gonna do?"

"Look, my parents will be back by Saturday, right?" He took his bowl and sat down at the breakfast bar. "And my cousin Nick, too. I figure they'll know how to deal with the police, how to get them off your tail and all. In the meantime, it would be really good if we could figure out who's trying to kill you."

"I don't know why anyone would want to kill me," Deirdre said, apparently giving up her own attempts at breakfast and coming to sit beside him. "The idea is crazy. Maybe I was just imagining things."

Seth stopped eating and looked at her. "Dee, someone blew up your apartment. That's more than imaginary."

"I know," she moaned, sinking her head in her hands. "It's just...so incredible."

"You know, if it was an accident or something...well, that would be bad, but we could still fix things. But, you have to tell me."

"An accident?" Deirdre raised her head and stared at him. "You think *I* did it?"

"It was either you or someone else," Seth pointed out gently.

"It wasn't me," she insisted. Seth nodded, feeling almost convinced. "Okay, so that leaves us back where we started. Who knew you were there? Who'd want to hurt you?"

Deirdre's hands were fisted on the counter. "No one."

"What about your father?"

"My father?" Color flared on her cheeks. "Impossible. Besides, how many times do I have to tell you? I don't know who he is. So, how could he be trying to kill me? And, and *why*?"

Seth shrugged. "I dunno. Maybe if he was a psycho or something."

"Seth! Do you have any idea how awful that would be?"

She looked so appalled that Seth didn't have the heart to continue questioning her. He threw an arm around her shoulders and kissed her cheek. "Look, don't worry about it. We'll leave it for the po to figure out, all right? They've got to be good for something. In the meantime, before I forget, you're invited to a birthday party tonight."

Deirdre looked bemused. "A birthday party? What are you talking about?"

"It's Cara's birthday today. She's ordered a fancy cake and I'm cooking dinner for her over at the inn. She invited you specially."

Deirdre's eyebrows rose. "She did?"

"Yup." Seth grinned. "See? She's not so bad once you get to know her."

"I guess," she replied, sounding none too sure.

"I have to go walk the dogs now," Seth told her as he got up. He carried his bowl back into the kitchen and put it in the dishwasher. "Do you want to get dressed and come with me?"

Deirdre shook her head. "I think I'll stay here and do some laundry."

"Okay." It wasn't exactly what he'd wanted, but perhaps it was better this way. "But, just in case, I'm gonna leave my dogs here with orders not to let anyone in," he told her as he crossed back to the bar where she was seated. "You don't have to be afraid of them. They're here to protect you."Deirdre nodded. "Okay," she answered faintly.

He bent and kissed her cheek again. "Great. I'll see you later then."

Deirdre sat very still after Seth left, too terrified to move, her thoughts a whirlwind of confusion. The idea that she needed protection from some crazy person who wanted to kill her was even scarier than the realization that she'd be stuck here for most of the day with the dogs trailing her every move.

Worse yet was the reminder—which she *hadn't* needed—that Seth still didn't completely trust her.

But worst of all was the issue she'd managed to deflect—for the moment. *Are you gonna let me have you*? Oh, how she wished she knew the answer to that. She'd never known it was possible to want something and to fear it in almost equal proportions until now.

She knew it was unlikely that making love with Seth would be as horrible as her first time. Certainly it couldn't hurt as much. But that one experience had left her feeling so violated, uncared for, misused. If sleeping with Seth left her feeling the same way, how would she bear it?

Cara fingered the flowers Seth had left for her. When she'd first seen them, she'd had the crazy hope– But Seth's note had put that to rest.

*From your friend.*

Well, Seth *was* her friend. Hadn't he proved that over and over again? Possibly the only real friend she'd ever had.

*See? What did I tell you*?

He'd told her he hadn't forgotten her birthday, and obviously, he'd been telling the truth. He couldn't have gotten them that morning, there wouldn't have been time. That meant he must have brought the flowers and balloons home with him last night, and sneaked them in here, sometime after she'd gone to sleep.

It was a lovely, thoughtful gesture, and it was wrong of her to feel disappointed, to wish they were from someone else. Someone like Liam.

But, all the same, she did.*Why don't you tell him how you feel*? Seth had asked last night, but she couldn't. If there was one thing she'd learned in the last year, it was that you shouldn't sell yourself too cheaply to the people you loved.

That was a good way to get hurt. That was a perfect way to destroy yourself.

It made very little difference what you did with people you didn't care that much about, but with the people who mattered—it made all the difference in the world, what you did to them, what they did to you.

Thanks to Gregg, Liam had seen far too much of her. He'd seen her exposed, vulnerable, humiliated. She'd offered herself to him and he'd rejected her. Now, she couldn't let him have anything more. Not unless he was willing to give her something in return. Something more than friendship. A whole lot more.

Sniffling, Cara wiped away the stupid tears that insisted on falling down her cheeks. What did she have to cry about anyway? Today was her birthday and she'd be celebrating tonight with a great cake and dinner and friends. And while it might not be the best scenario she could have imagined, it wasn't the worst one, either.

# 16

"Ah, there's the birthday girl," Chenoa called out cheerily when Cara entered the bakery later that morning. "I was wondering when you'd turn up."

"I'm not too early am I?" Cara asked as she approached the counter.

"Not at all." Smiling brightly, Chenoa slid a cake onto the counter. "So? Whaddaya think?"

Cara gasped in admiration. "It's beautiful."The round cake had been covered with a flawlessly smooth surface, just slightly shiny, pale blue flecked with brown, like a robin's egg. A string of pearls ran around the top edge and all along the side were feathers; soft plumes in shades of apricot, peach and white."Are those real?" Cara asked reaching out gingerly to touch one.

Chenoa grinned. "Nope. It's all edible. The feathers are made of spun sugar. The pearls are white chocolate dusted with an iridescent baker's food coloring powder that I–" She broke off chuckling. "Probably more than you wanted to know, right? Sorry. I always tend to get carried away when I start talking shop."

Cara still couldn't take her eyes from the cake. "No, that's okay. It's wonderful."

"Glad you like it. There's just one thing missing." Chenoa indicated the blank, ivory disk set into the top of the cake. "You never told me what name you wanted on it."

"It's Cara." The voice came from behind her, Cara stiffened at the sound. *Liam*. She turned in time to see him rise from his place at one of the tables near the window—to the left of the door, where she hadn't thought to look.

"Her name's Cara," Liam repeated, smiling as he walked toward them. Cara blushed, embarrassed that she'd walked right past him without noticing. "Happy birthday." Liam reached out a hand toward her shoulder.

Cara flinched away involuntarily. "Thanks."As Liam's hand dropped to his side Cara cringed inside at the look of disappointment that crossed his face. "Sorry," she mumbled, cheeks flaming.

"Cara. Is that with a C or a K?" Chenoa asked.

"With a C," Liam replied, smiling again, more sadly this time. "Just like caramel."

"Ahh, I gotcha." Chenoa whisked the cake away. "Just give me a sec."

"So, the big eighteen, huh? What do you have planned for the day?" Liam asked.

Cara shrugged. "Not too much. The cake. And my friend is cooking me dinner."

"You mean Seth?"

Cara's eyes widened. "Yeah. How'd you know?"

Liam grimaced. "Lucky guess. So, dinner? That's it?"

"Well, yeah." Cara felt herself blushing once again. It had seemed like a nice way to celebrate. Better than she'd hoped for. But now–

An awkward silence settled between them, broken only when Chenoa slid the cake, all boxed up and ready, back onto the counter. "Okay, all done."

Grateful, Cara fished in her bag for her checkbook. "How much do I owe you?"

"Put your money away," Liam said suddenly, moving the cake away from her. "You're not paying for this cake."

She looked at him in surprise. “But– Yes, I am. I- I have a good job now. I can afford it. What’s the problem?”

“No.” Liam shook his head. “And I don’t care how much money you make. I’m not going to let you buy your own birthday cake, and that’s final. I’ll take care of it.”

Cara stared at him, mortified. He was still thinking of her as a child. Even now. “But, Liam, I–”

“Okay, whoa. Time out,” Chenoa interjected, frowning at them both. “Cara, hon, it’s your birthday. I think if the *usually* charming young man wants to give you a present, it’s okay to let him, all right?”

Feeling miserable, Cara nodded. “Sure.”

“And you.” Chenoa turned to Liam. “Should ask. What do you think you’re doing ordering her around like that? It’s rude.”

Liam nodded, looking shamefaced. “Cara, would you please let me buy this cake for you? I would really like you to have it as a gift. Please?”

Cara nodded again, gulping back a sob.

“Good,” Chenoa said, sliding the cake back toward Cara and handing Liam the bill. “Now that that’s settled, here.” She extended a small, flat package toward Cara. “This is a little something I wanted you to have.”

“Th-thank you,” Cara said as she took reached for it. The package was wrapped in gold colored tissue paper and tied with a thin strip of soft, white leather.

“You can open it now or later,” Chenoa told her. “It’s your choice.

Cara nodded as she started to undo the tie. She opened the wrapping and once again gasped in admiration.

“It’s a dreamcatcher,” Chenoa explained as Cara held it up.

“I know,” Cara answered on a whisper. She’d learned about dreamcatchers in school the previous year. But she’d never seen one as beautiful as this.

“The hoop is made of grapevine,” Chenoa continued. “The stones are turquoise and white quartz, and those feathers at the bottom are flamingo.”

"Flamingo?" Liam glanced at her curiously. "I suppose there's some meaning to that?"

Chenoa smiled. "There's a meaning to everything, Liam. You should know that by now."[1]

Even with only one eye, Cara did not miss the look that passed between them. A look that spoke of intimacy, affection, respect; things she longed for, but never seemed to get.

"Thank you for the present," Cara murmured as she stowed the dreamcatcher carefully in her bag and reached for the box.

"It was my pleasure," Chenoa answered warmly. "And, don't be a stranger, okay? Stop by anytime."

"I will," Cara promised as she turned toward the door.

"Here, let me get that for you." Liam sprinted ahead of her, apparently determined to show Chenoa how well mannered he could be. "Can I walk you to your car?" he asked as he pulled the door open.

Cara shook her head, trying her best to sound adult, independent, capable, strong, and a whole lot of other things she was far from feeling, at the moment. "No, thank you. I can manage on my own."

"Of course you can," Liam murmured, watching as Cara limped away up the sidewalk. He jammed his hands into his pockets and fingered the card he'd torn from her bouquet this morning.

*With all my love, Liam.* That's what he'd written. That's what he'd really wanted to give her today. Not just cakes or flowers or balloons, but all the love his heart could hold. Funny thing was, she didn't appear to want anything from him, at all.

"So, that's her, huh?" Chenoa asked.

Liam turned. "What?"

"The girl from last spring. The one you claimed didn't exist. The one who had you all wound up for months."

Liam sighed. The girl who'd had him so wound up that he'd slept with Chenoa on the rebound. That's what she really meant. A magical evening. One he couldn't stop regretting. He was tempted to lie, to pretend he didn't know what she was talking about. But, while Chenoa wasn't an empath, she could read auras better than anyone he'd ever known. Besides, the least he owed her was the truth."Yeah. That's her."

"And you wouldn't touch her 'cause she was underage. Is that it?"

"Something like that." Liam sighed again. "I'm sorry. I– I should've just dealt with it on my own. I should never have involved you. It was my fault."

"Oh, lighten up." Chenoa shot him an exasperated glare. "You weren't the first one night stand I've had, you know, Liam. And I doubt you'll be the last. If you keep looking so gloomy whenever the subject comes up, I'm gonna think you didn't enjoy it. And then I *will* feel bad."

Liam smiled, feeling not one bit better. "You're really something. D'you know that?"

Chenoa grinned back at him. "I try."

"And I don't know what I would have done if I'd wrecked what we had, if you'd stopped being my friend. I would have hated that."

"Me, too. But it didn't happen. So, can't you please just get over it?"

"I'll try," he promised.

"So, this thing with you and Cara, was this before she got injured, or after?" she asked him after a moment.

"Before."

"What happened to her?" Liam shook his head. "Oh, just a madman tried to kill her, that's all. Stabbed her a bunch of times then nearly beat her to death."

"Tried to. Did someone stop him, or–?"

"Yeah. The kid who's fixing her dinner."

"Ah." Chenoa nodded. "Not you, huh?"

"No," Liam answered. "I was...detained." He'd been beaten, tied up, locked in a basement. None of which assuaged the guilt he felt at having failed her.

"And I bet you still feel real guilty about that, don't you?"

"Of course I feel guilty," Liam snapped. "Why shouldn't I feel guilty? I'm the idiot who set him after her in the first place."

"She doesn't hold it against you, you know."

Liam shrugged. "No? Well, maybe she should."

Chenoa frowned thoughtfully. "So, I don't get it. She's eighteen now. Why weren't you at her door at the crack of dawn this morning to tell her how you feel?"

"I was. Turns out she's living with someone else. The kid who *did* end up saving her. How can I compete with that?"

Chenoa frowned. "Are you sure about that? 'Cause I'm not picking up anything like that from her."

"Yes, I'm sure. I woke him up. She was still asleep. They were sharing a room. What conclusion would you have drawn?"

"But...living with someone? Liam, the girl can't stand to be touched. Surely you noticed?"

Liam laughed harshly. "You mean she can't stand for *me* to touch her, don't you? Yeah, I noticed, all right."

Chenoa shook her head. "No, it's not just you. I picked up on it the other day." She eyed him curiously. "You're an empath. Can't you tell how she feels about you?"

Liam shrugged. "Not really." His feelings for Cara were so strong that, whenever he was around her, they were all the emotions he could sense.

"I wouldn't give up on this, if I were you. I think she really likes you."

*Like*. It was such an insipid word, so far removed from how he wanted her to feel. Still, he'd had enough of this conversation.

"Well, why shouldn't she?" he asked, smiling brightly. "After all, I'm a very likable guy."

"Not that likeable, brah," a voice said from the doorway leading into the kitchen.

Liam grimaced. He recognized Chay's voice even before he was hit by the cold wave of dislike that always emanated from Chenoa's brother. Not that Liam blamed him. Chenoa might be fine with their 'one night stand', but, if so, she was the only one."Time to go," he murmured. Reaching across the counter, he took hold of Chenoa's hand and kissed it. "I'll see you."

"You'd better," Chenoa said as she gave his hand a squeeze.

Liam nodded and fled, before he lost any more of the balance and stability Chenoa had managed to give him.

As the door closed behind Liam, Chenoa turned on her brother. "Chay, what the hell do you think you're doing, frightening away all my customers?"

"Not all," Chay replied as he sauntered into the room, his eyes glued to the front window. "Just the ones who've hurt you."

"Oh, give it up already," Chenoa groaned. "I wasn't that hurt. Besides, it's not like he assaulted me, you know. I wanted it too."

"Doesn't matter. He had no business getting involved with you. He should have stayed away." Chay frowned suddenly. A moment later, he'd picked up his pace and disappeared out the front door. Chenoa stared after him, bemused. When he returned a few minutes later, he was still frowning.

"You know, Chay, instead of worrying about mine, why don't you concentrate on your own love life, for a change."

To her surprise, her brother nodded. "I am, actually."

Chenoa blinked. "Oh. Well, good. I told you months ago that it was time you settled down."

"Maybe you're right," Chay answered. "Maybe I agree with you. But maybe what you and I think doesn't matter, either."

Chenoa stared at him. Her brother was nervous. Her tough, cocky, sure of himself brother was nervous. "Oh, Chay. Relax, huh? You know Erin loves you, what are you so afraid of? She's not gonna turn you down."

Chay looked affronted. "Who says I'm afraid? But, I'm not so sure you're right, either. She was really moody right before she left town."

"Moods." Chenoa shrugged the idea away. "What's that mean? Everyone's got 'em." But she was only half listening anyway. Her mind was already at work designing a cake.

It would be shaped like a Indian wedding vase, decorated in a traditional pattern in shades of chocolate, mocha and vanilla; with a cascade of sugar flowers, all in white.

"What are you thinking about?" Chay asked suspiciously.

Chenoa smiled. "Nothing. Just daydreaming."

"Okay, well, I'll leave you to it, then. I gotta go."

Chenoa watched him leave. She still had no idea what he'd come for, but she was sure there'd been some purpose to it. Like she'd told Liam earlier, everything had a meaning. Just like the dreamcatcher she'd made for Cara.

Grapevine, flamingo, even the stones she'd used, all had to do with healing the heart. And if she'd ever met anyone who'd needed heart healing, Cara was it. The surface wounds were nothing. The real damage that had been done to the girl was deep inside.

Chenoa had a good idea that Liam held the key to that healing, but the two of them were both so steeped in misery, they couldn't see straight. It was a crapshoot whether they'd ever be able to give each other what they so desperately needed.

"Que sera, sera, I guess," she murmured shaking her head, sadly. Then she turned her mind to a happier subject. She had a wedding cake to design.

JACK'S HANDS were clutched so tightly around his car's steering wheel that his knuckles were white. As he drove back from the prison, back from his latest encounter with Gregg, he was shaking inside, although he couldn't decide whether it was fear or fury that he was feeling. Maybe both.

*"I'm disappointed in you, JJ," Gregg had told him, glaring at him from across the table with a look that had Jack thinking the interrogation room had never seemed so cold. "I give you one little task to do, one favor, and you screw it up."*

That motherfucking, slimebag punk, *Jack swore silently as he felt his gut tighten. The bastard had wasted no time in letting Gregg know about Jack's failure. "Look, Gregg, it's just a temporary setback. She'll surface in a few days and then I'll try it again."*

*Gregg shook his head. "You've had too many near misses already, Jack. How accidental is it gonna look if you stage another one? This time, you're gonna have to make her disappear. You're gonna have to find her* before *she surfaces—and then make damn sure she* doesn't. *Is that clear?"*

*"Sure, Gregg, sure. I'll take care of it. But, why are we talking about that? Why don't we discuss more important topics. Like how we can get your sentence reduced."*

*Gregg waved the subject away. "That's not your concern. We'll talk about what* I *want to talk about." He eyed him coldly. "There's something else you've been keeping from me, Jack. Cara. Seems she's been making time with* two *young pricks. I told you to keep an eye on her. How come I have to learn about this from someone else?"*

*Jack's eyes widened. "Two–? Gregg, I swear, I don't know what you're talking about."*

*"Sloppy, Jack. You've gotten very, very sloppy. That's not like you, is it? You've always been so careful, so attentive to detail, so...safe. But, lately?" Gregg shook his head. "Here's what I want you to do for me. The girl needs to be disciplined. I thought I'd fixed her so that no one else would ever want her. Apparently I was wrong. I'm going to get out of here soon, and when I do, she and I are gonna take up right where we left off. Someone needs to tell her that. Someone needs to make sure she understands. She's mine. And I don't want her with anyone else in the meantime. You understand me, Jack?"*

*Jack nodded. He thought the odds of Gregg getting out at all were slim enough.* Soon *was right out of the question. Except...if there was one thing he'd learned, it was never to underestimate his former mentor. It had been hard enough keeping Gregg in prison the first time. Now, even with all the charges lined up against him, who knew what kind of miracle he was capable of pulling off. "What do you want me to do?" he asked, his voice dull.*

*Gregg smiled. "Just what I said. Go out to that inn where she's staying and teach her a lesson."*

*"But, what–"*

*"I don't care what you do," Gregg snapped. "I'm confident you'll think of something...appropriate. Won't you?"*

*Jack nodded again.*

*Silence settled over the room. For a long moment Gregg studied him thoughtfully, while Jack quailed. He had a cold, nasty feeling in the pit of his stomach. Things were out of control and getting rapidly worse. He felt like a rat in a trap. No escape. No reprieve. No way out. He needed to find a way to extricate himself, to distance himself from this whole mess.*

*"You know, JJ, I think you and I may have made the same mistake," Gregg murmured softly.*

*"Mistake?" Jack eyed him questioningly.Gregg smiled. "My brother Glenn. I think we both underestimated the little cocksucker. Seems he was a lot more clever than either of us realized."*

*Jack shook his head. They were back to Glenn again? Not a good sign. But...clever? Glenn was devious, to be sure. But always in a rather straight-forward, simple-minded way, as far as Jack could determine.*

*"Of course, I should have realized that a long time ago," Gregg continued reflectively. "After all, look how long he managed to keep me locked up—with your help, I know."*

*Jack stared at him in alarm. "Gregg, no. I–"*

*Gregg put up a hand. "It's okay. I forgive you, Jack. I know you were just doing what you thought best. Isn't that so?"*

*Again Jack nodded, although he hardly knew what he was agreeing to this time.*

*"Too bad for you, you backed the wrong team. Here. Take a look." Gregg slid an envelope across the table to him. "I think you'll find this interesting."*

*Jack picked the envelope up warily. It contained a thick sheaf of paper. He removed the document, flattened it out and began to read. And, suddenly, he couldn't breathe. His heat skipped nervously in his chest and for a moment he wondered whether he was having a heart attack. The pages in his hand held a record of every fraudulent deal he'd ever made;*

*from the smallest infraction to the largest. It was all there in black and white. Every scheme. Every plan. He looked up at Gregg, horrified.*

*"Keep it," Gregg said kindly. "It's only a copy, after all. I'm sure you'll want to study it at your leisure. I still have the original, of course. Somewhere...safe."*

*Jack folded the papers back up and returned them to their envelope. Then he slipped the envelope into his jacket pocket where it felt like a piece of dry ice, burning a hole in his chest. "What do you want me to do?" he asked quietly.*

*Gregg's pale eyes gleamed brightly. "Oh, nothing we haven't already discussed. You're angry, aren't you Jack? You've been double crossed. All those years you thought you were safe. All those times you thought Glenn was your bitch. Turns out it was the other way around. That's enough to make any man furious. Especially when you consider the consequences."*

*Jack closed his eyes, shuddering in despair. He was going to end up here. Spending his life in prison. Right along with Gregg."Glenn fucked you over," Gregg whispered leaning forward. "But here's your chance at revenge. Take it!"*

*Jack opened his eyes and took a deep breath. "How?"*

*"Kill his daughter. Destroy his only chance at immortality. Fuck the bastard." Gregg leaned back in his chair again and smiled. "Or, if you don't, I'll make you wish you were the one who died three years ago, not Glenn. I promise."*

Now, as Jack approached the city limits, he still didn't have his breathing under control. He was going to kill the girl. There was no hesitation left. No room for any other considerations. It was either her, or himself and he was choosing himself. He just had to find her. And Cara...well, he'd do something to her, too, although he wasn't sure what.

Not that it mattered. He'd do what he could, whatever it took, to dot his "i"s and cross his "t"s and keep Gregg sweet for as long as possible.

Not that he harbored any real hope that Gregg would keep his word. No way, Jose. No, Jack was going to disappear. That was the only way out, at this point. Rio, he thought suddenly, that's where he'd go. He'd been there once, years ago, on vacation. He remembered good food, good nightlife, lots of culture, lots of nearly naked bodies basting on the beach.

It was a big city. An easy place to get lost in. A good place for a fresh start. But, best of all, extraditing someone out of it was exceedingly difficult to do.

"SETH! Long time no see, how're you doing, kiddo?"

Seth was picking out vegetables at his family's produce stand when a familiar, cheery voice greeted him. He looked up, startled. "Uncle Kenny, what are you doing here? I thought you'd gone camping?"

Kenny nodded. "I did. Had to come back early. Staffing problems." He punched his nephew lightly on the arm. "We really could use you around here, you know. When are you gonna decide to come back to work with us?"

"I dunno. I've got my own business now and I just–" He shrugged, not knowing how to continue. He felt torn, confused. Lost.

"Dogwalking. Yeah, I heard about that," Kenny said genially. "How's that working out for you?"

"It's great," Seth replied. "Really. I enjoy it and– I dunno, it's different." *But it's never going to support me,* he thought sadly. Not unless he expanded things a whole lot, hired people to walk more dogs for him, maybe took in dogs to board, now and then. He certainly couldn't do that in his present circumstances.

"And living at the winery. How's that going?"

Again Seth shrugged. "That's great too. But it's only temporary, you know. I'll have to move out soon and...I don't how I'll afford a place big enough for all my dogs."

His uncle nodded. "I hear that."

"So, how's the camping trip going?" Seth asked, desperate to change the subject.

Kenny smiled. "Surprisingly well, actually. You'll be happy to know that your Uncle Joe and your Cousin Nick have finally resolved that stupid feud of theirs."

Well that was something different. "They did? How'd that happen?"

"Joe told Nick that they were family, after all, and life was too short and too uncertain for them to stay away from each other and act like strangers and Nick agreed. 'Course it helped that Joey also admitted he'd been wrong about Scout. Said she was probably the best thing that ever happened to Nick." Kenny winked. "Nick agreed with that as well, and now they're back to being best of buds."

"Mom must be happy," Seth observed.

"Ah, you know our Lucy." Kenny chuckled. "She's taking credit for the whole damn thing."

Seth nodded. That sounded like his mom all right. Except, in this case, she was probably justified. She'd badgered everyone into going. Everyone but him.

*And thank God for that,* he thought, shuddering a little as he considered what might have happened to Deirdre if he hadn't been around to help her.

"Well, here's something for you to think about," Kenny said as they headed for the check stand. "Why don't you move your base of operations out here."

"Here?" Seth glanced around involuntarily. Kenny couldn't mean *here*.

"Out to the canyon," his uncle elaborated. "We've got tons of space and I'm sure your dad would spring for a portable unit to house your business, if you asked him to. That is, if you don't want to use one of the existing buildings. You know we've always got half a dozen sheds that we're not doing anything with."

"I never thought of that," Seth admitted, growing excited. Was it possible? If so, it would solve a whole lot of problems.

"Sure," Kenny continued. "You could put some pens up behind

the building for your dogs, although, to tell you the truth, we could probably use a few guard dogs around the place—especially at night."

"Really?" Seth looked at his uncle in surprise.Kenny shrugged. "Well, it's either that or replace miles and miles of fencing that's getting old. We're having a hell of a problem with deer lately. Not to mention raccoons. Besides, it would solve your housing problem too, wouldn't it?"

"Yeah, it would. I– I'll think about it."

"Well, good." Kenny slapped him on the back. "You do that. Now what's all this for?" He gestured at the basket of produce in Seth's hand. "Don't tell me you're going to eat all that yourself?"

Seth shook his head. "No. A friend of mine is having a birthday. I'm cooking."

"Oh, that's nice. Wish him a happy birthday for me."

"It's a her, actually," Seth answered reflexively.

Kenny's eyes twinkled. "Even better. Now, come on, let's get you bagged up."

"But, I haven't checked out yet," Seth protested.His uncle raised an eyebrow in surprise. "What are you talking about, Seth? You're family. You take what you need. You know that."

Thanks Uncle Kenny," Seth said as he followed his uncle toward the bagging station. Family. Come to think of it, it was kind of a nice thing to depend on after all. And, as his Uncle Joe had said, life was too uncertain to keep your distance from the people who cared about you.

DEIRDRE WAS in the laundry room, just inside the inn's back door, putting her clothes in the dryer when Cara got home. The two girls eyed each other for a long, uncomfortable moment.

Deirdre tried hard not to stare at the scars that laced the other girl's face and arms. Finally, she could stand the silence no longer. "You're Cara, right? Seth said it was okay if I did some laundry here."

Annoyance creased Cara's brow. "Oh, he did, did he?" She studied Deirdre thoughtfully for another minute and then shrugged. "Yeah, whatever," she muttered as she turned and hobbled into the kitchen.

Deirdre set the dryer to run and then followed after her, feeling somewhat hesitant. "So, I hear it's your birthday today?"

Cara turned from the table where she'd just placed the box she'd been carrying, her expression turned suddenly shy. "Yeah. You wanna see my cake?"

"Okay." Deirdre crossed the room to join her. She watched as Cara fumbled with the thin string that tied the box. It seemed her fingers were too stiff to get a purchase on it. Deirdre was tempted to offer to do it herself but, somehow, she doubted the gesture would be appreciated. At last, Cara mastered the tie and pushed open the box's cover with a little flourish. "Ta-da."

"Wow." Deirdre stared in amazement. "Are those feathers real?"

"Uh-uh. I asked that, too. But it's all sugar and chocolate and...oh, I forget what else she said. But you can eat all of it. Isn't it neat?"

"It's fantastic. It's almost too pretty to eat."

"I know," Cara murmured. "Too pretty to eat alone, anyway." She dropped the cover back into place and headed toward the refrigerator. "You want something to drink?"

"All right," Deirdre agreed, somewhat surprised by the offer. "Lemonade? Iced tea? Water..."

"Tea's good."Cara nodded. "Good. Me, too." She took out a pitcher, poured two glasses and then handed one to Deirdre. "So, how'd you and Seth meet, anyway."

Deirdre sighed. She should have known there was more behind the drink than simple hospitality. "I was here a couple of years ago visiting and... Oh, you know, we just... It's a long story," she ended lamely.

A long, sad story with too many parts she didn't want to think about, never mind discuss. Like the reasons why she'd run away, all the many things she'd done wrong, Seth's capture, Eric.

"Hmph." Cara studied her over the rim of her glass. "And so now you're back. For good this time?"

"Sort of." Deirdre shrugged. "I'm going to school at Abraxas. I mean, I will be in September. I moved down early to get used to the place."

"And then someone blew up your apartment? That sucks."

"Yeah." Deirdre sighed again, feeling her mood sink as she thought about it.

Cara shook her head. "I know how that is. I lost all my stuff in a fire last April. You know, all my clothes and, and everything? Funny, isn't it, how you'll be looking for something you want, sometimes for several minutes, before you remember it's gone, you don't have it anymore."

Deirdre knew just what she meant. "Does it get any easier?"

Cara shrugged. "Uh, no. Not so far." She took another sip of tea and then asked, "So was Sunday the first time you and Seth had seen each other again?"

"At the Faire," Deirdre answered in surprise. "Yeah. How'd you know about that?"

"I was there." Cara grinned suddenly. "He really pissed you off good, didn't he?"

Deirdre nodded and took refuge in her own glass. The Faire was yet another topic she didn't want to discuss.

"That's Seth for you," Cara mused. "He's a really great guy, but ya gotta watch out for that temper of his. No telling what he'll say if he gets in a bad enough mood."

"I've noticed," Deirdre replied dryly."Yeah, well, nobody's perfect, right? And he's usually sorry afterwards. But, he'd never hit you or anything, so...that's really not so bad, is it? I mean, if you think about it, he could be a whole lot worse."

Watching as the other girl flexed her stiff fingers, Deirdre had to ask, "How'd you get hurt?"

"See, that's what I'm talking about. The guy I was living with got ticked off about something. Actually, I'm not real sure what happened. My memory got fucked and I lost a few days. But, apparently he was trying to kill me."

"I'm sorry," Deirdre whispered.

Cara shrugged again. "Like I said, it could have been worse. Seth was there. He saved my life that night. He came in with his dogs and chased the bastard away from me."

Deirdre swallowed hard. "That was lucky."

"What was lucky was that it happened at his place. You know, that apartment over his parents' garage, where he used to live? I have no idea why I was there, but, if I'd been anywhere else, I'd probably be dead right now."

Deirdre's hand trembled as she lifted her glass to her lips. The apartment over the garage. No wonder Seth had seemed so freaked when he found her there the other morning. Suddenly, a lot of things were making sense. Sickening sense, but sense all the same.

"Hey, do you mind if we go and sit in the lounge?" Cara asked. "I gotta rest my leg and these chairs in here are hell."

"Sure," Deirdre replied, wondering what she'd gotten herself into. She really hadn't planned on spending the rest of the afternoon here, even though she'd already dressed for dinner, putting on the prettiest of the shirts she'd taken from the Nature Center; a soft knit, powder blue, with little cap sleeves and buttons all down the front.As they passed through the dining room, Deirdre couldn't help noticing the flowers arranged on the table. "Nice flowers," she observed.

"Yeah, aren't they?" Cara responded over her shoulder. "Seth gave me those."

"Really?" Deirdre stopped for a closer look. She felt her mood slip a notch lower. These weren't the type of flowers you would give a friend. They were too big, too extravagant, too...everything. "That was nice of him."

"Yep," Cara agreed as she sank into one of the couches and propped her leg up on the table. "It's like I said. He's a really nice guy...except when he's not."

Deirdre nodded. "Yeah." That was exactly what she was afraid of.

# 17

The girls were giggling together like old friends when Seth arrived back at the inn that evening. Surprised and relieved, he followed the sound of their laughter to the lounge and abruptly lost his temper. "Jesus. Cara– Crap. What the fuck are you doing?" he demanded.

There was an open bottle of wine on the coffee table, once again, and each of the girls held a full glass in her hand. "I thought we talked about this last night? I thought you weren't gonna do this anymore?"

"Oh, just chill!" Cara waved a hand at him dismissively. "What's one bottle more gonna hurt? Anyway—check it—I figured out what we can do. I'm gonna tell Sinead that I took all the wine out of the cooler in the kitchen 'cause I wanted to sort it. From light to dark—you know, like they do at the tastings? I'll tell her I had all the bottles lined up on the floor when you came in with the dogs and startled me. I got up too quick and tripped, 'cause of my bad leg, and four of the bottles got broken."

"Four?" There'd been two bottles last night, one now...what was he missing? His math skills weren't that bad. And neither were hers.

"Or, however many," Cara said with another negligent wave. "I'll tell her she can take the cost of the wine out of my pay, she'll probably say no, and that will be that. And, don't worry, I'll make sure she knows you didn't drink any of them. You just have to back me up about the dogs, 'kay?"

"You mean you want me to lie to her?" he demanded, growing angrier by the second.

"Oh, like you weren't gonna do that already?" Cara was quick to point out. "You were gonna let her think *you* drank them just to keep me from getting fired. How's this any different, other than it's a much better story and no one gets in any trouble?"

"I guess," he muttered, annoyed with how relieved he felt. It was a better story and he didn't want to get kicked out so soon. Still, this was an actual lie. It wasn't just fudging the truth to protect a friend. And it laid the fault on his dogs—who already had enough shit talked about them!

"Do you need help with the cooking?" Deirdre asked, smiling sweetly.

Seth scowled. "No. Why don't you two just...just set the table or something?"

He'd known too many girls who got turned on and horny after a couple of drinks. If Deirdre turned out to be one of those, he'd lose his mind for sure.

He went back to the kitchen and got rice started in the rice cooker. Then he went out to the terrace to fire up the grill. He'd bought strip steak and chicken tenderloins to go with the vegetables his uncle had given him: Japanese eggplants, zucchini, Portobello mushrooms, Visalia onions, teardrop tomatoes, along with four kinds of pepper and two types of Summer squash. Served with the rice and a Thai peanut dipping sauce that was just spicy enough to be interesting, he figured it would make a simple, festive meal.

When he went back to the kitchen to mix up the sauce he could hear the girls murmuring together in the dining room. He supposed he should be happy that they were getting along so well, but it was hard when he had the nasty suspicion that *he* was the topic of much of their whispered conversation.

"OH, WOW, THAT'S SPICY," Deirdre gasped, reaching for her wine and gulping down half the glass. Seth scowled. There was hardly any heat to the dish at all! Was this just another excuse not to eat?

Cara giggled. "I *told* you, didn't I? Seth likes *everything* hot."

Watching the smile that passed between the girls, Seth felt himself flush. Somehow, he didn't think they were talking just about food. "You know, you'd be better off drinking water, if you really want to cool things down," he told Deirdre angrily.

She frowned back at him. "Yeah, and maybe you should have some wine. It might put you in a better mood."

"I told you," he snapped as he shoveled more food in his mouth. "I don't drink."

"Oh, you do, too," she insisted. "Remember that night on the beach, the first time you kissed me? You were drunk then. And sweet and funny– I really miss that."

"Ooh, tell, tell," Cara urged, eyes sparkling.

Seth glowered. Funny? In the year and a half he'd been sober, he'd learned a painful truth. Drunks were never funny; they were just plain stupid.

"Well, I was chilling at the beach with my friends," Deirdre said, leaning closer to Cara and lowering her voice conspiratorially. "When guess who wanders up, with a big bottle of tequila and a big, goofy smile..."

Seth pushed his chair back from the table and got to his feet. "That's it. I'm outta here."

"What?" Cara glanced up at him, startled. "But, you can't! We haven't had the cake yet."

Seth shook his head. "I'm sure you two'll have no trouble dicing it up between you." Just like they'd already done to his ego, his heart, his memories...pretty much everything.

"Well, that sucks," Cara muttered as Seth stalked from the room.

Deirdre nodded. “I know. What the fuck’s his problem?”

To her surprise, Cara frowned at her crossly. “Well, you shouldn’t have teased him about his drinking, for one thing. You know how hard it was for him to stop.”

Deirdre blinked in surprise. “No, I don’t.”

“Huh?” For a moment Cara looked vaguely puzzled, then she shrugged. “Oh. Well, yeah, he had a real problem with it. Even went to rehab. Although I don’t know how he managed that, since, apparently, his folks never knew about it. He’d gotten addicted to meth, or something, and he was using the booze to kill the craving. I don’t know how he got started on that shit, though, ’cause it’s not like he ever did drugs for fun.”

“Oh.” Her appetite gone, Deirdre pushed her plate away. She knew how Seth had gotten addicted. In the two days Eric had held him captive, he’d been shot up numerous times. Eric’s plan was to kill him with an overdose, but he wanted to leave plenty of tracks to make it look like Seth had been using for a while.

“So, when are you gonna give him a break, anyway?” Cara asked.

Puzzled, Deirdre glanced at her. “What do you mean?”

“Well, that’s the other reason he’s so pissy. That cock tease routine of yours has to have him climbing the walls by now.”

“My what? I haven’t–”

“Oh, please.” Cara waved away her protests. “I’ve been watching you guys, you know. Like in the pool and all? The way you turn him on and off– Well, it’s just plain mean.”

Deirdre stared at her in surprise. She felt like she’d just been kicked in the head by Bambi.

“I should hate you, you know,” Cara continued reflectively. “We’d hooked up, Seth and I, I guess it was a little while after you guys met, and I was really into him. But, it didn’t mean dick to him, ’cause he was still so hung up on you.”

“He was?” Deirdre whispered faintly, feeling more confused than ever.

Cara nodded. “Hell, yeah. He even talked about becoming a

priest, at one point, 'cause he was sure you were never coming back and he didn't want anyone else."

Deirdre's legs were shaking as he got up from the table. "I have to go," she muttered as she fled the room.

"Well, that figures," Cara muttered, staring morosely at the ruins of her birthday party. She slid her plate away, put her arms on the table, and for the second night in a row, she wept.

SETH WAS LYING on the couch, surfing though the channels again, when Deirdre joined him in the pool house. He'd taken off his shirt and tossed it over the back of a chair and he was wearing only shorts. His body gleamed in the light of the TV. Deirdre paused just inside the doorway, trying to catch her breath.

"Seth," she murmured, her voice coming out all weird and breathy.

He glanced up at her and scowled. "Go away, Dee. I don't want to talk to you."

The night had turned unexpectedly chilly, she'd grabbed her hoodie from the dryer at the inn before crossing the terrace. Even so, she was shivering. But maybe it wasn't the temperature that caused her to tremble. Maybe it was the frost in his voice. Or maybe it was thinking about the step she was about to take.

Ignoring his rebuff, she crossed to the couch and seated herself on the edge of the coffee table."Remember how we were talking, the other day, about how we didn't think that much about each other these last two years?" she asked.

"You said that," Seth replied, his eyes never straying from the screen. "Not me.""Cara...Cara says that isn't true. She says you thought about me a- a lot."

Seth jerked erect, eyes blazing. "Yeah? Well, Cara talks too much.

She has a fucking, big mouth. Besides that, she's a big, fat liar." He punched the buttons on the remote. Click. Click. Click.

"Yeah, well. See, I was lying too," Deirdre admitted, swallowing hard. "I thought about you all the time."

Seth stilled. He turned to look at her, his eyes unreadable in the dim light.

Deirdre dropped her gaze to her hands which were twisted in her lap. "You asked me a question this morning. About whether I was going to let you have me?" She took a deep breath and raised her eyes to his face. "The answer's yes."

For a moment, Seth just continued to watch her. When he reached for her she jerked away. "No, not here," she said, getting quickly to her feet.

She jumped back half a step as he hurled the remote across the room, fisted his hands in his hair and howled. "Arrggh! Quit doing that!"

"No, I mean, in– in the bedroom," she explained, holding out her hand to him. "Please?"

He glared at her guardedly as he got up from the couch. Then he reluctantly took her hand. She led him across the room to the bedroom. When she opened the door, Snowball jumped from the bed and scurried to hide beneath it.

As Seth closed the door behind them, Deirdre crossed to the nightstand and lit the candles she'd placed there. When she turned back to face him, she found Seth staring at the bed.

"You did this earlier?" he asked, pointing at the flower petals she'd scattered on the covers.

Deirdre nodded as she moved to stand before him. "I've been planning it for a while. I just kept getting, I dunno, scared."

"Oh, no," he murmured as she pushed the hoodie off her shoulders and down her arms. Deirdre clutched at his waist, never noticing the way the fabric bunched on her forearms. "There's nothing to be afraid of," he promised as his fingers went to work on the buttons of her blouse. A moment later, it had joined her jacket.The front clasp of her bra came apart with a snap and as he slid the straps down her arms as well, Deirdre felt her nipples tighten, uncomfortably hard. Then he was pulling her close. As their chests met, skin to skin, she sighed in contentment.

Seth bent his head and kissed her, a mind bending kiss that left her breathless. Next thing she knew, he'd taken hold of her waist and tossed her lightly on the bed. He stripped off her shorts and panties, removed his own clothes as well, and then fell onto the bed beside her.

Only then did Deirdre discover that her hands were pinned to her side."Seth, wait," she gasped, wrenching her mouth away as he tried to kiss her.

"No," he groaned as pain etched his face. "Stop saying that! *Stop. Wait. Slow down.* You don't know what it does to me when you say those things. I'm out of my mind already tonight with wanting you." His eyes bored into hers. He swallowed hard, and she could feel the effort he was making to hold himself still. "Please. We are going to do this, aren't we? It's what you want, too—right?"

She stared at him for a moment, and then nodded.

"Then tell me," he pleaded. "I need to hear you say it. Please. Before I go crazy. Say that you want me, too."

But before she could answer, his mouth found hers again, giving her no chance to speak. Heat spread through her as his hand closed over her breast. *If I say no, will he stop?* she wondered, shaken by the thundering of her heart. *Will he at least slow down and let me catch my breath?*

But even for the sake of breathing, she could not give voice to the lie. "Yes." she whispered as his lips moved to her breast, "Yes, Seth. Yes, yes, yes!"

"How much?" he demanded in a voice almost as ragged as her own. "Tell me."

*How much?* She groaned as her mind tried and failed to find an answer. His lips trailed lower, setting fire to her blood. Denied any other purchase, her hands twisted frantically in the sheets. His hands slid between her legs, gently parted them, and then his tongue licked into her. She gasped. It felt wonderful, fantastic, better than anything she'd ever imagined.

"Tell me!" he repeated, but she could think of nothing beyond his voice vibrating against her skin, the feel of his lips as they closed around her and tugged at her flesh.

"I don't know." The words emerged as a whimper as her mind slid away entirely. She lifted herself against him, silently begging for more.

But he was already lifting his head and pulling away from her. "Not good enough," he moaned as he surged upwards along the length of her body to stare into her face with troubled eyes. "I want you more than anything, *ever*. And it gets worse each time I'm with you. When you tell me I can't have you, or you pull away, or you threaten to shut me out—it's like, it's like you're killing me. Like you've set fire to my soul, or something. It's like- Like this." He reached for one of the candles. The flame went out as he tilted it.

Too late, Deirdre realized his intention. "Seth, no!" she gasped as warm, melted wax splashed in a line from her shoulder to her elbow.

The spent candle hit the floor with a thud, but Seth's lips were already soothing away the heat. When he raised his head, his eyes were bleak. "I burn for you, Deirdre. I want you forever. And, if you let me, I swear I'll love you as long as I draw breath."[1]

SHE DIDN'T ANSWER RIGHT AWAY. She just stared at him, her eyes all wide and solemn. Seth lowered his gaze to her arm. His stomach dropped when he realized what he'd done. He picked the congealed wax away and kissed the still warm skin beneath. Shit. That had been a big mistake. What was wrong with him, that he kept messing up? Oh, God, he'd come so close, and now–He'd frightened her. He'd maybe hurt her. She was already scared; now she'd never feel safe with him. Never let him close again.

His muscles ached with the effort to withhold himself, to keep from plunging hard and fast into her hot, moist body, to keep from taking what he wanted, what he so desperately needed. What he was never going to have, now that he'd fucked things up between them. Again. *Loser!* The silence stretched on and on...Why wasn't she talking? Why couldn't she at least say...something?

*Like what, you moron,* a soft voice inside his head insisted on taunting. *What do you think she's gonna say?*

*Who cares? Anything would be better than this silence. Wouldn't it?*

*Leave. Good bye. Fuck off. Is that what you want to hear? 'Cause that's what she's likely to tell you. You really think that'll be an improvement?*

*No. No, not really.*

He swallowed hard, to keep from crying, to keep from begging for forgiveness. How many times could he say he was sorry in one week anyway? Whatever the limit was, he was sure he'd already exceeded it.

Still she said nothing, and he couldn't bring himself to meet her eyes. Maybe she wasn't ever going to answer, or talk to him again. Maybe she was just waiting for him to go. His muscles were taut with tension. And if he could just figure out some way to get them unlocked, he *would* leave, too. Just get up, get dressed, leave...and never come back. *Never.* He was pretty sure it would take that long before he'd trust himself to get anywhere near her again.

Finally, "Seth," she whispered. Her voice was like an echo from a million miles away.

Slowly he raised his gaze to her face. Her eyes shimmered, tears leaked slowly from the corners. He cringed at the sight. He *had* hurt her, hadn't he? He deserved for her to kick him out.

"Make love to me," she whispered. "Please."

Seth stared at her in surprise, convinced he'd forgotten how to breathe. His head pounded and his lungs felt paralyzed. Love? He wasn't sure he could.

*How can you make love to someone, unless you're in love with them*?

Jasmine had asked him that once. He was beginning to see her point. He'd had a lot of girls in the past two years but, in all that time, he'd loved only Deirdre. And she'd been gone. He'd never done this before.

"I'll try," he murmured, cradling her face in his hands and kissing her softly, determined to show her how gentle he could be.

She giggled suddenly. "You'll what? Try? Well, maybe if you get my hands free, I can help."

Her hands? He glanced at them and winced as he noticed for the first time how entangled her arms were in her clothes. Had he done that? God, he was clumsy. No wonder she thought he needed help. He lifted himself away from her, all ready to set her free, and then stopped.

She was laughing at him? He cocked his head to the side and gazed at her, challengingly. "You know, I think I kind of like things this way. I can do whatever I want, and you'll just have to trust me."

The smile disappeared from her face. Her eyes went wide again, and solemn. Seth closed his own eyes in despair. Oh, shit, shit, shit. He was screwing things up again. Why couldn't he just keep his fucking mouth shut? Would he never learn?

"Deirdre, I'm sorry. I didn't mean it. I–"

"No." She shook her head. "I do trust you, Seth. I do."

They stared at each other for a long, long time. Then he lowered his head and kissed her hard, giving her everything he had. "I thought about you, Dee," he murmured as he once again trailed kisses down her body. "All the time. More than you know. More than anyone knew. Every time– Every other girl I was with, I'd close my eyes and pretend she was you. It was always you I wanted. Only you. Ever."

Deirdre struggled for words, wanting to tell him she'd felt the same way, but his hands were parting her legs once again and the words were lost.

His tongue stroked her clit, and a small mew escaped from her lips. The heat spread fast. By the time he reached into the night table drawer for a condom she was half crazed with desire.

*Please don't hurt, please don't hurt*, she prayed silently as he got himself ready. When he rolled to take her she was trembling. *Please...*

She felt the tip of his cock probe her opening. Once. Twice. She held her breath, hoping. Then he slid inside and she sighed in relief.

There was no pain, no hurt, just a pleasant feeling of fullness. Then he began to move and what was pleasant became incredible.

Wanting more, she dug her heels into the bedding, hoping for better leverage, but the satin comforter was too slick. Still, Seth seemed to know exactly what she needed. He slipped a hand beneath her and tilted her hips up. Now, each thrust hit upon something so good that, before she knew it, she'd come undone, exploding all around him.

Through the spasms, she could feel him take hold of her hips and begin to thrust faster, harder than before. She felt his cock swell inside her. Then he went stiff, his head thrown back, his eyes squeezed shut. A low, satisfied groan erupted from his throat.

When he collapsed against her, she was so overcome with the rightness of it all that she pressed her face against his neck and began to cry.

# 18

The night was chilly and moonless and the wine had made her steps unsteady, but Cara didn't care about any of that as, towel in hand, she crossed the terrace heading for the back gate. The pool house was dark and quiet as she passed by, which she figured meant that the idiots inside were either sulking in separate rooms or had finally managed to hook up. Either way, she didn't want to think too much about it. It was just one more reminder of something she couldn't have.

She unlocked the gate and headed toward the creek. She almost lost her footing a few times on the loose, dry dirt that lined the slope, but she wasn't going to let that stop her, either. She was going to the pond. To the one place she could be alone and happy. The only place that felt like home.

THE MIDNIGHT BELL was crowded and noisy—definitely not Liam's usual type of hang out. As an empath, he sometimes found the press of other people's emotions unbearable. Tonight, however, was different. Tonight he welcomed the distraction, it beat being alone with his own sorry thoughts.

Suddenly, a hand clapped him on the back. "So, brah," a familiar and surprisingly friendly voice greeted him, "how's it going?"

Liam stifled a groan. Just perfect. He wasn't ready to leave yet, neither was he in the mood to deal with any more of Chay's hostility. He shook his head. "Look, Chay, let's cut through the bullshit, okay? You're upset about your sister. I don't blame you. I hurt her, and nothing can ever change that. But I didn't mean to do it, and I swear it's never gonna happen again. So, why don't you cut me some slack, okay?"

"Hmph." Chay studied him thoughtfully for a moment. Finally, he shrugged. "All right, fair enough. That's pretty much the same thing she said anyway, and I guess she knows what she's talking about. I suppose I should believe her."

"Terrific," Liam muttered, ignoring the suggestion that *his* word wasn't worth believing.

For the space of several minutes, they sat, side by side, and drank their beer in almost companionable silence until finally Chay spoke. "So, I have to ask myself, what makes you so interesting that a man would tail you all over town for several days?"

Liam frowned. "What are you talking about?"

"I've been watching you, brah," Chay replied. "You've got yourself a shadow. Tall, skinny, red-headed dude with something unpleasant in his aura. Sound familiar?"

A tall, skinny redhead with an unpleasant aura. Liam shook his head. "Nope, not really."

"Well, maybe he's working for someone else, then. You piss anyone off lately?"

"Not so far as I know." Liam eyed him curiously. "So, let me get this straight. You're saying someone's been following me?"

"Yeah, brah. And, I gotta tell you, I don't have a good feeling about it."

*Well, that makes two of us*, Liam thought. "And you know this... how?"

Chay met his eyes squarely. "It's like I said. I've been watching you."

Oh. Liam nodded. *Watching me? Great. Guess I don't have to ask 'how come'.* "Well, thanks for the heads up. I'll be sure to keep an eye out for this guy." *And, if I find him, I'll damn sure wring an explanation out of him.*

"Not a problem, dude. I just figured I'd better tell you, seeing as my sister's got such a soft spot for you. She'd be righteously pissed if I kept my mouth shut and something bad happened."

Another silence descended over them. Finally, "So is that what brought you in here tonight?" Liam asked. "You came to warn me I was being stalked?"

Chay shook his head. "Nah, brah. I'm here same as you, just drowning my sorrows."

Liam snorted. "What sorrows would those be?" As far as he understood from Chenoa, Chay was a no-worries kind of guy.

Chay chuckled softly. "Okay, you caught me out." He glanced around the bar for a moment, a small, bittersweet smile flickering over his lips. "Actually, I just dropped by to reminisce." He sighed wistfully then turned to Liam, a puzzled frown creasing his brow. "Do you know this place serves the weirdest damn drinks I've ever seen? Blue, green, yellow, pink—all of them bright as neon. What the fuck's up with that shit, anyhow?"[1]

"Ah, who knows," Liam replied, totally appreciating the other man's sentiments. He couldn't imagine actually drinking one of those bizarre concoctions, either. They looked semi-lethal. "Chicks like 'em, I guess."

"I suppose." Chay shook his head, apparently still puzzled.

"Well, that's it for me. I'm outta here," Liam said as he downed his beer and stood. He held out his hand. "Chay. Take it easy. See you around."

"Aho," Chay replied taking his hand in a firm grasp. "Hang loose, brah. And, hey: watch your back, eh?"

"Will do," Liam promised as he headed for the door.

Chay waited for a couple of beats, long enough to let the cop reach the sidewalk, then he put down his own bottle and exited the bar.The night was quiet and still. The streets of Oberon were all but deserted. Chay stood in the shadows and watched as Liam got into his car and drove away.

Then he waited some more, still watching, but, for once, the cop appeared to be unaccompanied. He sighed with relief. Good. That was one less thing for him to worry about tonight. He stood on the sidewalk for a moment longer, pondering his next move.

The long trek out to his cabin in the woods, several miles outside the city limits, didn't sound particularly appealing tonight. And, although he had the keys to Erin's apartment here in town, the thought of staying there alone held little comfort.

She'd been gone almost a month and he missed his mate. He missed her laughing eyes, the golden hair that rippled down her back, the feel of her body pressed against his own. When she got back, he hoped he could make her understand that his feelings had changed.

Or, no, that wasn't true, either. His feelings for her were as strong as ever, but his needs? Ah, those had definitely changed. They'd been happy together these past eight months, but now he needed more. More from her, or maybe more from life itself.

Wearily, he turned his steps towards his aunt's house. Camille was sure to nag him about something or other, but at least he wouldn't be alone. For once in his life, being alone was not something to look forward to.

It was too cold to swim, but Cara sat at the edge of the pond, paddling her bare feet in the water, watching the stars' reflection shimmer and letting the magic of the place soothe her spirits. So, her birthday hadn't gone so well. So what? There'd be other birthdays. And the cake would keep.

In fact, stored in the freezer, it would keep for months. Surely, in all that time, she could find someone with whom to share it? If not Liam, then maybe someone else.

She thought back to what she'd told Deirdre earlier about her feelings for Seth. She hadn't been quite honest. She'd been more than *into* him. He was her first love. And, for a long time, she didn't think she could ever love anyone else.

Funny how it wasn't making her feel one bit better knowing that her heart could recover from something like that. Not when the same damn thing was happening all over again with Liam!

She stared moodily at the pond, then stiffened when she realized that hers was not the only face reflected in the water. Startled, she turned her head. "Wh-where'd you come from?" she asked breathlessly of the young man seated cross-legged on the grass beside her.

He was barefoot, as well, dressed in shorts and a Hawaiian shirt. His bronze curls, a shade or two darker than her own, gleamed in the starlight as he smiled at her gently. "Don't be afraid."

*Afraid? Oh, no, of course not*, she thought, trying vainly to get her frozen muscles to move. *Why should I be?* After all, her last encounter with a stranger had worked out so well—not!

"You shouldn't be here," she said briskly, trying to bluff things out. "This happens to be private property, you know."

The stranger's smile didn't so much as falter. "I don't think that's an issue we need to worry about just now, do you? I only want to talk."

*Talk. Right. 'Cause that's what they always wanted.* And yet, despite the fact that she couldn't move, despite the fact that she knew first-hand the kind of danger she could be in, Cara was surprised to realize that she really *wasn't* afraid.

*Stupid, stupid, stupid*, she berated herself. *How many times do I have to go through this? Why can't I ever learn?* "Talk about what?"

"Things have been tough for you, haven't they? You've had a lot of challenges in your life, especially this last year. But, I've been watching you. You've handled them well."

*Oh, yeah, I've handled things real well,* Cara thought sourly. *That's why I ended up maimed.* "How d'you figure that? And, and what do you mean, you've been watching me?"

The stranger shrugged. "There were a lot of things you might have done differently. You could have run. You could have kept silent. You could have died. But, you didn't. You chose to stay in this world. You put yourself at risk, when you didn't have to. You did what was right, rather than what was easy."

Cara glanced at her scarred hands. "Yeah, and look what it got me."

The stranger chuckled. "I am looking," he said as he nodded at the pond.

Cara gazed into the water again and felt her eyes widen. Terrific. Another glitch in her eyesight. What next? She could still see her face reflected in the pond, she could still see the stars there, as well. But, for some reason, it now appeared as though the stars were circling her head like a crown. Uncomfortable with the thought—after all, what business did she have wearing a crown—she kicked at the water with her toe, to make the image disappear. [2]

"I was stupid," she said fiercely, turning back to the stranger.

His smile gone, the stranger shook his head. "No. You were brave. But, your ordeal is not yet over. You're going to have to be brave for a little while longer."

"What are you talking about?" she snapped. "What ordeal? How much longer?"

"You'll know when it happens," the stranger replied. He got to his feet with surprising gracefulness and stood looking down at her, his expression tender. "And, not for much longer. Soon, you'll have everything you've been praying for."

"Yeah, right." Like she could even remember the last time she'd prayed for anything. Or, like there'd ever been a point to it, in the first place. Things never worked out the way she wanted them to, no matter what she tried.

"Have faith," the stranger said, smiling once again. Then he turned and disappeared into the trees, causing not even a rustle in the underbrush.

Cara tucked her knees up under her chin and hugged them tight. She was shaking—and she was pretty sure it wasn't because she was cold.

"Whoever that guy was, he's fucking crazy," she muttered. Brave? She wasn't brave. And, she wasn't going to start now, either. Brave equaled stupid, and she was done with both of those.

"WHY ARE YOU CRYING?" Seth asked, working quickly to extricate Deirdre's hands from her clothes, not at all reassured when, after he'd finally freed her, she wrapped her arms around his neck and cried harder.

"Stop it, please," he begged. "C'mon, what's wrong? Tell me. What'd I do?"

Still gulping back tears, Deirdre pushed herself away from him. She shook her head. "No! Nothing's– That's not– It was wonderful. And you–"

He watched as she took a deep breath and tried again. "It's just, I was so afraid it wouldn't be. That it would be awful. That it would be like before. That I'd hate it."

"What? Oh, no. Shhh," he soothed, using his thumb to wipe the tears from her face, searching for the right words to make her understand. "How could it be awful? We were made for each other. Don't you know that?"

"Yes." Deirdre nodded, smiling tremulously. "I do."

"Awful." Seth shook his head. "How could you think something like that? I knew we'd be good together. I always knew. Always."

Deirdre sighed as a great wave of relief washed over her. She felt like she'd been holding her breath for two years, and had only now exhaled. What he was saying was everything she'd hoped for and dreamed of...and she could hardly believe that he could feel the same way.

Wordlessly, they stared at each other. Seth's hand stroked slowly down her body and then up again, caressing the curve of her waist. She felt something nudge her thigh and, looking down, was surprised to see that he'd grown hard again. She raised her gaze to his face. "Are you–? I mean, can you–? Already?"

Eyes gleaming wickedly, Seth grinned. "I'm ready if you are."

Deirdre felt a blush crawl up her cheeks as she bit her lips and gathered him close, loving the feel of his muscles beneath her hands, the way he nuzzled at her neck, and just...everything about him. "Yes," she whispered, feeling breathless with anticipation. "Oh, yes."

# 19

Deirdre sat at the breakfast bar the next morning wrapped in her robe, sipping her coffee and watching as Seth served up breakfast.

"Exactly what do you call an omelet like this, anyway?" she asked as he slid their two plates onto the counter. He'd added ham and bacon, mushrooms, tomatoes, onions, peppers, cheese and fried potatoes to the eggs as they cooked and then topped the whole thing off with slices of avocado, splashes of salsa and dollops of sour cream.

Seth shrugged. "I dunno. But, it's good. So, just eat it, okay? I don't think I've seen you finish a plate of anything yet."

Gingerly, she tried a bite. "Delicious," she said, smiling at him.

"Mm-hm. What'd I tell you?" Next thing she knew, he was reaching over, tugging at the lapels of her robe until her breasts were exposed."What are you doing?" she gasped, blushing as her nipples hardened under his gaze.

He smiled at her innocently. "Nothing. Just a little adjustment."

She took another bite of eggs, trying to pretend that there was nothing out of the ordinary going on, trying not to notice the way his eyes never left her chest, even as he ate and drank with apparent gusto.

But, it was getting harder and harder to breathe. She picked up her cup and took another sip of coffee and then, desperate to lighten the mood a little, she teased, "So, I suppose you're back to thinking I'm easy now, is that it?"

Seth stopped eating. Frowning slightly, he met her gaze. "Oh, c'mon. I apologized about that already, didn't I? Don't tell me you're *still* gonna hold that against me?"

She stared at him in surprise. She'd only meant it as a joke, after all.

"Besides," he continued. "I've forgiven you for sleeping with Eric, so I figured we're even."[1]

Suddenly, the food she'd just eaten felt like a lead ball in the pit of Deirdre's stomach. "Wh-what did you say?"

"Never mind." Sighing, he picked up his fork. "Forget it. I shouldn't have brought it up."

"No, really," she rasped. "I want to hear this."

He put his fork back down and gazed at her earnestly. "It was just so hard, you know? I don't suppose you even realized– I begged you not to leave me, but you went with him anyway. You went with *him*. Even after everything he'd– And, I could hear it all, you know? The wall was so thin, I had no choice but to lie there and listen to the two of you. Together. Going at it all night long. You broke my heart that night, Dee. It- it was torture."

The roar of blood in her ears was so loud Deirdre could barely hear her own voice. "You son of a bitch. Torture? Thin walls? I wish I had a wall between me and, and– No choice? You think *I* had a choice? You think I wanted that? That I wanted him?"

Seth frowned. "Well, yeah, what else was I supposed to think? It's not like anybody was forcing you to go with him. 'Least it sure didn't sound that way."

"I was a virgin, you asshole! You think I did that for *me*? You think *that's* what I wanted for my first time?" Her voice broke and she stared at him, waiting for him to speak; wishing he'd do or say something to fix things. But that was impossible, wasn't it? That was just another dream.

"Get out," she whispered hoarsely, finally finding her voice.

"What?" Seth's eyebrows rose.

"Get out," she said, her voice rising on every repetition. "Get out, get out, *get out*! I hate you. I never want to see you again!"

For an instant, Seth didn't move. Then he shot to his feet. "Fuck this shit," he muttered as he turned and stalked from the room. He grabbed his shirt from the back of the chair where he'd left it the night before, snatched his keys from the hook by the door, shoved his feet into his shoes, whistled for his dogs, and left.

Deirdre hurled his coffee cup after him, watching as it splintered on the cold, hard tile.

He'd forgiven her for sleeping with Eric? Deirdre shook her head in disbelief. *Incredible.* He'd forgiven her for sacrificing her innocence to save his life. "Big of him," she muttered, still shaking with rage. All the happiness she'd been feeling—only a few minutes earlier—had turned to pain.

As awful as that night with Eric had been, the one thing she'd never felt about it was betrayed...until now.

"I have to get out of here." Thrusting her hands into her hair, she tried to think. She couldn't count on Seth to keep her safe here, that was for certain. She couldn't count on him for anything after this, not ever. And she wouldn't wait around for his parents to get home, either.

Who knew what kind of crap *they* might decide to throw in her face?

No, she'd contact her own parents. That's what she should have done in the first place. At least she knew she could count on them to be on her side.She went into the bedroom, careful to avert her eyes from the bed. She couldn't believe she'd been so foolish, so stupid, so *wrong*. She sat at the desk and turned on Seth's computer.

She was momentarily nonplused when his desktop came up. It was a picture of her, one she'd posted on her blog months earlier. So. He really had thought about her while she was gone. Too bad that meant nothing to her now.

She logged onto her email and quickly typed a message, giving her parents just the bare details: What had happened, where she was, stressing several times that she was okay. She gave them the number here at the pool house and then, because it was new and she wasn't sure if they'd memorized it yet, she gave them her cell phone number, as well.

She hit send, logged off the computer and then sat for a moment, thinking hard. She couldn't leave just yet, much as she wanted to. She had to at least wait for their call. But, there had to be something she could do in the meantime; something, anything to make herself feel better.

A shower, she decided at last, that's what she needed. A hot, scalding shower to wash every trace of Seth from her body. She'd gathered up her clothes and was on her way to the bathroom when her cellphone began to ring.

Jack's heart pounded in anticipation as he gazed at his computer screen. At last! The extra work he'd put in the last couple of weeks was finally paying off. The keylogger he'd installed in the Shelton-Cooper girl's computer might have been incinerated, along with the rest of the girl's belongings, but the passwords and other information he'd harvested were still very much operational.

And now, according to the blinking icon on his screen, someone had just logged onto her email account.

He quickly keyed in the necessary commands and, in an instant, the message she was typing appeared on his screen. He scanned it with interest, jotting down numbers, murmuring in surprise at some of the information.

She'd done a fine job of hiding herself, these past few days; and in the last place he'd ever think to look. Finally, just before she hit send, he typed in a final command, ensuring that her message would be re-directed into cyber-trash.

It would be a shame to undo all her good work, after all. Four days ago, she'd gone missing. That's how it would stay. Mommy and Daddy would never have a clue what had happened to their little girl.

Of course, there might be a witness or two to eliminate, as well as a slight deviation to Gregg's big plan, but that was just too damn bad. For the first time in months, Jack finally had his priorities straight. He was looking out for number one, now. And, this time, he'd make no mistakes.

Smiling grimly, he turned away from his computer and reached for the phone.

COULD it be her parents calling already, Deirdre wondered as she raced for the phone, almost tripping over Snowball in her hurry. "Hello?" she said breathlessly.

"Yes, hello. I'm looking for a Miss Shelton-Cooper," an unfamiliar voice replied.

"This is she," Deirdre said, shocked into formality.

"Ah, Miss Cooper. At last. You're a very difficult young woman to get a hold of."

"Who is this?" she asked."I'm one of the lawyers handling your late father's estate," the voice explained. "We've been trying to reach you for several weeks now."

"M-my father?"

"Yes, that's correct. Glenn Gilchrist. We received a posthumous letter from your mother, a little over three months ago, informing us of your existence. Of course, we will have to ask that you submit to a few tests, but it's just a formality. Your mother provided birth details, proof of paternity, and all the other necessary documentation. Everything appears to be in order."

"You can tell me about my father?" Deirdre asked, still battling disbelief. Why would Paige do something like this? Deirdre had also received a letter several months ago. In it, Paige had claimed not to know the identity of Deirdre's father. *Maybe she only found out afterwards,* Deirdre thought wildly. *Maybe she died before she could write me a new letter, telling me what she'd learned.*

"Yes, of course," the voice on the phone assured her. "I can provide you with a complete dossier on Mr. Gilchrist, if you'd like."

"Yes, please. That would be wonderful."

"Of course, there are still some details to be worked out," the voice continued. "Papers to be signed and what not. And the sooner the better. Would it be possible for you to come to our offices today?"

"I don't have a car right now," Deirdre explained, cursing herself for her stupidity in leaving her car at Seth's house.

"Ah, well, that's no problem. I can come to you. Where are you staying?"

"The Morning Glory Inn. It's just outside town, at one of the wineries."

"Yes, I know it well. A charming accommodation. And, as it happens, I'm free this morning. Shall we say half an hour?"

"Yes. Okay," Deirdre mumbled breathlessly.

"Splendid," the voice purred as it signed off. "See you then."

Deirdre stared at the phone in her hand, hardly daring to believe it could be true. Her father. After all this time. Was it really possible?

THE MORNING WAS PERFECT, Liam decided as he stood on the sidewalk outside his apartment, surreptitiously scanning the street for the 'shadow' Chay had mentioned the night before, and finding nothing out of the ordinary.

A bright, warm day under a blue cloudless sky, he'd had big plans for the day. But, just like yesterday, all those plans were dependent on Cara. Without her, the perfect summer day was empty. Pointless. A waste. And, apparently, without even the small satisfaction of beating the crap out of the punk who'd been following him. Not that he was particularly violent by nature, but a man could only take so much frustration.

"Ah, Caramel," he sighed sadly. "Why couldn't you have waited for me?"

But, there was no sense dwelling on that, so he forced his mind back to its earlier topic. His shadow. On the surface, the idea seemed absurd. What had he done to anyone lately to make them want to tail him? Could someone be targeting him for something?

They had to be kidding, if they were. The gun tucked snugly at the small of his back offered pretty good assurance that he'd come out the victor in any confrontation. But he had a lot of respect for Chay's talents as a scout. If the man said that Liam was being stalked, the odds were good he was right.

"But why?" he muttered. And, if it really was the case, where was the punk now? Was he gone? Had he finished his task? Had Chay scared him away? Maybe he was busy this morning, off tailing someone else? That thought caused a scrap of conversation from earlier in the week to float to the surface of Liam's mind. His heart clenched.

*"Is there anything else you wanted to talk to me about?" he'd asked gently. Cara nodded. "What if there was a girl, a chick who'd had problems with the cops, or just didn't like 'em that much...what if Gregg was trying to have her, you know, killed or something."*

*"Some chick? You mean like you?"*

*"Yeah, you know. It's not like she did anything wrong, or anything. It's just–"*

*"Cara, are you worried about Gregg getting out of prison and coming after you?"*

*She blinked down at him; one eye widening in surprise, one eye staring over his shoulder, as though disinterested. "Well, yeah, sure. A little. I mean, who wouldn't be?"*

*He shook his head. "Well, don't be. I mean it. He's not getting out. Not ever."*

*She nodded again, still looking worried. "Still, he could maybe send someone else to do it, don't you think?"*

*"No. That'll never happen," he'd insisted. "You can't go through your whole life looking over your shoulder. You're safe now. It's over."*

But what if he'd been wrong?

Cara knew Gregg better than anyone. Why shouldn't she be right about this?

He opened the door of his car and got in. Either way, it wouldn't hurt to drive out to the inn and check on her safety. He stowed his gun in the glove compartment, checked to make sure he had a pair of handcuffs in there, as well. Just to be safe. And then started the car.

This would make two days in a row that he'd shown up at the inn unannounced. It could be that Seth wouldn't like that, but if he didn't, that was too damn bad. It wouldn't be much fun for Liam, either, after all, having to watch the little lovebirds bill and coo, but that was also unimportant. Cara's safety was paramount. Next to that, all other considerations paled.

Liam pulled slowly away from the curb, checking his rear view mirror again and again, hoping to see a car pull out behind him. But the road remained empty. Normally, he'd have counted that as a good thing. But, at the moment? Not so much.

SETH WAS STILL SEETHING when he pulled his truck into the beach parking lot. That girl was unbelievable; fucked up, crazy, cruel. He'd poured his soul out to her this morning, telling her things he'd never said aloud before, never told another person.

He'd shared his greatest heartache, confessed to how deeply she'd wounded him, and how had she reacted? With anger. With lies. With stupid attempts to deny that what he knew to be true had even occurred.

So, she wanted him gone? Well, good. That suited him fine, too.

He could use a little distance, right now, to mend the tattered shreds of his ego. And to decide if he could actually handle a relationship with anyone so certain to cause him nothing but pain.

He was halfway down the path that led to the little cove, so mired in his own unhappy thoughts he was oblivious to his surroundings, when Mouth's bark of greeting recalled his attention. Glancing ahead, he was surprised to see someone blocking the path.

*Rafe.* Speechless, he stared at the man. The early morning sunshine streamed through the trees, surrounding him in a halo of light. *What's he doing here*?

A likely explanation was not long in coming. Deirdre. No doubt she'd called her *friend* and asked him to intervene. Sure, she'd claimed to know neither his phone number nor address, but it wouldn't be the first time she'd lied.

"Go back," Rafe said quietly.

Seth shook his head. "No. Get out of my way."

"You're needed elsewhere," Rafe insisted.

Needed? Yeah, sure. Deirdre needed him when it suited her, but the rest of the time? "Fuck that."

Rafe gazed at him sadly. "Sometimes the truth is more complex than you realize, Seth. Sometimes you see part of a picture, and think you know all that it contains."

Seth glared at him. "Look, are you gonna get out of my way, or am I gonna have to make you?"

Rafe shook his head. "I'm afraid neither of those options are acceptable. There's something you need to hear," he said, as he opened his hand.

Seth stared blankly at the seashell resting in the other man's palm. "What the hell is that for?"

Rafe took a step forward. Seth tried to back up, and found that he couldn't move.

"Listen now," Rafe instructed as he pressed the shell against Seth's ear. There was a whir of noise in Seth's head, then his eyes snapped shut. Pain lanced through him and he found himself alone in the dark, lost in the memory that had haunted his dreams for two years...

*He was lying on a hard, stone floor; stiff and sore, aching with cold. Every breath he took was accompanied by a sharp, tugging pain in his ribs. His throat was parched. His eyes felt swollen. His head ached. He could barely even feel his fingers or his toes anymore.*

*The only touches of comfort were the blanket someone had spread over him, and the soft, fleecy bundle beneath his head.Suddenly, a face swam into view. Deirdre. He tried to smile, but then he heard it. Eric's voice, calling her name.*

*"Shit," she muttered scrambling to her feet. "I gotta go."*

*"No!" Vainly Seth tried to reach for her, only to find that his hands had been tied behind his back. "Don't go there. Don't–"*

*"I have to," she said, her voice shaking a little. "Don't you get it? It's the only way. Otherwise, he's just gonna come back in here and...and kick you around some more, or something."*

*"So what? I don't care. Let him try it," he answered wildly, not sure that he didn't mean it. "What's the difference? I'll probably just pass out again, anyway."*

*The idea of her going with Eric had been making him nuts since he'd first thought of it. The idea of her being with him now—that hurt a whole lot more than another kick in the head would have done. "I don't care what he does to me," he pleaded, again, his voice a whisper. "Just, please..."*

*She laughed, but it wasn't a cheerful sound. "Yeah? Well, lucky for you, I do care." She bent towards him and he felt something soft brush his face, then she slipped away. Light flared briefly as the door opened, and then it was gone.*

*"No," Seth moaned as the darkness blinded him.Within minutes, the sounds began. The murmur of voices. The rustle of clothes being removed. The grunts, the groans, the whimpers. The slap of flesh against flesh, over and over...*

"Make it stop," Seth begged as he felt his heart crumble once again.

"Shh," Rafe soothed. "Not yet. Open your mind."

*Suddenly, Seth found himself on the other side of the wall, feeling not just his own agony, but Deirdre's as well. If it weren't for the force that kept him immobile, he would have collapsed on the ground under the weight of all their suffering.*

*A sharp, sudden, burning pain had Deirdre gasping for breath. It felt like nothing Seth had ever imagined, or even considered before. She pushed and clawed at Eric's shoulders, trying to free herself, but, caught up in his own pleasure, he was mindless to her distress. His arms held her fast, trapped beneath him, as he thrust into her again and again.*

*Along with the pain came anger. Humiliation. A sickening sense of her own vulnerability. A wrenching feeling of loss. And through it all, over and above all the rest, there was fear: blind, shrieking terror that made everything else seem almost incidental.*

*But not for herself, Seth realized with a guilty start; her fear was for him. It was his safety, his life that had been her main concern. She'd done this for him.*

"Oh, God, please, make it stop," he whimpered.

"Peace," Rafe murmured, removing the shell. He slid a hand underneath Seth's elbow, steadying him as the stasis that had held him dissolved.Seth's chest heaved. He gulped back tears of anguish, straining to breathe.

"Slowly," Rafe instructed, staring deeply into his eyes until Seth finally managed to catch his breath. "That's better."

"Let me go," Seth begged when he could speak again.

Rafe nodded gravely. "Godspeed, Seth. But be careful."

"I will," Seth promised as he fled back up the path from which he'd come.

His hands were trembling as he secured the dogs in the truck. He jumped inside, started the engine and raced back toward the inn; praying he wasn't too late, that he hadn't already lost her.

# 20

Cara lay in bed, contemplating the view through the skylight over her head. It was empty and blue, which totally matched her mood. She had no reason to get up today. So maybe she wouldn't? Maybe she'd just turn over, go back to sleep, skip the whole miserable day and wake up tomorrow. At least tomorrow she'd be seeing Liam.

That happy thought was quickly followed by another, far more depressing one. It was possible that, tomorrow, she'd be seeing Liam for the very last time.

She'd been hoping all week that he'd express some interest in seeing her outside of class, but it hadn't happened. And, much as she longed to tell him how she felt, she wouldn't. Unless he said something, neither would she. She'd keep her mouth shut and just walk away and never let him know that, if he'd only let her, if he'd just give her a chance, she would love him with everything she had.

She was startled by the sound of the doorbell ringing downstairs. "Who could that be?" She certainly wasn't expecting anyone. Even more surprising, however, was the sound of footsteps crossing the foyer to answer the door. "What the fuck?"

She sat up to listen. Voices. A man's voice and a girl's. Deirdre. Well, that figured, didn't it?

"Give the bitch an inch and she takes a yard." First Seth, then the laundry, now the door– "What'll she want next, my job?"

Anger got Cara out of bed. She dressed quickly, determined to find out what was going on and put a stop to it. She was reaching for the door handle when another thought struck her. It wouldn't hurt to get some kind of idea who Deirdre's visitor might be. It was a long shot, but perhaps–

She crossed to the front deck, pushed open the glass door and stepped outside. She gazed down at the inn's driveway and promptly lost her breath. She recognized the car, all right. She remembered the countless times she'd buzzed it in through the gate at Gregg's 'church'. Jack Connolly, the slimebag. Gregg's lawyer.

"I knew it," she muttered as she fled back inside. Deirdre, Jack, Gregg; they were all in this together. And, whatever they were up to, it couldn't be anything good. "I have to get out of here." She was glancing around frantically, wondering what, if anything, she should pack, when another, more rational thought struck.

Oh, hell. What was she thinking? Deirdre probably wasn't in on this either. Cara could still remember Gregg's reaction to the email he'd received last April. He hadn't been pleased. Oh, he'd tried to hide his anger, but he was wearing that pissy look that always signaled trouble.

Well, that was sad, and she wished Deirdre well, but she was not gonna risk any more of her own skin to save someone else's. The front deck didn't make such a good escape route, but the back deck, on the other hand, held promise. There was the big live oak that dominated the terrace. Its branches shaded the deck and hung over the fence. Cara could climb up one branch and down another and be over the fence before anyone knew she was gone. It wouldn't be easy, but it could be done.

Once she was out, she could go anywhere: the winery, the pond.

Oh, shit.

"Oh, no, no, no," she moaned remembering the crazy stranger from last night, the one she'd almost convinced herself had been a dream. *You'll know when it happens*, he'd said, and damned if he wasn't right. But, she was scared, damn it. She didn't want to be brave, she just wanted to be safe.

"Please don't make me do this," she begged. "Please, please, please..." But, as usual, her prayers went unanswered. Resigned, she squared her shoulders, opened the door and headed downstairs.

SHE FOUND them in the lounge, which was just as she'd expected. "Hello, Jack," she said as she limped into the room. He turned to her with a smile. "Cara. How nice to see you again."

Cara felt her heart stall. He wasn't surprised to see her. That was bad news. That meant he knew she'd be here. And that meant this was likely a trap for her, as well. Shit. She should have known.

"What are you doing here?" she asked, hoping to at least stall for time.

"I just have a little business to transact with your friend," he answered smoothly.

"Right. Well, before you get started on that, Dee, can I see you in the kitchen for a minute?"

"Oh, I don't think that's a very good idea," Jack said, as Deirdre eyed them both warily. "Why don't you join us in here, instead? Come in. Sit down."

Cara smiled brightly. "Sure, that sounds great. But...after we talk, 'kay? It won't take long."

"I really think you should sit down," Jack repeated, as he reached into his jacket. Just then, the phone began to ring. Jack's face turned dark. "Don't answer that."

But Cara was already in motion. "Oh, I have to," she called over her shoulder. "I'll be right back."

*It's probably a sales call*, she thought despairingly. *It's probably a telemarketer, or something automated—nothing remotely helpful.* But, maybe, if she was very lucky– "Hello?"

"Hey, there, Caramel." Cheerful and confident, Liam's voice filtered through the phone, filling Cara with hope. "I thought maybe you could use some help studying for your test? I'm out your way and I thought I'd stop by, if that's okay."

"Yes, that's fine. Please do that," she said, trying to sound professional and unperturbed, just in case Jack was listening.

There was a moment's silence and then, "Cara? Is everything all right there?" Liam asked in a voice that radiated worry.

"Um, no, n-not really, as a matter of fact, I–" She clutched the phone tighter as she heard footsteps behind her. "Hurry," she whispered just before pain tore through her head and the floor rose up to meet her.

"Now, that was stupid, wasn't it?" Jack asked after he hung up the phone, but the girl at his feet was too stunned to respond. Blood trickled from a cut on her temple. Jack watched as she clutched at the table leg, trying to stand. He aimed a kick at her spine and watched as she went down again. It felt surprisingly good. Maybe Gregg was right after all. Disciplining the girl might be more fun than he'd ever imagined.

Too bad he was going to have to cut the lesson short. He tucked his gun back into his jacket, reached down and took hold of her arm and hauled her to her feet. Then he grabbed one of the dining room chairs and half dragged, half carried both girl and chair into the lounge.

"Wh-what happened?" The Shelton-Cooper girl's eyes were wide, startled.

"She's just feeling a little dizzy," Jack lied as he set down the chair and pushed Cara into it. "Why don't you come over here and give me a hand with her?"

"B–but sh-she's bleeding," the girl replied, not moving an inch. "H-how–?"

Sighing, Jack pulled his gun back out of his jacket. "Don't make me ask you again," he said as he leveled it at her.

The girl's face went white. Even from across the room he could see her trembling. "I don't understand," she whispered. "Wh-why are you doing this?"

"Never mind that now." Jack dug in another pocket and pulled out one of the lengths of rope he'd brought with him.

"Here," he said as he tossed it to her. "Tie her up, then I'll answer your questions."

"What?" Cara gazed up at him wide eyed. "No! Don't. Please, I can't–"

Annoyed and impatient, Jack smacked her again on the side of the head, and she went limp.

"Stop that!" Deirdre gasped, hurrying closer. "I'll do what you want, just leave her alone!"

Jack nodded. "Good. That's a better attitude."

"I'm sorry," Deirdre whispered to Cara as she pulled her hands behind her back and began to tie her to the chair. "This is all my fault." By the time she was done, she was sobbing in fear.

"Very nice," Jack said as he yanked her to her feet. "Now, I think it's time that you and I took a little drive."

"Why are you doing this?" she asked again, tearfully.He shook his head. "You took on the wrong man, little girl. Your father, if he really was your father, inherited part of a large estate when his mother died. After his death, that money reverted to his brother. Who, I'm afraid, does *not* like to share."

"If? You told me my mother wrote you. You said it was almost certain."

Jack clucked his tongue. "You really shouldn't believe everything you're told. I lied. There was never any letter. Now, let's go."He tightened his grip on her arm and then, just as he was about to push her toward the door, it slammed open.

"Police. Drop the gun," a voice demanded.

"No!" This couldn't be happening. Howling in fright and despair, Jack turned and fired. There was a second report and something slammed into his shoulder. The gun flew from his hand as he fell.

GUN DRAWN, Liam advanced into the room. "Are you all right?" he asked the dark haired girl. She looked about ready to pass out, but she nodded gamely. "Good. Go call 911."

He kicked the groaning gunman onto his stomach, tucked his gun back into his waistband and pulled out the handcuffs. "You have the right to remain silent," he began. He'd just snapped the cuffs into place when a sickening, unmistakable sound behind him made him freeze. It was the sound of a gun being cocked. *Jesus, what now?*

"Stand up nice and slow and turn around," an unfamiliar voice instructed. "And, oh, yeah, almost forgot. Keep your hands where I can see them."

The man on the floor writhed around to glare at the new arrival. "Make him get me out of these things. And get me something for my shoulder before I bleed to death."

The other man chuckled. "Sorry, Jack-o, no can do. I'm afraid you haven't quite got the whole picture, yet. You're not going anywhere."

*Oh, fuck.* Liam stared at the second gunman in dull surprise, taking in his tall, skinny build, his red hair. Liam didn't know much about auras but, as far as he could tell, there was *nothing* pleasant about the man.

The slimeball had the dark haired girl by the throat with his gun pressed against the side of her head. She gazed at Liam piteously.

"What are you talking about?" the man on the floor asked crossly. "I said, get me up. Now!"

The young punk smirked. "See, Jack, thanks to your recent activities, we've got enough evidence to pin the deaths of all these nice people on you; not to mention to tie you into the explosion at Gregg's crib last April.

Once the police finish putting all the pieces together, you're going down. And then Gregg will walk, just like he and I planned it."

Gregg. Of course. At the mention of the motherfucker's name,

Liam groaned inwardly. *Of course.* "And who the hell are you?" he asked, not really expecting an answer.

But the punk surprised him. He drew himself erect. A twisted smile curved his lips. "I'm Gregg's pet," he answered proudly. "That's all you need to know."

Liam felt his stomach turn, he had no doubt he was hearing the truth. The last person Gregg had called 'pet' was Cara. In build and coloring, she and the gunman were not all that dissimilar. Stunned, Liam stared at the man for another moment, until a flicker of motion outside the window caught his eye.

His brain began to race. The gun at the girl's head, that was the big problem. It was too dangerous, too big a risk. He'd have to do something about that. Unfortunately, his options were limited.

He waited until the very last instant, took a deep breath and then dove across the room, praying the gunman's aim would go wild.

After that, several things seemed to happen at once. There was the crack of a gun, the zing of a bullet passing over his head, with only inches to spare. There was a scream, a thunderous crash, ferocious growling, cries of pain and fury.

Liam rolled quickly to see what was going on, relieved to see that everything was as he'd hoped it would be.

The dark haired girl was okay, though she didn't appear able to stand on her own; she was safe in Seth's arms. One dog, snarling viciously, stood guard over the first gunman. The second gunman lay prone on the floor, pinned beneath the weight of a second dog who seemed intent on detaching the man's head from his shoulders.

"Seth," Liam ordered. "That's enough. Call him off!"

Seth uttered a short command and the dog subsided, though he kept his place on the gunman's back.

Getting to his feet, Liam hurried to where Cara sat tied to a chair. He undid the ropes and tossed them to Seth. "Here. Tie him up. And you," he addressed the girl, "let's try it again, okay? 911. Now!"

While the others hurried to comply with his demands, Liam gently pulled Cara's arms free of the chair and placed them in her lap. He stroked her face softly, fingered the cut on her temple.

"Cara, sweetie, can you hear me? It's time to wake up now."He rubbed her hands briskly, continuing to murmur encouragement until, finally, she began to respond. A shudder ran through her. She began to twitch and then to tremble. He rubbed harder, stroking up and down her arms as well.

A low moan escaped her lips, "Nooooo."

"Hey!" Seth called from across the room. "Cut that out! Don't touch her!"

Stung and furious, Liam turned on the boy, ready to blast him. But the pain and worry in Seth's eyes stopped him cold. He dropped his hands to his side and backed up a step. "Cara, it's okay," Seth soothed. "You're safe now."

Eyes still closed, Cara shook her head from side to side, whimpering softly, "Nooo."

"Yes, you are. Just open your eyes and you'll see."

She continued to gulp back tears for a moment, then her eyes fluttered open. She glanced around. "What happened?"

But there was no short answer to that. "Don't worry about that now," Liam told her. "Are you okay?"

She stared at him blankly, then nodded."All right. Good," he sighed. Careful to keep his hands to himself, he stalked from the room. Wherever that second girl had gone with the phone, she was taking too long. He'd called for backup from his car, but there were still calls to be made.

When Liam returned to the lounge, a few minutes later, Seth was nowhere to be found. He checked the ropes that bound the punk's hands and found them secure.

"My face," the young man moaned thickly. "My face."

Feeling angry and mean, Liam laughed at him. "Yeah, it's a real mess, all right. You'll prob'ly be scarred for life. Can't imagine who'll want you now, lookin' the way you do. Not much of anyone, I suppose."

A startled gasp behind him made him spin around. Cara was staring at him, eyes wide, a stricken expression on her face. *Oh, Jesus.*

"Cara, no," he groaned as he hurried toward her. "I didn't mean it like that." He reached for her, wanting to take her in his arms, but she flinched away.

Suddenly, Seth was there, rushing him; shoving him hard in the chest, pushing him backwards, shouting furiously. "Quit it, asshole! I told you to leave her alone! Can't you see how freaked out she is? Don't you know she can't stand being touched? What the fuck is wrong with you?"

"What?" Liam stared at him, appalled. Denial raged within him. It was the same thing Chenoa had said, but he hadn't believed her, and he really hadn't understood what it meant. Maybe because he hadn't wanted to.

Calming slightly, Seth nodded. "Sure. Ever since the attack. And then in the hospital, they just messed her up even more. So, just back the fuck off. I mean it."

"I hear you." Liam closed his eyes for a moment, remembering Cara as she used to be. Hers was such a bright, indomitable spirit. That was one of the first things he'd noticed, something he'd often marveled at and admired her for.

No matter what Gregg did to her, no matter how many times he tried to drag her down, she always emerged unmarred, undamaged. Fearless and...innocent, somehow.

It was killing him now, to think that her bold spirit had finally been crushed, that her improbable innocence had at last been destroyed.

"I'm sorry," he murmured, meeting her gaze. "I-I didn't know."

Though her lips were trembling, Cara angled her chin at him proudly. "I didn't want you to know."

And that, he thought sadly, was that. If she'd had any plans for continuing their relationship—even as friends—she would have realized he'd find out about it, at some point. And she'd have told him herself, straight out. But she hadn't, and the inference was clear: this week had been a fluke, a reprieve for him, a trial for her. And, after tomorrow, he was sure she'd keep her distance, and expect him to do the same.

"Excuse me," he muttered, averting his eyes. "They're gonna need me outside." It was true that he could hear the approaching sirens, and it would be useful to have someone out there, directing things, but it wasn't the real reason he was leaving. The real reason was simple: he couldn't bear to stay.

For the rest of the time he was there, he made sure to stay far away from her; just as he was sure she wanted him to do. And, when he left, it was without saying good-bye.

"HOW'S SHE DOING?" Deirdre asked, looking up from the couch where she'd been huddled, when Seth returned to the pool house, several hours later.

He sighed. "Better. I made her something to eat, now she's resting."

"And you still think she shouldn't be in the hospital?"

"Yeah, I'm positive." Seth crossed the room and sat down on the coffee table, uneasily aware that they'd sat in the reverse positions the night before. Maybe that was an omen, or a sign. But was it good or bad? "They messed with her too much, the last time she was in there. It would kill her to have to go back there now. Besides, she doesn't have a concussion. She's not sleepy, or anything. She just won't stop crying."

"Well, that's 'cause of that guy, right? The cop? I can't believe he just left like that."

"Yeah," Seth sighed wearily. "I know."

"You know what else I can't believe?"

He shook his head. "No. What?"

"You. I can't believe how you came back when you did, how you knew to come in through the front door. How'd you know that?"

Seth shrugged. The last thing he wanted was to tell her about the force that had taken control of his truck. How it had shut off his engine, turned the wheel in his hands, made him park the truck silently on the inn's side lawn, when he'd planned on roaring around to his usual parking place, at the back of the property.

Or to mention the voice in his head, the one that warned him to go in low, to send the dogs in first; that had told him to peek through the inn's front window before barging blindly inside.

But, most of all, he didn't want to tell her about the urge—entirely his own—that made him give Zeus an order he'd never once before given any of the dogs. The order to kill.

"I just got lucky I guess," he said at last.

"Well, whatever it was– You saved my life, you know that? You saved all our lives."

"Dee, don't." He gazed at her sadly. "You saved my life, too. So, maybe we should just call it even? Or, maybe we could both just... never need saving again."

"I don't understand," she whispered, her voice trembling."What are you saying?"

"Nothing. Forget it." He stared at her for another minute, looking grim and tired. Finally he sighed. "Look, we need to talk about this morning, about what happened, the things we said–"

Deirdre's eyes widened. "No, please. I didn't mean it. I should never have–"

"No!" He leaned forward suddenly and captured her hands in his. "Listen to me. I'm sorry. I didn't know. You should have told me. But, I meant what I said, back then. I'd rather he'd've killed me than to hurt you like that."

The tears that had been shimmering in Deirdre's eyes at last began to fall. "Oh, Seth...don't you get it yet? I couldn't let him hurt you any more. It was already my fault that you were there, in the first place!"

"No. That was my fault, not yours. I was stupid. I should've known better."

"And your addiction," she continued, starting to sob now. "I didn't know about that either un-until last night. That's my fault, too."

"Stop it, Dee. Don't say things like that. It wasn't."

She shook her head. "You were right this morning. It *was* my choice. It's just that it's been kind of hard to live with, you know? And, I guess...I was just hoping that you could–"

"What?" He slid to his knees and gazed at her imploringly. "What can I do? Tell me. How can I make it up to you?"

She smiled through her tears. "Make the memories go away?"

Seth closed his eyes in despair. She was asking for the impossible. He knew. He had those same memories too, now. Hard. Bitter. Indelible. "I can't," he whispered miserably."

You can," she insisted. "You did—last night."

He stared at her. Baffled. Confused. Hopeful. "How?"

"By giving me something else to think about when I, I– By showing me how different it could be. You made me feel safe. Happy. Loved. Won't you do that again for me? Please?"

For an instant, he couldn't move. Then he surged to his feet and swung her into his arms. "Yes," he promised as he carried her across the room. "Always."

He kicked the bedroom door closed behind him and fell on the bed, with her still in his arms.

This time, their clothes came off easily. No one got stuck or entangled. They both had their hands and their mouths free to rove and explore.

Somewhere in the course of the long night, Deirdre realized that things were different. It was not quite the same as it had been the night before and, perhaps, that would always be the case. Each time just a little bit different, with only the most important part staying the same: the knowledge that she was cherished, needed, loved.

And, maybe, if they were very, very lucky, that part would never change.

# 21

Another morning. And, once again, Deirdre was in her robe, in the kitchen, drinking coffee—or trying to drink it, anyway. "Stop!" she insisted, giggling as Seth grabbed her from behind and began to nuzzle her neck. "You'll make me spill!"

"No," he growled. "I won't stop. I can't. I love you so much, I think I'd die if I had to stop touching you now."

"Okay, well, we can't have that, I suppose." She sighed happily as he nibbled on her earlobe.

"You know what I'm thinking," he said as he raised his head, "I'm thinking that this might be a good time for you to say something back."

She craned her neck to look at him. "You mean, something like...I love you, too?"

He grinned at her. "Yeah. Something just like that."

"Well, you know I do," she teased. "So, why do I have to say it?

"Because." He spun her around and took hold of her robe's lapels. "I want you to."

"Careful! The coffee," she warned as he pulled her close. Just then, the door slammed open. They sprang apart in surprise.

"Well, there you are! And alive, thank God!"

Deirdre turned to see Seth's mother hurrying across the room, with his father right behind her.

"See? I told you he was all right," Dan said, although the worried look on his face implied otherwise.

"Sorry," Cara gasped, stumbling in behind them. "I tried to stop them."

Seth stared at his parents in dismay. "Mom, Dad, what are you doing here?"

"What are we doing here?" Lucy stopped in her tracks so suddenly that Dan nearly plowed into her. "Seth– We've just come from the house. The door to the apartment was left wide open, there's a strange car in the garage and the living room–"

"Oh, shit," Seth groaned. "The house. I forgot. I meant to go back and clean things up, but things got...well...a little busy around here."

"Hmph." Lucy's eyes shifted to Deirdre. "So I see."

Deirdre smiled sweetly. "Hi, Mrs. Cavanaugh." She knew the exact instant that Lucy recognized her: her face went blank with shock. "And Mr. Cavanaugh." Dan, on the other hand, looked only mildly surprised to see her. "Deirdre. It– it's very nice to see you again. Are you staying long?"

Deirdre nodded. "Yes, and I'm afraid the mess at your house is mostly my fault. See, my apartment blew up and I had nowhere to go. And then my cat got loose and the dogs started chasing him–

"Your apartment did what?" Lucy stared at her icily. "Is that my robe you're wearing?"

Seth took a step forward, partially blocking his mother's view of her. "Look, Mom, it's a really long story. Maybe I can come over later and we can talk about it?"

Lucy transferred her glare to him. "Later? Oh, no. I want to hear this now, Seth. All of it."

Deirdre put a hand on his shoulder and squeezed reassuringly. "I'll go get the coffee," she said, heading for the cabinet where the cups were kept.

Seth stared at his parents. How the hell was he ever going to explain everything that had happened in the past week? And, where should he start?

"Well, I'd love to stay and hear this," Cara said cheerfully. "But I have a test to take." She cocked her head to the side and smiled at Lucy. "But, hey, listen, before you get too upset with him, here's something to think about. It could've been worse, you know. It could've been me he hooked up with."

Seth groaned inwardly as his mother gave Cara a long, slow, considering look; the kind of look with which Seth was all too familiar. Finally, she spoke. "Oddly enough, that thought isn't nearly as frightening as it once might have been." As Cara blushed to the roots of her hair, Lucy smiled at her. "Now, go and ace that test of yours."

Cara nodded. "Yes, Ma'am."

As she hurried away, Seth gazed at his mother in surprise. "Mom. That was really nice of you."

"Nice?" His mother's eyes grew wide. "Well, I don't know why you should sound so surprised about that. When am I ever not nice?"

"You're always nice, babe." His father took hold of her shoulders and turned her to face him. "Haven't I been saying it for years?" Then he tilted her chin up and kissed her hard.

Seth stared at his parents enviously, wondering if he and Deirdre would ever learn to resolve their conflicts so easily.

"Coffee's ready," she said, returning with a tray. She took one look at his parents and her eyes went wide. "Oh. Okay, maybe not."

Smiling, Seth took the tray from her hands and slid it onto the counter. "C'mere," he whispered.

"Seth, no," she said, looking shocked. "We can't. Not now!"

He took hold of her arms and pulled her close. "Sure we can. Watch this."

"No," she murmured coming in quick, planting a tiny, chaste kiss on his lips, then pulling away again.

"Dee..."

"Later," she said, swooping in again, even quicker this time. Another kiss: too brief, too cool, barely worthy of the name. "I promise."

When she moved in for the third time, he caught her and kept her there, kissing her for real, this time, smiling inwardly when he felt her kiss him back. "That's better.""Mmm."

A promise, though, he liked the sound of that. Perhaps a promise to love each other for the rest of their lives? He felt like he'd been waiting his whole life to make such a promise. But he wanted it now, or at least very soon. Not later. They'd already waited two years, after all, and, the way he figured it, that was more than enough.

LIAM HAD PUT Cara's paper on the bottom of the stack. So that he'd grade it last. So that, when everyone else had gone, he could still spend a precious couple of minutes alone with her. It was selfish, he knew, but he was determined to milk this opportunity for all it was worth.

"So? C'mon, how'd I do?" she asked, standing beside his desk, shifting nervously from one foot to the other. "Tell me."

Finally, unable to draw out the moment any longer, he put his pencil down and handed her the paper. "Congratulations. An almost perfect score."

"Really? Omigod, are you kidding me?"

"Nope. I knew you could do it." He watched as she studied her score. Her eyes grew wide. A smile lit up her face. Her hands clutched the paper like they'd once clutched him. Once, but not now. Maybe not ever again.

He sighed as he remembered all the times he'd been forced to keep his distance, to push her away. Because of her age. Because of the danger they were both in. Because it was expected of him. Where was the reward for all his self restraint? Where was the pay off for having done what was right?

Her smile gone, Cara raised her eyes to his face. "So, I guess...I mean...is this it then?"

"This is it." He wished that it wasn't, though. He wished he could just– "So, tell me something, how're things with you and Seth? Does he treat you all right?"

He just needed to hear her say it. Her happiness was what mattered, after all. And, if she said she was happy, then fine. Great. He'd be happy, too. And, somehow, he'd find the strength to let her go.A tiny frown creased her forehead.

"Seth? Yeah, I guess. He made me dinner last night, because of my head and all."

Liam nodded. "Good. Glad to hear it." Well, he'd asked for it, hadn't he? And now was a fine time to realize that he'd been lying to himself. "But, you know, if he ever doesn't, you be sure and let me know about it, okay?"

"And, what then?" she asked looking angry and perplexed. "Are you gonna arrest him because, maybe sometimes, he gets in a bad mood and says stuff he feels bad about later? Gimme a break, Liam, that's just stupid."

"A bad mood?" *Gee, where have I heard that before? Oh, yeah. It's the same excuse she used to make for Gregg.* He scowled at her. "Jesus, Cara, I don't understand you. Why would you put up with shit like that?"

"What shit is that? You're the one who's getting all worked up about stuff. I don't have a problem with Seth."

"Well, maybe *that's* the problem then? You're always settling for so little. You deserve someone who's going to treat you...well, like you deserve to be treated."

Cara sighed. "Look, maybe you're right about that. But I still don't know why you're picking on Seth. He and I don't owe each other anything. We've both fucked up, but we've made our peace with it. We're square. We're friends now and...and perhaps that's all we were ever meant to be."

Liam's mouth dropped open. "Friends?"

The look on his face made Cara want to squirm. "Stop looking at me like that."

"You're not dating him?" Liam asked, ignoring her request, continuing to stare. *Figures.*

"Dating who? Seth?"

"Or anyone," he snapped. "Are you seeing anyone at all?"

Cara sighed. Oh, good. Another great topic. First Seth and now dating. What was next? Maybe they could talk about Chenoa and how great *she* was. "Liam, get a clue. How could I be dating anyone? Most guys have a funny habit of wanting to touch the girls they're dating. You know, to hold hands, to kiss, *something*? Right now, I don't even like to be looked at too hard. So, no. I'm not. Okay?"

There was a moment's silence. She could feel his surprise. "Cara," he said, softly, and, at the note of something dismayed in his voice, she felt herself cringe. *Oh, no, not that. No pity, please.*

"Hey, it's no big deal. There aren't that many guys I want to date, anyway." Just one, actually. "And, even if there were, well, what good would it do me?"

Even with only one good eye, she could see well enough when she looked in her mirror. She knew what she looked like now, and, if it happened that turned some guys off, then good. She'd had enough of those guys, anyway. But, she didn't need anyone feeling sorry for her—especially not Liam.

"Look, I have to go now," she said, as she turned away.

"Stop!" he ordered, reaching out a hand to grab her.

She jumped, jerking away from his touch, choking back a scream, all her nerves going crazy as memories—of pain and pain and more pain—flooded her system.

"Sorry," he mumbled, looking away, looking angry and embarrassed as his hand dropped to his side.

Cara struggled to get her breathing back under control. It took a moment to fight down the panic. "What is it?" she asked, very quietly, when she at last found her tongue again.

He said nothing, at first. And then, "Will you go out with me?"

She felt her eyes widen. "What?"

"You know, maybe have dinner? Or see a movie or something? Or coffee—do you have time to come have coffee with me right now?"

Hope sprouted in her heart, a tiny little shoot, yearning desperately for sunlight. She swallowed hard. "Why?"

Liam's eyebrows rose. "Why?"

"Yes why?" she snapped, trembling inside as she waited for his answer. "It's a simple enough question, isn't it? What is it you want from me?"

He looked perplexed for an instant, then he shrugged. "Everything."

Hope withered away. *Everything? Wow. Isn't that special.*

Yeah, she knew what everything meant, although he had to be crazy to think he could get it from her now. It was the same thing the guys had always wanted from her, wasn't it? And there'd been a time when she'd been okay with that, too. But, not now.

She tossed her head. "Well, you know what, Liam? It seems to me you had your chance for that last April. As I recall, you weren't that interested."

Liam sighed. "I was always *interested*, Cara. But, we've been over this, haven't we? I'm a cop. I was on a case. I couldn't compromise that. And, besides, you were under age."

She nodded. "Right. And, now, you're still a cop and I'm old enough to know better. So just...forget it."

His face grim, he nodded. "Okay. You're right. I'm sorry. Bad idea." Then he turned and walked away, just like he'd always done before. Like she was just that easy to put from his mind. He walked over to the window and stood with his back to the room, obviously more interested in whatever was happening in the parking lot, then he was with continuing their conversation.

Tears stung Cara's eyes, but she blinked them back. "So, is this why you wanted me to tell you if Seth wasn't treating me good? So that you could treat me like shit, too?"

Frowning, he turned back around to face her. "You know I'd never do something like that. It's just– I guess I was hoping, if you weren't seeing anyone else that...that you'd at least give me a chance to show you how you should be treated."

*Oh, goody. More lessons 'Cause I didn't get enough of those from Gregg.* "Really? And how's that, Liam? How should I be treated?"

He shook his head sadly. "Cara," he murmured reproachfully, as he walked back over to where she was standing. She crossed her arms over her chest. She lifted her chin. She waited. But he said nothing more.

"Well," she said, at last, when it appeared he was never actually going to finish the sentence, "that's a hell of an answer."

He shrugged again. "Maybe I don't know how to answer it. I only know that I don't ever want to see you hurt again." He reached out his hand again, slowly, questingly. Her heart fluttered out of control, but, this time, she stood her ground, although her breathing stalled and her eyes spasmed shut as he caressed her cheek with gentle fingers.

"You were right, you know," she murmured. "Remember all that stuff you used to tell me? About how I shouldn't let people use me, and...and I don't want that anymore either. So, if you're asking me out just to get laid, or out of pity, or because maybe I'll *learn something* from the experience—then forget it. Because I don't need that." *Not from you. Not from anyone, really, but, oh, definitely not from you.*

Liam shook his head. "You know that's not why I'm asking. And, I already told you what I wanted. I want everything."

*And, I still have no idea what you mean by that.* Were they still only talking about sex? Or, could it maybe mean more? "Yeah? So, what do I get out of it?"

His mouth curved up in a sad, little smile. "Me." Another riddle.

"You?"

Liam grimaced. "I know. It's not much of a trade, is it? Especially since, in reality, you've had me since March, Caramel."

She felt her cheeks flame. "Oh, bullshit, Liam. I have not."

"Yes, you have. Here." He pointed to his chest. "Put your hand right there and tell me if you can feel my heart beating."

She did as he asked. Her own heart was racing, but his was beating pretty hard, too. She nodded. "Yes. I feel it."

"Well, it's just 'cause you're here that it does that. I swear to God, when you're not around my whole chest feels empty."

She knew he didn't mean it—not literally, anyway. But, it was still just about the nicest thing anyone had ever said to her. It was the kind of thing she used to wish Seth would say, not that he ever would.

Her breath came out on a shaky little sigh. "Oh. th-that was really nice."

He smiled softly. "So, you never told me. Did you like your flowers?"

Cara felt herself stiffen. "F-flowers? Wh-what flowers?"

"And the balloons? For your birthday?"

"Th-those were from *you*?"He nodded. "Didn't Seth tell you? I had a card too, but then he answered the door and I thought you were with him so– I sent you some for your graduation, too, you know. And, then, when you were in the hospital I–" He broke off. "Cara? Sweetie, what's wrong?"

She was shaking from head to toe, too frightened to hope he was telling the truth. She'd wanted them to be from him. She'd hoped they might be. But, "Oh, please, you're not making this up are you? Because it would really, really...*hurt*...if you were just saying stuff."

"I'm not," he answered quickly. "I swear I'm not. I swear I mean every word I say." He stared at her for a moment, as though he were trying to make up his mind, trying to decide what to do next.

And then he kissed her, leaning across the gap that separated them, touching her with nothing but his lips. And it was the softest, sweetest kiss she'd ever imagined.

When she was a little girl she'd dreamed of being kissed like this, then she'd grown up and learned that every kiss was different. Some were nice and some were not and most were somewhere in between. She'd been kissed by a lot of different guys, in a lot of different ways. Even Liam had kissed her before. But, not like this. Never like this.

When it ended he put his hands on her shoulders and eased her close. He held her gently against his chest—no pressure, no force. She rubbed her cheek against the front of his shirt and wished she could melt right into him. It didn't even matter that it was a uniform shirt, that he was a cop—and she'd always gotten along so well with them—because it was also Liam. Her Liam. And, it really didn't matter what else he was.

Was it possible that, whatever else she was, whatever she'd done and despite everything that had been done to her, it didn't matter to him, either?

"I don't think you have any idea how special you are," he murmured. "Do you?"

She shook her head. "I don't know." Gregg used to say she was special, too. She winced just a little as she thought of that. But she knew, without ever needing to ask, that Liam meant something very different.

"Well, I do know. You're the most special person in the world to me."

Which was only everything she'd ever hoped to hear. "Oh. Well...you're pretty special, too."

"Only when I'm with you," he answered, and that was so exactly the right thing to say, she was surprised he even knew to say it.

"So, how about that coffee?" he asked after a minute or two had passed in silence.

Cara nodded. "I'd like that."

Liam sighed deeply, as if in relief. For just a moment he cupped her head in his palm, pressed another kiss against her hair, and murmured, "Thank you."

She was embarrassed by the tenderness of the gesture, by the humble, heartfelt gratitude in his voice. After all, "It's just a cup of coffee, Liam. We've had them before."

"No, it's not. It's more than that. It's a start."

"Yeah, I guess it is." It was the start of something good, she hoped, the start of something very, very special. She looked up at him and grinned. "So, Liam, how'd you like some cake to go along with that coffee?"[1]

SATURDAY NIGHT FOUND Chay on stage at the Temple Garden, sitting in with the owner's band. They were on their third set when a flicker

of movement near the door caught his eye. Glancing up, he was stunned to see Erin standing there, just inside the door. When the song ended, he whispered an excuse to Brent and jumped from the stage.

He caught a glimpse of Chenoa's satisfied smirk as he passed the table where she and Jasmine and Maya were seated, but he paid it no mind."You're back." He swept Erin into a big hug, and spun her around.

"I cut my trip short," she agreed as he released her.

Biting back a smile, he gazed at her solemnly. "Greetings, Rain Woman," he intoned, using the name he'd given her and the voice she loved him to use.

She grinned back at him. "How've you been, Star Man?"

"Better now that you're back." And then, deciding to throw caution to the wind, he added, "Listen, there's something I want to ask you."

Erin nodded. "Okay, and then there's something I need to tell you." She gazed at him expectantly.

"Not here." Chay took hold of her hand and pulled her back outside.

The street was deserted. He motioned her toward one of the cement planters that decorated the sidewalk. They sat down, side by side, and for a moment, neither of them spoke.

"Well?" she prompted, at last.

"I want you to marry me," he said. "I haven't worked out all of the details yet, like where we'll live, but I figure maybe those things will take care of themselves. I just– I want more. I want to make this permanent. I want–"

Erin nodded, a little absently. "I know." Pressing her hand against her belly, she stared into space, looking at nothing at all.

"You haven't answered yet," Chay reminded her, after several minutes had passed.

Brown eyes twinkled as she gazed up at him. "Oh, I'm sorry, was that a question?"

"Erin," he said, warningly.

She laughed merrily. "Of course, I'll marry you, Chay. As a matter of fact, it makes what I have to tell you a little easier to say.

"Okay. So?"

She took a deep breath. "I'm pregnant."

"You're what?"

Erin nodded. "At first, I thought it was the food that was making me sick. But then, I was too weeks late and I took a test and...please be happy about this."

"I am," he said faintly. "Of course, I am. It's just– A baby. Wow."

She smiled. "Hey, I've had several days to process it, and I'm still in the 'wow' stage myself. But, listen, about where we'll live, I thought we could stay at my place for now, because it's closer to the hospital and my doctor and stuff. Plus I can walk to stores and…well, wherever, when I get too big to drive. But then, maybe not right away, but when the baby's older, well, I can't think of any better place to raise a child than out in the country."

Chay nodded. "And I can use the time in between to build an extra room onto the cabin. Or, maybe two rooms."

"Exactly."

He smiled. "So. You've been thinking about this."

Erin shrugged. "It was a long flight back."

They sat for a moment, contemplating their future. Chay took hold of Erin's hand and gave it a squeeze. "Thank you."

She looked at him curiously. "For what?"

"For this. For everything. For agreeing to share your life with me."

"Oh, Star Man." Disentangling her hand from his, she wrapped her arms around his neck. "I agreed to that months ago. You mustn't have been paying attention."

Cara slid through the starlit water feeling happy and free, thinking about the events of the day.

Liam had followed her back to the inn. They'd had cake, they'd had coffee, they'd talked for hours. When it grew late, they'd raided the kitchen together, making a meal out of leftovers. And when he finally left, it was with a promise that he'd be back tomorrow.

She couldn't believe all the things he had told her. That he loved her at all still seemed like a miracle, but he claimed to have been in love with her for months! She turned on her back and floated for a bit, gazing up at the stars, but the air was too cool.

She got out of the water and dressed quickly. She'd toweled off her hair, and then, as she was wiping her feet dry, a shimmer of motion let her know she wasn't alone.She turned her head, not quite so surprised this time to see the same stranger seated on the grass beside her.

"Have you been here the whole time?" she asked, thinking she'd given him a hell of a show, if he had been.

He shook his head. "No."

"Oh. Well, good." She went back to wiping her feet. When she was finished, she turned to him again. "Well, I did it."

"And you did very well."

"I was really scared."

He smiled sadly. "There would be no need for bravery, if you weren't."

"I guess."

"So what is it that's troubling you now?" he asked her.

Cara sighed. "Nothing, really. There are just some things I wish I remembered, that's all."

Liam still swore that Gregg's attack on her had been his fault; that he'd scared her into flight, that she'd run to Seth to get away from *him*. The thought grieved him. And even thought she knew it wasn't possible that it could have been that way, with no clear memory of the event, she had no way to convince him he was wrong.

"Look at the water," the stranger suggested.

A soft breeze was ruffling the surface of the pond, distorting the reflections. When it cleared, Cara gasped in surprise. She could see herself, in the kitchen of Gregg's church, arguing with Liam. He wanted her to leave, but she was still reeling from the revelation that he was a cop, and she didn't want to go alone.

Finally, he agreed to go with her, but they still needed the remote control for the gate, which she'd left in the front hall. She left the kitchen to get it, and then...

*She was headed for the front door, about to cross the foyer, when voices on the landing above her head alerted her to the fact that she was not alone.*

*She skidded to a stop, plastered her back against the wall and held her breath, praying that whoever was up there would go back in their rooms. But, instead–*

*"Better wait until it's dark," she heard Gregg say. "That way, even if you're seen, you'll be harder to identify."*

*"Yes, Sensei." It was Steve, one of his followers, who answered.*

*"Here's the address," Gregg continued. "Remember, he lives in an apartment over the garage, so you shouldn't have any need to go near the house at all. Knock him out as quickly as you can, and don't leave any signs of a struggle. I want it to look like he left on his own. Understood?"*

*"Yes, Sensei."*

*"I'll leave the basement door unlocked. Bring him in that way when you come back. Tie him up and leave him there. And don't talk about this to anyone. I don't want anyone else to know he's here."*

Oh, God, oh, God, oh, God. *Slowly, Cara inched her way back into the dinning room, barely daring to breathe. They were talking about Seth. They had to be talking about Seth. And, omigod, they were going to kidnap him?*

*She breathed another silent prayer, thanking God that she'd found out in time. Thanking God she was leaving here anyway. She didn't even know if she believed in God—what had he done for her lately, anyway?*

*But, if He got her out of this mess, if she could make it to Seth's house in time...she'd be ready to believe in anything.*

*She waited until she heard footsteps coming down the stairs. The front door opened and shut, and she sighed in relief.* Okay, good. Time to go.

*She hurried out of hiding. The coast was clear, but just the same, there was no time to waste. She needed to get her remote, get back to Liam and go. The remote was on the table where she'd left it. She picked it up, took her bag from the hook in the front closet, turned back toward the kitchen, and ran smack into Gregg.*

*"Going somewhere, pet?"*

*"Yeah. I, I, uh, the grocery store?" she said, grasping at the first thing that came to mind.*

*"Now? It's almost time for dinner."*

*Cara nodded nervously. "I was just in the kitchen, and I didn't realize we were out of so much stuff. I need to go get some. Food. And, and stuff. Other stuff. Not food, just..."* Just what, you idiot? Think of something. Quick!

*Gregg frowned. "Can't it wait? Can't you make something else? We can't be completely out of food?"*

*"No, of course, we're not. But I, I...well, I guess I c-could. It's just that you were so mad this morning, and I thought...I thought I could make you something special?"'*

*"Something special, huh?" Gregg's lips curved upward in an eager smile. "Okay. What?"*

*"It-it's a surprise," she said, hoping to stall. She knew the real surprise would be if he bought that lie. And an even bigger surprise would be if she could dream up an actual answer before he demanded one.*

*"Well, you better get going." She bit her lip, trying to determine what her next move should be. Gregg was standing between her and the kitchen. Between her and Liam. Cara knew there was no way she could pull this off. She could either leave now, alone, through the front door. Or she could pretend to change her mind about dinner, go back into the kitchen...and wait for another time.*

*And that was exactly what she knew she should do. What she wanted to do. Except for one thing. Seth.*

'I won't be responsible for anyone else getting involved with Gregg.' *Liam's words from earlier that day came back to taunt her.* 'Or for anyone else getting hurt. Particularly not someone I consider a friend.'

*What kind of friend would she be to Seth, if she did nothing to help him now? It was her fault if anything happened to him. She'd put him on*

*Gregg's radar and now...now she had no choice but to warn him of the danger he was in.*

*If she did nothing, and something bad happened, she wouldn't be able to live with herself. And Liam would surely despise her for it.*

*"All right," she mumbled, swallowing hard, trying to force herself to do what she had to do. To walk away and...and leave Liam behind.*

*No. That was stupid. She couldn't think that way. She wasn't really leaving Liam. She'd just drive into town, warn Seth, pick up some groceries —and maybe, by the time she got there, she could even figure out something special to cook—and then she'd come back.*

*Gregg would be happy. Seth would be safe. And she and Liam could still leave here together, just later tonight.*

*"Pet?"*

*"Yeah, yeah. I'm going." She turned away from him, turned toward the door. Everything was okay, she reassured herself. Everything was fine. Just fine. Practically perfect, in fact...*

"That's enough for now, I think," the stranger said. He waved his hands through the water, and the images disappeared.

Cara stared at him. "I wasn't running away, after all. I went to warn Seth."

He nodded. "You were brave then, too."

Cara nodded thoughtfully. Maybe she was. Still, she was glad she couldn't recall the actual attack. She wasn't *that* brave. Besides, maybe some memories just weren't worth having. Maybe, someday, she'd be able to forget about it altogether. Someday when her scars had faded and her leg had healed.

There would always be her eye to remind her, however. She couldn't get away from that.

"Ah, I was almost forgetting." The stranger reached into his shirt pocket and pulled out a small, leather pouch.

"What's that?" Cara asked curiously as he dipped his fingers into it.

"Just something I find useful, from time to time." The grease on his fingers sparkled in the starlight, even brighter than the water.

"No," she gasped softly as he reached his hand toward her face.

"Please..." She tried to back away from him, only to find that, just like the first night, she couldn't move.

"Shh," he murmured softly as he touched the lid of her ruined eye. "Don't be afraid."

She closed both eyes and tried to relax, tried to breathe through the panic. In truth, the ointment he was applying to her eyelid felt wonderful, warm and slightly tingly.

He stroked her eye gently for several minutes and then, "How's that?" he asked, removing his hand from her face.

"Okay," she said as she opened her eyes. *Or, maybe not.* His image seemed to shift from right to left. She frowned and squinted and tried to focus. What had he done to her? Suddenly, it hit her. She was seeing out of both eyes. She gazed around her in disbelief—up, down, side to side. She tried blinking several times, closing first one eye and then the other– She stared at him in amazement.

"How–? Wh-what did you do?"

The stranger shrugged. "Your doctors will probably decide that the second blow to your head jarred things back into place. That won't make any sense to them, of course, but it's something they can believe in."

"Omigod."

"Yes. Even so." The stranger smiled as he got to his feet.

She gazed up at him. "Th-thank you."

But he shook his head. "No. Not me. I'm just the messenger." Gently he laid his hand on her head. "Be of good cheer," he told her, and then he left.

Cara sat by the pond for a long while, still gazing at everything, feeling grateful beyond measure, feeling happy just to be alive.[2]

# EPILOGUE

## Fourth of July

"So, you're saying it's over?" Dan asked. He was in the kitchen of the big old house that Scout had inherited from her stepmother, watching as Nick arranged pastries on a tray: mini cannolis, bite sized Tiramisu, cherry tarts. The soft, burbling sound of coffee brewing filled the air. "And you're sure about that?"

"Yup." Nick nodded. "It's over, all right. The fat lady sang."

"And, there's no chance they could, you know, beat it somehow? Maybe get paroled, or something?"

Nick smiled grimly. "With multiple charges of aggravated assault, attempted murder, conspiracy to commit murder, and who knows what else we'll be able to drum up? Not a chance. Those guys'll be dead long before they'll be eligible for a parole hearing—if they can even get one *that* soon."

"Good to know," Dan sighed. The door swung open and Mandy and Kate ran in, pausing only long enough to grab a couple of pastries before continuing on their way up to Kate's room.

Nick added a couple more tarts to the tray. Then, just as he finishing up, Bouncer, his big orange tomcat, jumped up on the table. He fed him a scrap of cannoli, then shooed him away, opened two bottles of beer and went to join his friend by the door. Together, they observed the scene outside.

Most of the women were gathered on the patio. Out on the grass, Sam and Ryan were playing catch with Marsha's twin boys. Adam, carrying baby Victoria, had strolled over to the sandbox to watch Cole play. The young people had all congregated in the gazebo.

Nick sighed. "So, it looks like Paige got what she wanted after all.

Dan eyed him curiously. "Oh? How d'you figure that?"

"Well, you're not Deirdre's biological father, but I guess she'll be calling you Dad soon, just the same."

"Yeah. How 'bout that?" Dan shook his head. "And, you know, I'm fine with it, really. I just wish they'd maybe wait a while."

Nick thought back to all the wasted years he'd spent waiting for Scout. "Screw that. Take it from me, waiting's highly overrated.

"Yeah, you would say that, wouldn't you?" Dan smiled. "I dunno, maybe you're right. Maybe age doesn't matter."

"You know, speaking of Deirdre's biological father...what's the word on that?"

Dan shrugged. "You got me. She's decided she doesn't want to know. All things considered, I'm not sure I blame her."

"Nope, me, neither. Sometimes, ignorance really can be bliss."

The door to the terrace opened once again and Liam came in. He nodded at the two men as he headed for the drink cooler. Nick briefly contemplated the mysteries of life. Given the animosity that had always existed between he and the younger officer, the idea that they might actually end up socializing like this, on a semi-regular basis, seemed almost inconceivable. And yet–

"What's up, McKnight?" he couldn't help taunting. "Looks like you've been robbing the cradle."

Liam took two sodas from the cooler and turned, frowning. "What can I tell you, Greco? I guess I'm just fated to follow in your footsteps in all sorts of ways."

Dan chuckled softly. Nick blinked in surprise as he thought about it. "Well, you could do worse," he said at last. "There's beer in the fridge if you want it."

Liam nodded. "Thanks. But, considering the crowd I'm hanging with, I think I'd better stick to soda."

"Probably for the best." Nick studied the young man for a moment. "By the way, that was good work last week."

Liam looked surprised. "Are you kidding me? It was a mess. I went in with no back up, no plan. The second gunman caught me completely by surprise. I had to totally wing it."

Nick shrugged. "Well, that's the job, sometimes, isn't it? Besides, I read the reports. You kept your head. You did what you had to do."

"Yeah, well, things wouldn't have turned out nearly as well, if I hadn't gotten some help." He looked at Dan. "Seth was the real champ. He and his dogs."

Dan nodded gravely. "Thanks."

After Liam left, Dan turned to Nick. "About the dogs..."

Nick smiled. "You know, a lot of folks thought we were taking a big risk two years ago, letting Seth keep those dogs. But, I have to say, it's paid off."

"Glad to hear it," Dan replied. "He's been a little worried, you know. I gather they'd bloodied one of the bad guys pretty good."

Nick snorted. "Damn near tore his face off, is what I heard. But, hey, he was attempting a kidnapping at the time and he'd just fired on an officer; I doubt anyone's gonna care all that much if one of the dogs got a little ambitious."

"That's a relief."For a moment, they drank their beer in silence.

And then, "You know, all things considered, this is shaping up to be a pretty good summer," Nick observed.

"That it is," Dan agreed. "It's already July and no one's died yet."

"Here's to things staying that way," Nick said as he raised his bottle.

"Amen to that," Dan replied as they hit the necks of their bottles together. "You think that coffee's about done now?"

"Probably." Nick drained his bottle, tossed it in the recycling bin and headed toward the stove. "If you want to take those pastries outside, I'll be right behind you."

Dan nodded as he threw his own empty in the bin. "Can do."

"So, the hero of the hour," Sinead greeted Seth as he crossed the lawn.

Seth blushed furiously. Hero. Shit, he'd come to hate that title. "Not really. I just got lucky, that's all. I'm real sorry about the mess, by the way."

Sinead shrugged. "Don't worry about it. At least it gave me an excuse to redecorate the lounge."

"And I'm sorry I moved Dee into the pool house without telling you," Seth continued, wanting to make a clean breast of things. "I just didn't know what else I could do."

Sinead studied him for a moment, then sighed. "Seth...Cara told me about the wine, you know. The *real* story, including how you offered to take the blame for it."

Seth gazed at her worriedly. "You're not gonna fire her, are you?"

"No." She shook her head. "I figure everyone's entitled to a screw up now and then. The point I'm trying to make is, considering the stress you were under, I think you all handled things pretty well. I'm proud of you."

"So, we're cool then?" Seth asked hopefully.

Sinead smiled. "Yeah, we're cool." Her gaze strayed toward the sandbox. "Well, I'd better go, and I'm sure you want to get back to your friends."

"Okay." Seth nodded. "Oh, and, hey, I almost forgot. Congratulations."

Sinead glanced at the antique ring on her left hand. "Yeah. Funny how things work out, isn't it? And I hear you might be taking the plunge soon, as well?"

Seth nodded, blushing again.

Sinead sighed. "Well, I'd warn you to be cautious, but it seems like maybe rushing into things is what you do best." She went up on her toes to kiss him on the cheek. "Remember, no matter what, you'll always be my Lancelot."

THE WOMEN at the table watched as Sinead went to join her new husband and Seth went back to be with Deirdre.

Scout nodded toward the young couple. "Think it'll last?"

Lucy sighed. "Considering how much like his father he is? Probably."

"And how do you feel about that?" Siobhan asked.

"I just want him to be happy," Lucy replied plaintively.

"He will be," Marsha said, using the confident tone that those who are used to seeing the future often employ. "You'll see."

"Thanks, Marsh." Lucy smiled at her gratefully.

Leaning back in her seat, Marsha studied each of the women in turn. "You know, when you think about it, these last few years have been really stressful—for everyone. And even though the good outweighed the bad in most cases, enough is enough. I'd say we're all due for a nice, long spell of peace and contentment. What do you all think?"

"Hear, hear," Siobhan said, raising her glass. "To peace and contentment."

"Peace and contentment," Lucy responded. "I'll drink to that." She turned and gazed expectantly at Scout who hadn't said anything. "Well?"

Scout looked around her, at all the familiar, happy faces; at the flowers in her garden, shimmering in the late afternoon sunlight; at the deep green lawn, the tall, dark trees, the azure smudge of sea in the distance.

Peace and contentment. She knew just what that would look like. Friends. Family. Love. And an endless string of bright, golden days in the only place she'd ever truly wanted to be. She raised her glass and smiled at the women gathered around her. "Peace and contentment. Count me in."[1]

# ABOUT THE AUTHOR

PG Forte inhabits a world only slightly less strange than the ones she creates; filled with serendipity, coincidence, love at first sight and dreams come true. Originally a Jersey Girl and forever a California Girl at heart, PG currently makes her home in the beautiful Texas Hill Country.

Learn more about PG and her books at www.PGForte.com

To stay up to date on new releases, access free reads, ARCs and more, please consider joining PG's reader group on Facebook at:
https://www.facebook.com/groups/TheCronesNest

Or sign up for her newsletter:
https://www.pgforte.com/newsletter

# WELCOME TO OBERON

Scent of the Roses
Oberon 1.0

For twenty years, Scout Patterson has tried to run from the mistakes in her past. Now, she's finally coming home—to face the ghosts she's never laid to rest, and the love she thought she'd lost forever. Reawakening that love would be a dream come true. Unfortunately, love is not the only emotion that can last forever.

Memories and dreams are the only things that have gotten Nick Greco through the past twenty years. Memories of the girl he loved and lost, and dreams of what his life would be like, if he could only find her again. And if he can bring himself to believe that anything she tells him is true.

Can the star-crossed lovers put aside the hurt and distrust they still harbor toward each other? Or will the evil which already nearly destroyed them once, triumph yet again?

https://books2read.com/ScentRoses

A Sight to Dream Of
Oberon 2.0

Sam Sterling is a man with problems. Including a partner who is trying to kill him, and a nosy reporter, who's just turned up dead! It's going to take a miracle to save him. Or, better yet, an angel.

Marsha Quinn is used to being called a witch. After all, her abilities as a psychic make a lot of people uncomfortable. But no one has ever called her an angel before!

Falling in love was not a possibility she'd ever envisioned, until Sam the skeptic arrives in Oberon, and teaches her to see past the scars she carries, and the lies he's told her, to the love that lies within their hearts and minds.

https://books2read.com/SightDream

Sound of a Voice That is Still
Oberon 3.0

Some wounds take a long time to heal, others never do. Four months after being wounded in the line of duty, Ryan Henderson is beginning to fear that his is of the latter variety. He's a patient man, but a poor patient. As winter drags interminably on, he's growing desperate for distraction—anything that might take his mind off his injury, and his fears for the future.

Siobhan Quinn could give the injured officer a lesson or two in living with pain. It's been ten years since her life was changed and her heart critically wounded as a result of the tragic accident that robbed her of her family. She knows firsthand how grief can cripple a soul and drive a sane mind over the edge.

Sometimes it seems like Spring will never come again. Sometimes, the only alternative to living in inner darkness, is death. Your own, or someone else's. In the depths of winter, Ryan and Siobhan will have to make a choice: to help each other heal, or die trying.

https://books2read.com/SoundVoice

# RETURN TO OBERON

A Taste Of Honey
Oberon Book 4.0

For Lucy Greco Cavanaugh, life is a dream come true. She has it all. The perfect family. The perfect husband. The perfect marriage. What more could she wish for? Other than the chance to do it all again. To experience once more the agony and ecstasy of falling in love with the man of her dreams. To recapture the joy and uncertainty that comes with starting over.

As far as Dan Cavanaugh is concerned, his life has become a nightmare. His storybook marriage is on the line when Deirdre Shelton-Cooper, the runaway daughter of a former girlfriend arrives in Oberon intent on proving Dan is her father. Even though he's convinced the girl's claims are false, Dan decides his only chance to keep from losing everything lies in keeping her very existence a secret from his wife and family.

But, sometimes, what you don't know can hurt you--and those you love. When Deirdre, masquerading as a surfer girl named Monica, accidentally hooks up with their son, Seth, Lucy and Dan are left to wonder: has their perfect, fairy-tale romance, turned into a classic Greek tragedy?

Sometimes you get exactly what you wish for. And it's more than you'd ever dreamed.

Touch of a Vanished Hand
Oberon 5.0

Sinead Quinn has always been something of a drifter. But now, with her ex-husband trying to blackmail her, and her ex-boyfriend's widow trying to put her in jail, she has no choice but to go to ground. What better place to hide than with your family? After all, what are sisters for? Especially when you're a twin.

But the first rule of hiding out, is to keep a low profile. And that does not mean kissing your sister's boyfriend (even if he can't tell the two of you apart); rescuing a troubled teen; or taking a highly visible job as hostess of Oberon's most celebrated new inn.

Adam Sasso has always dreamed big. But big dreams beget big complications. First, his goal to turn the vineyard he inherited from his grandfather into a world-class winery is threatened by a mysterious saboteur. Next, his plan to run the finest bed & breakfast Oberon has ever seen, is broadsided by a hostess who wants to run him. Finally, it seems his fondest wish, of finding love-everlasting with the soul mate of his dreams, is about to go up in smoke when he can't convince her that they're destined to be together.

This summer, it's going to take all the wizardry in Oberon to craft a happy ending for the drifter and the dreamer.

The Spirit of the Place
Oberon 6.0

'Tis the season to be jolly, but Jasmine Quinn is far from happy about her mother's latest folly: her upcoming wedding to former Wall Street financier, Sam Sterling. Jasmine doesn't like her future stepfather, or his values. Anybody with as much money as Sam, should be spreading it around, aiding worthy causes, making it count for something. Instead, he seems intent on using his wealth to embarrass her mother by throwing a ridiculously lavish wedding. But there's one thing about Sam that Jasmine can't help but admire, no matter how much she'd like to--the graduate student he's hired as an intern.

Brandon Ablemarle is also finding it hard to get into the holiday spirit. Especially since his dream job has just become a nightmare, thanks in part to the fiery redhead with some of the goofiest ideas he's ever heard of. But what else can you expect from the daughter of a self-proclaimed psychic? Marsha Quinn has a lot to answer for. Not only has she encouraged her daughter's esoteric craziness, she's also turned one of the most brilliant stock analysts Wall Street had ever seen into a nutcase as well. One who actually appears to believe that the answers to the stock market can be found in the stars!

It's a clash of ideologies when Jasmine and Brandon get together. Can the spirit of the season, and the spirit of the place help them to see beyond their differences?

# HAPPILY EVER AFTER IN OBERON

**Visions Before Midnight**
Oberon Book 7.0

Chay Johnson is a traditional man; and the educator, flute maker, apprentice shaman has a lot of traditions to uphold, especially when it comes to choosing a life mate.

Erin Allridge is a modern woman, with modern ideas about relationships and a painful personal history she has no intention of repeating.

When terror and tragedy strike the small town of Oberon, the pair are forced to re-think their visions for the future.

In this world of form and spirit it can be hard to find balance and harmony, but sometimes, particularly when the veil between the worlds is at its thinnest, love can find a way to bridge the gap.

Bonus Novella:
**Hungry Heart**

*Happily Ever After in Oberon*

*An Oberon Halloween Story*

Cara Matthews is trouble—with a capital T. That's one thing that pretty much everyone in Oberon can agree on—parents, teachers, other students, her on-again-off-again boyfriend, Seth Cavanaugh.

Well, if you give a dog a bad name they'll probably live up to it, right?

This Halloween, after one insult too many, Cara is hellbent on wreaking revenge—no matter who gets hurt in the process.

***Please note: This is a companion book to Visions Before Midnight. While it can stand on its own (and does contain scenes and material that does not appear in Visions) it's not a separate story. This is essentially Cara's version of events, which may or may not be accurate. Do you trust her?***

**Dream Under The Hill**

Oberon Book 8.0

The Spring Equinox falls in the month that nearly all Native Traditions recognize as being one of Big Winds—big changes. And big changes have certainly come to Oberon this spring, along with an ancient evil that must finally be laid to rest.

Cara Matthews is a girl with a troubled past and a very troubling present. The teenage girlfriend of Oberon's newest guru has always looked for love in all the worst places. And it doesn't get much worse than the Church of Truth, Light and Harmony.

Former cop Liam McKnight could have told her that, but he's infiltrated the cult in hopes of discovering some clue to the whereabouts of his missing family members, and he can't jeopardize his mission—not even for love.

In a month marked by birth, death and marriage, the inhabitants of Oberon must all come to terms with what's really important to each of them—important enough to die for. Only one thing is certain; when the winds of change finally stop blowing nothing, and no one, will be the same.

**And Shadows Have Their Ending**

Oberon Book 9.0

The last two years have not been kind to Seth Cavanaugh. But, he's suffered and grown and he finally feels ready to put his troubled past behind him. So, doesn't it just figure that the girl who caused all the trouble in the first place should pick now to return and cause him even more torment?

Deirdre Delaney Shelton-Cooper has spent the past two years trying to forget the events that marked her first visit to Oberon, but can you ever really forget the memory of your first love, no matter how painful those memories are? It's just her luck the boy she put herself through hell for has turned out to be such a loser.

After a disastrous reunion, they'd both be content to have nothing more to do with each other, if only fate—and one very determined angel—were not conspiring against them.

There are some wounds that time can't heal. There are some dreams that won't come true. But, sometimes, if you're lucky, shadows have their ending. And the love you'd just about given up on returns.

# MORE OBERON

Click the following links to learn more about:

The Oberon Series
The Oberon Novellas
The Oberon Christmas stories
The Oberon/LA Love Lessons Crossover Novellas

There's something magical about the little coast town of Oberon, California. Anything could happen here and all too often it does. It's a place filled with mystery, intrigue, mysticism and romance and while the location is fictional, the people populating it can seem all-too real.

The Oberon series is currently undergoing a re-boot. But you can read the prequel novella, *Such Fleeting Pleasures* now! Join my Facebook group, The Crone's Nest, for access to your free download!

Or learn even more about the series at any of these links:

Who's Who in Oberon
Oberon Chamber of Commerce

## Going Back to Oberon

*(A very short story)*

This story started out as a feature on Cabin Goddess's "Fourth Wall Friday" blog; in which authors were invited to put themselves into a scene where they interacted with their characters.

I had a great deal of fun imagining myself returning to the scene of my very first series. It started me thinking about all the Oberon stories I hadn't told yet. And it really motivated me to start getting some of those ideas out there.

You can download a copy HERE. Enjoy!

And Shadows Have Their Ending
Oberon: Book 9

20th Anniversary Edition

Cover Artist: PG Forte

digital ISBN: 978-1-880370-83-4
print ISBN: 978-1-880370-84-1
Published in the United States of America
Chapultepec Press



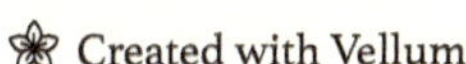
Created with Vellum

# NOTES

## Chapter 1

1. This is a nod to the old (I think it's from the 1700s) nursery rhyme, "Oh, No, What Can the Matter Be, rather than the Bonnie Rait song. I also love that the last book in the series echos the first book in that both main characters attend the Midsummer fair. I love my full-circle moments.
2. Does this count as a meet cute? Questionable. Seth is in a very bad place, and I wanted to put them at odds with each other right from the start.
3. This girl just keeps popping up! I do love this new friendship they've developed, though. It's sweet. Cara is the one person Seth can be himself with—she's seen the good and the bad and doesn't judge. Seth is Cara's only friend, at this point. and she trusts him implicitly. Doesn't mean they aren't going to argue, though...
4. Rafe was another surprise. I hadn't intended to bring angels back to Oberon—and now that I did, I can't get rid of them. They're ALL OVER the Christmas stories. But I guess Rafe felt like he had some work to do there this summer, because here he is again.
5. I also love how Seth is following in his father's footsteps, and Deirdre is following in her mother's. Which should be a recipe for disaster! But, instead...well. It's a romance. You know they're going to work things out!

## Chapter 2

1. Lucy is definitely having a little trouble letting go. Not that I blame her. It's been a rough few years for the Cavanaughs. BUT not as rough as it is in If Only in my Dreams—Scout's Wonderful Life vision of what Oberon would have been like if she'd never returned.
2. I think Lucy is a lot more psychic than anyone ever gives her credit for. lol I just wanted to point out, again, how I managed to get almost ALL the responsible adults out of the picture, so that when things go sideways—which they will!—the kids will have to figure things out for themselves.

## Chapter 3

1. I love the irony of Cara looking up to Sinead—the last woman who'd thwarted Gregg—as a role model. I'm not sure how much Sinead knows about Cara's involvement with Gregg—probably not too much. She would have been pre-occupied at the time. I'm quite sure Cara knows nothing of Sinead's involvement with him, however. Which is why makes the irony so delicious.

## Chapter 5

1. In reality, he probably wasn't that cool. But that's how Seth remembers it.
2. Now, you might be thinking that Seth's parents should have forced him to go to therapy. And they could have, but they couldn't have forced him to talk, so I'm not sure how much use it would have been. As we saw in book five, when he kept stonewalling Nick, Seth can be extremely stubborn when he wants to be. He gets it from his mother...actually, he probably gets it from both is parents. Dan spent sixteen years thinking if he didn't think about something it wouldn't come back to bite him in the butt. Much to his dismay, things didn't work out so well.
3. Yep. Back in the day there were daily papers and everyone read them.

## Chapter 6

1. I think this probably gives a fair approximation of what my house tended to look like during the period when I was writing the series.
2. This name was suggested by my daughter. In case you're not familiar, The Simpsons' first cat was white and was called Snowball. After Snowball died, Lisa acquired a second cat who she named Snowball II. The irony is that Snowball II was actually a black cat.

## Chapter 7

1. If there was another place Deirdre could go, Seth is definitely not going to think of it now. lol I think part of it is also that, on some level, he's afraid to let her out of his sight. PTSD is real.

## Chapter 8

1. Like everything to do with the inn, this all was inspired by the neighborhood where I lived in Paso Robles, CA. I wrote book three and part of book five during that time. I was also reading Julia Cameron's book The Artist's Way during that time, and taking a lot of walks around my neighborhood, noticing details. I was also working in a Veterinarian's office, getting up obscenely early and spending large amounts of my day walking dogs and cleaning out kennels. I think it shows. lol
2. Okay, this part—I believe—was based on a boutique hotel I stayed at once, either in Laguna Beach, or in Hollywood.

## Chapter 9

1. This is also an echo from the first Crone's Nest scene. At the time I wrote Scent of the Roses, I didn't really appreciate what that meant, why it was a curse. But it's taken on a whole new meaning for me in the last few years. I get it now.

## Chapter 12

1. None of the nature centers where I volunteered offered clothes to people whose own clothes got wet. Not even the one in Berkeley, where you'd think they would!

   I mean, *I* would. They have a "free box" in People's Park where people drop off clothes and household goods and other things they no longer need, and people can just sort through what's there and take what they need. They also have a Free Clinic, over a hundred Little Free Libraries; even a Little Free Pantry.

## Chapter 13

1. I picked up this info during my very brief stint as a dog walker. I've since heard it called predator drift (which makes more sense, I think) but this is what I was taught to call it.
2. Aw. Popular boy problems. lol!

## Chapter 14

1. That would be the field trip where she purposely triggered Scout's leftover post hypnotic suggestion.

## Chapter 16

1. Grapevine: relationships and connectivity. Because Chenoa could sense that Cara was feeling isolated. Turquoise: a stone with strong healing energy that is connected to the energy of water. Quartz: a stone that amplifies the energy of other stones. Flamingo: due to its color, flamingo is related to heart energy. It is said to be particularly healing for those who are getting out of a toxic relationship. People with flamingo as their totem animal tend to be flamboyant and truthful.

## Chapter 17

1. Does it spoil the moment if I mention that I'd originally intended this scene to be between Siobhan and Ryan, all the way back in **Sound of a Voice That is Still**? They were making love by candlelight, but it was in the middle of a winter storm, and I thought this scene with all the overwrought reactions matched the wildness of the weather. But eventually, I decided it sounded too young for Ryan--even though he's younger than Siobhan, by several years, and I did want to play that up more.

   And while it fit Ryan's occasionally fey moods, the reaction didn't really fit Siobhan (who probably would have drop-kicked him off the bed in a heartbeat).

   Deirdre has baggage, too, but it's an overnight bag compared to the steamer trunks that Siobhan walked around with for years.

   And yeah, Ryan's young; but he's still not as young, or as much of a loose cannon as Seth.

## Chapter 18

1. This, of course, is a nod to Chay's first meeting with Erin in the prologue of book seven, Visions Before Midnight.
2. I'm not really sure about the origin of this reference, but I do recall people jokingly tell someone to, "Think of all the stars in your crown," when they were reluctant to do something that could be construed as a "good deed."

## Chapter 19

1. Oh, Seth. SMDH

## Chapter 21

1. This scene right here, especially the kiss, is one of my favorite scenes ever. I got very sick while I was writing this book—pneumonia AND anemia. I was out of commission for weeks. But I had this scene in my head, and I'd play it over and over again in my mind. The need to get up and type it out was one of the biggest factors motivating me to recover.
2. I hope this doesn't come across as too ableist. But you can't just stick Raphael in a book with someone who's blind in one eye without his healing her. I mean, there's precedence, after all. See The Book of Tobit for details. lol!

## Epilogue

1. And we're done. Other than the sequel novellas, Christmas stories, and LA Love Lessons crossover books. I love this ending. Love how it mirrors the ending of the first book—with the whole group celebrating Fourth of July—but now they're at Scout's house, rather than Lucy's because she's become the center of the group, rather than the outsider.